"In the increasingly crowded field of kick-ass supernatural heroines, Mercy stands out as one of the best." —*Locus*

Shapeshifter Mercy Thompson has friends in high places—and in low, dark, scary ones. And in this must-have collection of stories, you'll meet new faces and catch up with old acquaintances—in all their forms . . .

In a time of fresh starts, Mercy is asked to use an old talent—ghost hunting—in the new story "Hollow." You'll learn what happens when an ancient werewolf on his last legs befriends a vulnerable adolescent ("Roses in Winter") and how Mercy's friend Samuel Cornick became a werewolf ("Silver"). The werewolf Ben finds "Redemption," and Moira, a blind witch, assists on a search in "Seeing Eye."

From Butte, Montana, the copper-mining town that vampire Thomas Hao calls home ("Fairy Gifts"), to Chicago, where the vampire Elyna buys and renovates the apartment she lived in while human ("Gray"), you'll travel the roads that originated with Mercy Thompson in the fertile imagination of Patricia Briggs. Roads that will lead you to places you've never been before . . .

"The characters and events in this world just keep getting better and better!" —*Fresh Fiction*

PRAISE FOR

SHIFTING SHADOWS

"*Shifting Shadows* is beautifully compiled, and all of the tales engaged me, making this a total win for Briggs's fans. I walked away with a smile and new books in my TBR pile." —*Caffeinated Book Reviewer*

"*Shifting Shadows* is everything fans of Patricia Briggs will like . . . There is no disputing that Ms. Briggs is a superb storyteller."

—*Fiction Vixen Book Reviews*

SHIFTING SHADOWS

Stories from the World of Mercy Thompson

Includes four new stories together with six all-time favorites

PATRICIA BRIGGS

ACE BOOKS, NEW YORK

ACE

An imprint of Penguin Random House LLC
375 Hudson Street, New York, New York 10014

Ace trade paperback ISBN: 978-0-425-26501-7

The Library of Congress has cataloged the Ace hardcover edition as follows:

Briggs, Patricia.
[Short stories. Selections]
Shifting shadows : stories from the world of Mercy Thompson / Patricia Briggs.—First edition.
pages cm
"Includes four new stories together with six all-time favorites."
ISBN 978-0-425-26500-0 (hardback)
1. Paranormal fiction.   I. Briggs, Patricia. Silver.   II. Title.
PS3602.R53165A6 2014
813'.6—dc23
2014016252

PUBLISHING HISTORY
Ace hardcover edition / September 2014
Ace trade paperback edition / September 2015

PRINTED IN THE UNITED STATES OF AMERICA

7th Printing

Cover art by Daniel Dos Santos.
Cover design by Judith Lagerman.

"Fairy Gifts" was previously published in the anthology *Naked City*.
"Gray" was previously published in the anthology *Home Improvement: Undead Edition*.
"Seeing Eye" was previously published in the anthology *Strange Brew*.
"Alpha and Omega" was previously published in the anthology *On the Prowl*.
"The Star of David" was previously published in the anthology *Wolfsbane and Mistletoe*.
"In Red, with Pearls" was previously published in the anthology *Down These Strange Streets*.

Penguin
Random
House

To Mercedes Athena Thompson Hauptman
and the rest of my imaginary friends.
Thank you for hanging out with me.
Here's to the adventures to come!

ACKNOWLEDGMENTS

Thanks to all the usual people—none of these stories would be worth reading without you.

CONTENTS

INTRODUCTION

Dear reader, you hold in your hand (or your e-book reader) the entirety of every short story ever published (plus four) that I have written in the world of Mercy Thompson. Short stories have allowed me to explore Mercy's world from different perspectives, to tell stories that couldn't be told in the books, and to go places the books do not.

We have organized the stories by the order in which they happen. There are a few that could have gone anywhere ("Gray") and a few that were difficult because they happened in different times, but we managed to find a place for each. I hope you enjoy the journey as much as I have.

—PATRICIA BRIGGS

SILVER

Herein is the ill-fated romance between Ariana and Samuel, the first half of the story that continues in *Silver Borne*. This is also an origin story of sorts, because how he met Ariana is also tied up with the story of the witch, his grandmother, who held Samuel and his father for such a long time. I have to say that if it had not been for the constant requests for this story, I, usually a teller of happier tales, would have left this one alone.

As a historical note—and for those who need to know how old Samuel and Bran are—Christianity came to Wales very early, perhaps as early as the first or second century with the Romans. When exactly the events of this novella took place, neither Samuel nor Bran could tell me. Bran just smiled like a boy without cares—so I knew it hurt him to remember—and said, "We didn't pay attention to time that way. Not then." Samuel told me, "When you get just so old, those first days blur together." I am not a werewolf, but I can, after all this time, tell when Samuel is lying to me.

I do know that the events in this story happen a long, long time before *Moon Called*.

ONE

SAMUEL

THREE WEEKS TO THE DAY AFTER I BURIED MY YOUNG- est child, and several days after I buried my oldest—a young woman who would never become older—someone knocked at my door.

I rolled off my sleeping mat to my feet but made no move to answer the knock. It was pitch-dark outside, and the only reason anyone knocked at my door in the middle of the night was because someone was ill. All of my knowledge of herb lore and healing had not been able to save my wife or my children. If someone was ill, they were better off without me.

"I can hear you," said my da's voice gruffly. "Let me in."

Another day, before the death of my family, I would have been surprised. It had been a long time since I'd heard my father's voice. But my da, he'd always known when I was in trouble. That insight had outlasted my childhood.

I was beyond caring about anything, expected or unexpected. Being used to doing what he asked, I opened the door and stepped back.

The man standing outside entered quickly, careful not to lose the heat of the evening's fire. The hearth in the center of my home was banked and covered for the night, and I wouldn't fuel it again until the morning. With the door shut, the room was too dark to see because the window openings were also covered against the cold night air.

I did not see how he did it because there was no sound of striking flint, but he lit the tallow candle. He had always kept a candle on the ledge, just inside the door, where one of the rocks that formed the walls of the house stuck out. After he had gone and left the hut to me, I found it practical to leave one there as well.

In that dim but useful light, he pulled down the hood of his tattered cloak, and I saw his lined face, which looked older and more weather-beaten than when I'd last seen him, a dozen or more seasons ago.

His hair was threaded through with hoary gray, and his beard was an unfamiliar snow-white. He moved with a limp that he hadn't had the last time I'd seen him, but other than that he looked good for an old man. He set down the big pack he carried on his back and the leather bag that held his pipes. He shrugged off his outerwear and hung it up beside the door where my da had always hung such things.

"The crows told me that you needed me," he said to my silence.

He seldom spoke of uncanny things, my da, and only to the family—which was down to just me, as my younger brother had died four years ago of a wasting sickness. But Da was better at predicting things and knowing things than the hedge witch who held sway in our village. He also had an easier time lighting fires or candles than any other person I knew, wet wood, poor tinder, or untrimmed wick—it didn't matter to him.

"I don't know how you can help," I told him, my voice harsh from lack of use. "They are all dead. My wife, my children."

He looked down, and I knew that it wasn't news to him, that the crows—or whatever magic had spoken to him—had told him about their deaths.

"Well, then," he said, "it was time for me to come." He looked up and met my eyes, and I could see the worry in his face. "Though I thought that I ran ahead of trouble, not behind."

The words should have sent a chill down my spine, but I foolishly believed that the worst thing that could happen to me already had.

"How long are you staying?" I asked.

He tilted his head as if he heard something that I did not. "For the winter," he told me at last, and I tried not to feel relief that I would not be alone. I tried not to feel anything but grief. My family deserved my grief—and I, who had failed to save them, did not deserve to feel relief.

IT WAS A HARSH WINTER, AS IF NATURE HERSELF mourned with me. My da, he didn't get in the way of my grieving, but he did make sure I got up every morning and did the things that were needful to get through the day. He didn't push, just watched me until I did the right thing. A man worked, and he tended those things that needed tending—I knew those lessons from my childhood. He wasn't a man people gainsaid, and that was as true of me as it was the rest of the village.

People came by to greet him. Some of the attention was because he'd been respected and liked, but more was because he could be coaxed to play for them. Music wasn't uncommon in our village, most folk sang and played a little drum or pipe. But most folk didn't sing like my da. When my mother died, no one had been surprised when he'd taken back to traveling, singing for his room and board, as he'd been doing when he first met her.

People brought him a little of whatever they had to pay for his music, and between that and the medicine I traded in barter, we had enough for winter stores even though I hadn't put things back as I usually did. I hadn't been worried about whether there was enough food to eat or enough wood to burn.

I hadn't worried about myself because I'd have as soon joined my little family in their cold graves. With my da here, that route now smacked of cowardice—and if I forgot that sometimes, my da's cool gaze reminded me.

It felt odd, though, not to have someone to take care of; for so long I had been the head of the family. I was not in the habit of worrying about my da: he wasn't the kind of person who needed anyone to fuss over him. He'd survived his childhood—not that he'd spoken of it to me beyond that it had been rough. But my ma, she'd known whatever it had been, and it had sparked fierce pride tinged with sorrow and tenderness. I knew only that he'd left his home while still a stripling boy. He had traveled and thrived in a world hostile to strangers.

He was tough, and it gave him confidence that had backed down my ma's folk when they objected to her marrying a man from outside the village. He was smart—and more than that, he was wise. When he spoke on village matters, which he didn't do often, the villagers listened to him.

He'd survived traveling the world after my mother's death—and he was still lit with the joy that made my home warmer than the logs on the hearth, though the chill left by the death of my little ones and their ma was deep.

My da, he could survive anything, and his example forced me to do the same. Even when I didn't want to.

TWO

SAMUEL

ON THE SHORTEST NIGHT OF THE YEAR, WHEN THE FULL moon hung in the sky, my grandmother came to us. I'd returned to my duties as village healer, so I didn't even think of not answering a knock in the dead of night. Da had gotten used to the middle-of-the-night summonses that were the lot of a healer. He didn't stir, though I was certain he was awake.

I opened the door to a stranger. She was a wild-looking young woman with hair that flowed in unkempt, tangled tresses all the way to the back of her knees. Her face was uncanny and so beautiful that I didn't pay much heed to the beast that crouched beside her, huge though he was.

"The son," she said to me. *The magic flows strongly in you.* Her voice echoed in my head.

"No," said my da, who had exploded to his feet the moment I opened the door. He stepped between us. "You will not have him."

"You shouldn't have run away," she told him. "But I forgive you because you brought a gift with you."

"I will never willingly serve you, Mother," my da said in a voice I'd never heard from him before. "I told you we are done."

"You speak as though I would give you a choice," she said. She glanced down, and the beast I had taken for a dog lunged at my da.

I grabbed the cudgel I kept beside the door, but the beast was faster than I was. It had time to bury its fangs in my da's gut and jerk him between us. The only reason I didn't brain Da was because I dropped the cudgel midswing. And after that, there was no chance to fight.

SHE TURNED US INTO MONSTERS—WEREWOLVES— though I didn't hear that term for many years. She bound us to her service with witchcraft and more cruelly through her ability to break into our minds—in this she had more trouble with Da than with the rest of her wolves. Though she looked like a young woman to all of my senses, I think she was centuries old when she came knocking on my door.

The first transformation from human to werewolf is harsh under the best of circumstances. I now know that most people attacked brutally enough to be Changed die. The witch had some way to interfere, to hold her victims to life until they became the beasts she desired. Even so, I would have died if my da had not anchored me. I heard his voice in my head, cool and demanding, and I had to obey him, had to live. That he was able to do this while undergoing a like fate to mine is a fair insight into the man my da is. That I lived was something that took me a very long time to forgive him for.

I do not know, nor do I wish to, how long I lived as a werewolf serving my grandmother. It could have been a decade or centuries, though I think it was closer to the latter than the former. It was long enough that I had time to forget my given name. I deliberately left it behind because I was no longer that person, but I had not thought to lose it altogether. My name was not the only memory I lost.

I no longer remembered my first wife's face or the faces of my children. Though sometimes in dreams, even all these centuries later, I hear the cry of "*Taid! Taid!*" as a child calls for his father. The voice, I believe, is that of my firstborn son. In the dream, he is lost, and I cannot find him no matter where I look.

My da likes to say that sometimes forgetfulness is a gift. Perhaps had I remembered them clearly, remembered what I'd once had, I would not have survived my time serving the witch. I learned to live in the moment, and the wolf who shared my body and soul made it easy: a beast feels no remorse for the past nor hope for the future.

THREE

ARIANA

ONCE UPON A TIME, THERE WAS A FAIR MAIDEN OF THE faerie courts who rode away from a hunting party, chasing something she could glimpse just ahead of her. Eventually she came to a glade where a strange and handsome man awaited her with food and drink. She ate the food and drank his wine and stayed with the lord of the forest even when the rest of her people found her, sending them back to the court without her.

Time passed, and she gave birth to a girl child who grew up as talented as she was wise. In a human tale, this couple would have had a happily-ever-after ending. But the fae are not human, and they live a very, very long time. Happily-ever-after is seldom long enough for them, and that was true for these two lovers. But for a time they were as happy as any.

They called their daughter Ariana, which means silver, as she early on had an affinity for that metal. As she grew up, it became apparent that her power harked back to the height of fae glory. By the time she reached adulthood, her power outshone even the forest lord's, and he was centuries old and steeped with the magic of the forest.

It is true that the high-court fae were notoriously fickle. It is also true that a forest lord has two aspects: the first is civilized and beautiful as any of the Tuatha Dé Danann, the second is wild as the forest he rules. The sidhe lady eventually grew bored, or perhaps her distaste for her lover's wilder half became too strong. Whatever the reason, she left her grown daughter and her lover without a farewell or notice, to return to the court.

The forest lord mourned his lover only briefly, for his kind, too, are as light in their affections as they are terrible in their hatreds. For a while after she left, he still loved his daughter and took joy in her. But when her power eclipsed his own, he grew jealous and spiteful. When the other fae took notice of her gifts and came to her with gold and jewels to entice her to share her magic, his jealousy outgrew his love and made it as nothing.

FOUR

SAMUEL

THE PACK CUSTOMARILY BEDDED DOWN IN THE WOODS behind the witch's cottage. It was mountainous there, but not particularly cold, though winter still held snow and autumn a fine frost. Our coats were thick, and the interior of the cottage was smoky, too warm, and reeked unpleasantly of rotting things both physical and spiritual.

I don't know about my da or the others, but I was happy to be out of the witch's way as much as possible. She kept us hidden from those who sought her services, both as unseen protection—because she dealt with powerful and dread beings—and as a precaution because she only *mostly* controlled us. My da she never let too near her unless she had some of the other, more obedient wolves nearby.

MY FATHER, CURLED UP BY HIMSELF, RAISED HIS HEAD as I came back from hunting. He stood and gave me a look before turning and trotting off into the woods where the leaves were ruddy and gold. I hesitated, but even then, the obedience was a part of our relationship. Instead of settling down to sleep until morning as I had planned, I stretched twice, then ran in his trail until I caught up. Though I didn't look behind me, I knew that the others followed—as they always did.

At first I thought the other wolves followed us to spy for the witch, but time had proven that wrong. There were six of us werewolves, seven really, though we all knew that Adda was dying—he had trouble stumbling down the trail into the hollow, and I would have to help him up it when we returned.

I had the impression that my father had known some of the wolves from his childhood, but he never confirmed or denied it. He

never spoke to them or of them when we were in human form—
and they never left their wolf shape.

Da had found a small sheltered hollow in the lee of a downed
oak shortly after the witch had brought us here. It served to keep
us hidden and offered some protection from the weather for our
naked bodies. Even though my human skin didn't get cold as it had
before the wolf entered my soul, skin was not as good as fur. It
wasn't winter yet, but the leaves had begun to change to autumn's
colors, and there was a bite to the air.

Da began his change as soon as we were in the oak's protection, but instead of following his example as I usually did, I hesitated. Life was easier when I let the wolf rule the man. The wolf
killed and killed, and it did not turn his stomach or make him
mourn for the creature he used to be.

Da saw that I was hesitating and growled at me—a demand the
wolf wouldn't disobey even if I wanted to.

It hurt. I don't know how my father even figured out that we
could change back to human. I didn't remember doing it the first
time—if I thought about it too long, there were a frightening number of things I couldn't remember very well. It had taken me a
while before I realized that, when my grandmother chose to use
my pain to feed her magic, she sometimes stole more than just
blood or flesh.

Skin absorbing fur felt like bee stings. The crack of bone was
no less painful than a real break. The witch didn't want her wolves
to turn human, but I didn't understand that then. Didn't understand how her magic fought the change to human—I just knew
that it hurt. She must have known we changed into our human
skins. I do not know why she didn't interrupt. Perhaps she was
more afraid of my father than she let on.

"Why are we still doing this?" I asked Da while I was still on
hands and knees and sweating from the required effort. "What
good does it do except to remind us of what we once were?"

He frowned at me. "I made a promise to your mother, boy.

When I told her what my blood was, I promised that I would never allow you to stay in my mother's hands. If you lose your humanity to the wolf—then my mother has won."

I stood up, waited until I was steady on my feet, then raised my hands and turned around slowly so he could see all of me, naked and filthy. "There is more to being human than the resemblance I bear to a man, Da. I have left humanity so far behind . . ."

"No," he growled. He jerked his chin toward the other wolves. "Not like they have. You know right from wrong. Good from evil."

"It would be easier if I could forget." I knew what he would say even before he said it; he was not fond of self-pity, my da.

"Easier doesn't mean better." He didn't say anything more. We never talked much at times like these, when he required me to take on human form. What was there to say? Neither of us wanted to talk of people long dead, nor of the day just past, or the one to come.

He believed that his mother would grow complacent and make a mistake. I had believed him long past foolish hope, but years and decades, and then tens of decades had worn my faith away as a river wears away stone. But I loved my da, and I would not hurt him more with my disbelief—let him believe in a better end than I saw. The end would come whatever we believed, and he found comfort in that future he saw for us. I did not tell him that even if we broke free—we would still be the monsters she had made us. My da, he was a smart man, he knew that as well as I did.

The other wolves waited, their eyes trained on my da. But it was the soft whine from Adda that my da acquiesced to. He sat down on the ground, threw back his head, and sang. I settled with my back to the oak and listened.

His voice had lost the old man's quaver I'd noticed in that last winter we'd spent together as humans, just as both of us had lost the silver hair and the aging skin. Made young again by my grandmother's magic or the bite of the wolf, I had no reason to ask or care.

My father had no instrument but that with which he was born, but that was fine indeed. When he sang, the others gathered around closely, but he only looked at the dying wolf, who laid his muzzle on my father's naked thigh and listened as his breath wheezed in and out. The music and the touch of my da's hand seemed to comfort him.

Witches use the suffering of others for their power, and a werewolf could suffer a great deal before he died. The first sign that Adda was dying was when his ears never grew back quite right. Healthy, we could regrow bits and pieces we lost. Instead of leaving him be, letting him get stronger as she'd done a time or two to others, she'd taken his left front paw when she needed to harvest his pain for her power. We all did what we could for him. When he died, she would spend time with all of us again, until someone started to weaken. Then she would single him out and kill him by inches.

There had been two other wolves who had died that slow death, but my father had not sung to them. Had not sung at all in all the years of our captivity until this wolf had appealed to him without words. I didn't know why this wolf was different—and I would not ask him.

After a while, I joined in Da's song. Our voices worked well together, as they always had. Music hurt more than the shift to human had because music recalled better days, days when I had loved and was loved in return, days when the turning of seasons had meaning. But it hurt worse not to sing. Moreover, when it brought my father some bits of joy, even in the darkest day, how could I not sing?

WHEN CHANGE CAME, IT SNUCK UP ON ME. I DID NOT recognize it for what it was when it began. Autumn ruled, still, but the nights were longer, and I could catch the acrid smell of snow in the air. Not today or the next day, but sometime in the next week there would be a storm.

I was not far from the cottage when I spied one of the fair folk coming to call on the witch. That was unusual because the fair folk, the Tylwyth Teg, had their own powers and usually would have no truck with witchcraft. He was, as they all were, beautiful: tall with eyes as deep blue as the winter sea under dark skies. His skin was silvery with cracks of darkness like the bark of the *bedwyn*.

Before my grandmother turned me into this beast I had never seen a fae, though I'd heard stories about them. They were still a rare enough sight to attract my interest. After a brief hesitation, I abandoned the rabbit's trail I'd been following to ghost behind the fae instead.

Tromping through the remains of the autumn leaves in the witch's woods with no weapon in his hand and looking neither left nor right, this one looked as though he would be easy prey.

I knew better.

The fae were tough, vicious, and deadly—especially the ones that strode through the forest as though they owned it. The lesser fae mostly stayed to the shadows and kept out of the way of things with big, sharp teeth. This one was not one of the Tuatha Dé Danann, the high-court lords, who, above all else, my grandmother feared, so I was under no obligation of her magical chains to report his intrusion. But he was a power; I could feel the forest's attention upon him.

I moved closer to let my nose get a better read on this one. His track smelled of bitterness and jealousy, small, sniveling emotions, though his body language and the forest alertness spoke of his power. I stayed out of his sight as he walked directly to the clearing where the witch made her home.

He rapped sharply on the door, and my grandmother opened it. She was dressed in a thin shift that left nothing to the imagination, and her thick sandy hair glimmered in the sun like honey pouring over her shoulders and hips. She raised her eyebrows when she got a good look, but she stepped back from the entry and let him in without protest.

Curiosity had me skulking to the side of the building and pressing my ear to the wall. *She* didn't know we could hear what went on in the cottage, and we weren't telling her.

"I am surprised," my grandmother said coyly, "to see one of your ilk here calling on such as me."

She was pretty, my grandmother, but not as beautiful as the fair folk; nor was she stupid. If she sounded coy, it was to make the fae believe her less than she was. Powerful things in his world didn't bow and scrape or creep; they attacked from the front with plenty of warning.

"I am the lord of this forest," he told her.

She believed the forest was hers; indeed, the locals called it the Witch's Woods.

"I know, I know," she said without hesitation, and her disdain was sly and hidden. "The birds whisper it to me, and the wind sings with your power. But two nights ago a pair of faery sight hounds came to me. They wore coats of white and rust, and in that way I knew them for fear hounds, the banehounds of old. So fearsome they were, as to stop the very heart in my chest. They came to my dreams and told me that they were gone away. That you could no more hold them obedient. They broke free of your leash. Such creatures do not make good slaves, so they told me." Her voice was innocent and light—but I could feel the malice in her intent.

"Take care, witch," he said.

"They left a promise and a warning for you," she said, her voice softening. "They said that the power you threw away to pad your vanity will not return to you because the followers of the sacrificed god have reached our shores. Already, Underhill writhes under their cold iron and colder prayers. In a few centuries, they will bind the magic in this land, and all the fae will be powerless before them."

I heard a noise, the sound of flat hand meeting cheek, and smirked inwardly because I cared not a smidgen for either of them. He had hit her, and he would pay dearly for it.

"You overstep yourself, witch," he snarled. "You are here on my sufferance, your presence debases my forest with foulness, and you draw the mortals who seek you through my lands."

There was a little silence.

I wondered if we would feast on a forest lord tonight. I licked my lips. Hunting had been lean within the area around the cottage where we could roam without leave from the witch, and she had not been inclined to allow us to forage farther afield.

"I meant no disrespect, sir," she said in an obsequious voice that managed to convey fear and respect. Oh, yes, I thought, we would dine on this one. "I only relay information I have been given. I thought you came because you needed something from me. Did you come to drive me away?"

I could hear the rustle of fabric as he paced.

"I *need* to call my hounds again," the fae lord said, his voice low and vicious. "I have a task to set them to. You will make it possible, or you will not need to worry about where you might live."

"Yes, yes, of course. I understand, sir," her voice was sweet and honey-soft. "Is your need life-and-death? Or simply desire?"

There was a long pause.

"I cannot help if you do not tell me," she pled. "My magic responds to need. I must know what you want and how much you want it." I wondered why the fae could not hear the lie as clearly as I could—but he did not know her, and she lied very well. The fae lied not at all, and so were not always good at seeing untruths when they were uttered.

"Yes," his answer to her was reluctant. "Life-and-death. My word has been given to someone who will destroy me if I cannot keep it."

"Then I can do something," said my grandmother briskly, as if a servile tone had never touched her voice. "I can give you power to call hounds. But, as I am sure you know, my power works on sacrifice. For this, the cost will be dear."

"Not just any hounds," he said sharply, thinking he saw her trap. The fae didn't lie, but deception was an art form to them. "The magical beasts."

I didn't need to see her smile to feel her satisfaction as he came to her trap without seeing it at all. He was prey, no matter how powerful he was. He was not clever enough to escape her—and she would forgive neither the slap nor the threat.

"Magical beasts in doglike form," she clarified. He hadn't listened to her. She'd told him that he wouldn't be able to call the fae dogs again. But she was not fae. She could lie all the time—and she did so when it suited her. But I could tell that she had not lied about that. Magical beasts in doglike form—that would be us.

She meant to let him call wolves when he expected his own hounds. Maybe, maybe if he had controlled the fae banehounds, who were fearsome beasts, he *could* control us. For a while.

"Yes," the forest lord said, not questioning her phrasing. After all, she was only responding to his request to clarify. He never thought to ask her what other magical doglike beasts there were nearby.

I didn't know if he was truly stupid, or if he did not recognize the threat she represented. The fae were proud, worse back in those days, when they ruled, and the humans feared. They did not easily take notice of threats that were not fae in origin.

"I can do that," she said slowly, as if after careful consideration. "You will pay me a pound of silver."

"Fine," he said easily, though it was more than she'd normally have seen in ten years of work.

"That is the cost you owe me," she told him. "But the magic will cost your hand—all witchcraft magic has a price, and I cannot bear that for you. You can decide if it is the left or right."

Silence enveloped the hut, and I left before that changed. If she realized I was there, she would make me do it—just because she knew it would hurt me. There was the faint possibility that she might do it herself; she enjoyed causing pain. But bones are hard to sever—and that one's wrath would focus on the one who took his hand. Probably it would be Dafydd, who led our pack. Let Dafydd chew the fae's hand off; he would enjoy it more than I.

Dafydd was not the name the leader of our wolf pack was born with, any more than my father was Selyf or I was Sawyl—David, Solomon, and Samuel. She changed our names each time she moved—which she did when the mood took her. Sometimes we moved every month for a year. Sometimes we stayed in a place, as we had here, for decades. This time in this place, it pleased my grandmother to use names found in the stories of the followers of the sacrificed god. I did not know why and did not care.

I had forgotten my own name. Sawyl or Samuel would do. Whatever name she called him by, though, my da, he was Bran— and she could not take that away from me.

FIVE

ARIANA

THE LITTLE HOBGOBLIN DID HER BEST TO FOLLOW orders no matter how her heart hurt. Haida cleaned the shivering, scared thing that used to be her lady, paying no attention to the way it flinched or gibbered or cried—just as she had been instructed. She also ignored the way the magic swirled around it, volatile and miserable and . . . deadly.

Haida covered the open wounds in salves that she had made herself this morning from plants she had gathered Outside. Neither she nor her lady trusted anything in their home: it was unstable, reflecting the madness of its lord. In an older time, this would not have been dangerous: Underhill was vast and had been robust, healing itself of spiritual wounds. But Underhill was losing its connection to the mundane world and becoming capricious. For those who dwelt in the forest lord's home in Underhill, the wise ate and drank nothing that had been in the cupboards overnight nor anything that had dwelt in the home as long as a day.

When the hobgoblin had done what she could for the wounds with her salves, she covered the shivering form with clothing and jewels strung on silver chains, then began the process of helping the creature to a stool where it could sit and eat.

"Don't think of me as a person when I'm like that," her lady had told her. "I know I look like myself, but it is not me. It is a beast. A dangerous beast. Be cautious and careful. You alone can help me defeat him."

Her lady was clever, much more clever than Haida, so she followed her rules to the letter. Food.

"Eat," the hobgoblin urged the thing that used to be her lady. Would be again. It had worked before; it had to work this time, too. "It's only a bit of bread and honeycomb. It will do you good."

Haida took a bite, to show the thing both that it was edible and that if it didn't eat soon, Haida might eat all the food. Whatever logic it used, the scarred and broken thing ate as soon as Haida swallowed. As it ate, the outwardly broken parts of it, bones and sinew, knit together and smoothed out into a more pleasing form, until the beast started to look more like Haida's lady again—outwardly at least.

Haida's lady, Ariana, was strong with magic from both sides of her bloodline. The magic allowed her to heal from things that would have killed a hobgoblin. Her father was a forest lord, an independent but powerful fae, her mother one of the high ladies of the highest courts—and would that she were here. But it had been years since she left, and not a word of reply to any message or plea sent by the hobgoblin who had once served her faithfully and now served her daughter.

Even as Haida thought about her grievance with her lady's mother, the building around them groaned and shifted. Disturbed by her fretting or, more likely, by the beast's turmoil. So much power in the hands of the angry and traumatized beast that wore

Ariana's body was not a happy thing, and Haida's anger was making their home worse. She could do something about both matters, and hopefully their place in Underhill would settle a little.

Haida focused her thoughts on her task and brought another tray of food to the table, food stolen this morning from three different villages to keep humans from taking too much notice. The food served the dual purpose of distracting the beast from whatever had the floor uneasy under her feet and further strengthening her lady.

The beast ate everything Haida could provide, then looked up at her with eyes that were solid black. In all other aspects, the beast looked like her lady now, though bruised and battered, but the eyes were always deep, fathomless, black.

"There is one more necessary thing," it told her in a voice made hoarse by screaming and slow from terror and exhaustion. That it spoke meant that her lady was near.

"Yes," Haida agreed, and prepared to pull a fog over the beast's recent memories.

Like most of the lesser fae, Haida had a few things she did very well. But hers was a wilder magic, not easily directed in small spells or bindings. Fogging the beast's memory was difficult for her, and if it fought her, she would not be able to do it at all. But she didn't need to keep the memories at bay for long, just for long enough.

Haida touched the beast's forehead, and the beast grabbed Haida's hand and growled. "Sawyl. Samuel. Samuel Whitewolf," the beast said.

Haida waited. The beast's magic was thick, and it flowed by the hobgoblin like a winter wind, biting and uncomfortable.

"Samuel," the beast murmured more gently, sounding too much like her lady. It released Haida and rubbed at its eyes as it whispered, "They come, the wolves. Death comes with them. Remember."

The beast had powers that her lady did not, powers more akin to Haida's own, though much more powerful. The hobgoblin had no doubt that the words meant something. It would probably be bad because nothing good could come out of the ugliness that was the beast—so her lady had told Haida, and so Haida believed.

When the beast did not seem inclined to say anything more, the hobgoblin touched the creature gently and continued with the task the talk of wolves had interrupted. When she had the proper shape of the magic within her, she settled her magic on the beast. She petted its forehead, and said, "Forget. Let the mists hide the worst and leave only the best."

Her magic snuck in and clothed the beast's memories in kindness, a thing possible only because the beast allowed it. The change was immediate—the terrible beast faded.

Instead of the horrible wounded thing, her lady blinked at Haida, the blackness shrinking down until it was pupil only and her eyes were wide and jewel green. Open wounds were absorbed by deep brown skin, scars hidden by glamour until she looked no different than she ever had.

"Hobgoblin?" she said, sounding a little confused but not distressed.

Her lady looked around the kitchen, Haida's domain. It was neat and tidy as always, if not so grand as the rest of the house. The hobgoblin felt the moss-covered walls of the kitchen, which had pulled back in distress at the beast's presence, ease back into place—but the stillness had a waiting feeling rather than that of a home at peace, and she worried.

"Yes, my lady," said the hobgoblin sadly, because the confusion in her lady's face was being replaced by worse things as the magic Haida had worked was dispelled, and memory resettled properly. Her lady only needed to forget for that breath of time, so that she would have courage to take back her power and body from the beast.

Her father the forest lord was dual-natured. He had the form of the sidhe, and another of a forest fae. Ariana's beast was born of that heritage, but had her father not brutalized her with pain and the terror of the hounds he commanded, it would never have materialized. The beast, a creature of the forest, unlike Ariana, could not disobey a direct order from the forest lord—what had started out as a punishment had borne useful fruit for Ariana's father.

Haida's lady sucked in a breath and looked at her hands, moving the fingers gently, then clenching them into fists.

"I don't remember everything the beast did this time," she said, her voice tight. "Did it do what he wanted us to do?"

Haida shook her head. "I don't know, Mistress. Your magic is beyond me. You will have to look at what it created yourself."

THE LITTLE HOBGOBLIN, GREEN-GRAY AND COVERED with wiry hair from head to feet, was closer to the Heart of Magic than the Tylwyth Teg, the greater fae like Ariana. Haida was like a shepherd who cared for the flocks and Ariana a weaver who worked tapestries with their yarn. One was not inherently more skilled or powerful than the other but differently able. Other fae did not see it as Ariana did, including Haida. To them, lesser fae were weak, but for her father, their home shivered and groaned, while only Haida could bring it comfort. If it had not been for Haida, Ariana knew she would have long ago been lost to the beast.

Ariana shed the last of the hobgoblin's veil of shadows, ready to face the results of her father's bidding and the beast's obedience. The first few times she'd been able to remember what she'd done after her father reduced her to that other aspect. But eventually, her memories had not been so clear. This time, like the time before, she could remember nothing after she'd broken under the wave of terror that was the banehounds' magic.

Her father would succeed in destroying her. All she could hope for was to ensure that he got no gain by it. She was so afraid that she would fail even in that.

She stood up carefully, but although she was dizzy and weak, the pain of her injuries was fading quickly.

"How long this time?" she asked Haida as Ariana walked out of the kitchen and down the hall with the poise her mother had drilled into her before she left. The advantage of moving with grace was that it kept her centered, so she didn't fall on her face. Every time her bare feet touched the floor, she drew magic from the earth to strengthen herself just as the food she'd eaten had strengthened her.

"Four days," Haida told her. "He left as soon as the dogs finished."

That was unusual. He liked to supervise her work, though what she did was so far outside of his forest-bound magic that he could not follow it. There was something she should remember about the dogs . . .

The color of old blood and snow, with fangs that tore, the hounds delivered pain and terror to freeze her forever. That was the gift of the white and red hounds of the forest lord, terror that stopped the breath and heart.

"My lady?"

Not *that*. She couldn't remember that, or she wouldn't stay in control. If she were reduced to her other aspect, the one who could only follow the orders of the power that gave a forest lord dominion over the beasts in his forest, all would be lost.

There was nothing left, now, of the father who had loved her. The one who had taken her on long walks in the woods and taught her to speak to the deep-voiced oaks and the quivering willow. No more than there was anything left of the daughter who had loved him and believed that he could do no wrong.

He'd told her that he had a commission for which he'd been well paid in favors and power—the power was what he craved, almost as much as he wanted to see her reduced to something that could only obey him, something he had no reason to be jealous of. She was to make a weapon that could be used to siphon the magic from any fae, sidhe, hobgoblin, and anything in between.

Her father couldn't or wouldn't see beyond his immediate goals to what such an artifact meant.

He was not the only fae who had lost power beneath the growing tide of iron, nor was he the most corrupt. The Tuatha Dé Danann who commissioned the work was powerful—but there were others yet stronger. By the artifact's very existence, it would cause a war that would not end until there was no one left who desired it. Ultimately it would bring an end to the fae and everything they would destroy in their wake.

Her father, blinded by need, was determined to force her to use her magic to make the artifact. She was more determined that she would not.

Ariana turned into her workroom and looked at the fist-sized lump of silver that lay on the table. As soon as she picked it up, she understood that she had failed.

"The main spell is set," she told Haida, her voice raw. She held the destruction of the world in her hand. "We are undone."

"Can you use it to destroy him?" asked the hobgoblin, ever practical.

"When the sight of him turns my knees to water?" Ariana said bitterly. "He has changed me. Made me a frightened and powerless creature who is as obedient to his command as any of his hounds ever were. I cannot move against him in his presence." Once, she'd been strong-willed and powerful, but now she was nothing, a shadow of what she had been—broken to her father's will except in these stolen moments.

But there was something about her father's hounds, something she should remember.

"Then we are undone," said Haida practically, licking delicately at her hand, then smoothing it over the hair on her cheeks. "If you have finished what he wanted, we should leave. He will follow—he cannot be what he is and not give chase. But he will play with his new toy first. It will give us a chance to lose ourselves in the world. I can keep us hidden from his hounds for many days. My magic is not powerful, but it is subtle."

Courageous hobgoblin. Haida always examined a problem and found the best path from where she found herself to somewhere she might survive.

Ariana drew upon her example and examined what had already been done and sealed within the silver. Until this time of awakening when her father was gone, she'd been able to destroy the work she'd done before he noticed. Once a spell was sealed into the silver, she could not unwork it—any more than anyone else could. She held her hand near and watched as the silver called her magic.

"As I said," she told Haida slowly, "this will eat the magic of any fae." She paused, examining the flow of the magic in the silver because there was something unexpected that she had to work out. "Maybe I can squeeze the flow until it is only a bare trickle. If it can only pull a little, how much harm can it do?"

The hobgoblin sank down on her haunches and smiled, revealing sharp green teeth. "I told you. Told you that you would outsmart him."

"When all he has to do to keep me stupefied with terror, obedient to his command, is call on his hounds?" Ariana asked. "You are overly optimistic. As long as he has the hounds . . ." And for an instant she knew why he'd left, knew that it was important, but she couldn't get past the thoughts of his hounds, and the reason for his departure trickled out of her grasp like water.

Survival meant that she pay attention to the embryonic artifact in her hands—and not pull the beast inside her back to the forefront by fretting about the hounds. She turned to Haida. "Even if I slow the draw to little more than nothing, eventually it will amass power. I can make it take years, centuries maybe, but eventually it will hold enough to be valuable."

"What it holds someone can take," the hobgoblin agreed. "Can you stop that?"

"No." She was powerful but not as powerful as some. To lay

such locks on the artifact that no one could break it open was beyond her. And it would be unwise, even if she could. If it did nothing but sit in the cottage and steal magic from the fae that passed near it—eventually it would eat all magic and concentrate it in the lump of silver that fit into her hand. She didn't know how much the metal could hold—but an explosive release when the silver could hold nothing more would be destructive on a scale she could almost not comprehend. Not as horrible as what would happen if it was able to hold all of the magic indefinitely—without magic, all life would cease.

"But I can make it so the magic it collects dissipates back to the Heart of Magic." The Heart of Magic was the center of the world. Magic held in the Heart did not come readily to anyone's hand but caused the wind to blow and the rain to fall. Ariana smiled fiercely at her little friend. "And—thus fulfilling the geas and thwarting my father." She considered how to do that. "I need you for this, Haida, and it will probably not be easy."

Haida bowed low. "It is my joy to aid you in any manner I might. But himself will be back soon—it is unlike him to be absent for long. Is there time?"

"Yes," said the beast that now dwelled within Ariana. "The hounds have fled, and he seeks the means to recall them."

Ariana closed her eyes and took in a shaky breath, waiting for the beast to subside. That was what she had needed to remember. His hounds were gone.

She should have felt relief but could not shake the feeling that her father was more dangerous than ever. Could not quiet her fear of him, and that fear made the beast stir again. She could not afford to let her beast take control, not with such delicate magic to embroider. She collected herself and looked at the hobgoblin, who was watching her warily.

"Haida, we can do this," she said with more confidence than she actually felt. "The hounds have been chafing under his leash, and they have left him. That's where he has gone—to reclaim the hounds. We might have enough time to do this thing."

USING HAIDA'S SENSE FOR THE WILD MAGIC THAT LIN-gered in the smallest thing and was closest to the Heart of Magic, Ariana worked until the hobgoblin made her stop and eat. Then she worked some more, the constant drain from the emerging artifact only a slight handicap.

The very slowness of its working was evidence that her other self was fully engaged in the attempt to mitigate the harm the artifact could cause, something she had not known for certain. The beast had seen the way to render this artifact mostly innocuous, just as Ariana had, and had shown itself to be an ally of sorts.

A fae of average power would have to keep the artifact the beast had crafted for weeks before it had an appreciable effect on his magic. So much the beast had managed.

She lost track of time, so tired she did not realize that it meant the beast had come to help. When she came to herself, she held a silver bird in her hand and just enough magic in her body to tell that it was an artifact, sealed and done. But she could not tell if she had accomplished her purpose or not.

She cupped the little silver bird in her hands, trembling with fatigue, as the walls trembled around her. This was her father's house, and it did not take joy in those who would work against him.

"It is done," she told Haida, who was hovering nearby. "Can you tell if it is for good or ill? I have burnt out my magic in its making."

"Leave the silver bird," said Haida. "It will distract him, and much good may it do him. I am not such as you to read an artifact. You have done what you could. Come, let us leave this place before it collapses apurpose. Underhill is no longer stable, and it is angry with us."

"Underhill is angry with the sidhe and not your kind," corrected Ariana tiredly, though she staggered to her feet. "Though my father's home is not best pleased with the two of us, that is also true."

Underhill had been necessary for her work. Magic did not lend itself to complicated things in the Outside, the land that now belonged to the short-lived, magic-blind folk.

"Underhill does not concern itself with sidhe or not," grumbled Haida, steadying Ariana when she would have fallen. "Only fae and not fae. And the fae are failing it, allowing the humans to bind what was not meant to be bound."

The hobgoblin was a great deal stronger than she looked, which was useful under the circumstances. But she was tired, too, so their travel was slow. If they could get out of her father's lands before he returned with his hounds, they might have a chance at eluding him for a short while.

But Ariana knew there would be no real escape. Artifact or no, it was her destruction that her father craved. So when the ground warned her, the trees whispering his name as flowers trembled—and then his horn sounded, summoning his hounds—she was not overcome with dismay. She would have had to have some hope to feel dismayed.

"We are finished," she told Haida, feeling fear rise like bile even without the magic of his hounds touching her. That he called to them meant that he must have found a way to win them back. "You need to flee."

The hobgoblin snarled at her.

"Do not make me make it an order," Ariana said—but it was already too late, for either of them.

"Ariana," purred her father's voice.

She turned around and faced him. He wore his wild aspect, stag horns reaching upward and tangling in the lower branches of the tree he stood under.

A shiver slid through her, a feeling of inevitability, as if this moment had been fated since her birth. That other part of her, the one she'd warned Haida to be careful of, stirred restlessly, ready to shield her from her father. The thought of the hobgoblin reminded her that Ariana was not the only one her father had reason to be angry at.

"Father." She stepped squarely in front of her little, faithful friend.

He looked around the woods, at Haida, at the grass at Ariana's feet—at everywhere other than Ariana herself—and smiled gently. "Did you think to flee me with the artifact still undone?"

"No, Father," she said staunchly. He would kill her. When he knew it all, he would kill her. "It is finished."

He held the little silver bird out to her. She hadn't realized that he'd been holding it.

"This?" He tossed it on the ground, and in a voice that carried the low rumble of distant thunder, he said, "This is garbage. You have broken your promise, your sworn word. To do so is death for the fae."

She raised her chin as triumph rushed through her. Whatever she and her beast had managed, it had thwarted her father's will. She might die, but he could not use her to destroy the world. "It does what I promised you it would. What the *thing* you turned me into by the tender care of your hounds promised you that the artifact would do. It eats the magic of any fae the wielder desires and allows it to be consumed again. Finished and sealed, so it cannot again be altered."

She could not lie and did not need to. The first part had been done when she and Haida had sought to deflect the artifact's purpose. The last she knew as well. However else the artifact functioned, she had not broken the word given by the beast.

He narrowed his eyes at her and snarled. The glimpse of the fangs in his mouth tightened her stomach and left her light-headed.

"You knew what I wanted," he said.

"Yes," she agreed, finding that the light-headedness had

brought with it a sort of sereneness—or maybe that had come from the earlier feeling that this meeting had been fated for them. He would kill her. Hopefully, it would not hurt too much, but there was nothing she could do to prevent it. "You knew that I did not want to build what you wanted. The strictures you gave me were loose enough that I could slide around them." Her father was powerful but not clever, not like her mother had been or Haida.

"You will make me another artifact, then," he said. "Or fix this one."

She shook her head. "The bird is finished. It is an artifact sealed and immutable. And I?" She smiled at him. "Artifacts demand a price. I do not have enough magic left in me."

Artificers were rare, even among the most powerful of the fae. He would not find another he could bend to his will before the terms of his agreement with one more powerful than he would come due. She closed her eyes and raised her face to the sun; she didn't expect to live long enough to see another day. Her only satisfaction was that he had not won: her magic would not destroy the fae—and her father would not outlive her by long.

Her father picked the bird up off the ground and rolled it around in his hand—and she saw that his right arm ended in a rough and bloody lump of bandaging.

"Father," she said before she considered the wisdom of it, "what did you do to your hand?"

SIX

SAMUEL

MY FATHER RAN HIS FINGERS THROUGH ADDA'S UN-healthy brown coat, and growled, "I thought you said she demanded the forest lord's hand to power the spell."

The witch had called Adda as soon as the forest lord—one arm wrapped in bandages—had left. She kept him until late in the afternoon, then dumped him outside when she was finished with him. As soon as he fell, my father and I had changed back to human. Adda needed help no wolf could render.

I brought the bowl of water to the weakened wolf and fed the water to him, one handful at a time. I made no answer to my da's accusation. His anger wasn't directed at me, and there was no way to answer the anguish in his eyes. Words didn't come to me as they once had, anyway.

Instead, I crooned to the suffering beast as he swallowed. Da patted my shoulder in mute apology for his sharpness, and I nodded an acknowledgment.

She'd mutilated Adda again.

His left front paw had not regrown from the last time; moreover, it was festering despite all I could do. I'd noticed that the wounds she made to feed her magic were more likely to rot than other, naturally acquired wounds, more difficult even for werewolves to heal.

To work the spell for the fae, tonight she'd taken Adda's right front paw, too. He could not walk in wolf form and he had not the strength to try to take on a human form, even if he knew how, which I was not certain of.

The wolf in my father's arms whined at him, and Da bent his head. "It will be well," he murmured. He looked at the cottage and the corners of his mouth whitened.

My mother's voice whispered in my ears. *Look now to your da. If you've never seen rage on his face, you have now. Those old fools won't know what hit them.*

I couldn't remember what long-ago conflict she'd been talking about, but I knew that she'd been right. Then. But this was a fight he could not win, and we all knew it. I began changing back to wolf. There was nothing more to do for Adda that my da wouldn't do, and I would be more use to him in my wolf form than as a weak human.

Dafydd made a soft sound, as gentle as I'd ever heard out of his mouth. The rest of the wolves hovered uncertainly.

"And a fat lot of help you have been," snarled my father at Dafydd. "He is your son, and you watch as she kills him."

Though Dafydd had always been quick to punish any sign of disrespect before, this time he didn't take any action at all. I couldn't read his emotions—of all the wolves, Dafydd was the most difficult to read. It was as though the only thing he ever felt was anger or fear of the witch, nothing else.

Adda woofed, catching Da's attention.

"I," my father said, "am through watching." He kissed Adda on the forehead, then broke the wolf's neck with a quick jerk of his hands.

It was so fast. One moment Adda had been panting in pain and the next he was gone.

That was when Dafydd finally growled, and the heat of his anger swept through the air.

Da stood up, let the dead wolf roll off his lap and onto the ground. He started the change that would turn him back to wolf. Dafydd and my da had disagreed before, even fought a time or two—and Da had always backed down before matters grew serious. But in my da's eyes, I could tell that he'd reached his breaking point. He was done.

I stepped between them, so Dafydd could not attack Da until Da was fully wolf. I didn't think it would happen, Dafydd was usually fair. But I stepped in anyway, just in case I was wrong.

A horn blew in the distance, a clear soft note that wrapped itself around my throat and tugged. The forest lord's call was more than any of us could resist, and I found myself running beside Dafydd, shoulder to shoulder. Da finished his change while we ran.

We would answer the fae's call and do his bidding if he could control us, and kill him if he couldn't—and I didn't much care which. When we were finished, there would be a reckoning either for my father's defiance or for Dafydd's complicity. The battle had only been delayed, not halted. Dafydd was huge and violent—only a little smaller than I was. My da was a little less than three-quarters of Dafydd's weight, but he was canny, my da. I did not know who would win.

I'd expected a short run to the fae, but it turned out to be a fair distance and I revised my estimates of his power—the chances of avoiding doing whatever he asked of us went down with each mile. It didn't bother me much. What could he ask that we had not already done for my grandmother? Any pretense of goodness that I ever claimed was spent long ago. The only thing that mattered to me was Da.

We topped a rise, and there was a small clearing laid out before our eyes. The fae lord was there, the bandage on his right arm red with his blood. He was less human-seeming out here in his woods. Antlers rose from his head and spread the width of his shoulders and more—and he was huge. He blew on his horn again, and it called songs from our throats.

We half slid, half ran down the backside of the rise and leaped over the creek on the bottom. Once across the water, Dafydd slowed to a cautious dogtrot, and the rest of us followed his lead into the meadow where the forest lord waited.

SEVEN

HAIDA

"MY HAND?" THE FOREST LORD SAID, RAISING THE STUMP of his arm. "*This* is the price I paid for what you have done to me." He threw the artifact Haida's lady had made at a tree. It hit and tore bark from the trunk, leaving a weeping wound. The little silver bird dropped to the ground out of sight.

He waited, but her lady was not such a fool as to say anything with her father in a towering rage. Not that her silence was likely to buy her safety in the long run. Haida understood that the lady had known that, really, since she made the decision to make sure that her little bird would never serve his purposes.

Haida said, her voice stinging with contempt, trying to draw his attention away from her lady, "You went to the crone by the white spring. To a witch. A human."

The forest lord hissed, his deerlike ears flattening with ire. He flung a hand out toward Haida, and the little hobgoblin stiffened her spine and prepared to accept the poison she'd spun.

But her lady stepped to the side and took the blow of magic herself. Haida wailed and started forward as the pain dropped her lady to her knees. The hobgoblin touched her lady's shoulder, trying to dilute the effect of the forest lord's anger.

"Go," said her lady with power in her voice. "Leave me. Hide." And such was the strength of the lady, even diminished as she was, that Haida could only follow her orders.

The forest lord, rage forcing a bellow like one of the great deer in rut out of his throat, threw another bolt of pain into his daughter. Hating herself for her inability to defend Ariana, Haida found a place under some bushes, where she could at least bear witness and give what aid she could.

The lord took the horn he wore on a thong around his chest and blew again, summoning his hounds.

The sound did what the pain had not. When Ariana raised her head, it was the beast who looked out of her eyes. The beast's lips curled back from white teeth, and it started to get to its feet. Haida felt a breathless instant of hope. The beast was more powerful in its way than her lady was. Haida could feel the power of the beast's magic, full and strong. Proof, if she'd needed it, that the beast and her lady were truly different from each other. Had the beast had more time, even a moment, it might have destroyed the forest lord—but the howls that answered the great horn caused the beast to freeze, and fear robbed it of its power. The beast rolled into a ball on the ground and waited for what would come.

The animals responding to the forest lord didn't sound like his hounds. Evidently the fae lord felt the same, for he paused, taking his attention off his daughter for a moment. If only her lady hadn't sent her away, Haida might have managed to make use of the momentary lapse, but she was too far away to do anything but watch.

EIGHT

SAMUEL

THERE WAS A MOMENT WHEN WE WERE FREE OF THRALL, after the forest lord blew his horn the second time, after we topped the rise, so he could plainly see that what had come to his call was not his hounds. While he stood in shock, we were free. I had not realized until then that the witch had given up her hold upon us when he summoned us with his horn.

I was of free will for the first time since she'd knocked upon my door and turned my father and me into monsters. We stopped, looking down upon them. Dafydd whined, and the others shuffled around, but my father and I stood frozen.

The forest lord's face twisted with anger, and he looked at us and closed his single fist. I felt his determination, his magic, roll over me. I snarled in protest, but we were his.

The forest lord turned his attention to the girl curled up on the ground in front of him. "You are of no further use to me." Next to his bulk, she looked frail and helpless. I could not see her face, only a long fall of pale silver hair touched with lavender that could not have belonged to a human. He looked at us then, smiled savagely, and said, "Direwolves. I had heard the witch had such to serve her. You are not my hounds, but you will suffice for this. Hurt this woman for me. She is meant to die today, but I want her to suffer first."

Slaved to his purpose, the pack ran to do his bidding. All except my father and I. Tantalized by that breath of freedom, I fought him, fought the magic that tried to hold me. And I failed. All I could do was slow my obedience so that the rest of them were already attacking the defenseless fae woman by the time I reached her, conscious that my father's pace was just a little slower than mine.

I closed my fangs on the fae woman's shoulder, biting deep, teeth scraping against bone. I had meant to crush her throat, and so to rebel against the fae lord's command—and save her from her suffering as my da had saved Adda. But the fae lord's magic was too strong for me.

Dafydd snarled at me and snapped his teeth in my direction. Maybe I was in his way, maybe he had seen what I tried to do. Dafydd believed in obedience. I released my grip and snarled back at him.

Which was why I saw Da attack the forest lord. Such a fae in his other form is a huge thing, heavier and taller than the biggest horse I'd ever seen. My father ran up the fae lord's side, digging in with claws like a cat climbing a tree. His fangs sank deep into the fae lord's neck—and the leash controlling us was no more.

I leaped away from the dying fae woman and dove to my father's aid. Dafydd hesitated. His prey was bleeding and helpless— but there was no longer anything forcing him to continue to hurt the woman.

For a moment, it was only Da and I. The forest lord broke my father's grip and tossed him to the ground. I leaped and got lucky, biting deep into the tendon behind his knee. The fae roared—and the forest answered. Magic, wild and painful, seared over my back like a swarm of angry bees.

But Da harried him from the other side, and the magic scattered as the forest lord lost concentration. He drew a bronze knife from his belt and swiped it at Da, who flowed away like water. Then he brought the blade back, so quickly I could tell it was an intentional strike, and I was the target he'd intended in the first place.

I could have dropped my hold, but I was close to crippling him. I wasn't afraid of death, had been waiting for it since my wife and children had died. To die as Adda had would be a release. I hung on grimly, feeling the tendon start to tear, but it would not give way before his knife found me.

Before it could connect, Dafydd's jaws closed on the fae lord's wrist and dragged the knife off course. The forest lord staggered, pulled off balance by Dafydd's unexpected weight and further off balance by the leg I'd damaged.

With a high-pitched scream that hurt my ears, he dropped the knife and grabbed Dafydd—and impaled him upon his sharp, pale ivory horns. One tine pierced Dafydd's throat and came out his eye. As I saw him die, I felt it, too. Like a tear in my chest that opened me to the pain he'd felt as he died.

For a moment, my eyes quit working, blinded by Dafydd's trauma. When I could see again, Pedr was dead. His head pulled off his body, and my own body convulsed as I felt that, too.

Adda had been my pack mate. But it had been his dying that had dwelt in us all, not his death, which had been a release. Dafydd's death, Pedr's death was no release. They had been vital and healthy, then dead, and their deaths rippled through bonds I had not realized were there until they hurt so.

This morning there had been seven of us—and now we were four—and our pack had no leader.

That last bothered my wolf, and if he had been in charge of our body, as he was during most battles I had engaged in since I was Changed, he would have disengaged and run. But neither witch, nor forest lord, nor wolf held my leash. I would not abandon my da to this creature.

My fangs severed the tendon, and I dropped to the ground, unable to keep hold where the fae's flesh had given way. The forest lord's leg collapsed, toppling him like a woodsman toppled an oak.

Unlike an oak, he did not lie still when he landed. He rolled, grabbed his knife, and stuck it into a wolf too distracted by the other wolves' deaths to get out of the way of the clumsy strike. Ieuan's belly ripped upward, spilling intestines and soft organs on the ground. Though the initial strike had been luck, the fae lord adjusted his grip and pulled the knife in a twisted path that ended in a thrust into the wolf's spinal column. So fast, Ieuan was dead, too.

This time, my pack mate's death didn't slow me down. It didn't hurt any less—but the shock of it was gone. I knew what it felt like now when one of our pack died.

From first impact to death was less than a breath's time. Ieuan was older than I and only a moment ago he was alive and unhurt. There had been times that I would have killed him myself if it had not been for the witch's hold upon me. I would not have thought I would mourn his death.

The fae lord was quick. So quick. Even half-crippled and one-handed, he dealt out painful wounds and the three of us who were left, Da, Deiniol, and I, learned to be swift and wary, to hit and *move*. If my first attack had not been from behind him, I'd already have joined Dafydd and the others in death. But the fae lord was too wary to let any of us behind him so easily again.

I suppose that time lasted no more than a few minutes, but it seemed like a long time that we fought with none of us gaining advantage. Then he stuck the knife deep in my da's hip. It caught there and he had to jerk to get it out. Deiniol dove to help Da—and I jumped and caught onto his mutilated right arm and ripped and tore with ferocity born of fear. He swung his arm, and I flew loose, my head hitting a tree like a smith hits an anvil. When I staggered to my feet, the forest lord was dead.

My father had torn out his throat.

Deiniol was dying, impaled, as Dafydd had been, on the forest lord's tines. The light dimmed in his eyes, and they fogged over with death's touch. His presence fell from my senses. My father howled in grief, and I echoed the sound.

I had not liked them, any of them. But they had been my pack, my family in spirit. Dafydd had led the others to our aid and given his life to save mine. I mourned them properly.

The fae lord's body moved, and I turned with a snarl to face another attack. He was still dead, but as ice melts into water, his body melted into the soil, leaving clothing and accouterments behind. In only a few moments, the only bodies left to rot on the forest floor belonged to my pack.

Da tried to stand up, but the fae lord's knife was still embedded in his hip. I nudged him ungently, telling him to quit moving.

Then I began my change to human. It should have been harder as I had changed earlier that day, but it wasn't. The pain was still there, but not so much of it, and the actual change felt . . . natural. Good.

In human skin again, I knelt beside my father. It had taken too long to change, and he'd already begun healing around the knife blade—just the flesh so far and not the bone, which would have been more complicated and more painful to fix.

"Quick, then," I told him, and held him down with one hand and jerked the blade free with the other.

He panted with the pain but made no other sound. He would heal now—and he wouldn't thank me for hovering. He didn't like being watched while he was in pain. None of my medical knowledge had ever done the werewolves much good—they either lived or they died. My experience told me that my father would live. Probably.

A crow had landed on Dafydd, and I drove it off. In response to my growl, the fae woman made a faint, pained noise.

I'd forgotten about her. I knew nothing of her but the taste of her blood in my mouth. I had not seen her face or heard her voice. She was nothing to me.

Nothing but my victim.

I did not know how long my freedom from the witch would last. Maybe if Da and I ran fast enough, we'd escape her entirely. I didn't believe that, but it was a faint possibility. But Da had to heal—and maybe in the meantime I could be of use to someone.

There was a fae creature of a kind I'd never seen beside the woman's body. She was maybe half the size of a human woman, no taller than my waist. Where her dress, which was silvery blue of a fine weave, did not cover, her body was covered with a coarse green-and-gray hair that thickened on the top of her head. She should have looked grotesque, but there was a rightness, a natural-ness to her form that made her oddly beautiful. She smelled female with a strong hint of power and growing things.

Her face was human enough for me to find expression on it, but it reminded me more of a fox's than a woman's, an impression not dispelled by triangular ears, now half-flattened along her skull. Her eyes were overly large, and she squinted like a being more used to shadows than light, wrinkling her nose and panting half in fear and half in desperation as I approached.

She hissed and bared sharp, weasel-like teeth and put herself between the wounded woman and me.

"I mean no harm, little one," I told her. "I have some training. Let me help."

"You would help my lady? You who hurt her?" The words were clear, if oddly accented.

"Before I was a monster, I was a healer," I told her. "This hurt I and my—" My what? Fellow monsters? It had been a long, long time since I'd talked to anyone but my da. It felt odd to put my thoughts into words, especially as I was distracted. "My pack. We were under duress and would not have hurt her otherwise." A lie. I did not lie. Once, it had been a matter of pride to me. So I amended my state-ment to make it truth. "*I* would not have hurt her otherwise."

She looked at me. Glanced over at my da, whose hip was scabbed over. I noticed that he was changing to human himself, and I stepped a little sideways, between her and Da. He was less able to protect himself effectively when changing.

She settled a little, as if my action had reassured her, and stepped aside.

I stripped the fae woman's body free of the rags of clothing our attack had left her. Her skin was darker than anything I'd seen on a human, a warm shade like a doe's summer coat. But the ridged scars that crossed and recrossed themselves like a macabre braid were white. Some looked as though they were put on her body with a whip, but more were the result of wounds very similar to the freshly open ones we'd given her.

In addition to the wounds from this day, there were a number of healing wounds. Bite wounds. Doubtless from the hounds that the forest lord had lost control of.

"Will she live?" The little creature crouched beside me and reached out to pet the wounded woman's arm.

"I don't know fae," I told her. "But she's lived through worse."

"She should be healing faster than this," the little creature said. "She always has before."

I thought of Adda and his festering wounds, and said nothing. The forest lord's body had gone to earth, but his clothing remained. I went to where he had died and appropriated his fine cloak, a bronze eating knife, and a flask filled with bracata—wort fermented with honey. I had found such alcohol good for cleaning wounds.

Returning to the woman, I cut the cloak into strips and used them to bind up the worst of the wounds.

"These should properly be stitched," I told the little creature. "But I don't have needles or thread. Without that, they will leave scars behind—like the other wounds have." I frowned at a nasty mass of scars on her ribs. "Why did he do this?" I asked.

She bowed her head. "She is two-natured, like you and her father, though not two-formed. This aspect, her sidhe aspect, is impervious to her father's commands. But her other self is closer to the natural world and must obey him. It rises to protect her from danger or harm. Her father needed her obedience to build a thing—a powerful and bad thing. She would not do it, so he tortured her with fear and pain until the other part of her rose."

"He was her father?" I asked.

She nodded.

The fae woman looked fragile and broken on the forest floor. But to resist such treatment, to have risen again, over and over— such a one was tougher than she looked.

"I can't do much," I told the fae creature. "I don't have the supplies. I can clean the wounds and stop the bleeding and give her the chance to heal. She needs to be somewhere out of the weather. There is snow coming."

"There is shelter." She bobbed her head. "And we have needles and thread. What else do you need?"

"Honey," I told her. "Willow bark. Water. How far away is the shelter?"

"Shelter is not far," she said. "Twenty minutes' walk. If you can bring her, I can take you. And also there might other items you mention be found, an Underhill wills it to be so." She sounded doubtful. "What is not there I can steal."

Promise of a shelter and supplies changed my to-do list. I finished stanching the bleeding. If the little creature could run, we could turn her twenty minutes to half that.

"Samuel." My da sounded tired. I looked at him, and his face was drawn and gray. The mark on his hip was still an angry red. "I'll find you after I dispose of the bodies."

I nodded and wrapped the remnants of the forest lord's cloak around myself, using the fabric to secure the flask of bracata and the knife and sheath. I picked up the woman. She was light in my arms, lighter than my wife had been, though she was taller.

I could remember the feel of my wife's weight in my arms, but I could not see her face. I staggered a step as my mind went blank in panic because I couldn't remember. Couldn't remember her face or her name, just glimpses of a lifetime. My breath caught in my throat with the terrible grief of loss. It had mattered a lot less while my grandmother had me on her leash. I'd lost more than my humanity while in my grandmother's hands—I'd lost my wife and my children and I had not recognized how terrible the loss was. I could not remember them, not their faces or their names.

"You are hurt?" asked the little fae creature tentatively.

"Yes," I said because I would not lie. "But not in the way that you mean."

My father said a name that slid off my ears. He waited a moment, then said, "Samuel?"

I must have looked a little wild-eyed when I turned to him. "She stole my memories. Stole my name."

He nodded once. "There will be a reckoning."

"Do you remember them? My wife and children?" I asked. When he nodded again, my panic eased. "As long as someone does, they aren't lost."

"They are not lost as long as I live," my father agreed. "I'll remember them for you. Go ahead, Samuel. I'll come by and by."

I nodded. I turned to the little fae creature. "I can run with her. Lead me as quickly as you can, and I will follow."

The fae creature ran. She stumbled a little here and there, and I had the impression that she was very, very tired. But she was quick, so it didn't take us long before we came upon a small hut that was less inviting than my grandmother's and looked as though no one had lived in it for years. She reached over her head and pulled a chain to release the latch. When she opened the door, I knew it for a fae residence because it was larger on the inside than on the outside.

As soon as I stepped into it, I felt an odd, hostile personality brush up against me. Letting my lips curl in a snarl, I pulled my patient closer to me in a futile effort to protect her from something I could not detect with any of my usual senses. The odd entity paused, then slid over my wolf in an exuberant and laughing run, and I smelled, for a very brief moment, the rich scent of summer flowers.

The little fae hesitated, then murmured, "The father is dead, so the lady is mistress here. I think we shall find what we need to tend her wounds. Follow me."

She took me to a large room and bade me lay the woman on a tick of straw that rested on ropes suspended on a carved wooden frame. She lit the fire in the room with a look and a word in a language I did not understand. Then left as I cut the bindings I'd put on the first and largest wound.

I cleaned the wound with the alcohol. By the time I was through, the little creature had returned with a bronze needle, fine thread, a jar of honey, several jars of salve, and a pitcher.

"The thread is too fine," I told her. "It will tear her skin. I need something more like thread to stitch leather."

She nodded and trotted away.

The pitcher was warm when I picked it up, and the brown liquid inside tasted strongly of willow bark. I set it aside and tested the salves, all but one of which I could identify the contents of. That one, I set aside with the pitcher.

The fae woman's little friend returned with appropriate thread and a bucket of water, and I began the tedious task of cleaning, stitching, and bandaging.

The woman didn't stir beyond a flutter of her eyelashes when I stitched up a particularly nasty tear over her hip. The worst hurt was a gash in her thigh that was too old to stitch. It would likely cause her trouble long after it healed. I covered it with a salve of fat, honey, yarrow, and comfrey that the little fae, who had shyly introduced herself as Haida, had brought back when I asked if she had such a thing.

"It was lurking on the shelves in her kitchen," she said, as if I'd asked for an explanation for why her kitchen could supply exactly the salve I'd asked for. "This is my lady's home now. And it approves of you." She gave me sharp look and a warning jerk of her chin. "For now."

Someone knocked briskly at the door, but before I could do

much more than stand up from where I'd been kneeling beside the bed, the door opened, and my da came striding into the room where I was working. He looked at the woman, then at me.

"Is she worth the death we have laid before her?" he asked me soberly.

"I do not know those of yours that died today. As for the forest lord, he well earned the ending of his life and no blame to my lady for it," Haida said. "But my lady is worthy of much. You have seen her scars."

"She's been treated badly," I told Da. "Torture over months, perhaps years."

Haida bobbed her head. "Yes. Torture to force her to build that which should never be made. She fought with what weapons were hers." Then she told us the forest lord's intent and the outcome her lady had seen for that artifact. So for years she had fought to deceive him, suffering horribly for her defiance.

My da bowed. "A worthy lady," he said wearily. "My da, if he were the man he was once, would have given his life happily to protect such a one. He died fighting for me, not knowing that we fought to save a woman of worth. But I do."

"Dafydd?" I said.

"Your grandda." Da grimaced. "Once, he was a power to challenge the witch, and also a good man. Adda was the youngest of us all, and his particular favorite. If he could not be moved to help him, then whatever humanity lurked inside the monster was too faint to attend to. Dafydd would have died today at my hands; instead, he died saving his grandson's life. It is a better outcome."

I nodded, cleaning my hands a final time. "If I pick her up, Da, can you strip the soiled blankets and help Haida spread new ones?"

In no time, we had the fae woman tucked back in clean, dry bedding, bandaged and treated to the best of my abilities. Being covered with dirt had not particularly bothered me when we'd changed to human in the forest, but here in the clean room, it felt wrong.

When I requested clean water to bathe in, Haida directed us to bedrooms, no less grand than the one in which the wounded fae lady rested. Though I had seen no signs of servants here, there were great copper tubs of hot water and clean clothes waiting for us (I ducked a head into both rooms before we separated).

I scraped away my beard with a knife so sharp that it did not nick my skin, though it had been a very long time since I had shaved. I washed my face again in an astringent that hadn't been on the table beside the bath when I started shaving.

Clean and dried, I put on the plain-made clothes left on the foot of the bed. The stitching might have been simple, but the fabric was rich and fine. If it felt odd to wear clothes again, it felt odder still to wear boots after so long barefoot.

But when Haida called us to the kitchen to eat, I did not think again about either boots or clothing. The food was plentiful and hot—and tasted fit for gods.

I almost felt human again.

For three days, Da and I took turns watching over the fae woman, Haida's lady, who did not wake, though several times she stirred. We poured cups of willow-bark tea and clear meat broth down her as often as we could. The second day, fever made her restless and me worried.

On that day, just after midday meal, I felt the witch's collar tighten around my throat. My da growled and surged to his feet while I dropped to my knees. Haida grunted, and the witch's call faded.

"It is a strange kind of magic," she said. "Powerful, and my power is limited. I will try to break it."

NINE

ARIANA

SHE AWOKE IN HER OWN BED WHEN SHE DIDN'T EXPECT to awake at all. She blinked and tried to get up and her body revolted—she felt the beast stir within her. She subsided hastily, breathing through her nose as she tried to remember what happened.

Her father . . . his missing hand—and then the beasts who came to his call. Not his hounds, with their overwhelming aura of terror, but these wolves who needed no magic to invite fear. She remembered teeth and snarls and . . . nothing. She was weak and vulnerable, empty of magic.

Unfamiliar feet scuffed on the floor of the hall outside her door. She forced herself to sit up, expecting something more threatening than the young human who bore a tray of soup in his hands.

"Ah," he said. "You are awake. Haida said she thought you'd be stirring soon."

"Who are you?" she asked as he set the tray on top of the leather-bound wooden chest. He was very tall. He had all of his teeth, and he moved well—balanced and more graceful than the humans she'd seen. He wasn't handsome, but she couldn't take her eyes from him. The beast inside her tried to tell her he was a threat, but the man's movements were slow and careful.

He dragged the chest over to the bed with a suspicious lack of effort. Humans, in her experience, were weak and fragile things prone to dying and breeding with about the same frequency. This one was stronger than he looked. The chest was heavy, and she could not have moved it on her own without magic. The beast warned her again that he was dangerous.

"I asked you a question, human," she said, fear making her cold.

He looked up, and his eyes, some shade between noon sky and moonlit waterfall, met hers. The expression in them held her prisoner. *I see your fear,* they told her, *but no harm will come to you by me.*

"I heard you," he said deliberately. "I was just considering the answer."

"It was not a difficult question," she said sharply.

He smiled, and the expression showed her that there was such sorrow inside him it made her heart ache.

"Not for most," he agreed. "My grandmother calls me Sawyl. Will that do?"

For a moment, a flash of insight caught her and she grabbed his hand where it rested on the handle of the tray while the beast tried to take her mouth and spill the True Names that she had for him: *Sawyl. Samuel Deathbringer. Samuel Whitewolf.* "Samuel Healer," she said, then managed to close her lips before more escaped.

He tilted his head, tossed an errant strand of long light brown hair out of his eye, and said, "Sometimes. I do warn you that calling me human is a little optimistic. I have not been simply human for a long time."

"*Wolf,*" she said, her throat closing as the Name was born on her tongue. "*Killer.*" She pulled her hand away from him as if his flesh were hot iron. The beast was riled, and the flash of the memory of fangs closing upon her left her too afraid to control it properly.

"Sometimes," he agreed again mildly, as if unaware of his danger. Maybe he didn't know. "But it was your father who tried to have us kill you. Happily, his control slipped, or my grandmother the witch did not give him enough control of us because he fair annoyed her. She does things like that. So we killed him instead of you."

She held still, all of her. The beast was silenced. The wolf sitting beside her was as nothing compared to what he told her. She felt as if time stopped, as if nothing moved inside her at all, not even her heart. "My father is dead?"

Samuel, who evidently was sometimes a wolf, though she'd

never heard of such a thing as a human who could turn into a wolf, said, "Yes. It wasn't an easy thing, not even for us. He killed the rest of the pack, all but my da and me. But your father is dead and returned to the forest."

Her heart started beating again, but it hurt, and she clasped her fist to her chest in an effort to stop it. Grief, rage, and relief fought for ascendance. Once, she had loved him, her father whose death changed so much.

Samuel sat on the edge of her bed and held up a carved wooden bowl that steamed and smelled of good things. "Drink this."

Her beast rose at his nearness, teetering on the brink of taking control. But when he simply did not move, she was able to breathe, and the thing her father had made of her subsided reluctantly. When she started to reach for the bowl, her hands shook, so she put them back down.

His mouth flattened, and the corner of his eyes tightened. "I did that," he said, as if the words pained him.

"What?"

"To your shoulder," he said. "It went bad—and the fever kept you sick for a while. Haida tells me that usually you heal faster but that you had used all your magic to thwart the forest lord's will. In any case, the shoulder will bother you for a while longer—I don't know how long. My patients were regular folk, not fae. Haida seems to think that you've been weakened by your magic working and might heal as slowly as a human. In that case, it will hurt for a few more days."

She blinked at him a moment. Her shoulder hurt, it was true, but compared to what she usually felt after her father had finished with her, it was nothing.

She might have said something, but he lifted the bowl to her lips. She contemplated another True Name she had not let escape: Samuel Silverheart. She was named for the metal—Ariana and silver were not always the same. But she feared that the name meant what it sounded like; she could not love a wolf.

"I am Ariana," she told him when the bowl was empty.

He bowed his head. "I wish that our first meeting had been different, lady. But upon this our second meeting, I say that I am happy to make your acquaintance."

SAMUEL'S EYES HELD SHADOWS THAT NEVER LEFT, though they lightened now and then—especially when he sang.

Ariana was not a hobgoblin, like Haida, to read emotions more easily than words. But despite the darkness born of sorrow and anger, he was gentle and patient with her sudden starts. When she fretted over staying in bed, he didn't argue as Haida did.

While the hobgoblin scolded, he left the room. Ariana had swung her legs off her bed, when he brought in a skin drum.

He frowned at her bare feet. She found herself tucking them up beneath her instead of getting up as she'd intended. Because her bare toes seemed more vulnerable than she liked in front of this man who was nearly a stranger. He sat on the side of her bed, and she scooted farther back, away from him and against the wall.

"Well, then," he said, not looking at her. "I saw this sitting around in the kitchen for no reason, and though it's been a while, I couldn't resist."

She didn't recognize the drum, which meant that Underhill had brought it for him—like a puppy seeking to please. It didn't reassure her completely—Underhill had served her father long—but it helped to make her more comfortable.

He struck up a soft, solemn rhythm and sang.

She'd heard sweeter voices; the fae have singers among them. But music loved his voice just the same. His song was about a wren singing in a field and a man who longed for his childhood home. When he was finished, he raised one eyebrow, set a quicker beat, and hopped directly into a song about a clever mouse and not so clever woman.

There *were* better singers among the fae, but he would have done well, even so, she thought, in the courts where her mother had lived.

At his orders, she stayed in bed for a few more days. When she grew restless, Haida brought her weaving to her. It was not her favorite task, but making cloth was a necessity even for the fae. Samuel came in while she was threading the warp—and he made her teach him. At first he made a mess of it, but his fingers were long and clever, and it wasn't long before he caught on. She thought it was another thing to keep her in bed. But when he later made Haida teach him to cook his favorite soups and sweets, she decided it was just curiosity.

If it hadn't been for his kindness to her little champion, she might have resisted him longer—no matter the serious attention he'd given to her women's work. He was human (*and wolf*, warned her beast, though it wasn't loud around Samuel). Ariana wasn't used to small kindnesses being dealt out by men, and she felt herself falling under the spell of the soft-spoken Samuel, just as Haida was.

The hobgoblin had initially resisted his intrusion into her kitchen—but then he proposed a trade. He taught her a song for every dish she taught him to make, finding pretty but simple tunes with limited range, so Haida could sing them well. Her little friend's pleasure in making her own music made him happier than learning to cook did.

He let Ariana get out of bed after three days—and then, contrary man, he became relentless in his demands for her to move, to bend and twist. An old wound in her leg bothered him the most. He told her to keep salve on it to soften the scar, made her move and bend until it hurt, then bend a little more.

It took her a week before she admitted that she'd named him true: Silverheart, Ariana's heart. Her body loved his form, but her heart loved the man within who had so much kindness inside him.

TEN

SAMUEL

HAIDA WAS SHY AND NERVOUS ABOUT MY BUMBLING around in her kitchen. But I needed something to keep my hands and mind busy. Ariana was healing much faster than I expected, and after the first few days, her care was not enough to keep me busy. I needed to do things to keep my mind off Da.

Haida had broken the hold my grandmother had on me, but the tie that bound my father to the witch was stronger than mine, either because he'd taken Dafydd's place as head of the pack, since he was closer in blood to her, or—and he'd said this was probable— because she'd had her claws into him longer. The witch would be enraged with the deaths of the rest of the pack and whatever Haida had done to free me—and my father was facing her alone. When I was certain that Ariana would heal without me, I would return to do for my father what Haida had done for me.

I would free him from the witch. I could all but taste her blood on my tongue—and it was a fine taste, one to look forward to.

In the meantime, I found things to keep me busy. If she had not loved music so much, Haida would never have let me into her kitchen. My wife . . . my wife had never let me help her cook.

As I worked grinding leaves to powder I thought about those lost memories. My da, he remembered my wife's name and my children's, too. I remember asking him about them and he told me, and their names and faces ran from me as if they could no longer stay within me.

The sound of Haida's singing soothed my sore heart. I don't know why she'd never sung on her own—her voice was lovely— but she treasured the songs I gave her more than my grandmother treasured power. After I'd been underfoot awhile, Haida quit being so quiet.

"I knew that you had it in you," I told her after she scolded me, then paused, almost cringing away from me. "Good. Now do it again."

"*You,*" she exclaimed in exasperated tones, but she stopped cringing. "You go. Do as I told you."

So I pounded and ground and stirred at her direction. Some of the ingredients were new to me. When I asked about those, Haida's eyes grew round, and she ducked her head, glancing around herself, as if asking for permission.

"That would be Underhill," she said. "This part of Underhill, anyway. It likes you. Brings out favorites to share with you."

Some of those ingredients I learned centuries later. Saffron, paprika, black pepper—spices from all over the world. It was there I first tasted oranges, bananas, and potatoes. Some of the foods I ate there I never knowingly tasted again.

I was crushing peppercorns with a mortar and pestle when she said to me, "You must be careful with my lady."

"I won't hurt her," I promised after sorting through several replies. Had Haida noticed how I looked at her sometimes? There was nothing that could come of it. I was a monster, and beyond that a simple village herbalist, and she a fairy princess. But a man could look and dream, couldn't he?

She made a chiding sound. "Of course you will. Everyone hurts everyone—it is a part of living. But I don't mean careful that way. She has a beast inside her."

"So do I," I told her, and as if that acknowledgment awakened it, the wolf inside me surfaced.

"Your heart beats with a wolf's rhythm," Haida said prosaically. "But it is not a monster. Not the way my lady's is—or your da's is, for that matter."

"My da is the same as I," I protested. "And Ariana is . . ." Words failed me for a moment. "Ariana is strong and true as a good oak tree."

Haida set her wooden spoon to rest on a small table and turned to look at me. "No," she said, heavily. "No, she is not. Once, she was lovely and sweet and, it hurts me to confess, spoiled. Beloved daughter. But immortality is more curse than blessing. All things pass away. Love may live for a month or a year, but sooner or later, it leaves."

I stopped working with the mortar. "No," I told her, because my heart knew better. "That is not true."

"Have you lived so long as I?" she asked.

"I don't know," I said. "But I have lived long enough to know that love doesn't die." I might not remember my wife's face or her name, but I remembered her smell, the touch of her hand, and the sound of her laughter. Not even the witch's magic could steal that from me. I loved my wife still, and the pain of her loss burned in my heart. "Not if you cherish it. Love, like any other living thing, needs to be fed. Only if you starve it will it die."

Haida blinked a little and leaned against the table where she had been working.

"But you were talking about Ariana," I said. "And not of love."

She nodded. "And not of love. Ariana's father ruined her. If you hurt her or scare her, the beast will attack. It is dangerous."

"So am I," I told her.

"It was afraid of her father and could not disobey him," she said. "But her father is no more, and it will do anything to protect her. Anything. And nothing you are is sufficient to protect yourself from it."

She meant it. I could smell her fear of the beast inside her lady.

"It doesn't matter," I said gently. "I am only here for a day or two more. As soon as I'm certain that she doesn't need me, I have to go to my da." And I would die. I might tell myself differently, but I had been with the witch for too long to believe in any other end.

Until then, I would continue to play human, to remember the man I had once been, even if I could not remember my family or my life, except in bits and pieces. I would take what I could, then do my best to save my da and to save me.

That night, as I turned wool into yarn as Ariana wove, she turned her head away from me with uncharacteristic shyness. "Do you really think love lives forever?"

"I think that you listen in doorways," I said lightly.

Her mouth curved up, but she still didn't look at me, her eyes paying closer attention to sliding her weft through the warp yarn in her loom. "I think that Underhill lets me hear what it chooses, even when I am tucked away and half-asleep. Answer my question."

I raised an eyebrow at the imperious demand.

She looked at me, laughed, and said, "Please?"

"I can only speak for myself," I said. "But there are none that I have ever loved who I no longer love. Wife, children, and parents, I love them still, though they have, with the exception of my father, been gone for a very long time."

She worked for a long time without speaking. Then she said, very quietly, "You worry about your father?"

"Yes," I said. "I will leave tomorrow to go to him."

We didn't speak again until she asked me to sing.

The next morning, I left Ariana sleeping and ventured into the kitchen. Haida was there before me, as she always was. She handed me a bowl of cooked grain sweetened with honey, her face stormy.

"What is it?" I asked.

"You will leave us," she said.

"The witch holds my da." I sat on a stool and started eating.

"They will come back for her," she said in a low voice, with an anxious glance toward the room where Ariana still slept. "The hounds spent three years with her as their prey, not allowed the kill. When they know that the forest lord is dead, they will come back and kill her."

"I will return, as fast as I am able," I told her. "But my father needs me."

She smiled, but she didn't mean it. "I know you will. And maybe they won't come. But I didn't worry about them until I knew you were going."

I finished the food and touched her hand. "I trust you to keep her safe."

It didn't take long for me to ready myself to go. I did not need a pack, just boots and a good woolen cloak. I should have changed forms because the wolf would have made the journey quicker. But I had only just regained my humanity and was loath to lose it. I stepped outside to put on my boots so the dirt on the soles wouldn't drop on the floor. The door opened again behind me.

"Samuel? You are leaving?"

I turned and saw her. The winter-morning sun lit her face and hair until she glowed the silver of her name. Like as not, she was centuries older than I, but she looked no more than a maiden.

"I told you I must," I said. "Da is still in thrall to the witch. I don't know what she did to him for our disobedience."

"Take this," she said, and she gave me a silver chain, long enough to wrap twice around my neck. "My home can be difficult to find. If you are wearing this chain in my father's . . . in this forest and say my name three times, you'll find yourself on my doorstep without delay."

The silver burned my hand, and I dropped it with a hiss. She picked it up.

"Silver burns evil," I told her.

"Nonsense," she said. "My father wore silver, and it never burned him." She ran the chain through her fingers once. "I don't have much magic left, but silver loves me. Try it now."

I took it, and it lay gently on my hands. And when I put the chain over my head and settled it around my neck, it did not burn. It was chill from her magic.

"I don't know that I will be able to come back," I said.

"If you will let me have a lock of your hair, with Haida's aid I can come to you," Ariana told me. "I may be without power, but Haida is more than a match for a mortal witch. I have a debt to settle."

"She is not mortal," I said. "Not anymore. And there is no

debt to settle between us. I but healed where harm was given. Haida freed me of my grandmother's leash. If there is a debt, it is between Haida and I—and it goes the other way."

She frowned at me, the expression making her look a lot less young. "Nonetheless," she said.

I hesitated, but in the end I let her cut some of my hair. And I admit to leaving her home with a lighter heart because of the silver chain and the loss of a few strands of hair.

ELEVEN

SAMUEL

IT TOOK ME THREE DAYS TO FIND THE WITCH'S HUT, though the distance I'd traveled to Ariana's home in the first place had not been nearly so long. Doubtless it was some sort of fae magic. I spent all three of those days working out how to sneak up on her.

It was then somewhat anticlimactic that when I reached the hut, it had been burned to the ground. Even when I shifted and let the wolf's nose test the ground, I could not find any sign of where my grandmother or my da had gone. Though I had been gone only a bit more than a week, the fire seemed seasons older.

I stayed wolf for three more days, searching for scent trails. On the fourth day, I went to the oak where my father used to make me change into human. I found nothing new there and was leaving the little hollow when my grandmother stepped out of the shadows.

"You return at last," she said. "I knew you would come."

I raised my head and met her gaze. She looked worn. Older by decades, not just a bare week. Her brown hair was spiderwebbed with gray, and her skin had forgone the blush of youth for dryer parchment.

"Underhill time doesn't run as ours. You've been gone a full year," she said, understanding my confusion full well. Da had told me she couldn't read every thought a person had, but she could pick through the surface of a mind fairly easily. "'Tis good for your da's sake that it wasn't two years, or I'd have lost patience and used him up."

She clicked her fingers, and my da crept around out of the trees. His head hung low, and he'd lost weight, a lot of it. His ribs showed, and so did the bones of his hips. His coat, which should have been thick and rich this time of the year, was starred and sparse.

A year. What had she done to him in a year?

Da didn't look at me. All of his attention was focused on the witch. Another person might have thought that she'd broken him as she had broken Dafydd. But I knew my da: if he'd ever looked at me with that expression, I'd have known my days on the earth were numbered on the fingers of one hand.

"You rescued a fairy maiden, Samuel," the witch purred. "She freed you, but she could not take your father from me as well." She smiled gently, rubbing her fingers through the hair on the base of Da's neck. "Between the two of you—you killed not only the fae lord but the rest of my wolves. I had plans for him—and for them."

I stared at her and concentrated hard on her words so that she would not pick out any other of my thoughts.

"Of course your father told me," she said. "Did you think him loyal to you?"

No. I thought him bound against his will, helpless to keep her from ruffling through his memories. How she could think I believed otherwise, with him pinned to her side like the crazed beast she'd made of him, I do not know. Maybe it had been so long since any had courage to call her on her lies that she thought we all believed every word out of her mouth.

"I will make a bargain with you," the witch told me. "By an oath of blood." She took out a knife and pricked her thumb so that a drop fell out. "You take me to this fairy lass, and I will free your da from my magic."

There were so many things wrong with what she promised that I could not hide my sneer.

"My blood oath," she said coaxingly, "my blood oath that your da will walk free of me to live his life, and you to live yours as well. All you need do is take me to the fairy." She shuddered and closed her eyes and licked her lips. "I wasted the fairy lord's pain, not realizing what I had until I had finished with it—the fool angered me too much, and I was not attending my business properly. He told me he was a great lord—but all the fae do that. I didn't believe him. I have never heard of a great fae lord losing his magic—not while Underhill still stands. They cannot lie, Sawyl, but they can stretch the truth into a lie. Assuming he was less than he claimed, I tried to use the magic his sacrifice gave me. It was too much, and I forfeited the power of it rather than destroy myself."

That explained the burnt hut. Magic's first child is always fire.

"Your da told me that the fairy lord is dead and his body gone to earth." She looked down at my da without fondness. "He said he also burned the wolves' bodies, so they are useless to me. And I must have power." She held up a wrinkled hand so we could both see it. "Without power, I age, Sawyl."

The witch smiled at me. "But the fae lord's daughter . . . and she owes you a debt. You will take me to her and bid her give what she owes you to me. Fae have to pay their debts." For a moment, her countenance showed such rapture as she contemplated the power she would gain from Ariana that it made my blood run cold. I was not certain that the witch would be able to take Ariana—and Haida. My experience with magic was nothing that would allow me to predict such things.

I could not, *would not* do as she bade me. I took a step backward.

She dragged the knife against my sire's side and raised the blade so I could see the blood upon it. "Come back here. If you leave, I will kill your father. Do not think I will not do as I claim."

Her fingers might belong to an old woman, but they were strongly wrapped around the haft of the knife. Da, for his part, stood utterly still beside her, not reacting to the pain at all. As I paced slowly forward, my eyes lingered on him.

Don't let her touch you. Do not give her access to the fae woman. She broke some larger spell when she threw away the fae lord's power. Without more fae blood, she will die. She must die.

I had only once heard my da's voice so clearly in my head, when he had held me alive when Dafydd's fangs had changed me into what I now was. The shock of it froze me where I stood.

Move.

I dodged aside, and she missed her grab.

I backed away from her a half dozen steps until I stood on the edge of the hollow. If she needed hair or skin to replace the shackles she'd held me with—as from what I knew of witchcraft seemed likely—I would give her no chance. If she took me prisoner, it would not matter if I could stand up to her or not, Ariana would come for me.

The witch surveyed me with cold eyes. "Fine. On your head be it." She looked down at my father, raised her knife, glanced at me, and I saw her change her mind.

Run.

"By blood bound you are to me, Bran son of Bran," she said. "Kill that wolf your son for me."

I was already sprinting away as quickly as I could. Driven, not only by my da's voice in my head but by the understanding of what it would do to my da if he was forced to kill me. He would resist her, I knew, and it would give me a chance to flee.

He had not left my mind, though there were no more words. Anger rose up from him, rage such as I had never felt before—not my rage, but his. Inflaming my blood so much that I was forced to quit running, held motionless in a murderous unthinking flood of fury. I do not know how long I stood there, heart pounding, growling and ready to rend everything around me into bloody pieces.

I felt him die.

We were bound together, not only by the witch's powers, but by that same thing that had bound us to Dafydd and the rest of the pack. It snapped, and his rage was gone as if it had never been. He was gone. I was alone. Utterly, remorselessly alone.

I howled, my cry breaking the silence that had fallen in the snow-covered woods. But no one answered me.

I ran, then, ran to Ariana. Retaining just enough of myself to change back to human as soon as I felt I was near enough to her to grip the chain I wore and chant her name.

TWELVE

ARIANA

THREE MONTHS AFTER HE LEFT, JUST AS SPRING WAS strewing her flowers over the forest, Ariana discovered Samuel naked upon the ground before the door to her home. His hands and feet were raw and muddied—he lay so still. She dropped to her knees beside him as he drew in a breath.

In that moment, when she knew that he lived, she understood what she had only worried over before. Human or not, she loved this man who had saved her from her father and washed away the despair of her home with his music.

When he wouldn't waken to touch or voice, she summoned Haida. Between the two of them, they got him in and laid him on her bed since it was closest to the door. Haida helped her clean him and cover him.

"Exhaustion," said Haida, her hands on his unshaven face. "And despair. Something terrible has happened."

He awoke in the middle of the night, when Ariana was sitting beside him. He didn't say a word, just looked at her with such sorrow that she crawled into bed beside him. When he turned to her, she gave him gladly what comfort he could take from her.

"He's gone," Samuel said afterward, his face buried in her hair where she could not see his pain. "My fault. The witch tried to get him to kill me, and when he rebelled, she killed him."

His pain was so different from hers when her father died that she didn't know what to say at first. She had never seen his father, though Haida had told her he'd had kind eyes and gentle hands.

"No guilt, surely," she said finally. "The witch killed him, and his blood is on her. If not for you, he would have lived in thrall to the witch for even longer."

"She will die now," he told her, and his body that had been clenched hard around her softened. "He would be satisfied with that, I think." And then, in the safe darkness of her room and bed, he told her the full tale, of which she knew only bits and pieces, of how he and his father came to be enslaved to a dark witch.

"Stay safe here," Ariana said when he was done. "She cannot come here without invitation. She will die, and your father's death will not be without meaning."

She held him through the night. Over the next week, she and Haida between them saw that he was seldom alone and never without something to keep his hands or head busy. His hurt was deep, but the wound of his father's murder did not fester nor mar the sweetness of his temperament. Gradually, as days passed, more laughter and music filled her house, and the nights were passion and fire, and her wounds of the spirit mended in his care.

One day, he set the drum he played aside and pulled her away from her loom and into the forest. Swinging her by the hand and singing at full voice, he pulled her into an impromptu dance of great silliness and more energy than grace. He stopped her and took her by the shoulders.

"You," he said, his blue eyes bright with heady joy.

"Yes?" She felt unaccountably shy, but he made her that way sometimes.

"You I love," he said, his voice a sweet rush that caused her heart to stumble.

Tears rose to her eyes, she who never cried. This was not a man who would forget that he loved someone in a fit of jealous envy or fear. Still, she couldn't help but whisper a question just to be certain. "Forever?"

His hands slid up to cup her jaw. "And always," he agreed hoarsely. He kissed her openmouthed, and there, in the forest that had once been her father's, he loved her in the sweet grass.

ARIANA WATCHED SAMUEL TEASE HER HAIDA AND SMILED to herself. He was one of those rare people who needed others to take care of. Once he'd decided that they were his, he was easier about his father's fate. He had a purpose and that suited him.

He suited her, too. When he held her at night, she didn't wake up cold and shaking, certain that the red hounds were on her again.

Like her, Samuel was not happy sitting around doing nothing; soon enough, the tasks around her house would not be enough for him. Already he was restless, getting up as soon as he sat down and pacing rather than sitting still. She decided she wasn't one for sitting idle, either. Perhaps they should do a little traveling.

"I think," she told him as he sang to them after dinner, "we should go traveling, we three."

Haida's eyes grew round. "Oh, they would never let the likes of us into a court, lady. You, of course. But I'm a hobgoblin and he a human. They treat humans with no gentleness."

"I'm not talking about visiting my mother," Ariana told her. "But why shouldn't we travel throughout the human kingdoms?"

Samuel smiled sharply, his hands keeping a restless rhythm on the drum. "A stir we'd make, that's for sure," he said, his voice oddly cadenced as he talked with the beat of his drumming. "They aren't used to fairy princesses and hobgoblins in human villages, my lady. Some warlord would try to claim you, and I'd have to take him down."

She pulled a glamour over her face and form and spread it over Haida just to watch his jaw drop. "Do you think that fae keep to themselves always, Samuel?" she said behind her guise of a pox-scarred, plain-faced woman. "Just because we are not seen doesn't mean that we do not go where we please."

"I thought your magic was gone," Samuel said, his face softening. "Is it back?"

"This isn't that kind of magic," she told him. She had expected her magic to start seeping back to her by now, but it had not. Sometimes she worried about that, but Samuel made her feel safe—and magic had brought her enough heartache that she would not be sad if she were never any more than what she was now. Samuel waited for her to explain herself, so she told him, "It's glamour—a part of me, like music is a part of you." Then she nodded at Haida. "I could only do that because she does not guard herself against me."

Haida put her hands on her cheeks. "Oh dear," she said, and squeaked when she sounded like an old woman. She laughed and ran off to find the polished-bronze mirror in the hallway to see what Ariana had done to her.

Samuel set the drum down, got up, and walked all the way around her. He stopped in front of Ariana and reached out to touch her nose. He slid his hands to her cheekbones, then to the corners of her eyes.

"It feels real," he said, drawing a deep breath. After a moment he relaxed. "But you smell like yourself."

"Samuel," Ariana said. "How would you like to earn our room and board as we travel from village to village? I can be your meek wife, and Haida can sing with you."

He rubbed his face and paced a bit.

"I have a hard time thinking with the moon singing in the sky," he said, as if it were a confession.

She tilted her head—it was still daylight, though the sun hung low in the sky. There were human things, phrases and aphorisms, that seemed odd to her; perhaps Samuel's odd comment was just such a thing as those.

"Samuel?" Ariana couldn't keep the concern out of her voice.

His eyes half closed. "I am restless tonight, I think. But travel appeals to me. Yes."

"We'll do it," she said. The floor moved just a little under Ariana's feet. So it was to her home she spoke the last bit. "Travel the summer and return for autumn and winter."

THIRTEEN

SAMUEL

I WOKE UP SUDDENLY, NOT TOO LONG AFTER I HAD GONE to sleep. Beside me, Ariana still slept deeply. I had tired her with my lovemaking this night, trying to drown the strange energy that filled me in her body. I had succeeded insofar that afterward I'd been able to sleep—only to be awakened by the moon's call.

I got up out of the bed carefully so as not to awaken Ariana and stepped to the open window, where the moon hung high in the sky. I had learned time passed differently in Ariana's home than it did in the outside world, but the moon's song had not changed between the world I knew best and Underhill. I lifted my hand toward the moon as if I might reach it.

And she reached back.

A sizzling, burning energy coursed through me, calling the wolf to hunt—and the wolf answered. It was a better change, now that the witch's power didn't fight the wolf. Over the years, I had learned to ease my way between wolf and human, but even so, it hurt.

I dropped to the floor and writhed under the moonlight as the wolf tore through my human flesh with as much care as he would have given the carcass of a deer. In all the years I had been a werewolf, I had never met the full moon in my human flesh. I had not realized that the moon would call the wolf, will I or no. Helpless, I held my silence as long as I could, but wolf and moon between them reft me of my humanity, and I cried out.

"Samuel?" Ariana's voice, full of worry and love and all those things that meant I wasn't alone, should not have filled me with dread.

The wolf, who eclipsed me in my own mind as he had not since the very early days of my running on four feet, rose to his feet and met Ariana's eyes. Ariana's beautiful green fae eyes. The wolf could see in darkness better than my human self. So he watched as her pupils expanded to eat her iris until her entire eye was black.

Ariana's scent changed until the smell of terror made the wolf drop his head and growl in pleasure. He bared his teeth, enjoying the spike of fear that followed. He was playing; he knew as well as I that she was not to be hurt. I, caught by surprise and thus overcome by moon-called wolf, was unable to do anything to reassure her.

Haida knocked on the door, "My lady? My lady?"

Ariana moved to get off the bed, and the wolf blocked her in, his countermove bringing him closer to the bed. Ariana made a sound then that I hope never to hear again. A keening, sorrowful sound like a rabbit who knows it will be dead before it draws another breath.

The door to the room opened, and the wolf snarled ferociously, angry at the intrusion into his game. The little hobgoblin stayed in the doorway, dropping her gaze.

"Samuel?" she said.

I felt the pull of my name, felt the wolf begin to give way to my control. I took a step toward Haida.

No!

The voice that uttered that word was not my Ariana, though it came from her throat. It was a roar more felt than heard, and it made my wolf think that we were under threat, and he turned again to face the bed and Ariana.

Her face was oddly distorted; I do not know if it was just the extremity of her fear or if there was some magic at work. Her dark skin was lit by scars that by a trick of magic, because that was thick in the room, or just some oddness of light looked the same color as her silver-lavender hair. The map of her pain was tattooed forever upon her skin, bared to the world.

My attention was caught by her for a moment too long. I didn't realize she was gathering more magic until the bed dissolved beneath her and she dropped to the floor. Walls crumbled around us as she pulled magic from Underhill to protect Haida from the wolf she thought was attacking her friend. When she thought Haida was threatened, she protected the little fae with all the power she could draw.

She thrust it at me in a deadly blast I could see, wine-dark power bearing the scent of death.

Haida stepped between us and let it hit her instead of me. She hung in the air for a moment, while the magic knocked me through the doorway and into the hall.

"My lady," she said and then the only thing left of the little fae who taught me to cook and gained such joy in music was a whiff of foul-smelling smoke.

The beast who had replaced my Ariana screamed hoarsely. I hesitated, caught by grief and unwilling to leave Ariana alone in her pain, but the wolf knew better than I. He bolted for the front door, which opened before us. A glance over our shoulder showed only a battered lean-to that collapsed as I watched.

I ran until the moon set, then I curled up in the shelter of an overhang where the last autumn's leaves were dry. I awoke human and naked as the day I was born, with the scent of Ariana in my nose and snow on the ground. I had expected her to come. She was not a coward; she would feel it necessary to face the consequences of last night.

I rose from my bed and went out barefoot in the weeks-old crusty snow to meet her.

She looked different. Her waist-length hair had been shorn to a finger's length, and she wore a gown of white, something that might have been worn in a king's court.

"Samuel Moon Called," she said, not meeting my eyes. I could smell her grief. "Well have I loved you."

"And I you, lady," I told her, sounding surprisingly steady for a man whose heart was bleeding with grief. Haida was worthy of mourning, and so was the future that Ariana and I had lost.

"And yet," she said, "and yet I would have killed you had not Haida sacrificed herself for you."

"Haida whom you also loved," I said. "It was not your fault, Ariana. She would not blame you."

She nodded and looked away. "I cannot risk destroying anyone else I love."

I wanted to drop to my knees and plead with her. I had no pack, they were all dead. My da was dead. He took with him the name I had been born with. He had kept the names of my lost family and their faces safe for me. And he was gone. Ariana was the only person I had left.

And without me, who would keep her safe? Who would hold her when the evil of what her father had done to her overwhelmed her dreams?

Yet between us lay the death of Haida, forming an impenetrable barrier between us.

"I will carry you in my heart until it beats no more," I told her, giving her the only thing I could think of that would not hurt her more.

Her eyes welled, and her mouth tried to smile, and still she did not look at me. Her eyes were fixed at my feet. "Spoken like a poet and singer, my dear Samuel. You'll forget things, forget me—this world does not easily hold the things best left Underhill." Her mouth trembled. "I need the chain I gave you."

I unwound the silver chain and held it out to her.

She took a half step closer, then closed her eyes and swallowed.

When her eyes opened, black was trying to consume the green. She took a full step back. She stretched out her arm, and I felt her magic burn my hand.

"If you ever need me," I told her, "I will come."

The silver chain unmade itself and fell to the ground from my hand, now a small pile of pebbles. She took out a small pouch and took out some of the hair inside, burning it as it nestled in her palm. When nothing except ashes were in her hand, she stepped closer, so that when she turned her hand over, the ashes fell onto the pebbles that had been her silver chain.

"Fare thee well, Samuel Silverheart," she said, turning away.

I waited until she had gone before I made my answer. I threw back my head and let the wolf sing our grief to the unkind moon.

FOURTEEN

SAMUEL

AFTER A DAY OF AIMLESS WANDERING IN MY WOLF'S skin, I found a task to turn my hand to and headed for the remains of the witch's hut. I no longer knew which direction Ariana's home was, but my wolf knew exactly where the witch had lived. The burnt hut looked just as it had when I'd last seen it. It smelled the same, too. Though weeks had passed in Ariana's world, here it was still the same winter that my da had died. I could smell my own scent as clearly as if I'd only been gone a few days.

I headed to the oak, driven by the need to destroy or be destroyed— and I didn't much care which. My grandmother had been staying somewhere nearby, or she would not have come out the last time I had been there. If it had only been days, then I could trail her and confront her. She could not reach Ariana through me anymore. If I could, I would kill her. If not, she would kill me, then die slowly for want of the power of fae pain and suffering anyway. Even dead, I would win.

As I approached the meadow, I smelled rotting flesh. I paused because it did not smell like wolf. It smelled like—

Pinning my ears I crept cautiously toward the source of the foul smell—and found the witch's body.

She had been savaged and half-eaten, but I would have known her if only a finger bone had been left. It had snowed once and melted since she died, but I knew wolf kill when I saw it.

My father was not dead.

I howled, calling for him, and the woods went still, recognizing a predator's voice. But my father gave me no answer, and gradually, the usual denizens of the winter forest went about their lives.

I slept near the hut that night and spent the next day building a fire hot enough to turn the witch's body to bits and pieces of bone, which I put in a sack with salt and buried under cold running water. My wife, whose name I had lost, had told me once that running water turns away evil.

I would wait for Ariana to call me, I thought, as I put a heavy boulder on top of the sack of the witch's ashes. Even if it took a very long time, I would wait for her. I would wait for her, and I would look for my da.

When I went to sleep that night, alone in the shelter of a downed tree, hope lived in my heart.

FAIRY GIFTS

I grew up in Butte, Montana. It is a town of about thirty-four thousand people that once had a population far greater—most of whom came to work the mines that started as gold mines, shifted to silver mines, and finally produced high-quality copper just as the country (and the world) began stringing copper wires for electricity. Butte was the third city in the world to have electricity—Paris, France, and New York City being the first two. The mining town once had a large Chinese population as well as Cornish, Irish, Welsh, Finnish, Italian, Serbian, and Greek.

When I was a child, the old tunnel mines had all been shut down, and the copper came from an open-pit mine that had eaten the suburbs of Meaderville, McQueen, and East Butte—and continued to grow until it ate the old amusement park Columbia Gardens. But there were all sorts of stories that were told about the "old days." Stories about the racetrack that had stood where East Junior High (now East Middle School) had been built. I heard tales of Shoestring Annie, Dirty-Mouth Jean, and the old madame who beat up Carrie Nation when she took her temperance crusade to the wrong bar.

So I just had to set a story in Butte.

The events in this story all happen before *Moon Called*.

Butte, Montana, present day, mid-December

COLD DIDN'T BOTHER HIM ANYMORE, BUT HE *REMEM-bered* how it felt: the sharp bite of winter on toes, fingers, nose, and ears. Even with modern adaptations, ten degrees below zero wouldn't be pleasant. Neither the temperature nor falling snow kept people out of the streets for the Christmas stroll, however. Hot apple cider, freshly made sausages, and abundant cookies under the streetlights strove to make up for the nasty weather—none of which were useful sustenance for him. He passed them by with scarcely a glance.

Well, then, he thought, impatient with himself, *what* are *you doing here?* He had no more answer now than he'd had two nights ago when he'd arrived.

The people who lived in the old mining town had always known how to party. In a hundred years that hadn't changed. Brutal climate, hard and dangerous work brought a certain clarity to the need for pleasure.

His Chinese face garnered a few looks—curiosity, no more. A century ago, Butte had had a large Chinese population. Then, the looks he'd garnered had been dismissive up on the street level but full of eagerness or fear down in his father's opium den in the mining tunnels where Thomas had been both guide and enforcer.

It was not just the looks that had changed. The streets were not cobbled, there were no trolleys, no horses. Steep streets had been somewhat tamed, and the town—once a bustling place—had a desolate air, despite the festive decorations. Buildings he remembered were abandoned or gone altogether, replaced by parking lots or parks. The few restored or well-kept buildings only made the rest look worse.

Some of the changes were vast improvements. The smelters and ore-processing plants now long closed meant that the sulfurous fog that had made it difficult to see across the street was gone. The air was immensely more pleasant to breathe. The night was free of the constant noise of the machinery that churned day and night.

The crowd that moved beside him on the sidewalks was a respectable size, though much smaller than those that had filled the streets of his memories. He hadn't decided whether to count that on the good side or the bad side of the changes.

He put his hands in front of his mouth and blew, a gesture to blend in, no more. Even had his hands been frozen, his breath wouldn't warm them.

He didn't know why he'd come back here. Just in time for the Christmas stroll, no less. He wasn't a Christian, despite the nuns who had ensured he could read and write: an education for her children was the only thing his quiet, obedient mother had ever stood up to his father for.

If . . . *if* he did believe, he'd have to believe he was damned, and had been since his father had brought him to the old man.

Butte, Montana, 1892, April

"*HERE* IS THE SON," HIS FATHER SAID, HIS VOICE LESS clear than usual. It was hard to talk with a mouth that had been hit so many times.

Last night his father had been set upon by a group of miners who wanted opium and had not wanted to pay for it. They had beaten Father and tied him up. It had been Thomas's day to protect the shop; his older brother, Tao, was away on other business. Thomas had been shot in the arm, and while he tried to stanch the blood, one of the miners had cracked his skull with a beer bottle.

When Thomas awoke, his mother had bandaged his hurts and was crying silently as she sometimes did. From Tao, because his father would not look at him nor talk to him, he learned that his father had given the men what they wanted and more: arsenic in the opium would ensure that they thieved from no one again. But despite the ultimate victory in the fight, his father felt that his honor and that of his family had been impinged. He made it clear that he blamed Thomas for the shame.

The next morning his father had left Tao in charge of the laundry and gone out to speak with friends. He'd been gone most of the day, and Thomas had worked hard despite his aching arm, seeking to assuage his disgrace with diligence. His uncles, his father's brothers, had stopped in with gifts of herbs, whiskey, and his grandmother's ginger cookies. They spoke to his mother in hushed whispers.

His father returned after the sun was down and the laundry storefront was closed. He hadn't said anything to the rest of the family gathered there. He'd only looked at Thomas.

"You," he'd said in English, which was the language he used when he was displeased with Thomas, because, to his father's horror, Thomas, born in America, was as fluent in English as in Cantonese. "You come."

According to his brother Tao, when Thomas was born a few weeks after his family had come to the New World, his father had given him an American name in a fit of optimism. It must have been true, but Thomas could never imagine his father being optimistic or excited about anything American.

Obediently, Thomas followed his father up the steep streets to a single-story house nestled between two new apartment build-ings. There was a dead tree in the yard. Maybe it had been planted in a fit of optimism.

His father entered the unpainted door without knocking and left it to Thomas to close it behind them. The incense burning on a small table didn't quite cover a sour, charnel-house smell. Thomas fol-lowed his father through a partially furnished front room and down the narrow and uneven stairs to the basement, where the odor of dead things was replaced by the scent of the dynamite that had been used to blast the basement into the granite that underlay the hillside.

The stairs ended in a small room lit only by a small beeswax candle. The floor beneath his feet was polished and well laid, a light-colored wood ringed by a pattern of darker. It seemed an expensive luxury to find in a basement room of a nondescript little house.

While he'd been looking at the floor, his father had continued on through a doorway, and Thomas hurried to follow. There was some-thing odd about this place that made his stomach clench and the hair on the back of his neck stand up. He didn't want to be left alone here.

He darted through the doorway and almost bumped into his father, who had stopped at a small entryway that dropped down a single stair and then opened up to a cavernous room. It too had only a single candle lighting it. Thomas couldn't make out the face of the man ensconced in some sort of big chair.

His father bent over with a pained grunt and set three twenty-dollar gold pieces on the floor.

"*Here* is the son," he said.

He put the flat of his hand on Thomas's back and thrust him toward the other man.

Not expecting the push, Thomas stumbled down the step, then turned to look at his father—only to see his sandaled feet disap-pear up the stairway.

"The son," said the man he'd been left with. His accent was Eastern European—Slavic, Thomas thought. The Slavs were among the latest immigrant wave that had washed over the mining town since Thomas Edison's electricity had made copper king. "Pretty boy. Come here."

Butte, Montana, present day

THOUGH THE SOUNDS OF THE CHRISTMAS CAROLS WERE pleasant enough, Thomas felt restless, impatient—the same feeling that had sent him driving here from San Francisco when he'd intended only an evening's drive.

Something was calling him here, and it certainly wasn't nostalgia. There wasn't much left of the town of his childhood. The last of the old whorehouses in the red-light district was falling down, and only a few buildings were left of the Chinatown where he'd grown up and died and been reborn a monster. No, he wasn't nostalgic for Butte.

This wasn't his home. He had a condo in San Francisco and another in Boston. None of his family remained here. There was nothing here for him—so why had it seemed so imperative to come?

"Hello, Tom."

He froze. It had been almost a century since he'd been in Butte. There weren't that many people who lived eighty years and still sounded so hale and hearty.

Fae.

That's why he'd had to come. He'd been called here by magic. If he hadn't been walking in the middle of a crowd, he would have snarled.

He didn't see anyone who looked familiar; the fae were like that. But he did find someone who was looking at him.

Leaning up against an empty storefront where a tobacco shop had once been was a balding man with an oddly fragile air about him. He was several inches shorter than Thomas—who wasn't exactly tall himself. The man's forehead was too large for the rest of him in the manner of some people who were born simple. Young blue eyes smiled at Thomas out of an old face. He wore new winter boots, red mittens and scarf, and a thick down jacket.

A couple, passing by, noticed Thomas's interest and stopped.

"Nick?" The woman half ducked her head toward the little man. "Are you warm enough? There are cookies and hot chocolate in the old Miner's Bank building at the end of the block."

The male half of the couple glared suspiciously at Thomas.

"I have good new gloves," said Nick in the voice of a man but with a child's intonations. "I'm warm. I had cookies. I think I'm going to talk with my friend Tom." He darted across the sidewalk and took Thomas's hand.

Thomas managed not to hiss or jerk his hand free. Nick, was it? His scent—at this close range—told Thomas that Nick was a hobgoblin.

"Do you live here? Or are you just visiting?" asked the man suspiciously.

"I'm visiting," said Thomas. He could have lied. Butte was smaller than it used to be, but, according to the lady who checked him into his hotel, it still had thirty thousand people living here.

His answer didn't please the man. "Nick's one of ours," he said, rocking forward on the balls of his feet like a man who'd been in a few real fights. "We watch out for him."

Ah, Tom thought. Butte's ties to Ireland had always been strong. In his day, the Irish here had set out cream in saucers outside their back doors to appease the fairies. Apparently the traditions of taking care of the Little People, changelings, and those who might be changelings were adhered to still—even if, as they clearly believed, the one they watched over was entirely human, just simpleminded.

"This is Ron," Nick the Hobgoblin said to Thomas. "He gives me rides in his yellow truck. I like yellow."

Ron who drove a yellow truck narrowed his eyes at Thomas, clearly telling him to go away, something Thomas was happy to comply with. He started to free himself.

"Tom likes tea," Nick informed them, his eyes as innocent as he was not. Not if he were a hobgoblin. "Tom likes the nighttime." He paused and with a sly smile added, "Tom likes Maggie."

Thomas's hand clenched on Nick's at hearing her name. He gave the hobgoblin a sharp look. How did the little man know about Margaret? Was *Margaret* the reason he'd been called here?

"Does he?" said the woman, with a sharp glance at Thomas. "Nick, why don't you come with us to see the singer at the old YMCA?"

Margaret.

Thomas decided that he would see what the hobgoblin wanted—and to that end, he'd have to allay the suspicions of Nick's protectors. He inclined his head respectfully toward Ron.

"Nick and I know one another," he said. "I went to school here." A long, long time ago.

"Oh," said the woman, relaxing. "Not a tourist, then."

The man looked down at his watch. "If you want to catch your brother's performance, we'd better go."

As soon as those two were gone, Thomas pulled his hand away from the hobgoblin's. Mindful of the watchful glances of the people around him—the couple weren't the only ones watching out for Nick—he was gentle about it.

"Tell me, hobgoblin," he said with soft menace. "What do you know about Margaret Flanagan?"

Butte, Montana, 1900

HE ESCORTED THE MEN THROUGH THE TUNNELS, KEEPing to the front of the group so that the lanterns they carried wouldn't damage his night vision. And also because it scared them that he didn't need a lantern to find his way.

The current location of his father's opium den was a few hundred feet from where they'd started, though he'd led them through alternate routes that had added a half mile and more to the trip. It was imperative that they—mostly experienced miners, though one was a merchant's son—not be able to find their way here without a guide. First, payment was made before they entered the mines, and anyone who made it to the den was assumed to have paid their fee. Second, it made it difficult for the police to find. To ensure the location remained a secret, the den was moved every couple of weeks.

Thomas took a final turn and opened the makeshift door in invitation. The light from a dozen lanterns inside illuminated the smoky haze within. It looked like the hell the nuns had promised him.

"Tap her light, Tommy," said one of the men he'd escorted, giving him the traditional farewell wishes of a miner: when forcing a stick of explosive into a drilled hole in the granite, a miner wanted to be very careful tapping it in with his hammer.

It caught Thomas by surprise, and he took a better look at the man's face. Juhani. He'd been a Finnish boy whose father worked with the timber crews when they'd gone to school together once upon a time—twenty years and more ago. Now they were both damned—Thomas as his father's monster, Juhani Koskinen as an opium addict.

For a moment they stared at each other, then Juhani stepped through the door into the den, followed by the rest of the men.

"Don't know why you talk to him, Johnny, my boyo," said one of them in a thick Irish lilt as Thomas closed the door, sealing them in. "He don't never talk."

Not since he'd returned from the Master as his father's new slave. What was there to say? Who would talk to him?

Even before his mother's brother, a famous scholar from a family of scholars, rescued his mother from his father's care, she had not looked upon his face if she could help it—not since he had become a monster. She had taken her other children with her when she returned to China with her brother. Thomas had been left behind.

For his father he had no words. Not that his father cared. He gave orders—and took him to the Master once a week to feed and be fed upon.

Thomas hoped his father regretted his bargain, regretted at least the necessity of the once-a-week twenty-dollar gold piece that was more than his father paid any of his workers, either in the laundry or in the opium den hidden down in the mine.

Alone, without a light of any kind, Thomas headed out deeper into the mines. The tunnels under the town were the labyrinthine result of more than three decades of every-day, round-the-clock mining. Aboveground, the gallows frames of the elevators that took men down and lifted them up again when their shifts were done clearly marked the different mines. Belowground, all of the mines interconnected.

He'd heard that there were thousands of miles of tunnels and it wouldn't surprise him if that were so. The other two men who ran dens sometimes took their nonpaying customers deep into the mines and left them in the maze of tunnels out of which they never found their way. His father's customers all paid ahead of time or they didn't get in.

He had always been good at finding his way around the mines. Since he'd been turned, he'd gotten a lot better.

He didn't need light, didn't need to see at all. He could feel the tunnel stretch around him—and the ones above, below, and beside him, too. He could sense the areas where miners were actively digging and the ones where no one had been for a very long time. He could tell north from south, up from down, and he knew where he was in relation to the city over his head.

He never got lost in the tunnels.

It was near three in the morning. His father had gone to sleep—the men Thomas had escorted in were the very last—and Thomas was free for the rest of the night. There were boys in the den whose job it would be to rouse their customers and escort them to the surface. Thomas never had to work in the den anymore: he scared the customers. He wasn't sure if they feared him because his father used him to hurt the ones who displeased him, or if some atavistic sense warned them that he was a dangerous predator.

Thomas walked to the nearest elevator shaft—he was safely

between shifts, so he didn't have to worry about the elevator cars—
and began climbing down.

The darkness soothed him, as did the growing heat. It was
always hot in the lower levels. He didn't need heat to survive anymore, but it had been such a luxury for him . . . before . . . that he
always took pleasure in it. He climbed down until it suited him to
stop a few levels above where they were actively mining. Descend-
ing the shaft pushed even his strength and abilities; he enjoyed it.

He was always alone, but somehow, deep in the heart of the
earth, with none but himself for company, he felt less so. Walking
down tunnels that might not have seen people for decades, he felt
comfortable in his skin and he relished it, even though it made it difficult to deny his growing hunger. Tomorrow he would have to feed.

He dreaded the feeding time. Afterward, his Master renewed his
orders and made certain his fledgling understood his place. Someday, Thomas was certain, someday he would be free. But for nearly
a decade he had been slave to his father and the demon-thing that
had, over a whole long year, turned him into what he was now.

He put out his hand and touched the damp earth. There was
water here, underground. A huge lake, he'd been told, and streams
that ran just as the creeks aboveground did. He couldn't feel the
water the way he felt the earth, which spoke to his bones.

Somewhere in the darkness in front of him chains rattled.

"Please?"

A woman's voice, and Irish.

He froze where he stood. Maybe she was one of the ones who
did not pay for her opium—though usually those were left much
higher than this. No one but he wandered alone down here. He
couldn't believe that either Mr. Wong or Mr. Luk would waste
money on chains for a nonpaying customer.

"Please, help me?"

He hadn't been walking particularly quietly. She knew he was
there.

The boy he'd been, Thomas Hao, would have run to the rescue.

But that boy had died a long time ago and left a monster in his place.

"What would you do for me in return?" he said, breathing in for the first time in a long time. He didn't have to, especially since he didn't speak. It made his father nervous when he didn't breathe, so he made a habit of letting his lungs sit empty.

He hadn't sensed her as he did the miners, and it bothered him. He'd assumed he could sense everyone in the tunnels, in his realm.

The chains rattled hard, agitated, as if the woman had not really believed there was someone else in the mine. "O lords and ladies, you are there," she said. "Please. My father is the Flanagan. The old one of high court. His element is fire. And I am accounted a power in my own right. Our gratitude will be yours, my word on it."

Fae. That's why he hadn't felt her. Now that he knew she was here he could sense her, but she felt so close to the sighs and groans of the earth that it was no wonder he hadn't noticed her before she'd spoken.

He avoided the fae when he could, and when he could not . . . well, the fae, unlike humans, knew exactly what he was, and they despised the monster almost as much as he despised himself.

"Please," she said.

If she were fae, chained down here, no human had done it, not this deep under the hill. He had no desire to find himself in the middle of a fae dispute.

"Sir?"

He could feel her listening. But he made no noise. This close to feeding day his heart only beat if he made it.

"You have nothing I want," he said, the words coming out hoarse and strange. He turned to go back the way he had come.

"Vampire."

He paused.

"They say there is a vampire who walks deep beneath the hill."

They must be the fae, because the humans didn't know. He didn't hunt: the Master forbade it. As a fledgling he could only take nourishment from another vampire, anyway. Taking the blood of humans did him no good at all. Every week the Master had him try it. The Master himself was agoraphobic, unable to leave his basement.

"Vampire," said the fae woman. "What do you wish most? I can grant you that."

Freedom, he thought. *If only the freedom to die.* The bleak knowledge that no one would be able to give that freedom to him until long after the remnants of Thomas Hao had been thoroughly eradicated, and there was nothing to free, made him angry with a rage that did not cloak his despair.

The sun. It had been so long since he'd walked in daylight that the hunger for it nearly eclipsed his growing thirst.

"I have power," she said. "Just tell me what you want?"

What I want, you cannot give me. And in the hopelessness of the thought, he found that he wanted her equally trapped, equally frantic, if only for a little while.

"You could feed me," he told her, his long-unused voice sharp and bitter. "I'm hungry."

"Come, then," she said. "Come and drink."

No hunting, was the command. *No unwilling victims.* Sometimes the Master forgot things or did not word things carefully enough. Maybe he'd never conceived that Thomas would find a willing victim.

If he intended to stay out of fae conflicts he should walk away—but a small part of him made him hesitate. It wasn't the hunger. It was the boy he had been who wanted the woman freed. He found he couldn't ignore the boy's necessities any more than he'd ever been able to ignore the Master's. It made the monster angry.

He gave her no chance to adjust, to brace herself. He dropped beside her, gripping her head and chin. He jerked her until her neck stretched out and bit down, sinking his fangs deep. He could have made it pleasant for her; his master insisted upon it being pleasant. But he wanted her to struggle, which would force him to stop and give him an excuse not to save her, to be the monster they—the Master and his father—had made him.

Other than a gasp as he struck, though, she was silent and still against him.

Her blood tasted nothing like the Master's. It reminded him of the taffy he'd eaten when he was human. Not in the flavor, but in the feeling of richness, of self-indulgence and satisfaction.

Feeding with the Master was *carnal* in its most profane sense— pleasure and pain. When it was over, it sent his senses into a stupor and left him feeling desperate for the bath that never really cleaned the stain from his soul no matter how hard he scrubbed.

This feeding was . . . as he imagined feeding from a dragon might be—sharp and not altogether comfortable, but rich with the bottomless power of fire and earth. The fire cleansed him, the earth restored him, leaving him raw and off balance—but not filthy.

It was the first time he'd fed from someone other than the Master, and it was hard to stop. *One more pull,* he thought, *just one more.* And one more became . . . He remembered the eyes of his old Finnish friend as he headed into the opium den. It gave him the strength to stop.

She was limp and unresponsive in his hold. He sealed the wounds he'd made, regretting the roughness of his attack and wondering if he had stopped too late. He lay beside her and listened to her heart beat.

When it continued past the first few minutes, he decided that she'd survive. His hands told him that they'd only chained her feet. He slipped his fingers inside the cuffs and broke them, one at a time. The flesh beneath was blistered, and her feet were bare. His clever hands told him also that she was young, far younger than she'd sounded—thirteen or fourteen, he thought, and clad in her nightdress. They'd taken her from her bed.

Poor thing.

He picked her up and carried her to the elevator shaft. She didn't wake up until he fed her sweet tea in his father's dark laundry.

She drank two cups before she said anything, her big gray eyes looking at the face of the monster he was.

He felt ashamed, and at the same time better than he had anytime these past twenty years or more, as if she had saved him, instead of the other way around.

He was not hungry at all.

"What is your name?" she asked. "I'm Margaret Flanagan. Maggie." Her voice sounded composed, but her hands were shaking so badly.

He was pretty sure she was scared of him. He had put his arm around her to brace her while he fed her tea. He expected his nearness made it worse, but he also expected that if he backed away from her right now, she'd fall off the stool.

For all that she was fae, she was a child.

He told himself that her fear didn't make him sad. He was confused and hid it behind his usual emotionless mask.

"I am Hao's monster," he told her abruptly. "Where is your father? I will take you home."

She tilted her head. She closed her eyes for one breath, heaved a sigh of heartfelt relief. When she looked up at him, she smiled, her face as bright as the sun he hadn't seen in years.

"He's coming," she said. "He'll be right here."

"Good," said Thomas, though he didn't know if that were true. If she had such power as he'd felt as he drank from her— earth and fire in abundance—then her father likely had more.

"Very true," said a man's voice, answering his thoughts— because Thomas had not spoken.

It took all of Thomas's considerable control not to show his surprise.

"Papa," said Margaret Flanagan, sounding for the first time as young as she looked. She pulled away from him and ran across the room to the arms of the man who stood in Hao's Laundry in a flannel shirt and dungarees, though the door was locked and the room had been empty when Thomas had carried her here.

The Flanagan didn't look imposing—only a few inches taller than Thomas, which made him short by the standards of the Irish in Butte. He didn't have the shoulders of a miner, though his hands showed the calluses of hard work.

"Vampire," he said, over his daughter's head. "I could destroy you, you're right. Fire is mine, and your kind are particularly vulnerable to it."

"Yes," acknowledged Thomas coolly. He might have been frightened, he thought, if he had really been afraid of death. Hell wasn't a pleasant thought, but then neither was a lifetime, possibly a hundred lifetimes, tied to the depraved thing that was his Master.

If a monster had taken advantage of someone he loved the way he had taken advantage of Margaret Flanagan, he would have killed that one and never felt regret. The wounds on her neck were closed, but his attack had been brutal and it would be a while before the red marks on her skin faded. The Flanagan stayed where he was.

Margaret turned her head until she could see Thomas.

"You have it now," she told him. "What will you do with it?"

"Have what?" asked Thomas.

"Freedom," she told him, and then collapsed in her father's arms.

He hadn't understood what she had done at first, not when he'd let her and her father out and relocked the laundry's door, not when he'd gone into the cupboard where he died for the day, not even when what had come to him had been sleep rather than death. He'd awakened and followed his father up the hill to the Master's house.

Hao Xun took him down the stairs to the basement as he always did, leaving Thomas with a gold coin at his feet.

"Pretty boy," said his Master. "Come here to me."

Obediently, Thomas stepped down the single stair. Above them, he heard his father walk out the door and shut it behind him.

"Give us a kiss, my sweet thing," the vampire told Thomas.

Thomas bent down to kiss his Master's cheek, one side and

then the other. As he did, he reached out with one hand to grasp the long, wooden candlestick that always sat on the little table beside the wing chair, though the candle it held was seldom lit.

"I'm so hungry for your blood," whispered his Master as Thomas pulled back.

As I hunger for yours, Thomas thought, thrusting the candlestick through the soft beeswax candle and into the old one's heart. He took two steps back, amazed that at long last he'd been able to do such a thing.

The old vampire leaned forward and smiled at him.

"Pretty boy," he said—and collapsed into himself.

Only then, staring at the dust that had been his Master, did Thomas understand the gift he'd been given.

Butte, Montana, present day

FREEDOM, THOMAS THOUGHT, FOLLOWING THE HOBGOB-lin up the hill to wherever Nick wanted him to go. He'd spoken to her with his lips, and Margaret had heard his heart.

Thomas had left Butte that very night, with his father's twenty-dollar gold piece in his pocket. He could not wait for Hao Xun to come and get him, because he didn't want to kill the man who had sired his human self the way he'd killed the thing that had sired his current flesh. If he'd seen his father again, he wasn't certain he could have helped himself.

He had never seen the two fae again, either, but unlike any of the vampires he'd met since then, he saw the sun every day and it did not burn him. He no longer needed to feed from a vampire in order to survive. Margaret had given him everything he'd desired as well as the feeding he'd asked for.

Nick stopped at a small well-kept house near the base of Big Butte, the hill that had given its name to the town—despite not being a butte at all. He let himself in the front door.

Thomas stopped on the porch. "If you want me inside," he told the hobgoblin, "you have to invite me in."

The little fellow stopped where he was and looked up at Thomas. "You mean no harm to me and mine, you will swear it."

"I'm not fae. Oaths have no power over me, Nick," he told the fae. "What I am is already damned."

The hobgoblin hissed and dismissed that with one hand.

"Don't throw Christian gobbledygook at me," he said. "Margaret told me you would come, told me you would help. You are here, so that is the first, but I wonder if the second is true. Vampire. I served her father most of my life. I can't afford to get this wrong."

The fae didn't like vampires. Thomas would have left because, with one exception, he didn't like the fae, either. But it hadn't been Nick who had brought him here; it had been Margaret. For her, he would do what he could.

"I owe Margaret Flanagan," said Thomas, who was better educated about fae than he'd been a hundred years ago. He knew what he was admitting—and that the fae would take it very seriously. "What she did for me was far more than what little I managed for her. I swear I mean no harm to her or hers."

"Come in and be welcome," said Nick after a pause, and turned to lead the way into his home.

THERE WERE FOUR OTHER PEOPLE IN THE LITTLE MAN'S living room, waiting for them, along with a blazing fire in the fireplace that gave out more light than heat.

One of the people, a big blond man, looked familiar, as though Thomas might have known him a long time ago. They were none of them human, and given that they were in a hobgoblin's house, Thomas was certain they were fae.

As soon as he entered the room on Nick's heels, everyone stood up—almost everyone. The kid on the piano bench just relaxed a little more. Thomas judged him the biggest threat: the really powerful ones often disguised themselves as something soft and helpless.

"Vampire," said the only woman. She was tall and muscular and spoke with a Finnish accent. "Is this the one?"

The big man's nose wrinkled as if he smelled something foul.

There was an old man—or one who looked old, since the fae could adopt any appearance that suited them. He peered at Thomas with nonjudgmental interest, which Thomas returned.

"It is him," said the boy on the piano bench. He was a beautiful young man, draped between the bench and the piano, his elbows on the cover that protected the keys. "Who else could it be? How many Chinese vampires do you think there are in Butte?"

"This is Thomas Hao," said Nick. "It is he who will find our Margaret."

He didn't introduce the others—hardly surprising, as names were odd things for the fae. Even a nickname, if held long enough, had power.

"Why does Margaret need finding?" Thomas asked.

The woman and the big man dropped their eyes and looked uncomfortable. Silence hung in the air for a moment.

"It is a long story," said Nick. "Will you take a seat?"

Thomas might be a vampire, but he had no way to judge the people in the room and was reluctant to sit down and put himself at a disadvantage.

The boy's smile widened as he slid off the bench and onto the floor. "Sit down, vampire, do—and the rest of you, too. Nick'll give him the rundown and then we'll see if she's right about the vampire."

The piano bench was hard and easy to rise from, unlike the overstuffed furniture in the rest of the room. It was acceptable—and it told Thomas something about the boy that he understood that.

Thomas sat on the bench. Once he was down, the fae took their seats. Nick sat on the floor opposite Thomas, though there was an empty chair.

"Let me begin this tale in its proper place—with the Flanagan," he said. "He was high-court fae. Do you know what that means, Tom?"

"Powerful," replied Thomas. "Though there is no high court any longer. There are only the Gray Lords, who rule all of the fae."

"Aye," agreed Nick. "Powerful. Also old—and smart. A person didn't survive long in the high court if he weren't smart." The little man looked down at his hands.

"That's not really where the story starts," said the boy sitting at Thomas's feet. "It starts with Butte. With fae who came here hiding among the humans. It probably won't surprise you to learn that all the fae don't get along together, will it, Mr. Hao?"

"We vampires are the soul of brotherly love," Thomas responded dryly. "I assumed that the fae were the same."

The boy laughed until tears ran out of his eyes.

"It was not as funny as all that," said the woman.

"Brotherly love," repeated the boy. "Ayah. I'll remember that. Anyway, the fae came. From northern Europe and the British Isles mostly, like the people. Norwegians, Swedes, Finns, Cornish, and Irish—they all came."

Italian, too, thought Thomas. *The Serbians, the Czech, the Ukrainians.*

The boy sat up straight now, his eyes on the woman and the big man, turned slightly away from Thomas. "Once upon a time, the Irish fae would have squashed them all, but then came the iron-mongers and their Christ and they bound the old places. Left us crippled and weak."

"It didn't hurt us as badly," said the woman softly. "We have more iron-kissed among us, we Finns and Nordic folk."

"Iron-kissed?" asked Thomas.

"Those who work metals: dwarves, hiisi—some of them anyway, metal mages. So for thirty years we controlled the land here, and among us was one, a hiisi, who . . . was not kind to the other fae."

The boy laughed as if he thought she were funny, too.

She looked at him. "Most of us were too afraid to object." It wasn't an apology . . . not quite. "He had a talent for finding what you held dear, and then using it to make you do his bidding."

"Yes," the boy said dryly. "You suffered too, didn't you, you poor things."

She bit her lip and turned away. Apparently she was ashamed.

"And then came the Flanagan," said the old man. He might look fragile and aged, but his voice told a different story. It rumbled in Thomas's ears—British with a hint of Welsh or Cornish.

"I knew we'd get to him sooner or later," said Nick. "Flanagan changed things."

"For the better," rumbled the giant. "Even we could see that."

The woman snorted inelegantly. "He pushed the hiisi—this was an old and powerful hiisi—into summoning the Iku-Tursas. The Flanagan could have worked something out, but he pushed and pushed and would not compromise."

Thomas frowned. Iku-Tursas. The name sounded familiar. He'd had some friends in school: Juhani Koskinen, Matti Makela, and another boy who was also Finnish. They told him a story once.

"The dragon," Thomas said. "But I thought it was a sea serpent."

The fae looked at him in surprise, except for the woman, who smiled and sat back. "Most people don't know Finnish stories."

"They didn't grow up here," said Thomas.

"The Tursas is a little more than a mere sea dragon, vampire," said the boy coolly. "It can take many forms. It attacked the Flanagan when he was down in the mines."

"No," said the big man at the same time the old man did. The bench under Thomas slid forward a little bit in eagerness, as if it wanted to go to the old man. Forest fae of some sort, he thought, setting his feet down a little firmer.

"It attacked the miners," said Nick. "Playing with them a little. The place where they'd be working would start leaking water.

It was the Speculator Mine—the one Flanagan was working for as a mining engineer. Modern, safe, well ventilated—the Flanagan insisted upon it."

"High-court fae always did love the silly humans," murmured the boy as if to himself.

The woman snorted again and reached out with a boot to nudge him hard. "I've heard you might come from high court yourself," she said.

He jumped up, fierce with indignation. "You take it back! You take that back right now."

She smiled at him. "Of course, I never believed it. Too much stupid, not enough looks."

He shook himself like a wet cat. "Damned piru," he snapped.

"Easy prey," she purred.

Piru, thought Thomas. Finnish fae, he remembered. But was it one of the witty demons prone to games of wit, or one of the air ladies who hung out and looked beautiful until something ticked them off? He looked at the woman and decided for the clever demon; she looked a little too substantial to be floating around.

"It picked groups of miners with fae among them to frighten," said Nick, picking up his story from where he'd left off. "Eventually one of them figured out that the water they'd been hitting wasn't just an accident of geology. He took the tale to the Flanagan."

"He was supposed to charge off to confront the Finnish fae who was tormenting his people," said the old man. "He would have, too, if certain people hadn't gone to him and told him that what he faced wasn't just any fae."

"There was betrayal on both sides," said the woman. "Some did not think that the Flanagan was strong enough to keep his promises and it would be the less powerful fae who would suffer. Others looked to him for justice and a way out from under the hiisi's thumb." She rubbed absently at the fabric of the couch where she sat. "It didn't matter. He went anyway."

"Aye," said the big man. "As he had to, being who he was. But he went armed and ready instead of oblivious. The Flanagan, he wouldn't back down for Tursas."

"Wait," said Thomas. "The Speculator. The Granite Mountain fire? The mining disaster, during World War One?"

"1917," said Nick. "When the fire broke out, we knew he'd won."

"In true Germanic fashion," said the giant morosely, "I suppose he had."

"He never came out," Nick told Thomas. "When the fires went out, we pulled out the bodies. Some of them were fae, most were human; some you couldn't tell. We didn't find the Tursas or the Flanagan."

"Afterward," said the woman, "we met. All of us. Summoning the Tursas from its exile, as if he were a dog to come to his master. If the Flanagan hadn't . . . hadn't done whatever he did, it might have eaten the world."

She believed that, Thomas thought.

"The fae killed him," rumbled the old man. "That hiisi who summoned the Tursas. He'd used so much power to do it, he was vulnerable. Even his allies turned on him. All the fae that were here: Cornish, Irish, Finn, German, Norwegian, Slav, and that little guy from Italy. We killed that hiisi who thought that his power was more important than the survival of all."

"We thought that was the end of it," the woman said. "Time passed. The city started to die, people left, and most of us left, too. Just a few stayed."

"But that hiisi had taken the Flanagan's daughter to make certain of his victory if the Flanagan, by some miracle, had destroyed the Iku-Tursas," the boy said. "Searches were made but . . . there are thousands of miles of tunnels. We thought her long dead. Then two years ago, she started to talk to us," said the boy. "A high-court trick, that, getting into your head. Unpleasant."

Thomas remembered.

"She's quite mad," whispered Nick. "Quite mad from all those years trapped in the earth."

"So what do you need me for?" Thomas asked.

"We need you to find her and kill her," said the big man.

"It is what she wants," said the boy, answering Thomas's raised eyebrow. "She tells me so, over and over. I've looked and looked and I can't find her anywhere."

"She's in the mines." Nick's voice was pensive. "We don't have an earth or iron-kissed fae left here to find her—not that they had much success when they looked before."

"And even if we did, she has a haltija." The woman looked out the window, and Thomas noted absently that the fae needed to replace the double-paned window because ice had formed around the edges of the inside of the glass.

"A what?" he asked.

She waved a hand. "A guard. This one is a kalman väki, we think—a dead man's spirit. He was probably killed and set to guard her when she was taken."

"A kalman väki," Thomas said slowly. "How do you know that, since you can't find her?"

"She told us." The big man glanced at Thomas searchingly and then looked away. Thomas knew he wouldn't read anything but mild interest in his face.

"We'd have to destroy it to get to her." The woman closed her eyes. "Even if we could find her, we could not get by that. A kalman väki holds the power of mortification: it kills with a touch; not even the immortal are immune. But you aren't exactly immortal, are you?"

"The mines were mostly filled when the company shut them down." The old man pulled his beard lightly. "The old timbers were rotting through and the tunnels collapsing. Was a time you could take a step off your back porch in the morning to find a hole four or five hundred feet down that hadn't been in your backyard when you went to bed. One tunnel collapsing on top of another, on top of another. Was quite the thing to fill them—expensive and time-consuming both. But some of it is left, where the tunnels were cut into granite mostly."

"So," said Thomas. "You want me—a vampire—to go looking in the old mines to find Margaret Flanagan, who has been trapped down there for a century. Because vampires are so good at . . . what? Dissolving into mist and sinking through the earth? I think you've been watching too many bad horror movies."

"She was never the same after she met you," Nick said. "She had such a touch with the earth: it came to her call and did as she bid. She had a little of her father's gift for fire, but it was the earth that knew her. She was able to call you here. If she can do that, she should be able to guide you to her down in the mines, where her power is greater."

"*Hello, vampire,*" said the big man softly—and his American accent turned lilting and softened. Thomas had only talked to Margaret for a few hours, one day out of the many years he'd lived, but he recognized her intonations in the man's deep voice.

The other fae moved away from the big man, but they didn't look startled. He knew that they would not perceive his surprise; his father had taught him well.

"*Or ill,*" the big man said, proving that her gift of reading thoughts that Thomas did not speak was still hers. The fae's clear blue eyes were not quite the same shade as Margaret's.

"They think I can find you," Thomas said carefully. "That because you called me here, you can lead me through the tunnels."

"*Like to like,*" she answered him. "*I don't know why you heard my call, just that you did. I could not have given you your wish if you had not been earth-touched.*"

He knew what she meant. How could he not? He remembered that sense he'd had of how she was a part of the earth that had held them together in its maw. He'd sensed it because the earth spoke to him, too.

Vampires develop abilities, the Master had told him. The Master could make humans do as he wanted even before a blood exchange—a rare gift, and useful.

Thomas's mother's family were scholars, back as far as their family history went—all the way, the stories said, to the dragon scholar who knew everything that dragons knew and turned into a man to see what men knew. Thomas's mother had told him that her family was founded by a dilong, an earth dragon. "Only a story," his father had said, rolling his eyes. He had never cared for anything that reminded him that his wife's family had higher status than his.

Thomas looked at the assembled fae. "Why do you say that she is mad?" he asked.

"My father's blood runs in the earth," the big man whispered in Margaret's voice. *"His fire consumes me. When I emerge I will burn them all to dust and beyond."*

"We think the Flanagan died two years ago," said the woman in subdued tones. She did not look at the man who sat next to her and spoke with Margaret's voice. "That he gave her his last strength so she could call out and find someone to help, so she could be saved, but it was too late."

"What would you expect of her?" asked the boy. "Alone for nearly a century. Trapped with only the dead for company, under the earth. Chained, without food or water. Neither dying nor living. And now she has the power of her father, who killed the Iku-Tursas." He shivered and hugged himself. "She will kill us all."

"No," said Thomas, coming at last to his feet. "I shall not allow it. The girl I knew would not want your deaths on her conscience." She had rescued him, a vampire who had hurt her, and still she rescued him. She did not need the blood of these fae on her hands.

IT TOOK HIM FOUR DAYS TO FIND A WAY TO THE PLACE she'd been kept. As the old man had promised, many of the tunnels he'd known were collapsed or filled, but his sense of the ways beneath the mining town was as good as it had ever been. He found a path.

As before, though, that earth sense he had did not betray her to him. It was the blood he'd taken from her. *Like calls to like,* she'd told him. While all the fae around her thought she was talking about her magic.

He rose in the absolute darkness and felt the shape of the last obstacle that stood between him and his goal. It was not just winter's chill, it was colder than that. He found himself wishing for a light to see the väki, but he'd never needed a light down here, so he hadn't brought one.

"Why come you smelling so of death?" It was a woman's voice; he hadn't expected her to be a woman.

"I am vampire," he told the kalman väki. "I bring death with me."

"Mine is the power of illness, of mortification of living flesh," she said. "But I would keep my charge though I have no power over the dead."

"No more than I do," he said gently. "I mean her no harm, guardian spirit. I killed those who did."

He'd killed them, her father's betrayers, so that Margaret wouldn't have to. They hadn't expected it, and he'd been careful to take out the boy first. Then the big man who could—Thomas was pretty sure—pick and choose how much Margaret could say through his lips.

He was a vampire, and these fae had believed he was their dog to do their bidding. They hadn't expected a monster, despite knowing what he was. Killing them had not taken him long.

Thomas had been raised in Butte, among the Irish, Finns, and all the other races who had come to pull the treasures of the Richest Hill on Earth. He might wear the face of a Chinese man, but he came from a family of scholars and lived among the people here for all of his childhood.

A väki of whatever kind was a protector of the treasure it guarded. No one would set such a creature to keep a prisoner in. Only a fae would think that a *vampire* would assume a väki of the grave would be an evil thing. Her father or perhaps the Finnish fae who had first warned the Flanagan of the dragon must have sent it to protect her. If they meant his Margaret no harm, the väki would not have prevented them from reaching her.

If Margaret had remained powerless in the heart of the earth, they would have left her there to rot. When her father's power came to her—or whatever had happened that she could tell their thoughts and return her own—she could finally take action against them; they had decided they had to kill her.

Somehow they'd discovered that she'd called him for help—perhaps she'd taunted them with it—that she *had* someone she could call for help. It didn't matter. What do you send against the spirit of the dead? A vampire. They had the weapon they needed; they just had to point it in the right direction. Once Thomas had dealt with the väki, they would have killed Thomas and Margaret both.

But Margaret hadn't told them everything about him. They assumed she could summon him because of the wish she'd granted him, that it had given her some sort of magical power over him. But it had been the blood. If she had trusted them—as they implied—she would have told them about that part. Telling him about the väki had been their first mistake. Not knowing that he'd bitten her and taken her blood had been the second.

Nick, who had served her father *almost* all his life, would have known a vampire saved her. But neither Margaret nor her father had told Nick the whole story.

The final, and greatest, mistake had been implying that Margaret had been driven insane, imprisoned in the earth. What was it Nick had said? "She's quite mad." A subtle word was *mad*. Nick had used it to imply one thing without a lie crossing his lips. Thomas would have been angry, too, imprisoned by his enemies. The earth was her element; it nurtured her and sustained her.

If he was wrong, if they had been innocent of all he suspected . . . ? Well, then, he was a vampire, after all—and they were fae. He would not regret their deaths.

But he had not been wrong, because he could feel the guardian move out of his path, satisfied by his answer. He slipped by it and found the fragile thing he searched for, little more than bones in chains.

"Please," she said, her voice as quiet as the whisper of the spring wind.

He broke the iron shackles first, throwing them as far from her as the confines of the tunnel allowed. He pulled a blanket out of the pack he carried and carefully, gently put her upon it.

"What would you do for me in return?" he said, raising her up and touching a damp cloth to her face. She pressed her face against it, sucking on the moisture. It would take her a long time to get water that way—and it would be slow enough not to make her sick from it.

When he pulled the cloth away and soaked it in water from his canteen again, she said, her voice hoarse, "Anything. My gratitude you have."

"Yes?" he said, pressing the cloth against her face again. "You gave me such a gift last time. Gratitude is a poor substitute. Perhaps I should give your gift back to you, shall I?" He picked her up, and she was such a light burden, lighter even than she'd been the first time he'd carried her out of the mine tunnels.

"Oh, yes," she sighed, understanding what he didn't say, as she had before. "I should love to see the sun again."

GRAY

This story, as some of my other stories have, started as an assignment from my writers' group. Take a color and a holiday and make a story out of it. As it was February, I chose Valentine's Day—but red would have been too obvious.

We lived in Chicago (a good long time ago now), and it remains one of my favorite big cities. It, like my hometown, has a colorful past and terrific people. Anyone who has been in Chicago in February, however, knows about those gray days, when everything is wet and cold and nasty, when it feels like it has been cold forever and spring will never come. Like those winter days, our heroine, Elyna, has been feeling cold and gray for a very long time.

The events in this story take place before *Moon Called*.

IT WAS RAINING, A DESULTORY, RELUCTANT, ANGRY RAIN
forced unwillingly from the gray clouds overhead. It dribbled with
the fiendish rhythm of a Chinese water torture. Drip. Drip. Drip.

Elyna's windshield wipers squeaked until she turned them off.
But the drops still came down to obscure her sight. From old habit,
she pulled into the space that had been hers.

She'd first parked there a couple of times because the space had
been open. When she'd moved in with Jack, a lifetime ago, it was
seldom open again because her car was in it. After a while if it
wasn't available for her little Ford, she'd curse the visitor who'd
stolen it and find some other, less convenient parking place. When
that happened, she'd go out to check before bedtime to see if it was
open. If it was, she'd repark her car where it would be happy.

"Cars just are, darlin'," Jack would tell her with a grin as he
escorted her out of the apartment to keep watch as she moved the
Ford. "They aren't happy or sad."

Jack had been in love with her, though, and was patient with
her little ways. He'd loved her and she'd loved him in that whole-
hearted eager fashion that only the young and innocent have—

secure in the knowledge that there was nothing so terrible it could tear them apart. Having successfully overcome her Polish and his Irish parents' objections to their match had only given her more confidence.

She was less innocent now.

Much, much less innocent.

Parking in that old spot had been habit, but it sat in her belly like a meal too cold. This was a bad idea. She knew it, but she couldn't give it up without trying to mend what she had . . . *lost* was the wrong word. *Destroyed* might have been a more apt one.

She rubbed her cold arms with colder hands, then turned off the motor. Without its warm hum, it was very quiet in the car.

She got out at last, locked the doors with the key fob, and left her car in the parking place that probably belonged to someone else now. Blinking back the aimless raindrops, she tromped through the slush from what must have been last week's snow on the sidewalk.

Only then did she look at the gray stone apartment building ahead. *Did they still call it an apartment building when all of the apartments were being sold as condominiums?*

It wasn't a particularly large building, three floors, six apartments, surrounded by a small front parklike area that had always managed to insert a little color in the summer without requiring maintenance or inviting anyone to linger. This evening, with winter still reigning despite the rain that fell instead of snow, there was no color to be had.

The cut granite edges of the steps were familiar and alien at the same time, worn in a way they hadn't been when this had been *their* home—and that strangeness hurt.

Next to the door, blown into the corner of the building, lay a little Valentine's Day card with a heart on it. The ink had run, fading out the *BE MINE* to a grayish semidecipherable mush. Only the name *Jack* scribed in black crayon was still clear. It was both irony and a sign, she thought, but she didn't know if a child's wet card was a good portent or not.

She looked up to the topmost windows with longing eyes and murmured, "Be mine, Jack?"

She rang the bell on the side of the door, a new plastic button surrounded by stainless steel, and a buzz released the door lock. The real estate agent must have beaten her here.

She wiped her tennis shoes off on the mat in front of the door and stepped into a small foyer. At first glance, she thought the room hadn't changed at all. Then she realized that the names written in Sharpie below the numbers on the boxes were different from the names she had known, and the wooden handrail next to the stairs had been replaced with the same polished steel as the doorbell.

"Our place, Elyna, just think of it!" Jack's voice rang in sudden memory, full of eagerness and life.

The wooden handrail had had a notch in it from when they'd hit it, she and Jack, with the sharp edge of her metal typist desk, carrying it up to their new home. She hadn't realized she had been looking forward to seeing that stupid notch until it wasn't there.

She looked down and saw that the new handrail was dented a little, too. She knew better than to do something like that; she had better control. But that notch had been a memory of laughter and . . . poor Jack had hated that desk, its industrial ugliness an affront to his artistic eye. Still, he'd helped her carry it all the way up the stairs to their third-floor apartment.

She'd paid him back, on top of the desk wearing (at least at first) a cream-colored lace teddy her mother had given her in a small, tastefully wrapped package with instructions to open it in private. Jack hadn't minded the desk so much after that.

And those kinds of thoughts weren't going to help Elyna tonight.

She continued up the stairs, trailing her hand over the new metal handrail, hard-won control keeping her hands open and light as they skimmed over the cold surface. On the third floor the real estate agent awaited her in a peacoat with damp shoulders. He had a closed rain-dampened umbrella in one hand.

"Ms. Gray," he said, taking a step forward and reaching out with his free hand. "I'm Aubrey Tailor."

"Yes," she said, shaking his hand gravely. "Thank you for making time to meet me here. When I saw the ad, I just knew that this was the place."

"You're cold," he said, sounding concerned. Delicately built and pretty, she tended to arouse protective instincts in some men. "There's no heat in the condo right now."

"It is February in Chicago," Elyna told him. "Don't worry, my hands are always a little cold."

"Cold hands, warm heart," he said, then flushed, because it was a little too personal when addressed to a single woman who was his client. He shook his head and gave her a sheepish smile. "At least that's what my mother always said."

"Mine, too," she agreed. She liked him better for losing the slick salesman front—which might have been his intention all along. He let her go into the apartment first, closing the door between them. He'd wait outside, he'd told her, while she looked her fill.

Here was change that made that handrail pale in comparison.

The old oak floors Elyna had polished and cursed, because keeping them looking good was an ongoing war, were scarred and bedecked with stains that she hadn't put on them. Her lips twisted in a snarl that made her grateful that the real estate agent had stayed outside.

Vampires are territorial and this was *her* home, the home of her heart.

One of the pretty leaded-glass windows that looked out on the street had been replaced with plain glass framed in white vinyl, giving the living room a lopsided look. Someone had started to tear down the plastered walls—messy work that had stopped about halfway. A piece of wallpaper showed where someone had broken through layers and layers of paper, plaster, and paint to a familiar scrap.

She pulled the chunk of plaster displaying that paper off the wall and sat down on the floor with the plaster in her lap. Was it her imagination or was there a rusty stain on the paper?

"Jack?" she said plaintively. "Jack?"

But, other than the normal sounds of a building with six apartments . . . condos . . . in it, five of them occupied, she heard nothing. She looked at the rest of the apartment—most of which she could see from where she sat—the gutted kitchen without the white cabinets, just odd-colored spots on the walls to show where they used to be. Bare pipes stuck out of the floor where the sink should have been, and wires dripped from the ceilings where once lights had illuminated her life.

Unable to look anymore, she put her forehead on her knees.

After a while she said, "Oh, Jack." Then she took a deep breath and worked at getting herself put back into some kind of public-ready shape. She'd fed before she drove over, but emotional distress makes the hunger worse, and her teeth ached and her nose insisted on remembering how good Mr. Aubrey Tailor had smelled when he'd blushed.

Something made a sighing noise in the empty apartment and she jerked her head up, all thoughts of hunger put aside. But nothing moved and there were no more sounds.

What had she expected? Time hadn't stopped for her; why would it have stopped for this apartment? Since seeing that first newspaper article about it, she'd done her research. She'd walked in here knowing that the stripping of the old had already been begun, awaiting replacement by the new. The in-progress remodel hadn't even bothered her until she saw it with her own eyes.

What was she doing here? The past was the past. She should strip it away just as the old plaster had been stripped from the living room wall. She should wash herself clean.

Outside, the rain slid down the windowpanes.

WHEN SHE HAD THE VAMPIRE WITHIN TAMPED DOWN until it would take another vampire to see what she was, she opened the apartment door.

"As you can see," the real estate agent said heartily—without looking at her—"it won't take much to get it ready to become whatever you'd like. It's good solid construction, built in 1911. You can put new flooring in, or strip the oak. It's three-quarter-inch oak; you don't see that in new construction. My client's price is very good."

"You had it sold twice this year," Elyna said, keeping the anxiety and need out of her voice. She had money. Enough. But not so much that bargaining wouldn't be a help.

"Ah." He looked disconcerted. No one expected someone who looked as young and frivolous as she did to have half a brain. He cleared his throat. "Yes. Twice."

"They both backed out before the papers were signed."

He frowned at her. "I thought you didn't have your own agent?"

"I took the downstairs neighbor, Josh, out to dinner yesterday." He was a nice man about ten years older than she looked. She'd treated him, despite his argument. It had been only fair that she pay for his dinner since she'd intended he should serve as hers afterward. He'd not remember the dinner clearly or what they'd discussed. Nor would he see that it was a problem that he didn't.

Elyna's Mistress had had a talent for beguilement. She could have given him a whole set of memories clearer than what had actually happened. Elyna, whose talents lay in other places, made use of the more common vampire ability to cloud minds and calm potential meals.

"I see." Elyna could tell from Aubrey's tone that he knew the story that Josh had related to her.

Even so, she laid it out for him. "He told me that the man who bought the building to turn it into condos stayed in this apartment and fixed the others, one at a time. He finished the one over there"—she tipped her head toward the door to the other third-floor apartment—"moved in, and started on this one. Only odd things started happening. First it was tools and small stuff disap-pearing. Then"—as the destruction increased—"it was perfectly stable ladders falling over with people on them. Sent an electrical contractor to the hospital with that one. Saws that turned them-selves on at the worst possible time—they managed to reattach that man's finger, Josh said. Chicago is a big city, but contractors do talk to each other. He couldn't get a crew in here to work the place." Elyna gave him a big friendly smile. "Some of that I already knew. I read the article in the neighborhood paper before I called you." That article was why she had called him.

She could see him reevaluate her. Was she a kook who wanted a haunted house? Or was she just looking for a real bargain?

"I'm older than I look," she told him, to help him make up his mind. "And I'm not a fool. Haunted or not, anyone looking at this apartment is going to start by getting appraisals from contractors. You haven't had an offer on this place in six months."

"A lot of bad luck doesn't a haunted place make," he said heartily, taking the bait. "All it takes is a few careless people. The man who lived here before my client, lived here for twenty years and never saw any ghost. I have his phone number and you can talk to him."

"It doesn't matter if I'm convinced it's not haunted," she told him. "It matters what the contractors think."

He looked grim.

"I'm willing to make an offer," she said. "But I'm going to have to pay premium prices to get anyone in to do the work, and that affects my bottom line."

And they got down to business. Aubrey had the paperwork for the offer with him. They took care of signatures, she fed from him, and then both of them went their separate ways in the night. Aubrey, with a new affection for Elyna, would be determined to make a good bargain for her regardless of the effect it might have on his commission. She felt guilty—a little—but not as much as she would have if he hadn't tried to take advantage of her supposed ignorance.

ELYNA'S PHONE RANG WHILE SHE WAS IN THE HOTEL shower. She answered it with her hair dripping onto the thick green carpeting. Only after she answered did she remember that she wouldn't be punished for not answering the phone right away anymore.

"Elyna," said Sean, one of the vampires who'd belonged to Corona with her. Without waiting for her greeting, he continued, "You are being foolish. There are plenty of places without seethes where you could settle. Colbert doesn't play nicely with others and you won't be able to hide from him forever."

Pierre Colbert was the Master of Chicago, and a nasty piece of business he was. He'd driven the Mistress and what he'd left of her seethe out of Chicago about thirty years ago. Elyna had met him only once, and that was enough. He wouldn't bother driving her out. He'd just destroy her—if he noticed she was in his territory.

"Elyna," coaxed Sean's voice in her ear. "Come back to Madison. Take your rightful place here."

Never. That much Elyna was certain of. Sean had been her lover sometimes—two frightened people finding what solace they could. Usually they'd been friends, too, and more often allies. But Elyna wasn't strong enough to hold the seethe—and Sean knew it. If she went back, he'd kill her to establish his power. Or maybe he was working for someone else, someone more powerful: there were several that came to mind.

"What of Sybil?" Elyna asked him. Sybil wouldn't need to kill Elyna to take power, but she'd enjoy doing it.

"Sybil's been dealt with," Sean said with considerable satisfaction.

"Good," Elyna said, meaning it. If Corona had been brutal, Sybil, her lieutenant, was fiendish.

Sybil had enjoyed hurting others: vampires or regular people, she didn't care. She had a special hatred of men, and Sean had suffered under her hand as much as any in the seethe except maybe Fitz. Fitz was ash and gone, but he'd provided Sybil with months of entertainment. "That's good. With her gone, Brad or Chris can take over as Master."

"Where are you staying?" said Sean.

Elyna sighed, making sure he heard it. He was being too obvious. Ah, the joys of vampire politics. No one even made an attempt to hide the bodies.

"I'm not really as dumb as I look," she told him gently. "I would have thought that you, of all the seethe, would know that."

"Colbert will find you," he told her. "That's his talent, you know, finding vampires when he wants them. You'll be dead anyway and we'll be in the middle of a fucking civil war—"

She ended the call while he was speaking—answering rudeness with rudeness. She didn't approve of swearing. Or prolonging conversations with stupid people. She hadn't thought Sean was one of the stupid people, and it hurt.

She walked over to the mirror on the bathroom door and stared. Did she really look so gullible and helpless? She blinked at herself a few times. She could admit she looked harmless, but surely not stupid.

Colbert could find vampires, any vampire. She'd known that when she'd come here.

Still staring at herself, Elyna flexed her hands, then fisted them. All vampires had talents of one sort or another. There were some magics that almost all of them who'd survived past the first few months had to one degree or another, such as the ability to cloud minds. Vampires who had to kill everyone they fed from were eliminated as a threat to the rest of them. Too many dead bodies brought too much attention.

There were rarer talents, like Colbert's ability to track other vampires. Her former Mistress Corona's ability with minds was rare only in how powerful she had been.

Elyna had a rare talent, too. She could hide in plain sight. As long as she didn't move, she was invisible in a room full of vampires. She'd kept that quiet, once she'd understood the implications. Finding the will to use it had taken a long, long time. A lifetime and more—because a vampire must obey her maker.

That was the first thing she had learned. If her Mistress had taken control of her a day earlier, or if her Mistress had made more certain of the rope she'd tied Elyna's dead body with, things would have been different. To Corona's credit, most vampires take years of mutual feeding to change from human to vampire. She'd had Elyna only a couple of weeks when someone slipped up and drained her dry. As Corona told Elyna when she'd finally tracked her down, they had assumed that Elyna was as dead as she looked; the rope had been merely a precaution. Sometimes, the Mistress had told her, there were people who turned much easier than others. Who knew why?

Stubborn Pole, Jack had called her when at his most exasperated. Fair enough; she'd called him a hotheaded Mick in return, and there had been more than a cup of truth in both epithets.

So, stubborn Pole that she was, despite expectations, Elyna had awoken tied up in a shed in Corona's backyard. The ropes had taken her a little while to break. Confused and dazed by the transformation from human to dead to vampire, she had run home, where Jack had been waiting.

If she survived to be a thousand, she would never forget the joy on his face when she'd opened the door.

But she hadn't been Elyna O'Malley, Jack O'Malley's wife, anymore, not then. She had been vampire, and she'd been hungry.

She'd fed and then fallen comatose into their bed until Corona found her the following evening. By chance the bedroom's thick curtains had been drawn and kept the sun at bay, or else Elyna would never have awoken again. It was a long time before she quit being bitter about those heavy curtains.

Corona wouldn't let her kill herself on purpose, so Elyna settled for second best. She couldn't kill Jack's murderer, so she decided instead to kill Corona, who'd made her and not made sure that Jack was safe from her. So she'd learned to control the vampire, learned to be the best vampire she could, learned to be Elyna Gray instead of Jack O'Malley's wife.

Four weeks ago, the time had been right. The ties that kept her loyal to her Mistress broke at last. Elyna's stubbornness had been rewarded and she was free.

Elyna moved from the bathroom. Her hotel room was eleven stories to the ground and had a fine view of the Loop and the big lake beyond that.

In contrast to the thirst for vengeance that had driven her since her death, hope seemed such a fragile thing.

IN THE END, SHE PAID A LITTLE TOO MUCH FOR THE apartment turned condo, but a lot less than she'd been willing to pay.

She moved into a furnished efficiency apartment whose greatest assets were its location a few blocks from her home, its basement entrance where no one would see her comings and goings, and a storage room with no windows.

She went shopping at a few thrift stores and then took her newly acquired laundry to the nearest Laundromat. Three middle-aged women eyed her as she sorted her laundry. When she put the first load in, a grandmotherly woman came up to her and explained the ins and outs of the neighborhood laundry.

By the time she'd folded the last of her towels, Elyna had learned a nifty trick to get lipstick out of washable silk; that there was a scary-looking man who washed his clothes on Tuesdays who was a retired Marine, horribly shy, and a dear, sweet man, so she wasn't to let him frighten her; and that there was a local man, someone's cousin's sister-in-law's nephew, who was a contractor.

PETER VANDERSTAAT WAS A NEIGHBORHOOD MAN, A police officer who ran remodel jobs with his partner and a half dozen other people on the side. He'd agreed to meet Elyna at her condo and look at it, even though what she wanted wasn't the kind of project they looked for. He usually bought a place, fixed it up, and sold it at a profit, but he was between projects.

He looked to be in his midforties with tired, suspicious eyes. Short and squat, Jack would have said—built like a wrestler. Peter didn't talk a lot, just grunted, until they came back to the living room.

"Where is the money coming from?" he asked. "I don't want to have my men put hours in and then not get paid."

Elyna had money. She'd started by stealing a little bit from her victims and continued with investments. Investments she'd successfully hidden from Corona.

"My family has money," she told him. "I can pay you."

She had been painfully honest when she had been human. Lying was one of those skills she'd had to learn to be a successful vampire.

Vanderstaat bought her story, turning his attention back to the apartment. He frowned at the mismatched windows. "You want me to match the vinyl?"

"*Please*, no," she said, involuntary horror in her voice.

He looked at her and lifted a shaggy eyebrow.

"Vinyl is good. I'm sure that would look terrific in a modern place, but . . ." She let her voice trail off.

"But," he agreed. "What do you intend to do with the floors? Some of those boards can't be saved, expensive to find replacement boards of the same quality. There are some very good laminates on the market; I can get you fair prices."

"Can't you fix the floors?" she asked in a small voice.

That time she got a grin. "A girl after my own heart," he said. "Not the most profitable way to go—but we're in it for fun, too. No fun slapping together crap no matter how much more money you make at it."

Peter and his men worked evenings, he told her, five days a

week but not on Saturday or Sunday. They'd stop at ten every night for the neighbors' sake, which made for a long remodel—the reason they usually didn't take on a contract like this. They shook hands on it and agreed that he would start in two days to give him time to put together his crew.

GHOSTS AND CATS DON'T LIKE VAMPIRES. DOGS, ON THE other hand, didn't mind Elyna—which was good because more often than not, Peter brought his yellow Lab as one of the crew. Peter was initially dubious of Elyna's need to help, but when she proved useful, he started ordering her around like he did the rest of his crew.

The first job was finishing the demolition, clearing out the old for the new. They started with the bedrooms and moved forward. Some nights it was just Peter and Elyna; other nights they had as many as eight or ten men.

"Hey, you guys," said Simon, a twentysomething rookie cop and drywall man who had pulled down a chunk of plaster from the living room wall and held it up for everyone to see. "Look how this is stained. Do you think this is blood? My mom says that back in the late twenties a man was killed up here in this apartment. Or at least he left a lot of blood behind and disappeared."

No one was looking at Elyna, which was a good thing.

"I remember that story," agreed one of the other men. "Something to do with the gangsters, wasn't it? And the Saint Valentine's Day Massacre."

"The massacre was 1929," commented Peter.

"Yeah," agreed Simon. "The guy who lived here was an architect just hired by John Scalise—one of Capone's men. Story was that the architect's wife went missing a few weeks before Valentine's Day. Right after the massacre, the neighbor across the hall and several police officers broke down the door—"

Everyone, even Elyna, looked at the front door, which showed all sorts of damage. If it wasn't the door that had been there when she'd lived here, someone had found an exact match. And then aged it for eighty-plus years.

"But"—Simon dropped his voice and whispered—"all they found was blood. Lots and lots of blood."

There was a crash in the kitchen.

Peter whacked Simon upside the head. "Kid, Elyna's going to be living here. You think she needs that in her head?" And then Peter tromped off to see what the noise in the kitchen had been.

"Sorry, Elyna," Simon told her sheepishly. "Boss is right. I wasn't thinking."

"No worries," Elyna said, straining her ears to listen for any more noises. "I've heard the story before. I did my research before I bought this place."

She must not have been convincing, because he followed her around like Peter's dog for the rest of the evening, mistaking grief and guilt for fear. Peter couldn't figure out what had made the noise, but they decided it was one of the tools falling off some precarious perch. Even so, Peter's crew was jumpy for the rest of the night.

Weeks passed without further incidents. They moved from tearing down to rebuilding the plumbing and electric. And Peter started to schedule times when he, his right-hand man Frankie, and Elyna would sit down with catalogs to choose what the apartment would look like when it was finished.

As soon as the bathroom and most of the electric was finished, Elyna put up blackout curtains in the master bedroom and moved in. She didn't have much more than would fit into a pair of suitcases.

The first thing she bought after moving in was a twin bed. The second thing was a small bookcase, followed by a double handful of books. She kept the efficiency apartment for the coming summer days when the sun's setting time meant Peter's crew would be arriving in daylight. She encouraged Peter to assume that was where the rest of her things were, waiting for the floors to be finished so she wouldn't have to move the stuff around. Peter, Frankie, and the rest of the guys had gotten quite protective of her.

Other than something falling in the kitchen while Simon was telling his ghost story, there had been no sign that the apartment was haunted, let alone haunted by Elyna's dead husband. Sometimes, sitting on her bed and reading a book, Elyna would pretend that Jack was just in another room.

Reading was something they'd shared. It had started when he caught her reading E. M. Hull's *The Sheik*. The scandalous book had left her blushing like a ninny and him rolling his eyes.

"Bastard needed to be put down like a mad dog," he'd told her. "Instead he gets to keep the girl he kidnapped and raped. Doesn't sound right to me. Is that the kind of hero you really want?"

So he'd read *Tarzan of the Apes* to her, and she'd agreed that the ape man would be a much better choice than the sheik—and that had led to a merry few minutes with Jack jumping around on the furniture and her laughing her fool head off until the neighbors knocked on the walls.

They read every odd thing: Charles Darwin, Zane Grey, F. Scott Fitzgerald. Sometimes they read them separately, and sometimes they read them to each other.

She hadn't read in the seethe. She hadn't wanted to give Corona even so much as a glimpse into her real thoughts—and Jack always had said you knew a person by the books they read . . . or didn't read.

When Elyna went shopping for books now, she was bewildered by the offerings. She found a copy of *Tarzan*, but the rest were all new to her.

She'd been reading *The Sackett Brand* for about fifteen minutes before she realized it was something Jack would have liked. She turned back to the beginning and started over out loud, reading for hours. She read *Tarzan* next, commenting on some of the things that science had proven since it was written. But she also went out and got twelve more books by Louis L'Amour for Jack.

As she read to him, she pictured her husband sitting in his favorite chair, eyes closed with that intent expression on his face that meant he was enjoying the book.

Reading wasn't the only pleasure she regained. It had been a long time since she'd had a friend. Inside Corona's seethe, Elyna hadn't been able to trust anyone. She could only show them the broken, fragile thing they all thought her to be. Someone to be discounted. She couldn't afford to care too deeply. The lover who gave her solace one day would torture her the next, because no one disobeyed the Mistress. Even the few who could have done so successfully (because they were older, stronger, or not of the Mistress's making) didn't disobey her. At least not after the Mistress gave Fitz, who had been her favorite, to Sybil.

To Elyna's lonely heart, Peter and his moonlighting friends were like a warm blanket on a cold night. She knew she couldn't afford friends, not if she was a stray living surreptitiously under the radar in Colbert's territory. More accurately, her friends could not afford her. But she couldn't help the affection she felt for them.

Between the books and work on the apartment, Elyna's time fell into a pleasant order that was so much better than anything that had happened to her in a very long time. One evening she woke up and realized she was happy. It was a very disconcerting feeling.

ELYNA LISTENED TO THE IRREGULAR RHYTHM OF THE jazz guitar and breathed in the scent of sixty or so humans crowded together in the dark drinking mixed drinks and listening to the music.

A smart vampire doesn't feed in her own backyard if she can help it. Elyna had been hunting in a small club district several miles away from her home. Unfortunately, even a big city is composed of dozens of smaller places. When the bartender of the Irish pub that she'd been going to nodded at her and set a screwdriver on the bar in front of Elyna without asking, she knew she had to move on.

That was why she was sitting in a popular jazz club in the Loop. The Loop attracted tourists, and it was easier to blend in. At least that was her working theory. She'd come to this club four times in the last week; not feeding, just getting the lay of the land.

Anywhere she thought to be good hunting ground was going to appeal to Colbert, too, but she'd seen no sign of any other vampires. So tonight she'd come dressed to kill. She'd picked up the white sheath dress at a thrift store, but it was real silk and suited her flat stomach. When she'd been human she'd always carried an extra few pounds, but keeping the weight off was not a problem anymore.

She closed her eyes and let a soft smile stretch her lips as she nodded her head to the music. *Come here,* she announced without saying anything at all, *come here and I might be yours.* She didn't use any magic yet, just human mating rituals.

Corona had been bitterly envious of Elyna's ability to attract men this way—Corona had been in her seventies when she died. Though she had once been beautiful—stunning, Elyna suspected— she continued her life-after-death as an old woman. Corona lured her prey by vampire magic, which meant she had to feed more often and more deeply than Elyna, who could usually find someone willing to follow her to a dark corner without use of coercion or power. She wasn't beautiful the way Corona once had been, but she was attractive enough.

"Hey, doll," said a rough tenor voice next to her. "You look like you're having a good time."

She hated this. Making connection, making small talk, getting a glimpse inside someone she'd never see again. She understood the vampires who kept menageries of sheep: humans no one would miss. Menageries reduced the risk of being found out, of having to go hunting, of feeding from strangers, and they served as a sort of crèche from which new vampires were born. After a while, the sheep could be made to forget who they had been, and most of them learned to love their vampire, who slowly killed them. Maybe that had been the problem. Elyna hadn't been a sheep for long enough to learn to love the monsters. Sure as God made little fishies, she couldn't be made to keep humans as sheep just to save herself from a little risk and distaste.

"I am now," she said to the man sitting next to her.

He told her his name was Hal, and she had no trouble coaxing him out into the dark outside the club despite the gold ring on his finger. He had no qualms about following her around the back to a small, dark space of privacy that had made her finally determine that this was the club where she would hunt. Hal would have hesitated to follow a man, but she was half his weight and a foot shorter: he didn't find her threatening.

He laughed when she nuzzled his neck.

When she finished feeding and blurring his memory, she eased him down on the ground. Crouched beside him, one knee on the ground to brace herself against his weight, she felt them.

Vampires.

Elyna moved as fast as she could into the little bit of half-alley trap, no bigger than ten feet by twenty, then froze against the outside wall as flat as she could, thinking, *No one here, no one here.* Power flickered over her and she felt the drain touch her faintly. An hour was the longest she'd ever held this magic to her, and it had left her weak and violently hungry.

She heard their footsteps stop when they spotted her victim. It was dark here, but vampires can see in the dark.

"Not from our seethe," said the woman, her vowels a little rich with the same accent that had colored Elyna's Polish mother's voice.

"None of ours would feed from anyone in Colbert's favorite club," agreed the man. "He's not been here more than a few minutes."

They did a meticulous search of her hiding place. Elyna stood with the stillness of the dead, all of her attention focused on her high-heeled raspberry sandals—not the easiest thing to do when deadly enemies are less than a handspan away. Vampires can feel people who look at them too hard or pay too close attention to them. It means survival in a world that would destroy them if possible.

After far too long the female vampire turned to her comrade. "Not here anymore. Damn. I could have sworn I saw something move in here, just before we found this guy."

"I've heard some of the old ones can fly," said the second vampire.

"Don't be stupider than you have to be," the woman said. "If a vampire that old and powerful had come to town, Colbert would know it. He'll find this one, too. Time to go inside and let him know."

Chicago was huge, but that wouldn't save Elyna, not once he knew she was there.

"Life is what you do next," she whispered to herself as soon as the other vampires had left. It was one of Jack's favorite sayings. She walked quickly toward the L. She'd left her car at her condo because it was hard to make a quick getaway in a parking garage when monsters were after you.

Safely on the train, she shivered and tried not to look at the other passengers—in short, acting just like everyone else. She got off one stop early and walked through alleys and side streets until she made it home.

Home.

She locked the door behind her and sat down on the floor with her back to it. Vampires could not cross the threshold of a home— unless it was their home, which was why she had been able to get in to kill Jack all those years ago. Thresholds were made of life and love—all those things that turn a dwelling place into a home. She hoped that her threshold would hold them out.

But even if it did, it would not be enough. Once Colbert knew where she lived, he had only to wait until she left to feed. She was under no illusions. If he knew she was here, it was only a matter of time until he caught her: her death warrant was signed. Her only escape was to leave.

She could do that. Find some place that had no seethes. They were out there; vampires were not so common as fae or the weres. But it would mean leaving Jack again.

Jack was probably not here anyway.

She looked through the living room entranceway and stared out the window, where the sun was just beginning to lighten the sky. She had a third choice. Perhaps it would be enough penance for her crime if she died here, too. Popular knowledge was that vampires had no souls. Popular knowledge also said that ghosts were not souls of the dead, just leftover bits and pieces that remembered what they had been once. Maybe if she died here, her leftover bits could find Jack's leftover bits as well.

Gold touched the edges of the rooftops across the road from her and washed over the now-matching windows in her front room. She smiled and took one last deep breath as the pain from the sunlight reached her at last.

She had to close her eyes against the light.

"I'm sorry, Jack," she said. "I love you."

Because her eyes were closed, she didn't see the living room blackout curtains snap shut—just heard them the instant before her body died for the day.

SHE AWOKE IN A CRUMPLED HEAP IN FRONT OF THE door. The skin on her face was tight from the sunburn, but the bathroom mirror assured her that the curtains had shut before the sun had done much damage.

Staring at her wide-eyed reflection in the mirror, she said, "Jack?"

He didn't answer, not then.

But when she and Peter were deciding which of several designs were closest to her original cabinets, a stray breeze fingered through the pages of a catalog they'd set aside and left it opened to a sleek modern style in hickory. She liked those, she thought, pulling the catalog in front of her. But she was trying to recreate her old home, not build a new one.

Maybe she could do both.

"What do you think of this one?" she asked Peter.

"Not very vintage," he told her. "But they would look fine with the countertops you picked out. Good wood goes with almost anything."

A FEW NIGHTS LATER SHE FINISHED THE BOOK SHE'D been reading to Jack and replaced it in the bookshelf. The next night there was a book sitting on her chair, ready for her to begin: an Ellery Queen mystery.

The next evening, Jack rearranged the cardboard cutouts that Peter had made to let Elyna see how her kitchen would come together. She put them back as she'd had them, but he was relentless. He never moved them while she was in the kitchen, but if she left for more than a few minutes they were back the way he wanted them.

"And you called me stubborn," she sputtered at him finally, standing in the empty room. "I'm a vampire, Jack. I don't care where the stove is. Why should you?"

Something fluttered lightly on her lips, like a butterfly's kiss. She froze. "Jack?"

But there was no further sign that she wasn't alone in the room. She touched her lips with light fingers.

PETER ROLLED HIS EYES WHEN SHE TOLD HIM THAT she'd changed her mind on the kitchen layout. Frankie just laughed, a great big booming laugh that filled the air.

"Hah," he said. "Told Peter it wasn't natural the way you just let him dictate your kitchen. Never was a woman yet who let a man arrange her kitchen."

"Hmm," said Elyna.

The kitchen progressed rapidly after that. Stainless steel sinks, marble countertop, and all. Elyna bought a teddy bear for Simon's new son and told Frankie what to buy his wife for their anniversary.

When the men came in to lay the kitchen flooring, they were grim-faced and unhappy. Elyna, as she had done before, coaxed the story out of them. Being police officers in Chicago was not for the faint of heart. Vampires are territorial, and somehow this group of hardworking men had become hers just as the home they'd helped her put together was hers. Her mother had taught her to take care of what was hers. She had to use a touch of persuasion to get a name and address.

"Sorry to invite this in here," Peter murmured to her as they were getting ready to leave for the night. "Evil belongs out in the street, not in your home."

Elyna looked down at her hands. "Evil exists everywhere," she told him.

That night she broke the neck of a murderer who had gotten free on a technicality, just as she had killed the drug dealer who'd handed a ten-year-old the heroin to overdose on and the lawyer who liked to kill prostitutes.

THEN CAME THE EVENING THAT PETER DIDN'T COME.

"You get a call, Elyna?" Frankie asked her. "He told me he was going to be coming here after his shift."

She shook her head. Everyone became increasingly worried as an hour crept by without word. Peter didn't answer his cell phone, and as he was ten years divorced, no one was home to answer the phone. They called the station and were told that Peter had left at his usual time.

Finally Frankie stood up and stretched, cracking his spine. "We're getting nothing done here, sweetie," he told Elyna. "We need to go out and look for him. He has a few mates and some places he goes to for a bite or glass."

"Call me when you find him."

"As long as it's not too late," Frankie promised, and he and the rest left Elyna alone in her home.

There were all sorts of reasons why Peter might not have made it over tonight. But the one she believed was that she had made him hers—and Colbert had noticed.

She remembered quite clearly how easily Colbert had ousted Corona and her seethe from this city. Half her seethe, anyway; the other half was gone to ashes and sunlight, never to rise again.

She pulled out her cell phone and dialed. "Sean," she said, "get me Colbert's phone number, would you?"

She felt his hesitation through the phone lines. He was angry with her—and would happily have sacrificed her on his road into power. But she had killed his Mistress, and for a while more the urge to obey would stay strong, even with the physical distance between them. She snapped her phone closed, confident that Sean could get the information and would call her back.

She walked into the living room, where Jack had died at her hands, and touched the floor where the wood was just a little darker than the boards around it, despite sanding and staining.

"My fault, Jack. I was mad because you were late again. Jealous, maybe. You were the newest rising star among the architects of Chicago, and I was a housewife. There was a new singer at that speakeasy we used to go to, and you'd promised to take me there. When you couldn't, I decided to go by myself."

The air in the apartment was still and hot despite the new HVAC system. Waiting.

"My fault. I knew it was stupid when I did it." Her eyes burned, but no tears fell. "The new singer was an old woman with a voice like a lark. She came to my table and said, 'You're all alone here, aren't you? I think I'll take you home with me tonight.' If I'd waited until you could go with me, she'd have left us both alone."

Elyna bowed her head. "She and her fellow vampires fed on me for a couple of weeks. I don't remember a lot about that time. Someone got careless and I died. It's unusual for someone to turn after such a short time; mostly they just die."

Stubborn Pole.

Elyna turned slowly, unsure whether her mind had supplied that voice or she'd really heard it.

"When vampires rise the first time, we are nearly mindless, and hungry. *Scared.*" She remembered that most of all. She'd been so scared. "I ran home and you were waiting for me." She swallowed. "Thing is, Jack, I don't think I'll be coming back here after tonight. The local vampires have taken Peter." Peter might already be dead, though certainly they'd have toyed with him while they were waiting for her to figure out what had happened. "I just . . . wanted you to know that my death wasn't your fault. I wish . . . I wish you'd had a chance to marry again, to grow old and watch over your grandchildren, never knowing what had become of me."

In the silence, her phone's ring was very harsh.

"Elyna," she answered.

"Elyna," said a man's voice, "I heard that you wanted to call me."

When she was through talking to Colbert, she slipped the phone back into her pocket. It was traditional for vampires to dress up when they treated with each other, a convention that traced back to older times. Elyna didn't bother changing out of her work clothes.

She opened the door to leave, paused, and said, "I love you, Jack."

THE JAZZ CLUB WASN'T THE SAME ONE WHERE SHE'D run into Colbert's vampires. This one had a CLOSED FOR REMODEL-

ING sign on the door and wasn't in nearly as nice a neighborhood. Elyna got out of the cab and paid the driver.

"You sure you want off here?" he asked, a fatherly man who'd entertained her all the way here with stories of his daughter's almost-disastrous dance recital. "It's late and there's no one here."

She smiled at him. "I'll be fine."

The cab waited, though, until she opened the club door before driving off.

She took a step into the dark room, and with a click someone turned a spotlight on her. With the light in her face, she couldn't see them, but the vampires could see her just fine.

"Such a lot of trouble for such a little girl," purred a man's voice. Over the years, he'd lost most of the French accent she remembered. Colbert sounded a lot more like a TV newscaster than the eighteenth-century vintner he had once been.

"You have someone who belongs to me," she said, tired of playing games. Corona had liked games, too. "Show me that he is alive or this ends now."

Something heavy was tossed onto the floor in front of her, a body.

She went down to one knee and felt the body in front of her. She still couldn't see, but one hand touched something wet. She brought her fingers up to her mouth and licked the moisture away. It was Peter's blood. The body it had come from still breathed. She petted him gently and stood up.

"What do you want?" she asked. "And would you turn off the stupid light? You can't possibly be that afraid of me."

He laughed. The spotlight was turned off, and others were turned on.

Elyna found herself in a large room full of tarps, sawhorses, and tools. The walls had been newly painted a burnt orange. She didn't allow herself to look down and see how much damage they'd done to Peter, just stared at the vampires.

Colbert didn't look imposing. He was only a little taller than she was, wiry rather than bulky. His face looked as if he'd been turned as a teenager, though his dark hair was thinning on top. Only the expense of his attire hinted at his power.

Two vampires stood with him—a woman who was taller than he by four or five inches and a black man with the eyes of a poet and the body of a Chippendales dancer. Both of them were pretty enough to be models.

Arm candy, she thought. There were others here, on the other side of the wall to her right. Sheetrock was not much of a barrier to vampires, but it hid them from sight and made them easy to forget about. Not that it mattered. Doubtless either of his arm candy guards could wipe the floor with her, if Colbert didn't choose to do it himself.

"I am Pierre Colbert," he said.

The way he said it, it rhymed.

"You find something funny?" Colbert asked coolly.

She waved her hands around the building, leaving her right hand pointing at the wall behind which he had more of his people waiting, so he'd know that she understood they were there.

"All of this," she said, "for me."

"Elyna Gray," he said. "Who killed Corona and refused to take her seethe."

"I struck her from behind," Elyna said. "If I'd faced her in a proper fight I'd be ash. If I'd tried to take over the seethe, I'd have been dead in two days."

"Still," said Pierre, "you killed your Mistress and then came into my territory."

"I killed the monster who made me, and then I ran home," Elyna told him. "I admit it is a subtle difference, but significant to this conversation."

"Ah, yes," he purred. "Now, that wasn't smart, Elyna Gray who was Elyna O'Malley. If you'd found somewhere else to live, it might have taken me longer to find you—you've been very discreet in your hunting habits other than coming into my favorite club a few weeks ago. I thought perhaps you had a menagerie, but that sheep"—he indicated Peter—"was a virgin pure."

His words accomplished what she'd tried avoiding by not looking at Peter. Rage rushed in and she felt her skin tighten and her eyes burn with fire. Someone looking at her would know that they were in the presence of Vampire.

"Mine," she said, barely recognizing her own voice. "He was one of mine and you harmed him."

"He tasted *mmm* so good," said the woman. "Bitch."

Behind Elyna something fell to the ground with a sharp crack. She took a quick look behind her to where a sawhorse lay on the floor, two legs on one side broken off.

"Now," said Colbert in an interested voice, "how did you manage that?"

Elyna had thought it was someone on his side. She shrugged.

The pretty man turned in a slow circle. "Master," he said, biting out the word as if he found it distasteful. "Master, there is a ghost in this room, can you feel it?"

"Elyna." Colbert looked at her. "You are just full of surprises. But the ability to control ghosts is not uncommon; why do you think they hide from us? And, as it happens, I am very good at it." He looked around the room. "Come out, come out, wherever you are."

Familiar big hands landed on Elyna's shoulders.

"Jack," she said, horrified. "Jack, you have to get out of here."

"Too late," said Colbert, smiling. "Jack, is it? Break her neck."

No.

The pretty black man looked from Elyna to the ghost behind her and started to smile.

"Jack, come here." The Master of Chicago's voice cracked with power. His pretty pet woman took a step forward and so did Elyna.

Jack patted her shoulder and then moved around her. His

hands had been so solid, she thought that the rest of him would look that way, too. Instead, he looked more like a mist of light, a shimmering presence mostly human-sized but not human-shaped.

She'd done this to Jack, brought him to be enslaved by this vampire. She had to do something about it. Everyone in the room was paying attention to Jack and to Colbert. No one was looking at her.

You aren't interested in me, she thought, calling on all the power she had to fade out of notice in this fully lit room full of vampires.

Colbert extended his hand until it touched the cloud of light that was Jack. "Mine," he said in a voice of power.

But vampires can move fast, and Elyna had already crossed the room and found a weapon.

"*You*"—Elyna hit the Master vampire across the back with a piece of the broken sawhorse and knocked him away from her husband—"leave him alone."

Colbert turned on her—and there was nothing human left of him. "You *dare*—" He would have said more, but another piece of the wooden sawhorse emerged from his chest. He looked down, opened his mouth, then collapsed.

It took Elyna a moment to realize that Jack had used the other leg.

Beside Elyna, the black man threw back his head and laughed in utter delight. When he stopped laughing, it cut off abruptly, leaving echoing silence behind. His face free of emotion, he turned his attention to Elyna. He gave her such an empty look that she took two steps away from him until she hit the solid-feeling bulk that had been Jack O'Malley.

"He forgot," said the man who had been Colbert's. "Evil has no power over love." He smiled, his fangs big and white against his ebony skin. "And we are evil, aren't we, Elyna Gray?"

She didn't say anything.

"What now?" he asked her. "Do you want this seethe, Elyna? Do you want to be Mistress of Chicago?"

"No." Her response was so fast and heartfelt that it caused him to laugh again. His laugh was horrible, so much joy and beauty coming out of a man with such empty eyes.

"Then what?"

Elyna looked at the woman, Colbert's other minion, who had fallen to the ground in that utter obeisance sometimes demanded of them by their Mistress or Master.

"Who is the strongest vampire in your seethe?" she asked.

"Steven Harper," he told her. "That would be me."

Jack's reassuring presence behind her, she smiled carefully. "Steven Harper, I would seek your permission to live in your city, keeping the laws and rules of the old ones and bearing neither you nor yours any ill will. Separate and apart with harm to none. Yours to you and mine to me—and this human"—she tilted her head to indicate Peter, who was lying very still just where he had been dropped—"is mine."

The new Master of the Chicago seethe looked at Peter, then over Elyna's shoulder at Jack, and finally to the floor, where a splintered piece of wood stuck out of Colbert's limp body. "You have done me a great favor," he said. "I swore never to call anyone Master again, and now I no longer have to. Come and be welcome in my city—with harm to none."

Elyna bowed, keeping her eyes on him. "Thank you, sir." She took a step back, paused, and said, "The really old ones turn to dust when they are dead and gone."

He looked down at Colbert's body. "I guess he lied about how old he was."

"Or he is not, quite, gone." Elyna had made a point of finding out things like that. Corona had been ash before she touched the floor.

"Ah," Steven said, pushing the corpse with his toe. "My thanks."

A pair of Steven Harper's vampires drove her to her apartment building and helped her negotiate the way into her apartment while she carried Peter, unwilling to trust him to anyone else. She could no longer see Jack, but she knew he was with her by the occasional light touches of his hands.

Harper's vampires didn't try to come in, nor did they speak to her. She set Peter down on her bed, since she didn't have anywhere else to put him. Then she went back out and locked the door. When she returned to the bedroom Peter was sitting up. She'd been pretty sure that he was more awake than it had appeared, because a smart man knows when to lie low.

Without a word, she cut the ropes and helped peel off the duct tape that covered his mouth. Then she got a wet hand towel and brought it to him.

"There's blood on your face and neck," she told him.

He took it from her, stared at it a moment, and then wiped himself clean. The wounds had closed, she noticed, as vampire bites do. They hadn't actually hurt him very badly—not physically, anyway.

They stared at each other awhile.

"Vampire," he said.

She nodded. "If you tell anyone, they'll think you're crazy."

"Could you stop me? Make me not remember? Isn't that what vampires are supposed to be able to do?"

She shrugged, but chose, for his sake, not to give him the whole truth. He'd sleep better at night without it. "Hollywood vampires can do lots of things we can't," she told him instead. "You don't have to worry about Harper coming after you, though. He agreed that you are one of mine, and he won't hurt you. We vampires take vows like that very seriously."

"You don't look like a vampire," he said.

"I know," she agreed. A stray breeze brushed a strand of hair off her cheek. "We're like serial killers; we look just like everyone else."

Peter grunted, looked down at his hands, and then made another sound—something she couldn't interpret.

Then he said, "That man who killed his girlfriend's baby, the one where the evidence got bungled and the charges were dismissed a few weeks ago. The one who turned up dead in a place full of people who never were sure who killed him. That was you?"

Elyna nodded. He eyed her thoughtfully, then nodded.

He cleared his throat. "There were others after that, just a couple. The ones we talked about while we worked. Like the well-connected lawyer who liked to pick up hookers and beat them to death. Fell down his stairs and died a month or so back. That was you, too?"

She ducked her head. "Vampires don't have to kill people," she told him. "Especially once we are older, more in control of ourselves. I try not to. But . . . it doesn't bother me very much, not when they are"—she looked him in the eye and gave him an ironic smile—"evil."

"In my business," Peter said slowly, "you come into the job seeing the world in black-and-white. Most of us who survive, the good cops, learn to work in shades of gray." He smiled slowly at her. "So, Ms. Gray. What have you decided about the lighting fixtures in the kitchen?"

The brass lights are nice, but I think the bronze will look better, Jack whispered, his lips brushing the edge of her ear.

"I think I like the bronze," she told Peter.

SEEING EYE

I was invited to submit a story for P. N. Elrod's *Strange Brew*. I had intended to write a story about the witches at some point in time, and this invitation seemed tailor-made for it. In Mercy's world, good witches are few and far between—and mostly on the run from the dark witches. I thought about how a white witch could gain enough power to stand up to the evil ones, and Moira was born. A moment later, Tom knocked at my (figurative) door, full-fledged and ready to go. I am going to write more about Tom and Moira eventually. But for those who want more now, they also have a guest appearance in *Hunting Ground*.

Tom and Moira had been together for some time when they appeared in *Hunting Ground*, so the events in "Seeing Eye" take place about a year before those in *Moon Called*.

THE DOORBELL RANG.

That was the problem with her business. Too many people thought they could approach her at any time. Even oh-dark thirty, even though her hours were posted clearly on her door *and* on her Web site.

Of course, answering the door would be something to do other than sit in her study shivering in the dark. Not that her world was ever anything but dark. It was one of the reasons she hated bad dreams—she had no way of turning on the light. Bad dreams that held warnings of things to come were the worst.

The doorbell rang again.

She slept—or tried to sleep—the same hours as most people. Kept steady business hours, too. Something she had no trouble making clear to those morons who woke her up in the middle of the night. They came to see Glinda the Good Witch, but after midnight, they found the Wicked Witch of the West and left quaking in fear of flying monkeys.

Whoever waited at the door would have no reason to suspect how grateful she was for the interruption of her thoughts.

The doorbell began a steady throbbing beat, ring-long, ring-short, ring-short, ring-long, and she grew a lot less grateful. To heck with flying monkeys, *she* was going to turn whoever it was into a frog. She shoved her concealing glasses on her face and stomped out the hall to her front door. No matter that most of the good transmutation spells had been lost with the Coranda family in the seventeenth century—rude people needed to be turned into frogs. Or pigs.

She jerked open the door and slapped the offending hand on her doorbell. She even got out a "Stop that!" before the force of his spirit hit her like a physical blow. Her nose told her, belatedly, that he was sweaty as if he'd been jogging. Her other senses told her that he was something *other*.

Not that she'd expected him to be human. Unlike other witches, she didn't advertise, and thus seldom had mundane customers unless their needs disturbed her sleep and she set out one of her "find me" spells to speak to them—she knew when they were coming.

"Ms. Keller," he growled. "I need to speak to you." At least he'd quit ringing the bell.

She let her left eyebrow slide up her forehead until it would be visible above her glasses. "Polite people come between the hours of eight in the morning and seven at night," she informed him. Werewolf, she decided. If he really lost his temper, she might have trouble, but she thought he was desperate, not angry—though with a wolf, the two states could be interchanged with remarkable speed. "Rude people get sent on their way."

"Tomorrow morning might be too late," he said—and then added the bit that kept her from slamming the door in his face: "Alan Choo gave me your address, said you were the only one he knew with enough moxie to defy them."

She should shut the door in his face—not even a werewolf could get through her portal if she didn't want him to. But . . . *them*. Her dream tonight and for the past weeks had been about *them*, about *him* again. Portents, her instincts had told her, not just nightmares. The time had come at last. No. She wasn't grateful to him at all.

"Did Alan tell you to say it in those words?"

"Yes, ma'am." His temper was still there, but restrained and under control. It hadn't been aimed at her anyway, she thought, only fury born of frustration and fear. She knew how that felt.

She centered herself and asked the questions he'd expect. "Who am I supposed to be defying?"

And he gave her the answer she expected in return. "Something called Samhain's Coven."

Moira took a tighter hold on the door. "I see."

It wasn't really a coven. No matter what the popular literature said, it had been a long time since a real coven had been possible. Covens had thirteen members, no member related to any other to the sixth generation. Each family amassed its own specialty spells, and a coven of thirteen benefited from all those differing magics. But after most of the witchblood families had been wiped out by fighting among themselves, covens became a thing of the past. What few families remained (and there weren't thirteen, not if you didn't count the Russians or the Chinese, who kept to their own ways) had a bone-deep antipathy for the other survivors.

Kouros changed the rules to suit the new times. His coven had between ten and thirteen members . . . He had a distressing tendency to burn out his followers. The current bunch descended from only three families that she knew of, and most of them weren't properly trained—children following their leader.

Samhain wasn't up to the tricks of the old covens, but they were scary enough even the local vampires walked softly around them, and Seattle, with its overcast skies, had a relatively large seethe of vampires. Samhain's master had approached Moira about joining them when she was thirteen. She'd refused and made her refusal stick at some cost to all the parties involved.

"What does Samhain have to do with a werewolf?" she asked.

"I think they have my brother."

"Another werewolf?" It wasn't unheard of for brothers to be werewolves, especially since the Marrok, He-Who-Ruled-the-Wolves, began Changing people with more care than had been the usual custom. But it wasn't at all common, either. Surviving the Change—even with the safeguards the Marrok could manage—was still, she understood, nowhere near a certainty.

"No." He took a deep breath. "Not a werewolf. Human. He has the *sight*. Choo says he thinks that's why they took him."

"Your brother is a witch?"

The fabric of his shirt rustled with his shrug, telling her that he wasn't as tall as he felt to her. Only a little above average instead of a seven-foot giant. Good to know.

"I don't know enough about witches to know," he said. "Jon gets hunches. Takes a walk just at the right time to find five dollars someone dropped, picks the right lottery number to win ten bucks. That kind of thing. Nothing big, nothing anyone would have noticed if my grandma hadn't had it stronger."

The *sight* was one of those general terms that told Moira precisely nothing. It could mean anything from a little fae blood in the family tree or full-blown witchblood. His brother's lack of power wouldn't mean he wasn't a witch—the magic sang weaker in the men. But fae or witchblood, Alan Choo had been right about it being something that would attract Samhain's attention. She rubbed her cheekbone even though she knew the ache was a phantom pain touch wouldn't alter.

Samhain. Did she have a choice? In her dreams, she died.

She could feel the intensity of the wolf's regard, strengthening as her silence continued. Then he told her the final straw that broke her resistance. "Jon's a cop—undercover—so I doubt your coven knows it. If his body turns up, though, there will be an investigation. I'll see to it that the witchcraft angle gets explored thoroughly. They might listen to a werewolf who tells them that witches might be a little more than turbaned fortune-tellers."

Blackmail galled him, she could tell—but he wasn't bluffing. He must love his brother.

She had only a touch of empathy, and it came and went. It seemed to be pretty focused on this werewolf tonight, though.

If she didn't help him, his brother would die at Samhain's hands, and his blood would be on her as well. If it cost her death, as her dreams warned her, perhaps that was justice served.

"Come in," Moira said, hearing the grudge in her voice. He'd think it was her reaction to the threat—and the police poking about the coven would end badly for all concerned.

But it wasn't his threat that moved her. She took care of the people in her neighborhood; that was her job. The police she saw as brothers-in-arms. If she could help one, it was her duty to do so. Even if it meant her life for his.

"You'll have to wait until I get my coffee," she told him, and her mother's ghost forced the next bit of politeness out of her. "Would you like a cup?"

"No. There's no time."

He said that as if he had some idea about it—maybe the *sight* hadn't passed him by, either.

"We have until tomorrow night if Samhain has him." She turned on her heel and left him to follow her or not, saying over her shoulder, "Unless they took him because he saw something. In which case, he probably is already dead. Either way, there's time for coffee."

He closed the door with deliberate softness and followed her. "Tomorrow's Halloween. Samhain."

"Kouros isn't Wiccan, any more than he is Greek, but he apes both for his followers," she told him as she continued deeper into her apartment. She remembered to turn on the hall light—not that he'd need it, being a wolf. It just seemed courteous: allies should show each other courtesy. "Like a magician playing sleight of hand, he pulls upon myth, religion, and anything else he can to keep them in thrall. Samhain—the time, not the coven—has power for the fae, for Wicca, for witches. Kouros uses it to cement his own, and killing someone with a bit of power generates more strength than killing a stray dog—and bothers him about as much."

"Kouros?" He said it as if it solved some puzzle, but it must not have been important, because he continued with no more than a breath of pause. "I thought witches were all women." He followed her into the kitchen and stood too close behind her. If he were to attack, she wouldn't have time to ready a spell.

But he wouldn't attack; her death wouldn't come at his hands tonight.

The kitchen lights were where she remembered them, and she had to take it on faith that she was turning them on and not off. She could never remember which way the switch worked. He didn't say anything, so she must have been right.

She always left her coffeepot primed for mornings, so all she had to do was push the button and it began gurgling in promise of coffee soon.

"Um," she said, remembering he'd asked her a question. His closeness distracted her—and not for the reasons it should. "Women tend to be more powerful witches, but you can make up for lack of talent with enough death and pain. Someone else's, of course, if you're a black practitioner like Kouros."

"What are you?" he asked, sniffing at her. His breath tickled the back of her neck—wolves, she'd noticed before, had a some-what different idea of personal space than she did.

Her machine began dribbling coffee out into the carafe at last, giving her an excuse to step away. "Didn't Alan tell you? I'm a witch."

He followed; his nose touched her where his breath had sensi-tized her flesh, and she probably had goose bumps on her toes from the zing he sent through her. "My pack has a witch we pay to clean up messes. You don't smell like a witch."

He probably didn't mean anything by it; he was just being a

wolf. She stepped out of his reach in the pretense of getting a coffee cup, or rather he allowed her to escape.

Alan was right: she needed to get out more. She hadn't so much as dated in . . . well, a long time. The last man's reaction to seeing what she'd done to herself was something she didn't want to repeat.

This man smelled good, even with the scent of his sweat teasing her nose. He felt strong and warm, promising to be the strength and safety she'd never had outside of her own two hands. Dominant wolves took care of their pack—doubtless something she'd picked up on. And then there was the possibility of death hovering over her.

Whatever the ultimate cause, his nearness and the light touch of breath on her skin sparked her interest in a way she knew he'd have picked up on. You can't hide sexual interest from something that can trail a hummingbird on the wing. Neither of them needed the complication of sex interfering in urgent business, even assuming he'd be willing.

"Witchcraft gains power from death and pain. From sacrifice and sacrificing," she told him coolly, pouring coffee in two mugs with steady hands. She was an expert in sacrifice. Not sleeping with a strange werewolf who showed up on her doorstep didn't even register on her scale.

She drank coffee black, so that was how she fixed it, holding the second cup out to him. "Evil leaves a psychic stench behind. Maybe a wolf nose can pick up on it. I don't know, not being a werewolf myself. There's milk in the fridge and sugar in the cupboard in front of you if you'd like."

SHE WASN'T AT ALL WHAT TOM HAD EXPECTED. THEIR pack's hired witch was a motherly woman of indeterminate years who wore swami robes in bright hues and smelled strongly of patchouli and old blood that didn't quite mask something bitter and dark. When he'd played Jon's message for her, she'd hung up the phone and refused to answer it again.

By the time he'd driven to her house, it was shut up and locked with no one inside. That was his first clue that this Samhain's Coven might be even more of a problem than he'd thought, and his worry had risen to fever pitch. He'd gone down to the underpass where his brother had been living and used his nose through the parks and other places his brother drifted through. But wherever they were holding Jon (and he refused to believe Jon was dead), it wasn't anywhere near where they kidnapped him.

His Alpha didn't like pack members concerning themselves with matters outside of the pack ("Your only family is your pack, son"). Tom didn't even bother contacting him. He'd gone to Choo instead. The Emerald City Pack's only submissive wolf, Alan worked as an herbalist and knew almost everyone in the supernatural world of Seattle. When he told Alan about the message Jon had left on his phone, Alan had written this woman's name and address and handed it to him. He'd have thought it was a joke, but Alan had better taste than that. So Tom had gone looking for a witch named Wendy—Wendy Moira Keller.

At his first look, he'd been disappointed. Wendy the Witch was five foot nothing with rich curves in all the right places and feathery black hair that must have been dyed, because only black Labs and cats are that black. The stupid wraparound mirrored glasses kept him from guessing her age exactly, but he'd bet she wasn't yet thirty. No woman over thirty would be caught dead in those glasses. The cop in him wondered if she was covering up bruises— but he didn't smell a male in the living-scents in the house.

She wore a gray T-shirt without a bra, and black pajama pants with white skull-and-crossbones wearing red bows. But despite all that, he saw no piercings or tattoos—like she'd approached mall Goth culture, but only so far. She smelled of fresh flowers and mint. Her apartment was decorated with a minimum of furniture and a mishmash of colors that didn't quite fit together.

He didn't scare her.

Tom scared everyone—and he had even before their pack had

a run-in with a bunch of fae a few years ago. His face had gotten cut up pretty badly with some sort of magical knife and hadn't healed right afterward. The scars made him look almost as dangerous as he was. People walked warily around him.

Not only wasn't she scared, but she didn't even bother to hide her irritation at being woken up. He stalked her, and all she'd felt was a flash of sexual awareness that came and went so swiftly, he might have missed it if he'd been younger.

Either she was stupid or she was powerful. Since Alan had sent him here, Tom was betting on powerful. He hoped she was powerful.

He didn't want the coffee, but he took it when she handed it to him. It was black and stronger than he usually drank it, but it tasted good. "So why don't you smell like other witches?"

"Like Kouros, I'm not Wiccan," she told him, "but 'and it harm none' seems like a good way to live to me."

White witch.

He knew that Wiccans consider themselves witches—and some of them had enough witchblood to make it so. But witches, the real thing, weren't witches because of what they believed, but because of genetic heritage. A witch was born a witch and studied to become a better one. But for witches, real power came from blood and death—mostly other people's blood and death.

White witches, especially those outside of Wicca (where numbers meant safety), were weak and valuable sacrifices for black witches, who didn't have their scruples. As Wendy the Witch had noted—witches seemed to have a real preference for killing their own.

He sipped at his coffee and asked, "So how have you managed without ending up as bits and pieces in someone else's cauldron?"

The witch snorted a laugh and set her coffee down abruptly. She grabbed a paper towel off its holder and held it to her face as she gasped and choked coffee, looking suddenly a lot less than thirty. When she was finished, she said, "That's awesome. Bits and pieces. I'll have to remember that."

Still grinning, she picked up the coffee again. He wished he could see her eyes, because he was pretty sure that whatever humor she'd felt was only surface deep.

"I tell you what," she said, "why don't you tell me who you are and what you know? That way I can tell you if I can help you or not."

"Fair enough," he said. The coffee was strong, and he could feel it and the four other cups he'd had since midnight settle in his bones with caffeine's untrustworthy gift of nervous energy.

"I'm Tom Franklin and I'm second in the Emerald City Pack." She wasn't surprised by that. She'd known what he was as soon as she opened her door. "My brother Jon is a cop and a damn fine one. He's been on the Seattle PD for nearly twenty years, and for the last six months he's been undercover as a street person. He was sent as part of a drug task force: there's been some nasty garbage out on the street lately, and he's been looking for it."

Wendy Moira Keller leaned back against the cabinets with a sigh. "I'd like to say that no witch would mess with drugs. Not from moral principles, mind you. Witches, for the most part, don't have moral principles. But drugs are too likely to attract unwanted attention. We never have been so deep in secrecy as you wolves like to be, not when witches sometimes crop up in mundane families— we need to be part of society enough that they can find us. Mostly people think we're a bunch of harmless charlatans—trafficking in drugs would change all that for the worse. But the Samhain bunch is powerful enough that no one wants to face them—and Kouros is arrogant and crazy. He likes money, and there is at least one herb-alist among his followers who could manufacture some really odd stuff."

He shrugged. "I don't know. I'm interested in finding my brother, not in finding out if witches are selling drugs. It sounded to me like the drugs had nothing to do with my brother's kidnap-ping. Let me play Jon's call, and you make the determination." He pulled out his cell phone and played the message for her.

It had come from a pay phone. There weren't many of those

left, now that cell phones had made it less profitable for the phone companies to keep repairing the damage of vandals. But there was no mistaking the characteristic static and hiss as his brother talked very quietly into the mouthpiece.

Tom had called in favors and found the phone Jon used, but the people who took his brother were impossible to pick out from the scents of the hundreds of people who had been there since the last rain—and his brother's scent stopped right at the pay phone, outside a battered convenience store. Stopped as if they'd teleported him to another planet—or, more prosaically, thrown him in a car.

Jon's voice—smoker-dark, though he'd never touched tobacco or any of its relatives—slid through the apartment: "Look, Tom. My gut told me to call you tonight—and I listen to my gut. I've been hearing something on the street about a freaky group calling themselves Samhain—" He spelled it, to be sure Tom got it right. "Last few days I've had a couple of people following me that might be part of Samhain. No one wants to talk about 'em much. The streets are afraid of these . . . "

He didn't know if the witch could hear the rest. He'd been a wolf for twenty years and more, so his judgment about what human senses were good for was pretty much gone.

He could hear the girl's sweet voice clearly, though. "Lucky Jon?" she asked. "Lucky Jon, who are you calling? Let's hang it up, now." A pause, then the girl spoke into the phone. "Hello?" Another pause. "It's an answering machine, I think. No worries."

At the same time, a male, probably young, was saying in a rapid, rabid flow of sound, "I feel it . . . Doncha feel it? I feel it in him. This is the one. He'll do for Kouros." Then there was a soft click as the call ended.

The last fifty times he'd heard the recording, he couldn't make out the last word. But with the information the witch had given him, he understood it just fine this time.

Tom looked at Choo's witch, but he couldn't tell what she thought. Somewhere she'd learned to discipline her emotions, so he could smell only the strong ones—like the flash of desire she'd felt as he sniffed the back of her neck. Even in this situation, it had been enough to raise a thread of interest. Maybe after they got his brother back, they could do something about that interest. In the meantime . . .

"How much of the last did you hear, Wendy?" he asked.

"Don't call me Wendy," she snapped. "It's Moira. No one called me Wendy except my mom, and she's been dead a long time."

"Fine," he snapped back before he could control himself. He was tired and worried, but he could do better than that. He tightened his control and softened his voice. "Did you hear the guy? The one who said that he felt *it* in him—meaning my brother, I think. And that he would do for Kouros?"

"No. Or at least not well enough to catch his words. But I know the woman's voice. You're right: it was Samhain." Though he couldn't feel anything from her, her knuckles were white on the coffee cup.

"You need a Finder, and I can't do that anymore. Wait—" She held up a hand before he could say anything. "I'm not saying I won't help you, just that it could be a lot simpler. Kouros moves all the time. Did you trace the call? It sounded like a pay phone to me."

"I found the phone booth he called from, but I couldn't find anything except that he'd been there." He tapped his nose, then glanced at her dark glasses and said, "I could smell him there and backtrail him, but I couldn't trail him out. They transported him somehow."

"They don't know that he's a cop, or that his brother is a werewolf."

"He doesn't carry ID with him while he's undercover. I don't see how anyone would know I was his brother. Unless he told them, and he wouldn't."

"Good," she said. "They won't expect you. That'll help."

"So do you know a Finder I can go to?"

She shook her head. "Not one who will help you against Samhain. Anyone, *anyone* who makes a move against them is punished in some rather spectacular ways." He saw her consider sharing one or two of them with him and discard it. She didn't want him scared off. Not that he could be, not with Jon's life at stake. But it was interesting that she hadn't tried.

"If you take me to where they stole him, maybe I can find something they left behind, something to use to find them."

Tom frowned at her. She didn't know his brother, he hadn't mentioned money, and he was getting the feeling that she couldn't care less if he called in the authorities. "So if Samhain is so all-powerful, how come you, a white witch, are willing to buck them?"

"You're a cop, too, aren't you?" She finished her coffee, but if she was waiting for a reaction, she wasn't going to get one. He'd seen the "all-knowing" witch act before. Her lips turned up as she set the empty cup on the counter. "It's not magic. Cops are easy to spot—suspicious is your middle name. Fair enough."

She pulled off her glasses, and he saw that he'd been wrong. He'd been pretty sure she was blind—the other reason women wore wraparound sunglasses at night. And she was. But that wasn't why she wore the sunglasses.

Her left eye was Swamp Thing–green without pupil or white. Her right eye was gone, and it looked as though it had been removed by someone who wasn't too good with a knife. It was horrible—and he'd seen some horrible things.

"Sacrifice is good for power," she said again. "But it works best if you can manage to make the sacrifice your own."

Jesus. She'd done it to herself.

She might not be able to see him, but she read his reaction just fine. She smiled tightly. "There were some extenuating circumstances," she continued. "You aren't going to see witches cutting off their fingers to power their spells—it doesn't work that way. But this worked for me." She tapped the scar tissue around her right eye. "Kouros did the other one first. That's why I'm willing to take them on. I've done it before and survived—and I still owe them a few." She replaced her sunglasses, and he watched her relax as they settled into place.

TOM FRANKLIN HADN'T BROUGHT A CAR, AND FOR OBVI-ous reasons, *she* didn't drive. He said the phone was only a couple of miles from her apartment, and neither wanted to wait around for a cab. So they walked. She felt his start of surprise when she tucked her arm in his, but he didn't object. At least he didn't jump away from her and say "ick," like the last person who'd seen what she'd done to herself.

"You'll have to tell me when we come to curbs or if there's something in the way," she told him. "Or you can amuse yourself when I fall on my face. I can find my way around my apartment, but out here I'm at your mercy."

He said, with sober humor, "I imagine watching you trip over a few curbs would be a good way to get you to help Jon. Why don't you get a guide dog?"

"Small apartments aren't a good place for big dogs," she told him. "It's not fair to the dog."

They walked a few blocks in silence, the rain drizzling unhappily down the back of her neck and soaking the bottoms of the jeans she'd put on before they started out. Seattle was living up to its reputation. He guided her as if he'd done it before, unobtrusively but clearly, as if they were waltzing instead of walking down the street. She relaxed and walked faster.

"Wendy." He broke the companionable silence with the voice of One Who Suddenly Comprehends. "It's worse than I thought. I was stuck on Casper the Friendly Ghost and Wendy the Good Little Witch. But Wendy Moira . . . I bet it's Wendy Moira Angela, isn't it?"

She gave him a mock scowl. "I don't have a kiss for you, and I can't fly—not even with fairy dust. And I *hate Peter Pan*, the play, and all the movies."

His arm moved, and she could tell he was laughing to himself. "I bet."

"It could be worse, Toto," she told him. "I could belong to the Emerald City Pack."

He laughed out loud at that, a softer sound than she'd expected, given the rough grumble of his voice. "You know, I've never thought of it that way. It seemed logical, Seattle being the Emerald City."

She might have said something, but he suddenly picked up his pace like a hunting dog spotting his prey. She kept her hand tight on his arm and did her best to keep up. He stopped at last. "Here."

She felt his tension, the desire for action of some sort. Hopefully she'd be able to provide him the opportunity. She released his arm and stepped to the side.

"All right," she told him, falling into the comfortable patter she adopted with most of her clients—erasing the odd intimacy that had sprung up between them. "I know the girl on your brother's phone call—her name used to be Molly, but I think she goes by something like Spearmint or Peppermint, Somethingmint. I'm going to call for things that belong to her—a hair, a cigarette—anything will do. You'll have to do the looking. Whatever it is will glow, but it might be very small, easy to overlook."

"What if I don't see anything?"

"Then they didn't leave anything behind, and I'll figure out something else to try."

She set aside her worries, shedding them like a duck would shed the cool Seattle rain. Closing her senses to the outside world, she reached into her well of power and drew out a bucketful and threw it out in a circle around her as she called to the essence that was Molly. She hadn't done this spell since she could see out of both eyes—but there was no reason she couldn't do it now. Once learned, spells came to her hand like trained spaniels, and this one was no exception.

"What do you see?" she asked. The vibration of power warmed

her against the cold autumn drizzle that began to fall. There was something here; she could feel it.

"Nothing." His voice told her he'd put a lot of hope into this working.

"There's something," she said, sensations crawling up her arms and over her shoulders. She held out her right hand, her left being otherwise occupied with the workings of her spell. "Touching me might help you see."

Warmth flooded her as his hand touched hers . . . and she could see the faint traces Molly had left behind. She froze.

"Moira?"

She couldn't see anything else. Just bright bits of pink light sparkling from the ground, giving her a little bit of an idea what the landscape looked like. She let go of his hand and the light disappeared, leaving her in darkness again.

"Did you see anything?" she asked, her voice hoarse. The oddity of seeing anything . . . She craved it too much, and it made her wary because she didn't know how it worked.

"No."

He wanted his brother and she wanted to see. Just for a moment. She held her hand out. "Touch me again."

. . . and the sparkles returned like glitter scattered in front of her. Small bits of skin and hair, too small for what she needed. But there was something . . .

She followed the glittering trail, and as if it had been hidden, a small wad of something blazed like a bonfire.

"Is there a wall just to our right?" she asked.

"A building and an alley." His voice was tight, but she ignored it. She had other business first.

They'd waited for Tom's brother in the alley. Maybe Jon came to the pay phone here often.

She led Tom to the blaze and bent to pick it up: soft and sticky, gum. Better, she thought, better than she could have hoped. Saliva would make a stronger guide than hair or fingernails could. She released his hand reluctantly.

"What did you find?"

"Molly's gum." She allowed her magic to loosen the last spell and slide back to her, hissing as the power warmed her skin almost to the point of burning. The next spell would be easier, even if it might eventually need more power. Sympathetic magic—which used the connections between like things—was one of those affinities that ran through her father's bloodlines into her.

But before she tried any more magic, she needed to figure out what Tom had done to her spell. How touching him allowed her to *see*.

SHE LOOKED UNEARTHLY. A VIOLENT WIND HE HAD NOT felt, not even when she'd fastened on to his hand with fierce strength, had blown her hair away from her face. The skin on her hands was reddened, as if she held them too close to a fire. He wanted to soothe them—but he firmly intended never to touch her again.

He had no idea what she'd done to him while she held on to him and made his body burn and tremble. He didn't like surprises, and she'd told him that he would have to look, not that she'd use him to *see*. He especially didn't like it that as long as she was touching him, he hadn't wanted her to let him go.

Witches gather more power from hurting those with magic, she'd said . . . more or less. People just like him—but it hadn't hurt, not that he'd noticed.

He wasn't afraid of her, not really. Witch or not, she was no match for him. Even in human form, he could break her human-fragile body in mere moments. But if she was using him . . .

"Why are you helping me?" he asked as he had earlier, but the question seemed more important now. He'd known what she was, but *witch* meant something different to him now. He knew enough about witches not to ask the obvious question, though—like what it was she'd done to him. Witches, in his experience, were secretive about their spells—like junkyard dogs are secretive about their bones.

She'd taken something from him by using him that way . . . broken the trust he'd felt building between them. He needed to reestablish what he could expect out of her. Needed to know exactly what she was getting him into, beyond rescuing his brother. Witches were not altruistic. "What do you want out of this? Revenge for your blindness?"

She watched him . . . appeared to watch him, anyway, as she considered his question. There hadn't been many people who could lie to Tom before he Changed—cops learn all about lying the first year on the job. Afterward . . . he could smell a lie a mile away an hour before it was spoken.

"Alan Choo sent you," she said finally. "That's one. Your brother's a policeman, and an investigation into his death might be awkward. That's two. He takes risks to help people he doesn't know—it's only right someone return the favor. That's three."

They weren't lies, but they weren't everything, either. Her face was very still, as if the magic she worked had changed her view of him, too.

Then she tilted her head sideways and said in a totally different voice, hesitant and raw, "Sins of the fathers."

Here was absolute truth. Obscure as hell, but truth. "Sins of the fathers?"

"Kouros's real name is Lin Keller, though he hasn't used it in twenty years or more."

"He's your father." And then he added two and two. "Your *father* is running Samhain's Coven?" Her father had ruined her eye and—Tom could read between the lines—caused her to ruin the other? Her own father?

She drew in a deep breath—and for a moment he was afraid she was going to cry or something. But a stray gust of air brought the scent of her to him, and he realized she was angry. It tasted like a werewolf's rage, wild and biting.

"I am not a part of it," she said, her voice a half octave lower than it had been. "I'm not bringing you to his lair so he can dine upon werewolf, too. I am here because some jerk made me feel sorry for him. I am here because I want both him and his brother out of my hair and safely out of the hands of my rat-bastard father so I won't have their deaths on my conscience, too."

Someone else might have been scared of her, she being a witch and all. Tom wanted to apologize—and he couldn't remember the last time that impulse had touched him. It was even more amazing because he wasn't at fault: she'd misunderstood him. Maybe she'd picked up on how appalled he was that her own father had maimed her—he hadn't been implying she was one of them.

He didn't apologize, though, or explain himself. People said things when they were mad that they wouldn't tell you otherwise.

"What was it you did to me?"

"Did to you?" Arctic ice might be warmer.

"When you were looking for the gum. It felt like you hit me with a bolt of lightning." He was damned if he'd tell her everything he felt.

Her right eyebrow peeked out above her sunglasses. Interest replaced coldness. "You felt like I was doing something to you?" And then she held out her left hand. "Take my hand."

He looked at it.

After a moment, she smiled. He didn't know she had a smile like that in her. Bright and cheerful and sudden. Knowing. As if she had gained every thought that passed through his head. Her anger, the misunderstanding between them was gone as if it had never been.

"I don't know what happened," she told him gently. "Let me try re-creating it, and maybe I can tell you."

He gave her his hand. Instead of taking it, she put only two fingers on his palm. She stepped closer to him, dropped her head so he could see her scalp gleaming pale underneath her dark hair. The magic that touched him this time was gentler, sparklers instead of fireworks—and she jerked her fingers away as if his hand were a hot potato.

"What the heck . . . " She rubbed her hands on her arms with nervous speed.

"What?"

"You weren't acting as my focus—I can tell you that much."

"So what was going on?"

She shook her head, clearly uncomfortable. "I think I was using you to *see*. I shouldn't be able to do that."

He found himself smiling grimly. "So I'm your Seeing Eye wolf?"

"I don't know."

He recognized her panic, having seen it in his own mirror upon occasion. It was always frightening when something you thought was firmly under control broke free to run where it would. With him, it was the wolf.

Something resettled in his gut. She hadn't done it on purpose; she wasn't using him.

"Is it harmful to me?"

She frowned. "Did it hurt?"

"No."

"Either time?"

"Neither time."

"Then it didn't harm you."

"All right," he said. "Where do we go from here?"

She opened her right hand, the one with the gum in it. "Not us. Me. This is going to show us where Molly is—and Molly will know where your brother is."

She closed her fingers, twisted her hand palm down, then turned herself in a slow circle. She hit a break in the pavement, and he grabbed her before she could do more than stumble. His hand touched her wrist, and she turned her hand to grab him as the kick of power flowed through his body once more.

"They're in a boat," she told him, and went limp in his arms.

SHE AWOKE WITH THE FAMILIAR HEADACHE THAT USU-ally accompanied the overuse of magic—and absolutely no idea where she was. It smelled wrong to be her apartment, but she was lying on a soft surface with a blanket covering her.

Panic rose in her chest—sometimes she hated being blind.

"Back in the land of the living?"

"Tom?"

He must have heard the distress in her voice, because when he spoke again, he was much closer and his voice was softer. "You're on a couch in my apartment. We were as close to mine as we were to yours, and I knew I could get us into my apartment. Yours is probably sealed with hocus-pocus. Are you all right?"

She sat up and put her feet on the floor, and her erstwhile bed indeed proved itself to be a couch. "Do you have something with sugar in it? Sweet tea or fruit juice?"

"Hot cocoa or tea," he told her.

"Tea."

He must have had water already heated, because he was quickly back with a cup. She drank the sweet stuff down as fast as she could, and the warmth did as much as the sugar to clear her headache.

"Sorry," she said.

"For what, exactly?" he said.

"For using you. I think you don't have any barriers," she told him slowly. "We all have safeguards, walls that keep out intruders. It's what keeps us safe."

In his silence, she heard him consider that.

"So, I'm vulnerable to witches?"

She didn't know what to do with her empty cup, so she set it on the couch beside her. Then she used her left hand, her seeking hand, to *look* at him again.

"No, I don't think so. Your barriers seem solid . . . even stronger than usual, as I'd expect from a wolf as far up the command structure as you are. I think you are vulnerable only to me."

"Which means?"

"Which means when I touch you, I can see magic through your eyes . . . with practice, I might even be able just to see. It means that you can feed my magic with your skin." She swallowed. "You're not going to like this."

"Tell me."

"You are acting like my familiar." She couldn't feel a thing from him. "If I had a familiar."

Floorboards creaked under his feet as his weight shifted. His shoulder brushed her as he picked up the empty cup. She heard him walk away from her and set the cup on a hard surface. "Do you need more tea?"

"No," she said, needing suddenly to be home, somewhere she wasn't so dependent upon him. "I'm fine. If you would call me a taxi, I'd appreciate it." She stood up, too. Then realized she had no idea where the door was or what obstacles might be hiding on the floor. In her own apartment, redolent with her magic, she was never so helpless.

"Can you find my brother?"

She hadn't heard him move, not a creak, not a breath, but his voice told her he was no more than a few inches from her. Disoriented and vulnerable, she was afraid of him for the first time.

He took a big step away from her. "I'm not going to hurt you."

"Sorry," she told him. "You startled me. Do we still have the gum?"

"Yes. You said she was on a boat."

She'd forgotten, but as soon as he said it, she could picture the boat in her head. That hadn't been the way the spell was supposed to work. It was more of a "hot and cold" spell, but she could still see the boat in her mind's eye.

Nothing had really changed, except that she'd used someone without asking. There was still a policeman to be saved and her father to kill.

"If we still have the gum, I can find Molly—the girl on your brother's phone call."

"I have a buddy whose boat we can borrow."

"All right," she told him after a moment. "Do you have some aspirin?"

SHE HATED BOATING. THE ROCKING MOTION DISRUPTED her sense of direction, the engine's roar obscured softer sounds, and the scent of the ocean covered the subtler scents she used to negotiate everyday life. Worse than all of that, though, was the thought of trying to swim without knowing where she was going. The damp air chilled her already cold skin.

"Which direction?" said Tom over the sound of the engine.

His presence shouldn't have made her feel better—werewolves couldn't swim at all—but it did. She pointed with the hand that held the gum. "Not far now," she warned him.

"There's a private dock about a half mile up the coast. Looks like it's been here awhile," he told her. "There's a boat—*The Tern*, the bird."

It felt right. "I think that must be it."

There were other boats on the water; she could hear them. "What time is it?"

"About ten in the morning. We're passing the boat right now."

Molly's traces, left on the gum, pulled toward their source, tugging Moira's hand toward the back of the boat. "That's it."

"There's a park with docks about a mile back," he said, and the boat tilted to the side. "We'll go tie up there and come back on foot."

But when he'd tied the boat up, he changed his mind. "Why don't you stay here and let me check this out?"

Moira rubbed her hands together. It bothered her to have her magic doing something it wasn't supposed to be doing, and she'd let it throw her off her game: time to collect herself. She gave him a sultry smile. "Poor blind girl," she said. "Must be kept out of danger, do you think?" She turned a hand palm up and heard the whoosh of flame as it caught fire. "You'll need me when you find Molly—you may be a werewolf, but she's a witch who looks like a pretty young thing." She snuffed the flame and dusted off her hands. "Besides, she's afraid of me. She'll tell me where your brother is."

She didn't let him know how grateful she was for the help he gave her exiting the boat. When this day was over, he'd go back to his life and she to hers. If she wanted to keep him—she knew he wouldn't want to be kept by her. She was a witch, and ugly with scars of the past.

Besides, if her dreams were right, she wouldn't survive to see nightfall.

SHE THREADED THROUGH THE DENSE UNDERBRUSH AS if she could see every hanging branch, one hand on his back and her other held out in front of her. He wondered if she was using magic to see.

She wasn't using him. Her hand in the middle of his back was warm and light, but his flannel shirt was between it and skin. Probably she was reading his body language and using her upraised hand as an insurance policy against low-hanging branches.

They followed a half-overgrown path that had been trod out a hundred feet or so from the coast, which was obscured by ferns and underbrush. He kept his ears tuned so he'd know it if they started heading away from the ocean.

The Tern had been moored in a small natural harbor on a battered dock next to the remains of a boathouse. A private property rather than the public dock he'd used.

They'd traveled north and were somewhere not too far from Everett, by his reckoning. He wasn't terribly surprised when their path ended in a brand-new eight-foot chain-link fence. Someone had a real estate gold mine on their hands, and they were waiting to sell it to some developer when the price was right. Until then, they'd try to keep out the riffraff.

He helped Moira over the fence, mostly a matter of whispering a few directions until she found the top of it. He waited until she was over and then vaulted over himself.

The path they'd been following continued on, though not nearly so well traveled as it had been before the fence. A quarter mile of blackberry brambles ended abruptly in thigh-deep damp grasslands that might once have been a lawn. He stopped before they left the cover of the bushes, sinking down to rest on his heels.

"There's a burnt-out house here," he told Moira, who had ducked down when he did. "It must have burned down a couple of years ago, because I don't smell it."

"Hidden," she commented.

"Someone's had tents up here," he told her. "And I see the remnants of a campfire."

"Can you see the boat from here?"

"No, but there's a path I think should lead down to the water. I think this is the place."

She pulled her hand away from his arm. "Can you go check it out without being seen?"

"It would be easier if I do it as a wolf," Tom admitted. "But I don't dare. We might have to make a quick getaway, and it'll be a while before I can shift back to human." He hoped Jon would be healthy enough to pilot in an emergency—but he didn't like to make plans that depended upon an unknown. Moira wasn't going to be piloting a boat anywhere.

"Wait," she told him. She murmured a few words and then put her cold fingers against his throat. A sudden shock, like a static charge on steroids, hit him—and when it was over, her fingers were hot on his pulse. "You aren't invisible, but it'll make people want to overlook you."

He pulled out his HK and checked the magazine before sliding it back in. The big gun fit his hand like a glove. He believed in using weapons: guns or fangs, whatever got the job done.

"It won't take me long."

"If you don't go, you'll never get back," she told him, and gave him a gentle push. "I can take care of myself."

It didn't sit right with him, leaving her alone in the territory of his enemies, but common sense said he'd have a better chance of roaming unseen. And no one tackled a witch lightly—not even other witches.

Spell or no, he slid through the wet overgrown trees like a shadow, crouching to minimize his silhouette and avoiding anything likely to crunch. One thing living in Seattle did was minimize the stuff that would crunch under your foot—all the leaves were wet and moldy without a noise to be had.

The boat was there, bobbing gently in the water. Empty. He closed his eyes and let the morning air tell him all it could.

His brother had been in the boat. There had been others, too—Tom memorized their scents. If anything happened to Jon, he'd track them down and kill them, one by one. Once he had them, he'd let his nose lead him to Jon.

He found blood where Jon had scraped against a tree, crushed plants where his brother had tried to get away and rolled around in the mud with another man. Or maybe he'd just been laying a trail for Tom. Jon knew Tom would come for him—that's what family did.

The path the kidnappers took paralleled the waterfront for a while and then headed inland, but not for the burnt-out house. Someone had found a better hideout. Nearly invisible under a shelter of trees, a small barn nestled snugly amidst broken pieces of corral fencing. Its silvered sides bore only a hint of red paint, but the aluminum roof, though covered with moss, was undamaged.

And his brother was there. He couldn't quite hear what Jon

was saying, but he recognized his voice . . . and the slurring rapid rhythm of his schizophrenic-mimicry. If Jon was acting, he was all right. The relief of that settled in his spine and steadied his nerves.

All he needed to do was get his witch . . . Movement caught his attention, and he dropped to the ground and froze, hidden by wet grass and weeds.

MOIRA WASN'T SURPRISED WHEN THEY FOUND HER—TEN in the morning isn't a good time to hide. It was one of the young ones—she could tell by the surprised squeal and the rapid thud of footsteps as he ran for help.

Of course, if she'd really been trying to hide, she might have managed it. But sometime after Tom left it had occurred to her that if she wanted to find Samhain, the easiest thing might be to let them find her. So she set about attracting their attention.

If they found her, it would unnerve them. They knew she worked alone. Her arrival here would puzzle them, but they wouldn't look for anyone else—leaving Tom as her secret weapon.

Magic called to magic, unless the witch took pains to hide it, so any of them should have been able to feel the flames that danced over her hands. It had taken them longer than she expected. While she waited for the boy to return, she found a sharp-edged rock and put it in her pocket. She folded her legs and let the coolness of the damp earth flow through her.

She didn't hear him come, but she knew by his silence whom the young covenist had run to.

"Hello, Father," she told him, rising to her feet. "We have much to talk about."

SHE DIDN'T LOOK LIKE A CAPTIVE, TOM THOUGHT, WATCH-ing Moira walk to the barn as if she'd been there before, though she might have been following the sullen-looking half-grown boy who clomped through the grass ahead of her. A tall man followed them both, his hungry eyes on Moira's back.

His wolf recognized another dominant male with a near-silent growl, while Tom thought that the man was too young to have a grown daughter. But there was no one else this could be but Lin Keller—that predator was not a man who followed anyone or allowed anyone around him who might challenge him. He'd seen an Alpha or two like that.

Tom watched them until they disappeared into the barn.

It hurt to imagine she might have betrayed him—as if there were some bond between them, though he hadn't known her a full day. Part of him would not believe it. He remembered her real indignation when she thought he believed she was part of Samhain, and it comforted him.

It didn't matter, couldn't matter. Not yet. Saving Jon mattered, and the rest would wait. His witch was captured or had betrayed him. Either way, it was time to let the wolf free.

The change hurt, but experience meant he made no sound as his bones rearranged themselves and his muscles stretched and slithered to adjust to his new shape. It took fifteen minutes of agony before he rose on four paws, a snarl fixed on his muzzle—ready to kill someone. Anyone.

Instead he stalked like a ghost to the barn where his witch waited. He rejected the door they'd used, but prowled around the side, where four stall doors awaited. Two of them were broken with missing boards; one of the openings was big enough for him to slide through.

The interior of the barn was dark, and the stall's half walls blocked his view of the main section, where his quarry waited. Jon was still going strong, a wild ranting conversation with no one about the Old Testament, complete with quotes. Tom knew a lot of them himself.

"Killing things again, Father?" said Moira's cool disapproving voice, cutting though Jon's soliloquy.

And suddenly Tom could breathe again. They'd found her somehow, Samhain's Coven had, but she wasn't one of them.

"So judgmental." Tom had expected something . . . bigger from the man's voice. His own Alpha, for instance, could have made a living as a televangelist with his raw fire-and-brimstone voice. This man sounded like an accountant.

"Kill her. You have to kill her before she destroys us—I have seen it." It was Molly, the girl from Jon's message.

"You couldn't see your way out of a paper bag, Molly," said Moira. "Not that you're wrong, of course."

There were other people in the barn, Tom could smell them, but they stayed quiet.

"You aren't going to kill me," said Kouros. "If you could have done that, you'd have done it before now. Which brings me to my point: Why are you here?"

"To stop you from killing this man," Moira told him.

"I've killed men before—and you haven't stopped me. What is so special about this one?"

MOIRA FELT THE BURDEN OF ALL THOSE DEATHS UPON her shoulders. He was right. She could have killed him before— before he'd killed anyone else.

"This one has a brother," she said.

She felt Tom's presence in the barn, but her look-past-me spell must still have been working, because no one seemed to notice the werewolf. And any witch with a modicum of sensitivity to auras would have felt him. His brother was a faint trace to her left— something his constant stream of words made far more clear than her magic was able to.

Her father she could follow only from his voice.

There were other people in the structure—she hadn't quite decided what the cavernous building was: probably a barn, given the dirt floor and faint odor of cow—but she couldn't pinpoint them, either. She knew where Molly was, though. And Molly was the important one, Kouros's right hand.

"Someone *paid* you to go up against me?" Her father's voice was faintly incredulous. "Against us?"

Then he did something, made some gesture. She wouldn't have known except for Molly's sigh of relief. So she didn't feel too bad when she tied Molly's essence, through the gum she still held, into her shield.

When the coven's magic hit the shield, it was Molly who took the damage. Who died. Molly, her little sister, whose presence she could no longer feel.

Someone, a young man, screamed Molly's coven name—Wintergreen. And there was a flurry of movement where Moira had last sensed her.

Moira dropped the now-useless bit of gum on the ground.

"Oh, you'll pay for that," breathed her father. "Pay in pain and power until there is nothing left of you."

Someone sent power her way, but it wasn't a concerted spell from the coven, and it slid off her protections without harm. Unlike the fist that struck her in the face, driving her glasses into her nose and knocking her to the ground—her father's fist. She'd recognize the weight of it anywhere.

Unsure of where her enemies were, she stayed where she was, listening. But she didn't hear Tom; he was just suddenly there. And the circle of growing terror that spread around him—of all the emotions possible, it was fear that she could sense most often—told her he was in his lupine form. It must have been impressive.

"Your victim has a brother," she told her father again, knowing he'd hear the smugness in her tone. "And you've made him very angry."

The beast beside her roared. Someone screamed . . . Even witches are afraid of monsters.

The coven broke. Children most of them, they broke and ran.

Molly's death followed by a beast out of their worst nightmares was more than they could face, partially trained, deliberately crippled fodder for her father that they were.

Tom growled, the sound finding a silent echo in her own chest as if he were a bass drum. He moved, a swift, silent predator, and someone who hadn't run died. Tom's brother, she noticed, had fallen entirely silent.

"A werewolf," breathed Kouros. "Oh, now there is a worthy kill." She felt his terror and knew he'd attack Tom before he took care of her.

The werewolf came to her side, probably to protect her. She reached out with her left hand, intending to spread her own defenses to the wolf—though that would leave them too thin to be very effective—but she hadn't counted on the odd effect he had on her magic. On her.

Her father's spell—a vile thing that would have induced terrible pain and permanently damaged Tom had it hit—connected just after she touched the wolf. And for a moment, maybe a whole breath, nothing happened.

Then she felt every hair under her hand stand to attention, and Tom made an odd sound and power swept through her from him— all the magic Kouros had sent—and it filled her well to overflowing.

And she could see. For the first time since she'd been thirteen, she could see.

She stood up, shedding broken pieces of sunglasses to the ground. The wolf beside her was huge, chocolate-brown, and easily tall enough to leave her hand on his shoulder as she came to her feet. A silvery scar curled around his snarling muzzle. His eyes were yellow-brown and cold. A sweeping glance showed her two dead bodies—one burnt, the other savaged—and a very dirty, hairy man tied to a post with his hands behind his back, who could only be Tom's brother Jon.

And her father, looking much younger than she remembered

him. No wonder he went for teens to populate his *coven*—he was stealing their youth as well as their magic. A coven should be a meeting of equals, not a feeding trough for a single greedy witch.

She looked at him and saw that he was afraid. He should be. He'd used all his magic to power his spell—he'd left himself defenseless. And now he was afraid of her.

Just as she had dreamed. She pulled the stone out of her pocket—and it seemed to her that she had all the time in the world to use it to cut her right hand open. Then she pointed it, her bloody hand of power at him.

"*By the blood we share*," she whispered, and felt the magic gather.

"You'll die, too," Kouros said frantically, as if she didn't know.

"*Blood follows blood*." Before she spoke the last word, she lifted her other hand from Tom's soft fur that none of this magic should fall to him. And as soon as she did so, she could no longer see. But she wouldn't be blind for long.

TOM STARTED MOVING BEFORE HER FINGERS LEFT HIM, knocking into her with his hip and spoiling her aim. Her magic flooded through him, hitting him instead of the one she'd aimed all that power at. The wolf let it sizzle through his bones and returned it to her, clean.

Pleasant as that was, he didn't let it distract him from his goal. He was moving so fast that the man was still looking at Moira when the wolf landed on him.

Die, he thought as he buried his fangs in Kouros's throat, drinking his blood and his death in one delicious mouthful of flesh. This one had moved against the wolf's family, against the wolf's witch. Satisfaction made the meat even sweeter.

"Tom?" Moira sounded lost.

"Tom's fine," answered his brother's rusty voice. He'd talked himself hoarse. "You just sit there until he calms down a little. You all right, lady?"

Tom lifted his head and looked at his witch. She was huddled on the ground, looking small and lost, her scarred face bared for all the world to see. She looked fragile, but Tom knew better, and Jon would learn.

As the dead man under his claws had learned. Kouros died knowing she would have killed him.

Tom had been willing to give her that kill—but not if it meant her death. So Tom had the double satisfaction of saving her and killing the man. He went back to his meal.

"Tom, stop that," Jon said. "Ick. I know you aren't hungry. Stop it now."

"Is Kouros dead?" His witch sounded shaken up.

"As dead as anyone I've seen," said Jon. "Look, Tom. I appreciate the sentiment, I've wanted to do that anytime this last day. But I'd like to get out of here before some of those kids decide to come back while I'm still tied up." He paused. "Your lady needs to get out of here."

Tom hesitated, but Jon was right. He wasn't hungry anymore, and it was time to take his family home.

ALPHA AND OMEGA

Charles appeared in my life three-dimensional and in possession of an entire history. He stalked onto the pages of *Moon Called*, Bran Cornick's younger son, and he told me who he was. He didn't care that there were already far too many characters in the book—and that major characters needed to be introduced earlier. There he was.

So I sketched in a bare-bones appearance and promised him his own story. When my editor asked me to write a novella for an anthology of four novellas (two from paranormal-romance writers, two from urban-fantasy writers), I told her I'd write her a story about Charles, Samuel's younger brother. She read the story and asked if I thought I could write a series based on these characters—and the rest is history.

The events in "Alpha and Omega" take place during the events in *Moon Called*.

ONE

THE WIND WAS CHILL AND THE COLD FROZE THE ENDS
of her toes. One of these days she was going to break down and buy
boots—if only she didn't need to eat.

Anna laughed and buried her nose in her jacket, trudging the
last half mile to her home. It was true that being a werewolf gave
her greater strength and endurance, even in human form. But the
twelve-hour shift she'd just finished at Scorci's was enough to make
even *her* bones ache. You'd think that people would have better
things to do on Thanksgiving than go eat at an Italian restaurant.

Tim, the restaurant owner (who was Irish, not Italian for all
that he made the best gnocchi in Chicago), let her take extra shifts—
though he wouldn't let her work more than fifty hours a week. The
biggest bonus was the free meal she got each shift. Even so, she was
afraid she was going to have to find a second job to cover her
expenses: life as a werewolf, she had found, was as expensive finan-
cially as it was personally.

She used her keys to get into the entryway. There was nothing
in her mailbox, so she got Kara's mail and newspaper and climbed
the stairs to Kara's third-floor apartment. When she opened the

door, Kara's Siamese cat, Mouser, took one look at her, spat in disgust, and disappeared behind the couch.

For six months she'd been feeding the cat whenever her neighbor was gone—which was often, since Kara worked at a travel agency arranging tours. Mouser still hated her. From his hiding place he swore at her, as only a Siamese could do.

With a sigh, Anna tossed the mail and newspaper on the small table in the dining room and opened a can of cat food, setting it down near the water dish. She sat down at the table and closed her eyes. She was ready to go to her own apartment, one floor up, but she had to wait for the cat to eat. If she just left him there, she'd come back in the morning to a can of untouched food. Hate her he might, but Mouser wouldn't eat unless there was someone with him—even if it was a werewolf he didn't trust.

Usually she turned on the TV and watched whatever happened to be on, but tonight she was too tired to make the effort, so she unfolded the newspaper to see what had happened since the last time she'd picked one up a couple of months ago.

She skimmed through the headline articles on the front page without interest. Still complaining, Mouser emerged and stalked resentfully into the kitchen.

She turned the page so Mouser would know that she was really reading it—and drew in a sharp breath at the picture of a young man. It was a head shot, obviously a school picture, and next to it was a similar shot of a girl of the same age. The headline read: "Blood Found at Crime Scene Belongs to Missing Naperville Teen."

Feeling a little frantic, she read the article's review of the crime for those, like her, who had missed the initial reports.

Two months ago, Alan MacKenzie Frazier had disappeared from a high school dance the same night his date's body had been found on the school grounds. Cause of death was difficult to determine as the dead girl's body had been mauled by animals—there had been a pack of strays troubling the neighborhood for the past few months. Authorities had been uncertain whether the missing boy was a suspect or not. Finding his blood led them to suspect he was another victim.

Anna touched Alan Frazier's smiling face with trembling fingers. She knew. She knew.

She jumped up from the table, ignoring Mouser's unhappy yowl, and ran cold water from the kitchen sink over her wrists, trying to keep nausea at bay. *That poor boy.*

It took another hour for Mouser to finish his food. By that time Anna had the article memorized—and had come to a decision. Truthfully, she'd known as soon as she read the paper, but it had taken her the full hour to work up the courage to act upon it: if she'd learned anything in her three years as a werewolf, it was that you didn't want to do anything that might attract one of the dominant wolves' attention. Calling the Marrok, who ruled all the wolves in North America, would certainly attract his attention.

She didn't have a phone in her apartment, so she borrowed Kara's. She waited for her hands and her breathing to steady, but when that didn't seem to be happening, she dialed the number on the battered piece of paper anyway.

Three rings—and she realized that one o'clock in Chicago would be considerably different in Montana, where the area code indicated she was dialing. Was it a two-hour difference or three? Earlier or later? She hastily hung up the phone.

What was she going to tell him, anyway? That she'd seen the boy, obviously the victim of a werewolf attack, weeks after his disappearance, in a cage in her Alpha's house? That she thought the Alpha had ordered the attack? All Leo had to do was tell the Marrok that he'd come upon the kid later—that he hadn't sanctioned it. Maybe that was how it happened. Maybe she was projecting from her own experience.

She didn't even know if the Marrok would object to the attack. Maybe werewolves were allowed to attack whomever they pleased. That's what had happened to her.

She turned away from the phone and saw the boy's face looking out at her from the open newspaper. She looked at him a
moment more and then dialed the number again—surely the Marrok would at least object to the publicity it had attracted. This time
her call was answered on the first ring.

"This is Bran."

He didn't sound threatening.

"My name is Anna," she said, wishing her voice wouldn't
quiver. There was a time, she thought a little bitterly, when she
hadn't been afraid of her own shadow. Who'd have thought that
turning into a werewolf would turn her into a coward? But now she
knew the monsters were real.

Angry with herself she might have been, but she couldn't force
another word out of her throat. If Leo knew she'd called the Marrok, she might as well shoot herself with that silver bullet she'd
bought a few months ago and save him some trouble.

"You are calling from Chicago, Anna?" It startled her for a
moment, but then she realized he must have caller ID on his phone.
He didn't sound angry that she'd disturbed him—and that wasn't
like any dominant she'd ever met. Maybe he was a secretary or
something. That made better sense. The Marrok's personal number wouldn't be something that would be passed around.

The hope that she wasn't actually talking to the Marrok helped
steady her. Even Leo was afraid of the Marrok. She didn't bother
to answer his question—he already knew the answer. "I called to
talk to the Marrok, but maybe you could help me."

There was a pause, then Bran said, a little regretfully, "I am
the Marrok, child."

Panic set in again, but before she could excuse herself and hang
up, he said soothingly, "It's all right, Anna. You've done nothing
wrong. Tell me why you called."

She sucked in a deep breath, conscious that this was her last
chance to ignore what she'd seen and protect herself.

Instead she explained about the newspaper article—and that

she'd seen the missing boy in Leo's house, in one of the cages he kept for new wolves.

"I see," murmured the wolf at the other end of the phone line.

"I couldn't prove that anything was wrong until I saw the newspaper," she told him.

"Does Leo know you saw the boy?"

"Yes." There were two Alphas in the Chicago area. Briefly she wondered how he'd known which one she was talking about.

"How did he react?"

Anna swallowed hard, trying to forget what had happened afterward. Once Leo's mate had intervened, the Alpha had mostly quit passing her around to the other wolves at his whim, but that night Leo had felt that Justin deserved a reward. She didn't have to tell the Marrok that, surely?

He saved her the humiliation by clarifying his question. "Was he angry that you had seen the boy?"

"No. He was . . . happy with the man who'd brought him in." There had still been blood on Justin's face and he stank with the excitement of the hunt.

Leo had been happy when Justin had first brought Anna to him, too. It had been Justin who had been angry—he hadn't realized she'd be a submissive wolf. Submissive meant that Anna's place was at the very bottom of the pack. Justin had quickly decided he'd made a mistake when he Changed her. She thought he had, too.

"I see."

For some reason she had the strange feeling that he did.

"Where are you now, Anna?"

"At a friend's house."

"Another werewolf?"

"No." Then realizing he might think she'd told someone about what she was—something that was strictly forbidden—she hurried to explain. "I don't have a phone at my place. My neighbor is gone and I'm taking care of her cat. I used her phone."

"I see," he said. "I want you to stay away from Leo and your pack for right now—it might not be safe for you if someone figures out you called me."

That was an understatement. "All right."

"As it happens," the Marrok said, "I have recently been made aware of problems in Chicago."

The realization that she had risked everything unnecessarily made his next few words pass by her unheard.

"—I would normally have contacted the nearest pack. However, if Leo is murdering people, I don't see how the other Chicago Alpha wouldn't be aware of it. Since Jaimie hasn't contacted me, I have to assume that both Alphas are involved to one degree or another."

"It's not Leo who's making the werewolves," she told him. "It's Justin, his second."

"The Alpha is responsible for the actions of his pack," replied the Marrok coolly. "I've sent out an . . . investigator. As it happens he is flying into Chicago tonight. I'd like you to meet him."

Which was how Anna ended up naked between a couple of parked cars in the middle of the night at O'Hare International Airport. She didn't have a car or money for a taxi, but, as the crow flies, the airport was only about five miles from her apartment. It was after midnight and her wolf form was black as pitch and smallish as far as werewolves were concerned. The chances of someone seeing her and thinking she was anything but a stray dog were slight.

It had gotten colder, and she shivered as she pulled on the T-shirt she'd brought. There hadn't been room in her small pack for her coat once she'd stuffed it with shoes, jeans, and a top—all of which were more necessary.

She hadn't ever actually been to O'Hare before, and it took her a while to find the right terminal. By the time she got there, *he* was already waiting for her.

Only after she'd hung up the phone had she realized that the

Marrok had given her no description of his investigator. She'd fretted all the way to the airport about it, but she needn't have. There was no mistaking him. Even in the busy terminal, people stopped to look at him, before furtively looking away.

Native Americans, while fairly rare in Chicago, weren't so unheard of as to cause all the attention he was gathering. None of the humans walking past him would probably have been able to explain exactly why they had to look—but Anna knew. It was something common to very dominant wolves. Leo had it, too—but not to this extent.

He was tall, taller even than Leo, and he wore his black, black hair in a thick braid that swung below his bead-and-leather belt. His jeans were dark and new-looking, a contrast to his battered cowboy boots. He turned his head a little and the lights caught a gleam from the gold studs he wore in his ears. Somehow he didn't look like the kind of man who would pierce his ears.

The features under the youth-taut, teak-colored skin were broad and flat and carried an expression that was oppressive in its very blankness. His black eyes traveled slowly over the bustling crowd, looking for something. They stopped on her for a moment, and the impact made her catch her breath. Then his gaze drifted on.

CHARLES HATED FLYING. HE ESPECIALLY HATED FLYING when someone else was piloting. He'd flown himself to Salt Lake, but landing his small jet in Chicago could have alerted his quarry—and he preferred to take Leo by surprise. Besides, after they'd closed Meigs Field, he'd quit flying himself into Chicago. There was too much traffic at O'Hare and Midway.

He hated big cities. There were so many smells that they clogged his nose, so much noise that he caught bits of a hundred different conversations without trying—but could miss entirely the sound of someone sneaking up behind him. Someone had bumped by him on the walkway as he left the plane, and he'd had to work to keep from bumping back, harder. Flying into O'Hare in the middle of the night had at least avoided the largest crowds, but there were still too many people around for his comfort.

He hated cell phones, too. When he'd turned his on after the plane had landed, a message from his father was waiting. Now instead of going to the car rental desk and then to his hotel, he was going to have to locate some woman and stay with her so that Leo or his other wolves didn't kill her. All he had was a first name— Bran hadn't seen fit to give him a description of her.

He stopped outside the security gates and let his gaze drift where it would, hoping instincts would find the woman. He could smell another werewolf, but the ventilation in the airport defeated his ability to pinpoint the scent. His gaze caught first on a young girl with an Irish-pale complexion, whiskey-colored curly hair, and the defeated look of someone who was beaten on a regular basis. She looked tired, cold, and far too thin. It made him angry to see it, and he was already too angry to be safe, so he forced his gaze away.

There was a woman dressed in a business suit that echoed the warm chocolate of her skin. She didn't look quite like an Anna, but she carried herself in such a way that he could see her defying her Alpha to call the Marrok. She was obviously looking for someone. He almost started forward, but then her face changed as she found the person she was looking for—and it was not him.

He started a second sweep of the airport when a small, hesitant voice from just to his left said, "Sir, have you just come from Montana?"

It was the whiskey-haired girl. She must have approached him while he'd been looking elsewhere—something she wouldn't have been able to do if he weren't standing in the middle of a freaking airport.

At least he didn't have to look for his father's contact anymore. With her this close, not even the artificial air currents could hide that she was a werewolf. But it wasn't his nose alone that told him that she was something far rarer.

At first he thought she was submissive. Most werewolves were more or less dominant. Gentler-natured people weren't usually cussed enough to survive the brutal transformation from human to werewolf. Which meant that submissive werewolves were few and far between.

Then he realized that the sudden change in his temper and the irrational desire to protect her from the crowds streaming past were indications of something else. She wasn't a submissive, either, though many might mistake her for that; she was an Omega.

Right then he knew that whatever else he did in Chicago, he was going to kill whoever had given her that bruised look.

UP CLOSE HE WAS EVEN MORE IMPRESSIVE; SHE COULD feel his energy licking lightly over her like a snake tasting its prey. Anna kept her gaze fully on the floor, waiting for his answer.

"I am Charles Cornick," he said. "The Marrok's son. You must be Anna."

She nodded.

"Did you drive here or catch a cab?"

"I don't have a car," she said.

He growled something she didn't quite catch. "Can you drive?"

She nodded.

"Good."

SHE DROVE WELL, IF A LITTLE OVERCAUTIOUSLY—WHICH trait he didn't mind at all, though it didn't stop him from bracing one hand against the dash of the rental. She hadn't said anything when he told her to drive them to her apartment, though he hadn't missed the dismay she felt.

He could have told her that his father had instructed him to keep her alive if he could—and to do that he had to stick close. He didn't want to scare her any more than she already was. He could have told her that he had no intention of bedding her, but he tried not to lie. Not even to himself. So he stayed silent.

As she drove them down the expressway in the rented SUV, his wolf-brother had gone from the killing rage caused by the crowded airplane to a relaxed contentment Charles had never felt before. The two other Omega wolves he'd met in his long lifetime had done something similar to him, but not to this extent.

This must be what it is like to be fully human.

The anger and the hunter's wariness that his wolf always held was only a faint memory, leaving behind only the determination to take this one to mate—Charles had never felt anything like that, either.

She was pretty enough, though he'd like to feed her up and soften the stiff wariness in her shoulders. The wolf wanted to bed her and claim her as his own. Being of a more cautious nature than his wolf, he would wait until he knew her a little better before deciding to court her.

"My apartment isn't much," she said in an obvious effort to break the silence. The small rasp in her voice told him that her throat was dry.

She was frightened of him. Being his father's chosen executioner, he was used to being feared, though he'd never enjoyed it.

He leaned against the door to give her a little more space and looked out at the city lights so she'd feel safe stealing a few glances at him if she wanted to. He'd been quiet, hoping she would get used to him, but he thought now that might have been a mistake.

"Don't worry," he told her. "I am not fussy. Whatever your apartment is like, it is doubtless more civilized than the Indian lodge I grew up in."

"An Indian lodge?"

"I'm a little older than I look," he said, smiling a little. "Two hundred years ago, an Indian lodge was pretty fancy housing in Montana." Like most old wolves he didn't like talking about the past, but he found he'd do worse than that to set her at ease.

"I'd forgotten you might be older than you look," she said apologetically. She'd seen the smile, he thought, because the level of her fear dropped appreciably. "There aren't any older wolves in the pack here."

"A few," he disagreed with her as he noted that she said "*the* pack," not "*my* pack." Leo was seventy or eighty, and his wife was a lot older than that—old enough that they should have appreciated the gift of an Omega instead of allowing her to be reduced to this abased child who cringed whenever he looked at her too long. "It can be difficult to tell how old a wolf is. Most of us don't talk about it. It's hard enough adjusting without chatting incessantly about the old days."

She didn't reply, and he looked for something else they could talk about. Conversation wasn't his forte; he left that to his father and his brother, who both had clever tongues.

"What tribe are you from?" she asked before he found a topic. "I don't know a lot about the Montana tribes."

"My mother was Salish," he said. "Of the Flathead tribe." She snuck a quick look at his perfectly normal forehead. Ah, he thought, relieved, there was a good story he could tell her. "Do you know how the Flatheads got their name?"

She shook her head. Her face was so solemn he was tempted to make something up to tease her. But she didn't know him well enough for that, so he told her the truth.

"Many of the Indian tribes in the Columbia Basin, mostly other Salish peoples, used to flatten the foreheads of their infants—the Flatheads were among the few tribes that did not."

"So why are they the ones called Flatheads?" she asked.

"Because the other tribes weren't trying to alter their foreheads, but to give themselves a peak at the top of their heads. Since the Flatheads did not, the other tribes called us 'flat heads.' It wasn't a compliment."

The scent of her fear faded further as she followed his story.

"We were the ugly, barbarian cousins, you see." He laughed.

"Ironically, the white trappers misunderstood the name. We were infamous for a long time for a practice we didn't follow. So the white men, like our cousins, thought we were barbarians."

"You said your mother was Salish," she said. "Is the Marrok Native American?"

He shook his head. "Father is a Welshman. He came over and hunted furs in the days of the fur trappers and stayed because he fell in love with the scent of pine and snow." His father put it just that way. Charles found himself smiling again, a real smile this time, and felt her relax further—and his face didn't hurt at all. He'd have to call his brother, Samuel, and tell him that he'd finally learned that his face wouldn't crack if he smiled. All it had taken to teach him was an Omega werewolf.

She turned into an alley and pulled into a small parking lot behind one of the ubiquitous four-story brick apartment buildings that filled the older suburbs of this part of town.

"Which city are we in?" he asked.

"Oak Park," she said. "Home of Frank Lloyd Wright, Edgar Rice Burroughs, and Scorci's."

"Scorci's?"

She nodded her head and hopped out of the car. "The best Italian restaurant in Chicago and my current place of employment."

Ah. That's why she smelled of garlic.

"So your opinion is unbiased?" He slid out of the car with a feeling of relief. His brother made fun of his dislike of cars since even a bad accident was unlikely to kill him. But Charles wasn't worried about dying—it was just that cars went too fast. He couldn't get a feel for the land they passed through. And if he felt like dozing a bit as he traveled, they couldn't follow the trail on their own. He preferred horses.

After he got his suitcase out of the back, Anna locked the car with the key fob. The car honked once, making him jump, and he gave it an irritated look. When he turned back, Anna was staring hard at the ground.

The anger that being in her presence had dissipated surged back full force at the strength of her fear. Someone had really done a number on her.

"Sorry," she whispered. If she'd been in wolf form, she'd have been cowering with her tail tucked beneath her.

"For what?" he asked, unable to banish the rage that sent his voice down an octave. "Because I'm jumpy around cars? Not your fault."

He was going to have to be careful this time, he realized as he tried to pull the wolf back under control. Usually when his father sent him out to deal with trouble, he could do it coldly. But with a damaged Omega wolf around, one that he found himself responding to on several different levels, he was going to have to hold tight to his temper.

"Anna," he said, fully in control again. "I am my father's hit man. It is my job as his second. But that doesn't mean that I take pleasure in it. I am not going to hurt you, my word on it."

"Yes, sir," she said, clearly not believing him.

He reminded himself that a man's word didn't count for much in this modern day. It helped his control that he scented as much anger on her as fear—she hadn't been completely broken.

He decided that further attempts to reassure her were likely to do the opposite. She would have to learn to accept that he was a man of his word. In the meantime he would give her something to think about.

"Besides," he told her gently, "my wolf is more interested in courting you than in asserting his dominance."

He walked past her before he smiled at the way her fear and anger had disappeared, replaced by shock . . . and something that might have been the beginning of interest.

She had keys to the outer door of the building and led the way through the entry and up the stairs without looking at him at all. By the second flight her scent had dulled of every emotion besides weariness.

She was visibly dragging as she climbed the stairs to the top floor. Her hand shook as she tried to get her key into the dead bolt of one of the two doors at the top. She needed to eat more. Werewolves shouldn't let themselves get so thin—it could be dangerous to those around them.

HE WAS AN EXECUTIONER, HE SAID, SENT BY HIS FATHER to settle problems among the werewolves. He must be even more dangerous than Leo to have survived doing that job. She could feel how dominant he was, and she knew what dominants were like. She had to stay alert, ready for any aggressive moves he might make—ready to handle the pain and the panic so she didn't run and make him worse.

So why was it that the longer he was around, the safer he made her feel?

He followed her up all four flights of stairs without a word, and she refused to apologize again for her apartment. He'd invited himself, after all. It was his own fault that he'd end up sleeping on a twin-sized futon instead of a nice hotel bed. She didn't know what to feed him—hopefully he'd eaten while he traveled. Tomorrow she'd run out and get something; she had the check from Scorci's on her fridge, awaiting deposit in the bank.

There had once been a pair of two-bedroom apartments on her floor, but in the seventies someone had reapportioned the fourth floor into a three-bedroom and her studio.

Her home looked shabby and empty, with no more furniture than her futon, a card table, and a pair of folding chairs. Only the polished oak floor gave it any appeal.

She glanced at him as he walked through the doorway behind her, but his face revealed very little he didn't want it to. She couldn't see what he thought, though she imagined his eyes lingered a little on the futon that worked fine for her, but was going to be much too small for him.

"The bathroom's through that door," she told him unnecessarily, as the door stood open and the bathtub was clearly visible.

He nodded, watching her with eyes that were opaque in the dim illumination of her overhead light. "Do you have to work tomorrow?" he asked.

"No. Not until Saturday."

"Good. We can talk in the morning, then." He took his small suitcase with him into the bathroom.

She tried not to listen to the unfamiliar sounds of someone else getting ready for bed as she rummaged in her closet for the old blanket she kept in it, wishing again for a nice cheap carpet instead of the gleaming hardwood floor that was pretty to look at, but cold on bare feet and sure to be hard on her backside when she tried to sleep.

The door opened while she was kneeling on the floor, folding the blanket into a makeshift mattress as far as she could from where he would be sleeping. "You can take the bed," she began as she turned around and found herself at eye level with a large reddish-brown werewolf.

He wagged his tail and smiled at her obvious surprise before brushing past her and curling up on the blanket. He wiggled a bit and then put his head down on his forepaws and closed his eyes, to all appearances dropping off immediately to sleep. She knew better, but he didn't stir as she went into the bathroom herself or when she came out dressed in her warmest pair of sweats.

She wouldn't have been able to sleep with a man in her apartment, but somehow, the wolf was less threatening. *This* wolf was less threatening. She bolted the door, turned out the light, and crawled into bed feeling safer than she had since the night she'd found out that there were monsters in the world.

THE FOOTSTEPS ON THE STAIRS THE NEXT MORNING didn't bother her at first. The family who lived across from her was in and out at all times of the day or night. She pulled the pillow over her head to block the noise out, but then Anna realized the brisk, no-nonsense tread belonged to Kara—and that she had a werewolf in her apartment. She sat bolt upright and looked at Charles.

The wolf was more beautiful in the daylight than he had been at night, his fur really red, she saw, set off by black on his legs and paws. He raised his head when she sat up and got to his feet when she did.

She put a finger to her lips as Kara knocked sharply on the door.

"Anna, you in there, girl? Did you know that someone is parked in your spot again? Do you want me to call the tow truck or do you have a man in there for once?"

Kara wouldn't just go away.

"I'm here, just a minute." She looked around frantically, but there was nowhere to hide a werewolf. He wouldn't fit in the closet, and if she closed the bathroom door, Kara would want to know why—just as she'd demand to know why Anna suddenly had a dog the size of an Irish wolfhound and not nearly as friendly looking in her living room.

She gave Charles one last frantic look and then hurried over to the door as he trotted off to the bathroom. She heard it click shut behind him as she unbolted the door.

"I'm back," said Kara breezily as she came in, setting a pair of bags down on the table. Her dark-as-night skin looked richer than usual for her week of tropical sun. "I stopped on the way home and bought some breakfast for us. You don't eat enough to keep a mouse alive."

Her gaze caught on the closed bathroom door. "You do have someone here." She smiled, but her eyes were wary. Kara had made no secret of the fact that she didn't like Justin, who Anna had explained away, truthfully enough, as an old boyfriend.

"Mmm." Anna was miserably aware that Kara wouldn't leave until she saw who was in the bathroom. For some reason Kara had taken Anna under her wing the very first day she'd moved in, shortly after she'd been Changed.

Just then, Charles opened the bathroom door and stepped just through the doorway. "Do you have a rubber band, Anna?"

He was fully dressed and human, but Anna knew that was impossible. It had been less than five minutes since he'd gone into the bathroom, and a werewolf took a lot longer than that to change back to human form.

She cast a frantic glance at Kara—but her neighbor was too busy staring at the man in the bathroom doorway to take note of Anna's shock.

Kara's rapt gaze made Anna take a second look as well; she had to admit that Charles, his blue-black hair hanging free to his waist in a thick sheet that made him look strangely naked despite his perfectly respectable flannel shirt and jeans, was worth staring at. He gave Kara a small smile before turning his attention back to Anna.

"I seem to have misplaced my hair band. Do you have another one?"

She gave him a jerky nod and brushed past him into the bathroom. How had he changed so fast? She could hardly ask him how he'd done it with Kara in the room, however.

He smelled good. Even after three years it was disconcerting to notice such things about people. Usually she tried to ignore what her nose told her—but she had to force herself not to stop and take a deep lungful of his rich scent.

"And just who are you?" Anna heard Kara ask suspiciously.

"Charles Cornick." She couldn't tell by the sound of his voice whether he was bothered by Kara's unfriendliness or not. "You are?"

"This is Kara, my downstairs neighbor," Anna told him, handing him a hair band as she slipped by him and back into the main room. "Sorry, I should have introduced you. Kara, meet Charles Cornick, who is visiting from Montana. Charles, meet Kara Mosley, my downstairs neighbor. Now shake and be nice."

She'd meant the admonition for Kara, who could be acerbic if she took a dislike to someone—but Charles raised an eyebrow at her before he turned back to Kara and offered a long-fingered hand.

"From Montana?" asked Kara as she took his hand and shook it firmly once.

He nodded and began French-braiding his hair with quick, practiced motions. "My father sent me out here because he'd heard there was a man giving Anna a bad time."

And with that one statement, Anna knew, he won Kara over completely.

"Justin? You're gonna take care of that rat bastard?" She gave Charles an appraising look. "Now, you're in good shape, don't get me wrong—but Justin is a bad piece of business. I lived in Cabrini-Green until my mama got smart and married her a good man. Those projects, though, they grew a certain sort of predator—the kind that loves violence for its own sake. That Justin, he has dead eyes—sent me back twenty years the first time I saw him. He's hurt people before and liked it. You're not going to frighten him off with just a warning."

The corner of Charles's lip turned up and his eyes warmed, changing his appearance entirely. "Thank you for the heads-up," he told her.

Kara gave him a regal nod. "If I know Anna, there's not an ounce of food to be found in the whole apartment. You need to feed that girl up. There's bagels and cream cheese in those bags on the table—and no, I don't mean to stay. I've got a week's worth of work waiting on me, but I couldn't go without knowing that Anna would eat something."

"I'll see that she does," Charles told her, the small smile still on his face.

Kara reached way up and patted his cheek in a motherly gesture. "Thank you." She gave Anna a quick hug and pulled an envelope out of her pocket and set it on the table next to the bagels. "You take this for watching the cat so I don't have to take him to the kennels with all those dogs he hates and pay them four times this amount. I find it in my cookie jar again, and I'll take him to the kennels just for spite because it will make you feel guilty."

Then she was gone.

Anna waited until the sound of her footsteps reached the next landing, then said, "How did you change so fast?"

"Do you want garlic or blueberry?" Charles asked, opening the bag.

When she didn't answer his question, he put both hands on the table and sighed. "You mean you haven't heard the story of the Marrok and his Indian maiden?" She couldn't read his voice, and his face was tilted away from her so she couldn't read that, either.

"No," she said.

He gave a short laugh, though she didn't think there was any humor behind it. "My mother was beautiful, and it saved her life. She'd been out gathering herbs and surprised a moose. It ran over her and she was dying from it when my father, attracted by the noise, came upon her. He saved my mother's life by turning her into a werewolf."

He took out the bagels and set them on the table with napkins. He sat down and waved her to the other seat. "Start eating and I'll tell you the rest of the story."

He'd given her the blueberry one. She sat opposite him and took a bite.

He gave a satisfied nod and then continued. "It was one of those love at first sight things on both their parts, apparently. Must have been looks, because neither one of them could speak the other's language at first. All was well until she became pregnant. My mother's father was a person of magic and he helped her when she told him that she needed to stay human until I was born. So every month, when my father and brother hunted under the moon, she stayed human. And every moon she grew weaker and weaker. My father argued with her and with her father, worried that she was killing herself."

"Why did she do that?" Anna asked.

Charles frowned at her. "How long have you been a were-wolf?"

"Three years last August."

"Werewolf women can't have children," he said. "The change is too hard on the fetus. They miscarry in the third or fourth month."

Anna stared at him. No one had ever told her that.

"Are you all right?"

She didn't know how to answer him. She hadn't exactly been planning on having children—especially as weird as her life had been for the last few years. She just hadn't planned on *not* having children, either.

"This should have been explained to you before you chose to Change," he said.

It was her turn to laugh. "No one explained anything. No, it's all right. Please tell me the rest of your story."

He watched her for a long moment, then gave her an oddly solemn nod. "Despite my father's protests, she held out until my birth. Weakened by the magic of fighting the moon's call, she did not survive it. I was born a werewolf, not Changed as all the rest are. It gives me a few extra abilities—like being able to change fast."

"That would be nice," she said with feeling.

"It still hurts," he added.

She played with a piece of bagel. "Are you going to look for the missing boy?"

His mouth tightened. "No. We know where Alan Frazier is."

Something in his voice told her. "He's dead?"

He nodded. "There are some good people looking into his death, they'll find out who is responsible. He was Changed without his consent, the girl who was with him was killed. Then he was sold to be used as a laboratory guinea pig. The person responsible will pay for their crimes."

She started to ask him something more, but the door to her apartment flew open and hit the wall behind it, leaving Justin standing in the open doorway.

She'd been so intent on Charles, she hadn't heard Justin coming up the stairs. She'd forgotten to lock her door after Kara left. Not that it would have done her much good. Justin had a key to her apartment.

She couldn't help her flinch as he strode through the door as if he owned the place. "Payday," he said. "You owe me a check." He looked at Charles. "Time for you to go. The lady and I have some business."

Anna couldn't believe that even Justin would take that tone with Charles. She looked at him to gauge his reaction and saw why Justin had put his foot in it.

Charles was fussing with his plate, his eyes on his hands. All his awesome force of personality was bottled up and stuffed somewhere it didn't show.

"I don't think I'd better go," he murmured, still looking down. "She might need my help."

Justin's lip curled. "Where'd you pick this one up, bitch? Wait until I let Leo know you've found a stray and haven't told him about it." He crossed the room and took a handful of her hair. He used it to force her to her feet and up against the wall, shoving her with a hip in a gesture that was both sexual and violent. He leaned his face into hers. "Just you wait. Maybe he'll decide to let me punish you again. I'd like that."

She remembered the last time he'd been allowed to punish her and couldn't suppress her reaction. He enjoyed her panic and was pressed close enough that she could feel it.

"I don't think that she's the one who is going to be punished," Charles said, his voice still soft. But something in Anna loosened. He wouldn't let Justin hurt her.

She couldn't have said why she knew that—she'd certainly found out that just because a wolf wouldn't hurt her didn't mean he would stop anyone else from hurting her.

"I didn't tell you to talk," Justin snarled, his head snapping away from her so he could glare at the other man. "I'll deal with you when I'm finished."

The legs of Charles's chair made a rough sound on the floor as he stood. Anna could hear him dust off his hands lightly.

"I think you are finished here," he said in a completely different voice. "Let her go."

She felt the power of those words go through her bones and warm her stomach, which had been chill with fear. Justin liked to hurt her even more than he desired her unwilling body. She'd fought him until she realized that pleased him even more. She'd learned quickly that there was no way for her to win a struggle between them. He was stronger and faster, and the only time she'd broken away from him, the rest of the pack had held her for him.

At Charles's words, though, Justin released her so quickly that she staggered, though that didn't slow her down as she ran as far away from him as she could get, which was the kitchen. She picked up the marble rolling pin that had been her grandmother's and held it warily.

Justin had his back to her, but Charles saw her weapon and, briefly, his eyes smiled at her before he turned his attention to Justin.

"Who the hell are you?" Justin spat, but Anna heard beyond the anger to fear.

"I could return the question," said Charles. "I have a list of all the werewolves in the Chicago packs and your name is not on it. But that is only part of my business here. Go home and tell Leo that Charles Cornick is here to talk with him. I will meet him at his house at seven this evening. He may bring his first five and his mate, but the rest of his pack will stay away."

To Anna's shock, Justin snarled once, but, with no more protest than that, he left.

TWO

THE WOLF WHO SCARED ANNA SO BADLY HADN'T
wanted to leave, but he wasn't dominant enough to do anything
about it as long as Charles was watching. Which was why Charles
waited a few seconds and then quietly followed him down the stairs.

The next flight down, he found Justin standing in front of a
door, prepared to knock on it. He was pretty sure it was Kara's
door. Somehow it didn't surprise him that Justin would look for
another way to punish Anna for his forced retreat. Charles scuffed
his boot on the stairs and watched the other wolf stiffen and drop
his arm.

"Kara's not home," Charles told him. "And hurting her would
not be advisable."

Charles wondered if he should just kill him now . . . but he had
a reputation that his father couldn't afford for him to lose. He only
killed those who broke the Marrok's rules, and he only did it after
their guilt was established.

Anna had told his father that Justin was the wolf who Changed
Alan MacKenzie Frazier against his will, but since there were so
many things wrong in this pack there might have been mitigating
circumstances. Anna had been a werewolf for three years and no
one had told her that she could not have children. If Anna knew so
little, then it was more than possible that this wolf didn't know the
rules, either.

Whether the wolf was ignorant of his crimes or not, Charles
still wanted to kill him. When Justin turned around to face him,
Charles let his beast peer out of his eyes and watched the other
wolf blanch and start back down the stairs.

"You should find Leo and give him the message," Charles said.
This time he let Justin know that he was following him, let him
feel, a little, the way it was to be prey for a larger predator.

He was tough, this Justin. He kept turning around to confront
Charles—only to meet his eyes and be forced away again. The chase

aroused his wolf; and Charles, still angry at the way Justin had manhandled Anna, let the wolf out just a little more than he should have. It was a fight to stop at the outside door and let Justin go free. The wolf had been given a hunt and it was much, much too short.

Brother Wolf hadn't liked seeing Anna frightened, either. He'd staked his claim and it had taken all of Charles's control not to just kill Justin in Anna's apartment. Only the strong suspicion that she'd go back to being afraid of him had allowed him to stay seated until he was sure he could control himself.

Climbing four flights of stairs should have given him enough time to silence the wolf. It might have, except that Anna was waiting for him, rolling pin in hand, on the landing below her apartment.

He paused halfway up the stairs, and she turned around without a word. He stalked her back to her apartment and into the kitchen area, where she set the rolling pin on its stand—right next to a small pot that held a handful of knives.

"Why the rolling pin and not a knife?" he asked, his voice raspy with the need for action.

She looked at him for the first time since she'd seen his face on the stairs. "A knife wouldn't even slow him down, but bones take time to heal."

He liked that. Who'd have thought he'd get turned on by a woman with a rolling pin? "All right," he said. "All right."

He turned abruptly and left her standing in front of the counter because if he'd stayed there he would have taken her, seduced her. The apartment wasn't large enough either to pace or to get much distance between them. Her scent, blended with fear and arousal, was dangerous. He needed a distraction.

He pulled one of the chairs around and sat on it, leaning back until it was propped on two legs. He folded his arms behind his head and assumed a deliberately relaxed posture, half closed his eyes, and said, "I want you to tell me about your Change." He hadn't missed the clues, he thought, watching her flinch a little. There was something wrong with how she'd been Changed. He focused on that.

"Why?" she asked, challenging him—still caught up in the adrenaline rush of Justin's visit, he imagined. She caught herself and turned away, cringing as if she expected him to explode.

He closed his eyes entirely. Another moment and he was going to put all the gentlemanly behavior his father had taught him aside and take her, willing or not. Oh, that would teach her not to be afraid of him, he thought.

"I need to know how Leo's pack is run," he told her patiently, though at the moment he couldn't have cared less. "I'd rather do that through your impressions first, and then I'll ask you questions. It'll give me a better insight into what he's doing and why."

ANNA GAVE HIM A WARY LOOK, BUT HE HADN'T MOVED. She could still smell the anger in the air, but it might just have been a remnant from when Justin had been there. Charles was aroused, too— and she found herself responding to it, though she knew it was a common result of victorious confrontations among males. He was ignoring it, so she could, too.

She took a deep breath, and his scent filled her lungs.

Clearing her throat, she tried to find the beginning of her story. "I was working in a music store in the Loop when I first met Justin. He told me he was a guitarist like me, and he started coming in a couple of times a week, buying strings, music . . . small-ticket stuff. He'd flirt and tease." She gave an exasperated huff for her foolishness. "I thought he was a nice guy. So when he asked me out for lunch, I said sure."

She looked at Charles, but he looked as though he might have fallen asleep. The muscles in his shoulders were relaxed and his breathing was slow and easy.

"We dated a couple of times. He took me to this little restaurant near a park, one of the forest preserves. When we were finished he took me for a walk in the woods. 'To look at the moon,' he told me." Even now, with the night long over, she could hear the tension in her voice. "He asked me to wait a minute, said he'd be right back."

He'd been excited, she remembered, almost frantic with suppressed emotion. He'd patted his pockets, then said he'd left something in his car. She'd been worried that he had gone to get an engagement ring. She'd practiced gentle ways of saying no while she waited. They had very little in common and no chemistry at all. Though he seemed nice enough, she'd been getting the feeling that there was something a little off about him, too, and her instincts told her that she needed to break it off.

"It took longer than a minute, and I was just about to go back to the car myself when I heard something in the bushes." The skin on her face tingled with fear, just as it had that night.

"You didn't know he was a werewolf?" Charles's voice reminded her that she was safe in her apartment.

"No. I thought that werewolves were just stories."

"Tell me about after the attack."

She didn't need to tell him about how Justin had stalked her for an hour, herding her back from the edge of the preserve every time she came close to getting out. He only wanted to know about Leo's pack. Anna hid her sigh of relief.

"I woke up in Leo's house. He was excited at first. His pack only has one other woman. Then they discovered what I am."

"And what are you, Anna?" His voice was like smoke, she thought, soft and weightless.

"Submissive," she said. "The lowest of the low." And then because his eyes were still closed she added, "Useless."

"Is that what they told you?" he asked thoughtfully.

"It's the truth." She ought to be more upset about it—the

wolves who didn't despise her treated her with pity. But she didn't want to be dominant and have to fight and hurt people.

He didn't say anything so she continued her story, trying to give him all the details she could remember. He asked some questions:

"Who helped you gain control of the wolf?" (No one, she'd done that on her own—another black mark against her that proved she wasn't dominant, they'd told her.)

"Who gave you the Marrok's phone number?" (Leo's third, Boyd Hamilton.)

"When and why?" (Just before Leo's mate stepped in and stopped him from passing Anna around to whatever male he wanted to reward. Anna tried to avoid the higher-ranking wolves—she had no idea why he'd given her that number and no desire to ask.)

"How many new members have come into the pack since you?" (Three, all male—but two of them couldn't control themselves and had had to be killed.)

"How many members of the pack?" (Twenty-six.)

When she finally wound down to a stop she was almost surprised to find herself sitting on the floor across the room from Charles with her back against the wall. Slowly Charles let his chair drop back to the floor and pinched the bridge of his nose. He sighed heavily and then looked at her directly for the first time since she'd begun speaking.

She sucked in her breath at the bright gold of his eyes. He was very near a change forced by some strong emotion—and despite seeing his eyes, she couldn't read it in his body or his scent—he'd managed to mask it from her.

"There are rules. First is that no person may be Changed against their will. Second is that no person may be Changed until they have been counseled and passed a simple test to demonstrate that they understand what that Change means."

She didn't know what to say, but she finally remembered to drop her eyes away from his intense stare.

"From what you've said, Leo is adding new wolves and missing others—he didn't report that to the Marrok. Last year he came to our annual meeting with his mate and his fourth—that Boyd Hamilton—and told us that his second and third were tied up."

Anna frowned at him. "Boyd's been his third for as long as I have been in the pack and Justin is his second."

"You said that there is only one female in the pack besides you?"

"Yes."

"There should have been four."

"No one has mentioned any others," she told him.

He looked over at the check on her fridge.

"They take your paycheck. How much do they give you back?" His voice was bass-deep with the heat of the change behind it.

"Sixty percent."

"Ah." He closed his eyes again and breathed deeply. She could smell the musk of his anger now, though his shoulders still looked relaxed.

When he didn't say anything more, she said quietly, "Is there anything I can do to help? Do you want me to leave or talk or turn on music?" She didn't have a TV, but she still had her old stereo.

His eyes stayed closed but he smiled, just a twitch of his lips. "My control is usually better than this."

She waited, but it seemed to get worse rather than better.

His eyes snapped open and his cold yellow gaze pinned her against the wall where she sat as he uncoiled and prowled across the room.

Her pulse jumped unsteadily and she bowed her head, curling up to be smaller. She felt rather than saw him crouch in front of her. His hands when they cupped her face were so hot she flinched—and regretted it when he growled.

He dropped to his knees, nuzzling against her neck, then rested his body, now taut as iron, against hers, trapping her between him and the wall. He put his hands on the wall, one to each side of her, and then quit moving. His breath was hot on her neck.

She sat as still as she could, terrified of doing anything that might break his control. But there was something about him that kept her from being truly scared, something that insisted he wouldn't hurt her. That he never would hurt her.

Which was stupid. All the dominants hurt those beneath them. She'd had that beaten into her more than once. Just because she could heal quickly didn't make getting hurt pleasant. But no matter how much she told herself she ought to be frightened of him, a dominant among dominants, a strange man she'd never seen before last night (or, more accurately, very early this morning), she couldn't be.

Though he smelled of anger, he also smelled like spring rain, wolf, and man. She closed her eyes and quit fighting, letting the sweet-sharpness of his scent wash away the fear and anger aroused by telling this man about the worst thing that ever happened to her.

As soon as she relaxed he did as well. His rigid muscles loosened and his imprisoning arms slid down the wall to rest lightly on her shoulders.

After a while, he pulled away slowly, but stayed crouched so his head was only slightly higher than hers. He put a gentle thumb under her chin and raised her head until she gazed into his dark eyes. She had the sudden feeling that if she could look into those eyes for the rest of her life, she would be happy. It scared her a lot more than his anger had.

"Are you doing something to me to make me feel like this?" She asked the question before she had time to censor herself.

He didn't ask her how he made her feel. Instead, he tilted his head, a wolflike gesture, but kept eye contact, though there was no challenge in his scent. Instead, she had the impression he was almost as bewildered as she was. "I don't think so. Certainly not on purpose."

He cupped her face in both of his hands. They were large hands, and callused, and they trembled just a little. He bent down until his chin rested on the top of her head. "I've never felt this way before, either."

HE COULD HAVE STAYED THERE FOREVER, DESPITE THE discomfort of kneeling on the hardwood floor. He'd never felt anything like this—certainly not with a woman he'd known less than twenty-four hours. He didn't know how to deal with it, didn't want to deal with it, and—most unlike himself—was willing to put off dealing with it indefinitely as long as he could spend the time with her body against his.

Of course there was something he'd rather do, but if he wasn't mistaken there was someone else coming up the stairs. Four flights of stairs were, evidently, not enough to keep intruders away. He closed his eyes and let his wolf-brother sort through the scents and identify their newest visitor.

There was a knock at the door.

Anna jerked back out of his hold, sucking in her breath. Part of him was pleased that he'd managed to distract her so much that she hadn't noticed anything until then. Part of him worried at her vulnerability.

Reluctantly, he stood up and put a little distance between them. "Come in, Isabelle."

The door opened and Leo's mate stuck her head in. She took a good look at Anna and grinned mischievously. "Interrupting something interesting?"

He'd always liked Isabelle, though he'd tried hard not to show it. As his father's executioner, he'd long ago learned not to get close to anyone he might someday have to kill—which made his circle of friends very small: his father and his brother for the most part.

Anna stood up and returned Isabelle's smile with a shy one of her own, though he could tell she was still shaken. To his surprise, though, she said, "Yes. There was something very interesting going on. Come in anyway."

Once the invitation had been issued, Isabelle blew in like the March wind, as she usually did, simultaneously shutting the door and holding out a hand to Charles. "Charles, it is so good to see you."

He took her hand and bowed over it, kissing it lightly. It smelled of cinnamon and cloves. He'd forgotten that about her, that she used perfume with an eye toward the sharpness of werewolf senses. Just strong enough to mask herself and so give her some protection from the sharp noses of her fellow wolves. Unless she was extremely agitated, no one could tell how she felt from her scent.

"You look beautiful," he said, as he knew she expected. It was true enough.

"I should be looking a nervous wreck," she said, running the hand Charles had kissed through her airy, feathery-cut hair that, combined with her fine features, made her look like a fairy princess. She was shorter than Anna and finer-boned, but Charles had never made the mistake of thinking of her as fragile. "Justin came boiling in with some nonsense about a meeting tonight. He was all but incoherent—why did you enrage the boy like that?—and I told Leo I'd drop by to see what you were doing."

This was why he didn't make friends.

"Leo received my message?" Charles asked.

She nodded. "And looked quite frightened, which is not a good look for him, as I told him." She leaned forward and put a too-familiar hand on his arm. "What has brought you to our territory, Charles?"

He stepped back. He didn't much like to touch or be touched—though he seemed to have largely forgotten that while he was around Anna.

His Anna.

Forcefully he brought his attention back to business. "I have come to meet with Leo tonight."

Isabelle's usually cheerful face hardened, and he waited for her to blow up at him. Isabelle was as famous for her temper as she was for her charisma. She was one of the few people to blow up in the Marrok's face and get away with it—Charles's father liked Isabelle, too.

But she didn't say anything more to him. Instead she turned her head to glance at Anna, whom, he suddenly realized, she'd been pointedly ignoring up to that point. When she returned her gaze to Charles, she began speaking, but not to him.

"What tales have you been carrying, Anna, my dear? Complaining about your place in the pack? Choose a mate, if you don't like it. I've told you that before. Justin would take you, I'm sure." There was no venom in her voice. Maybe if Charles hadn't already met Justin, he'd have missed the way Anna's face paled. Maybe he wouldn't have heard the threat.

Anna didn't say anything.

Isabelle continued to stare at Charles, though she was careful to keep from meeting his eyes. He thought she was studying his reactions, but he knew that his face gave nothing away—he'd been prepared for the way his Brother Wolf surged up in anger to defend Anna this time.

"Are you sleeping with him?" Isabelle asked. "He's a good lover, isn't he?"

Though Isabelle was mated, she had a wandering eye and Leo let her indulge herself as she pleased, a situation almost unique among werewolves. That didn't mean *she* wasn't jealous; Leo couldn't so much as look at another woman. Charles always felt it was an odd relationship, but it had worked for them for a long time. When she'd made a play for him a few years ago, he'd allowed himself to be caught, knowing that there was nothing serious about her offer. He hadn't been surprised when she'd tried to get him to talk his father into letting Leo expand his territory. She had taken his refusal in good humor, though.

The sex had meant nothing to either of them—but it meant

something to Anna. He'd have had to be human to miss the hurt and mistrust in her eyes at Isabelle's thrust.

"Play nicely, Isabelle," he told her, abruptly impatient. He put a little force in his voice as he said, "Go home and tell Leo I'll talk to him tonight."

Her eyes lit with rage and she drew herself up.

"I am not my father," he said softly. "You don't want to try the shrew act with me."

Fear cooled her temper—and his, too, for that matter. Her perfume might have hidden her scent, but it didn't hide her eyes or her clenched hands. He didn't enjoy frightening people—not usually.

"Go home, Isabelle. You'll have to swallow your curiosity until then."

He shut the door gently behind her and stared at it for a moment, reluctant to face Anna—though he had no idea why he should feel so guilty for doing something long before he'd ever met her.

"Are you going to kill her?"

He looked at Anna then, unable to tell what she thought about it. "I don't know."

Anna bit her lip. "She has been kind to me."

Kind? As far as he could tell kindness had been pretty far from anything that had happened to Anna since her Change. But the worry in her face had him swallowing his sharp reply.

"There is something odd going on in Leo's pack," was all he said. "I'll find out exactly what it is tonight."

"How?"

"I'll ask them," he told her. "They know better than to think they can lie to me—and refusal to answer my questions, or refusal to meet with me, is admitting guilt."

She looked puzzled. "Why couldn't they lie to you?"

He tapped a finger on her nose. "Smelling a lie is pretty easy, unless you are dealing with someone who cannot tell truth from lie, but there are other ways to detect them."

Her stomach growled.

"Enough of this," he said, deciding it was time to feed her up a little. A bagel was not enough. "Get your coat."

He didn't want to take the car into the Loop, where it would be difficult to find parking, because his temper was too uncertain around her. He couldn't talk her into a taxi, which was a new experience for him—not many people refused to listen when he told them what to do. But then, she was an Omega, and not constrained by an instinctive need to obey a more dominant wolf. With an inward sigh, he followed her down a few blocks to the nearest L station.

He'd never been on Chicago's elevated train before, and, if it weren't for a certain stubborn woman, he wouldn't have ridden one this time. Though he admitted, if only to himself, that he rather enjoyed it when a rowdy group of thugs disguised as teenagers decided to give him a bad time.

"Hey, Injun Joe," said a baggy-clothed boy. "You a stranger in town? That's a foxy lady you have there. If she likes her meat brown, there's plenty here to go 'round." He tapped himself on his chest.

There were real gangs in Chicago, raised in the eat-or-be-eaten world of the inner city. But these boys were imitators, probably out of school for the holidays and bored. So they decided to entertain themselves by scaring the adults who couldn't differentiate between amateurs and the real deal. Not that a pack of boys couldn't be dangerous under the wrong circumstances . . .

An old woman sitting next to them shrank back, and the smell of her fear washed away his tolerance.

Charles got to his feet, smiled, and watched their smugness evaporate at his confidence. "She's foxy, all right," he said. "But she belongs to me."

"Hey, man," said the boy just behind the one who had spoken. "No hard feelings, man."

He let his smile widen and watched them shuffle backward.

"It's a nice day. I think that you should go sit in those empty seats up there where you see your way more clearly."

They scuttled to the front of the car and, after they had all taken a seat, Charles sat back down next to Anna.

THERE WAS SUCH SATISFACTION IN HIS FACE WHEN HE sat down that Anna had to suppress a grin for fear that one of the boys would look back and think she was laughing at one of them.

"That was a prime example of testosterone poisoning," she observed dryly. "Are you going to go after Girl Scouts next?"

Charles's eyes glinted with amusement. "Now they know that they need to pick their prey more cautiously."

Anna seldom traveled to the Loop anymore—everything she needed she could find closer to home. He evidently knew it better than she did, despite being a visitor. He chose the stop they got off at and took her directly to a little Greek place tucked in the shadow of the L train tracks, where they greeted him by name and took him to a private room with only one table.

He let her give her order and then doubled it, adding a few dishes on the side.

While they were waiting for their food, he took a small, worn-looking, leather-bound three-ring notebook from his jacket pocket. He popped the rings and took out a couple of sheets of lined paper and handed them to her with a pen.

"I'd like you to write down the names of the members of your pack. It would help if you list them from the most dominant and go to the least."

She tried. She didn't know everyone's last name and, since everyone outranked her, she hadn't paid strict attention to rank.

She handed the paper and pen back to him with a frown. "I'm forgetting people, and other than the top four or five wolves, I could be mistaken on rank."

He set her pages down on the table and then took out a couple of sheets with writing already on them and compared the two lists, marking them up. Anna took her chair and scooted it around the table until she sat next to him and could see what he was doing.

He took his list and set it before her. "These are the people who should be in your pack. I've checked the names of the ones who don't appear on your list."

She scanned down it, then grabbed the pen back and marked out one of his checks. "He's still here. I just forgot about him. And this one, too."

He took the list back. "All the women are gone. Most of the rest who are missing are older wolves. Not *old*. But there's not a wolf left who is older than Leo. There are a few younger wolves missing as well." He tapped a finger on a couple of names. "These were young. Paul Lebshak, here, would have been only four years a werewolf. George not much older."

"Do you know all the werewolves?"

He smiled. "I know the Alphas. We have yearly meetings with all of them. I know most of the seconds and thirds. One of the things we do at the meetings is update the pack memberships. The Alphas are supposed to keep the Marrok informed when people die, or when new wolves are Changed. If my father had known so many wolves were gone, he would have investigated. Though Leo's lost a third of the pack membership, he's done a fair job of replacing them."

He gave back the list she'd written—a number of names, including hers, were also checked. "These are all new. From what you've told me, I'd guess that they are all forced Changes. The survival rate of random attack victims is very poor. Your Leo has killed a lot of people over the past few years in order to keep the number of his pack where it is. Enough that it should have attracted the attention of the authorities. How many of these people were made wolves after you?"

"None of them. The only new wolf I've seen was that poor boy." She tapped the paper with her pen. "If they didn't leave bodies and spread out the hunt, they could have easily hidden the dis-appearance of a hundred people in the greater Chicago area over a few years."

He leaned back and closed his eyes, then he shook his head. "I don't remember dates too well anymore. I haven't met most of the missing wolves, and I don't remember the last time I saw Leo's old second except that it was within the last ten years. So whatever happened was after that."

"Whatever happened to what?"

"To Leo, I'd guess. Something happened that made him kill all the women in his pack except Isabelle and most of his older wolves—the wolves who would have objected when he started attacking innocent people, or quit teaching new wolves the rules and rights that belong to them. I can see why he'd have to kill *them*—but why the women? And why didn't the other Chicago Alpha say anything to my father when it happened?"

"He might not have known. Leo and Jaimie stay away from each other, and our pack is not allowed to go into Jaimie's territory at all. The Loop is neutral territory, but we can't go north of here unless we get special permission."

"Oh? Interesting. Have you heard anything about why they aren't getting along?"

She shrugged. There had been a lot of talk. "Someone told me that Jaimie wouldn't sleep with Isabelle. Someone else said that they had an affair and he broke it off, and she was insulted. Or that he wouldn't break it off and Leo had to step in. Another story is that Jaimie and Leo never got along. I don't know."

She looked at the checks that marked the newer wolves in her pack and suddenly laughed.

"What?"

"It's just stupid." She shook her head.

"Tell me."

Her cheeks flushed with embarrassment. "Fine. You were look-ing for something that all the newer wolves had in common. I was just thinking that if someone wanted to list the most handsome men in the pack, they would all make the cut."

Both of them were surprised by the flash of territorial jealousy that he didn't bother to hide from her.

It was probably a good time for the waiter to come in with the first course of food.

Anna started to move her chair back to where it had been, but the waiter sat his tray down and took it from her, seating her properly before he got back to setting out the dishes.

"And how have you been, sir?" he said to Charles. "Still haven't given up and moved to civilization?"

"Civilization is vastly overrated," Charles returned as he put the sheets of paper into his notebook and shut the cover. "As long as I can come up once or twice a year and eat here, I am content."

The waiter shook his head with mock sadness. "Mountains are beautiful, but not as beautiful as our skyline. One of these days I'll take you out for a night on the town and you'll never leave again."

"Phillip!" A bird-thin woman stepped into the room. "While you are here chatting with Mr. Cornick, our other guests are going hungry."

The waiter grinned and winked at Anna. He dropped a kiss on the woman's cheek and slipped through the door.

The woman suppressed a smile and shook her head. "That one. Always talking. He needs a good wife to keep him in line. I am too old." She threw up her hands and then followed the waiter.

The next twenty minutes brought a series of waiters and waitresses who all looked as though they were related. They carried food on trays and never said anything about it being odd that two people should eat so much food.

Charles filled his plate, looked at hers, and said, "You should have told me you didn't like lamb."

She looked at her plate. "I do."

He frowned at her, took the serving spoon, and added to the amount on her plate. "You should be eating more. A lot more. The change requires a lot of energy. You have to eat more as a werewolf to maintain your weight."

After that, by mutual consent Anna and Charles confined their conversations to generalities. They talked about Chicago and city living. She took a little of a rice dish and he looked at her until she took a second spoonful. He told her a little about Montana. She found he was very well spoken and the easiest way to stop a conversation cold was to ask him about anything personal. It wasn't that he didn't want to talk about himself, she thought, it was that he didn't find himself very interesting.

The door swung open one last time, and a girl of about fourteen came in with dessert.

"Aren't you supposed to be in school?" Charles asked her.

She sighed. "Vacation. Everyone else gets time off. But me? I get to work in the restaurant. It sucks."

"I see," he said. "Perhaps you should call child welfare and tell them you're being abused?"

She grinned at him. "Wouldn't that get Papa riled up. I'm tempted to do it just to see his face. If I told him it was your suggestion, do ya suppose he'd get mad at you instead of me?" She wrinkled her nose. "Probably not."

"Tell your mother that the food was perfect."

She braced the empty tray on her hip and backed out the door. "I'll tell her, but she already told me to tell you that it wasn't. The lamb was a little stringy, but that's all she could get."

"I gather you come here often," Anna said, unenthusiastically picking at a huge piece of baklava. Not that she had anything against baklava—as long as she hadn't eaten a week's worth of food first.

"Too often," he said. *He* was having no trouble eating more, she noticed. "We have some business interests here, so I have to come three or four times a year. The owner of the restaurant is a wolf, one of Jaimie's. I sometimes find it convenient to discuss business here."

"I thought you were your father's hit man," she said with interest. "You have to hunt down people in Chicago three or four times a year?"

He laughed out loud. The sound was rusty, as if he didn't do it very often—though he ought to, it looked good on him. Good enough that she ate the forkful of baklava she'd been playing with and then had to figure out how to swallow it when her stomach was telling her that it didn't need any more food sent its way.

"No, I have other duties as well. I take care of my father's pack's business interests. I am very good at both of my jobs," he said without any hint of modesty.

"I bet you are." He was a person who would be very good at whatever he decided to do. "I'd let you invest my savings. I think I have twenty-two dollars and ninety-seven cents right now."

He frowned at her, all amusement gone.

"It was a joke," she explained.

But he ignored her. "Most Alphas have their members give ten percent of their earnings for the good of the pack, especially when the pack is new. This money is used to ensure there is a safe house, for instance. Once a pack is firmly established, though, the need for money lessens. My father's pack has been established for a long time—there is no need for a tithe because we own the land we live on and there are investments enough for the future. Leo has been here for thirty years: time enough to be well established. I've never heard of a pack demanding forty percent from its members—which leads me to believe that Leo's pack is in financial trouble. He sold that young man you called my father about, and several others like him, to someone who was using them to develop a way to make drugs work on us as well as they work on humans. He had to kill a number of humans in order to get a single survivor werewolf."

She thought about the implications. "Who wanted the drugs?"

"I'll know that when Leo tells me who he sold the boy to."

"So why didn't he sell me?" She wasn't worth much to the pack.

He leaned back in his chair. "If an Alpha sold one of his pack, he'd have a rebellion on his hands. Besides, Leo went to a lot of trouble to get you. There haven't been any pack members killed or gone missing since you became a member."

It wasn't a question, but she answered him anyway. "No."

"I think maybe you are the key to Leo's mystery."

She couldn't help a snort of derision. "Me? Leo needed a new doormat?"

He leaned suddenly forward, knocking his chair over as he swept her off of her own and stood her on her feet. She'd thought she was used to the speed and strength of the wolves, but he stole her breath.

As she stood still and shocked, he prowled around her until he came back around the front and kissed her, a long, dark, deep kiss that left her breathless for another reason entirely.

"Leo found you and decided that he needed you," he told her. "He sent Justin after you, because any of his other wolves would know what you were. Even before your Change, they'd have known. So he sent a half-crazy wolf because any other would have been unable to attack you."

Hurt, she flinched away from him. He made her sound special, but she knew he was lying. He sounded like he was telling the truth, but she was no prize. She was nothing. For three years she had been nothing. He had made her feel special today, but she knew better.

His hands, when they came down on her shoulders, were hard and impossible to resist. "Let me tell you something about Omega wolves, Anna. *Look* at me."

She blinked back tears, and, unable to resist his command, raised her eyes to glare at him.

"Almost unique," he said and gave her a little shake. "I work with numbers and percentages all the time, Anna. I might not be able to figure the odds exactly, but I'll tell you that the chances that Justin picked you out to Change by sheer chance are almost infinitesimal. No werewolf, acting on instincts alone, would attack an

Omega. And Justin strikes me as a wolf who acts on very little else."

"Why not? Why wouldn't he have attacked me? And what is an Omega?"

It was evidently the right question because Charles stilled, his former agitation gone. "You are an Omega, Anna. I bet that when you walk into a room, people come to you. I bet complete strangers tell you things they wouldn't tell their own mothers."

Incredulous, she stared at him. "You saw Justin this morning. Did he look calm to you?"

"I saw Justin," he agreed slowly. "And I think that in any other pack he would have been killed shortly after he was made because his control is not good enough. I don't know why he was not. But I think you allow him to control his wolf—and he hates you for it.

"You should not be ranked last in your pack." His hands slid down her shoulders until he held her hands. Oddly that felt more intimate than his kiss had. "An Omega wolf is like the Indian medicine men, outside of the normal pack rankings. They had to teach you to lower your eyes, didn't they? To submissive wolves, such things are instinctive. You, they had to beat down.

"You bring peace to all those around you, Anna," he said intently, his eyes on hers. "A werewolf, especially a dominant wolf, is always on the edge of violence. After being shut in an aircraft with too many people for hours, I came into the airport craving bloodshed like a junkie craves his next fix. But when you came up to me, the anger, the hunger left."

He squeezed her hands. "You are a gift, Anna. An Omega wolf in the pack means that more wolves survive the Change from human to wolf because they can find control easier with you there. It means that we lose fewer males to stupid dominance fights because an Omega brings a calmness to all those around him. Or her."

There was a hole in his argument. "But what about earlier, when you almost changed because you were so angry?"

Something happened to his face, an emotion she didn't know him well enough to read, except to know that it was strong.

When he spoke it was with visible effort, as if his throat had tightened. "Most werewolves find someone they love, get married, and spend a long time with their spouse before the wolf accepts her as his mate." He dropped her gaze and turned away, walking across the room and giving her his back.

Without the warmth of his body, she felt cold and alone. Scared.

"Sometimes it doesn't happen that way," he told the wall. "Let it rest there, for now, Anna. You have been through enough without this."

"I am so tired of being ignorant," she spat, suddenly hugely angry. "You've changed all the rules on me—so you can *damned* well tell me what the new rules are." As abruptly as the anger had come, it was gone, leaving her shaky and on the verge of tears.

He turned and his eyes had gone gold, reflecting the dim light of the room until they glowed. "Fine. You should have let it be, but you want truth." His voice rumbled like thunder, though it wasn't very loud. "My Brother Wolf has taken you for his mate. Even if you were *nothing* to me, I would have never allowed such abuse as you have suffered since your Change. But you are mine, and the thought of you hurt, of being able to do nothing about it, is an anger that even an Omega wolf cannot easily soothe."

Well, she thought, stunned. She'd known he was interested in her, but she'd assumed it had been a casual thing. Leo was the only mated wolf she knew. She didn't know any of the rules. What did it mean that he said his wolf had decided she was his mate? Did she have a choice in the matter? Did the way he aroused her without trying, the way he made her feel—as if she'd known him forever and wanted to wake up next to him for the rest of her life, though she'd known him only hours, really—was that his fault?

"If you had let me," he said, "I'd have courted you gently and won your heart." He closed his eyes. "I didn't mean to frighten you."

She should have been frightened. Instead, suddenly, she felt very, very calm, like the eye in a hurricane of emotion.

"I don't like sex," she told him, because it seemed like something he ought to know under the circumstances.

He choked and opened his eyes, their bright color giving way to human dark as she watched.

"I wasn't enthusiastic before the Change," she told him plainly. "And after being passed around like a whore for a year, until Isabelle put a stop to it, I like it even less."

His mouth tightened, but he didn't say anything, so she continued. "And I won't be forced. Never again." She pulled up the sleeves of her shirt to show him the long scars on the underside of her arm, wrist to elbow. She'd made them with a silver knife, and if Isabelle hadn't found her, she'd have killed herself. "This is why Isabelle made Leo stop making me sleep with whatever male pleased him enough. She found me and kept me alive. After that I bought a gun and silver bullets."

He growled softly, but not at her, she was pretty sure.

"I'm not threatening to kill myself. But you need to know this about me because—if you want to be my mate—I won't be like Leo. I won't let you sleep around with anyone else. I won't be forced, either. I've had enough. If that makes me a dog in the manger, so be it. But if I am yours, then you *damned* well are going to be mine."

"A dog in the manger?" He let out a gusty breath of air that might have been a half laugh. He closed his eyes again and said in a reasonable tone, "If Leo survives tonight, I shall be very surprised. If I survive you, I'll be equally surprised." He looked at her. "And very little surprises me anymore."

He strode across the floor, picking up his chair and setting it where it belonged as he passed it. He stopped just in front of her and touched her raised chin gently, then laughed. Still smiling, he tucked a piece of her hair behind her ear. "I promise you will enjoy sex with me," he murmured.

Somehow she managed to keep her spine straight. She wasn't ready to fall into a puddle at his feet quite yet. "Isabelle said you were a good lover."

He laughed again. "You have no need for jealousy. Sex with Isabelle meant no more to me than a good belly scratch and rather less to her, I think. Nothing worth repeating for either of us." There was a whisper of sound outside the room and he took her hand. "Time for us to go."

He paid polite compliments to the meal as he handed over a credit card to a young-looking man who called him "sir" and smelled of werewolf. The owner of the restaurant, Anna supposed.

"So where would you like to go next?" she asked as she stepped out onto the busy sidewalk.

He pulled his jacket on the rest of the way and dodged a woman in high heels who carried a leather briefcase. "Somewhere with fewer people."

"We could go to the zoo," she suggested. "This time of year it's pretty deserted, even with the kids out of school for Thanksgiving."

He turned his head and started to speak when something in a window caught his attention. He grabbed her and threw her on the ground, falling on top of her. There was a loud bang, like a backfiring car, and he jerked once, then lay still on top of her.

THREE

IT HAD BEEN A LONG TIME SINCE HE'D BEEN SHOT, BUT the sizzling burn of the silver bullet was still familiar. He hadn't been quite fast enough—and the crowd of people made sure that he couldn't go after the car that had taken off as soon as the gun had fired. He hadn't even gotten a good look at the shooter, just an impression.

"Charles?" Beneath him, Anna's eyes were black with shock and she patted his shoulders. "Was someone shooting at us? Are you all right?"

"Yes," he said, though he couldn't really assess the damage until he moved, which he didn't want to much.

"Stay where you are until I can get a look," said a firm voice. "I'm an EMT."

The command in the EMT's voice forced Charles to move—he didn't take orders from anyone except his father. He pushed himself off of Anna and got to his feet, then leaned down and grabbed her hand to pull her up from the frozen sidewalk.

"Damn it, man, you're bleeding. Don't be stupid," snapped the stranger. "Sit down."

Being shot had enraged the wolf in him, and Charles turned to snarl at the EMT, a competent-looking middle-aged man with sandy hair and a graying red moustache.

Then Anna squeezed his hand, which she still held, and said, "Thank you," to the EMT and then to Charles, "Let him take a look"—and he was able to hold back the snarl.

He did growl low in his throat, though, when the stranger looked at his wound: never show weakness to a possible enemy. He felt too exposed on the sidewalk; too many people were looking at him—they had acquired quite an audience.

"Ignore him," Anna told the EMT. "He gets grumpy when he's hurt."

George, the werewolf who owned the restaurant, brought out a chair for him to sit on. Someone had called the police; two cars came with flashing lights and sirens that hurt his ears, followed by an ambulance.

The bullet had cut through skin and a fine layer of muscle across the back of his shoulders without doing a lot of damage, he was told. Did he have any enemies? It was Anna who told them that he'd just flown in from Montana, that it must have been just a drive-by shooting, though this wasn't the usual neighborhood for that kind of crime.

If the cop had had a werewolf's nose, he would never have let her lie pass. He was a seasoned cop, however, and her answer made him a little uneasy. But when Charles showed him his Montana driver's license, he relaxed.

Anna's presence allowed Charles to submit to cleaning and bandaging and questioning, but nothing would make him get into an ambulance and be dragged to a hospital, even though silver-bullet wounds healed human-slow. Even now he could feel the hot ache of the silver as it seeped into his muscles.

While he sat beneath the hands of strangers and fought not to lose control, he couldn't get the image of the shooter out of his head. He'd looked in the window and saw the reflection of the gun, then the face of the person who held it, wrapped in a winter scarf and wearing dark glasses. Not enough to identify the gunman, just a glimpse—but he would swear that the man had not been looking at him when his gloved finger pulled the trigger. He'd been looking at Anna.

Which didn't make much sense. Why would someone be trying to kill Anna?

They didn't go to the zoo.

While he used the restaurant bathroom to clean up, George procured a jacket to cover the bandages so Charles wouldn't have to advertise his weakness to everyone who saw him. This time Anna didn't object when he asked her to call a taxi.

His phone rang on the way back to Anna's apartment, but he silenced it without looking at it. It might have been his father, Bran, who had an uncanny knack for knowing when he'd been hurt. But he had no desire to talk with the Marrok while the taxi driver could hear every word. More probably it was Jaimie. George would have called his Alpha as soon as Charles was shot. In either case, they would wait until he was someplace more private.

He made Anna wait in the taxi when they got to her apartment building until he had a chance to take a good look around. No one had followed them from the Loop, but the most likely assailants were Leo's people—and they all knew where Anna lived. He hadn't recognized the shooter, but then he didn't know every werewolf in Chicago.

Anna was patient with him. She didn't argue about waiting but the cabdriver looked at him as though he were crazy.

Her patience helped his control—which was shakier than it had been in a long time. He wondered how he'd be behaving if his Anna hadn't been an Omega whose soothing effect was almost good enough to override the protective rage roused by the attempt on her life. The painful burn of his shoulders, worsening as silver-caused wounds always did for a while, didn't help his temperament, nor did the knowledge that his ability to fight was impaired.

Someone was trying to kill Anna. It didn't make sense, but somewhere during the trip back to Oak Park, he'd accepted that it was so.

Satisfied there was no immediate threat in or around the apartment building, he held out his hand to Anna to help her out of the taxi and then paid the fare, all the while letting his eyes roam, looking for anything out of place. But there was nothing.

Just inside the front door of the lobby, a man who was getting his mail smiled and greeted Anna. They exchanged a sentence or two, but after a good look at Charles's face, she started up the stairs.

Charles had not been able to parse a word she'd said, which was a very bad sign. Grimly he followed her up the stairs, shoulders throbbing with the beat of his heart. He flexed his fingers as she unlocked her door. His joints ached with the need to change, but he held off—only just. If he was this bad in human form, the wolf would be in control if he shifted.

He sat on the futon and watched her open her fridge and then her freezer. Finally she dug in the depths of a cabinet and came out with a large can. She opened it and dumped the unappealing contents into a pot, which she set on the stove.

Then she knelt on the floor in front of him. She touched his face and said, very clearly, "Change," and a number of other things that brushed by his ears like a flight of butterflies.

He closed his eyes against her.

There was some urgent reason he shouldn't change, but he'd forgotten it while he'd been watching her.

"You have five hours before the meeting," she said slowly, her voice making more sense once his eyes were shut. "If you can change to the wolf and back, it will help you heal."

"I have no control," he told her. That was it. That was the reason. "The wound's not that bad—it's the silver. My changing will be too dangerous for you. I can't."

There was a pause and then she said, "If I am your mate, your wolf won't harm me no matter how much control you lack, right?" She sounded more hopeful than certain, and he couldn't think clearly enough to know if she was correct.

DOMINANTS WERE TOUCHY ABOUT TAKING SUGGESTIONS from lesser wolves, so she left Charles to make up his own mind while she stirred the beef stew to keep it from burning. Not that burning would make it taste any worse. She'd bought it on sale about six months ago, and had never been hungry enough to eat it. But it had protein, which he needed after being wounded, and it was the only meat in the house.

The wound had looked painful, but not unmanageable to her, and none of the EMTs had seemed overly concerned.

She took the metal ball out of the pocket of her jeans and felt it burn her skin. While the EMTs had been working on his back, Charles had caught her eye and then looked at the small, bloody slug on the sidewalk.

At his silent direction, she'd pocketed it. Now she set it on her

counter. Silver was bad. It meant that it really hadn't been a random shooting. She hadn't seen who fired the shot, but she could
only assume that it had been one of her pack mates, probably
Justin.

Silver injuries wouldn't heal in minutes or hours, and Charles
would have to go wounded to Leo's house.

Claws clicked on the hardwood floor and the fox-colored wolf
who was Charles walked over and collapsed on the floor, near
enough to rest his head on one of her feet. There were bits and
pieces of torn cloth caught here and there on his body. A glance at
the futon told her he hadn't bothered to strip out of his clothes,
and the bandages hadn't survived the change. The cut across his
shoulder blades was deep and oozing blood.

He seemed more weary than wild and ravenous, though, so she
assumed his fears about how much control he'd have had not been
borne out. An out-of-control werewolf, in her experience, would
be growling and pacing, not lying quietly at her feet. She put the
stew in a bowl and set it in front of him.

He took a bite and then paused after the first mouthful.

"I know," she told him apologetically, "it's not haute cuisine. I
could go downstairs and see if Kara has any steaks or roasts I
could borrow."

He went back to eating, but she knew from healing her own
wounds that he'd be better off with more meat. Kara wouldn't be
home, but Anna had a key, and she knew Kara wouldn't mind if
she borrowed a roast as long as she replaced it.

Charles seemed to be engrossed in his meal so she started for
the door. Before she was halfway there, he'd abandoned the food
and stalked at her heels. It hurt him to move—she wasn't quite
sure how she knew that, since he neither limped nor slowed visibly.

"You need to stay here," she told him. "I'll be right back."

But when she tried to open the door, he stepped in front of it.

"Charles," she said and then she saw his eyes and swallowed
hard. There was nothing of Charles left in the wolf's yellow gaze.

Leaving the apartment wasn't an option.

She walked back to the kitchen and stopped by the food bowl she'd left him. He stayed at the door for a moment before following her. When he had finished eating she sat down on the futon. He jumped up beside her, put his head in her lap, and closed his eyes with a heavy sigh.

He opened one eye and then closed it again. She ran her fingers through his pelt, carefully avoiding the wound.

Were they mated? She thought not. Wouldn't something like that have a more formal ceremony? She hadn't actually told him that she accepted him—no more than he had really asked her.

Still . . . she closed her eyes and let his scent flow through her and her hand closed possessively in a handful of fur. When she opened her eyes, she found herself staring into his clear gold ones.

His phone rang from somewhere underneath her. She reached down to the floor and snagged the remnant of his pants and pulled the phone out and checked the number. She turned it so he could see the display.

"It says 'father,'" she told him. But evidently the wolf was still in control, because he didn't even look at the phone. "I guess you can call him back when you're back to yourself." She hoped that would be soon. Even with silver poisoning, he ought to be better in a few hours, she hoped.

The phone quit ringing for a moment. Then started again. It rang three times. Stopped. Then rang three more times. Stopped. When it rang again she answered it reluctantly.

"Hello?"

"Is he all right?"

She remembered the werewolf who had brought out a chair for Charles to sit on while the EMTs worked on him. He must have called the Marrok.

"I think so. The wound wasn't so bad, pretty much a deep cut across his shoulder blades, but the bullet was silver and he seems to be having a bad reaction to it."

There was a little pause. "Can I speak to him?"

"He's in wolf form," she told him, "but he is listening to you now." One of his ears was cocked toward the phone.

"Do you need help with Charles? His reaction to silver can be a little extreme."

"No. He's not causing any problems."

"Silver leaves Charles's wolf uncontrolled," crooned the Marrok softly. "But he's giving you no problems? Why would that be?"

She'd never met the Marrok, but she wasn't dumb. That croon was dangerous. Did he think she had something to do with Charles being shot and was now holding him prisoner somewhere? She tried to answer his question, despite the possible embarrassment.

"Um. Charles thinks that his wolf has chosen me as a mate."

"In less than one full day?" It did sound dumb when he said it that way.

"Yes." She couldn't keep the uncertainty out of her voice, though, and it bothered Charles. He rolled to his feet and growled softly.

"Charles also said I was an Omega wolf," she told his father. "That might have something to do with it as well."

Silence lengthened and she began to think that the cell phone might have dropped the connection. Then the Marrok laughed softly. "Oh, his brother is going to tease him unmercifully about this. Why don't you tell me everything that has happened. Start with picking Charles up at the airport, please."

HER KNUCKLES WERE WHITE ON THE STEERING WHEEL, but Charles was in no mood to ease Anna's fears.

He'd tried to leave her behind. He had no desire to have Anna in the middle of the fight that was probable tonight. He didn't want her hurt—and he didn't want her to see him in the role that had been chosen for him so long ago.

"I know where Leo lives," she told him. "If you don't take me with you, I'll just hire a taxi and follow you. You are not going in there alone. You still smell of your wounds—and they'll take that as a sign of weakness."

The truth of her words had almost made him cruel. It had been on the tip of his tongue to ask her what she thought she, an Omega female, could do to help him in a fight—but his Brother Wolf had frozen his tongue. She had been wounded enough, and the wolf wouldn't allow any more. It was the only time he could ever remember that the wolf put the restraints on his human half rather than the reverse. The words would have been wrong, too. He remembered her holding that marble rolling pin. She might not be aggressive, but she had a limit to how far she could be pushed.

He found himself meekly agreeing to her company, though as they got closer to Leo's house in Naperville, his repentance hadn't been up to making him happy with her presence.

"Leo's house is on fifteen acres," she told him. "Big enough for the pack to hunt on, but we still have to be pretty quiet."

Her voice was tight. He thought she was trying to make conversation with him to keep her anxiety in check. Angry as he was, he couldn't help but come to her aid.

"It's hard to hunt in the big cities," he agreed. Then, to check her reaction because they'd never had a chance to really finish their discussion about what she was to him, he said, "I'll take you for a real hunt in Montana. You'll never want to live near a big city again. We usually hunt deer or elk, but the moose populations are up high enough that we hunt them sometimes, too. Moose are a real challenge."

"I think I'd rather stick to rabbits, if it's all the same to you," she said. "Mostly I just trail behind the hunt." She gave him a little smile. "I think I watched *Bambi* one too many times."

He laughed. Yes, he was going to keep her. She was giving up without a fight. A challenge, perhaps—he thought about her telling him that she wasn't much interested in sex—but not a fight. "Hunting is part of what we are. We aren't cats to prolong the kill, and the animals we hunt need thinning to keep their herds strong and healthy. But if it bothers you, you can follow behind the hunt in Montana, too. You'll still enjoy the run."

She drove up to a keypad on a post in front of a graying cedar gate and pushed in four numbers. After a pause the chain on the top of the gate began to move and the gate slid back along the wall.

He'd been here twice before. The first time had been more than a century ago and the house had been little more than a cabin. There had been fifty acres then and the Alpha had been a little Irish Catholic named Willie O'Shaughnessy who had fit in surprisingly well with his mostly German and Lutheran neighbors. The second time had been in the early twentieth century for Willie's funeral. Willie had been old, nearly as old as the Marrok. There was a madness that came sometimes to those who live too long. When the first signs of it had manifested in him, Willie had quit eating—a display of the willpower that had made him an Alpha. Charles remembered his father's grief at Willie's passing. They— Charles and his brother, Samuel—had been worried for months afterward that their father would decide to follow Willie.

Willie's house and lands had passed on to the next Alpha, a German werewolf who was married to O'Shaughnessy's daughter. Charles couldn't remember what had happened to that one or even his name. There had been several Alphas here after him, though, before Leo took over.

Willie and a handful of fine German stonemasons had built the house with a craftsmanship that would have been prohibitively expensive to replace now. Several of the windows were rippled, showing their age. He remembered when those windows had been new.

Charles hated being reminded how old he was.

Anna turned off the engine and started opening her door, but he stopped her.

"Wait a moment." A hint of unease was brushing across the senses bequeathed to him by his gifted mother, and he'd learned to pay attention. He looked at Anna and scowled—she was too vulnerable. If something happened to him, they'd tear her to bits.

"I need you to change," he told her. Something inside him relaxed: that was it. "If something happens to me, I want you to run like hell, get somewhere safe, then call my father and tell him to get you out of here."

She hesitated.

It was not his nature to explain himself. As a dominant wolf in his father's pack, he seldom had to. For her, though, he would make an effort.

"There is something important about you being in wolf form when we go in there." He shrugged. "I've learned to trust my instincts."

"All right."

She took a while. He had time to open his notebook and look at her list. He'd told Justin that Leo could have Isabelle and his first five. According to Anna's list, other than Isabelle, of those six only Boyd was on the list of names his father had given him. If Justin was Leo's second, then there wasn't a wolf other than Leo who was a threat to him.

The ache of his wound gave lie to that thought, so he corrected it. There were none of them who would give him a run for his money in a straightforward fight.

Anna finished her change and sat panting heavily on the driver's side seat. She was beautiful, he thought. Coal black with a dash of white over her nose. She was on the small side for a werewolf, but still much larger than a German shepherd. Her eyes were a pale, pale blue, which was strange because her human eyes were brown.

"Are you ready?" he asked her.

She whined as she got to her feet, her claws making small holes in the leather seat. She shook herself once, as if she'd been wet, then bobbed her head once.

He didn't see anyone watching them from the windows, but there was a small security camera cleverly tucked into a bit of the gingerbread woodwork on the porch. He got out of the SUV, making sure that he didn't show any sign of the pain he was in.

He'd checked in the bathroom of Anna's house and he didn't think the wound would slow him appreciably now that the worst of the silver poisoning had passed. He'd considered acting more hurt than he was—and he might have if he'd been sure that it was Leo who was responsible for all the dead. Acting wounded might lead Leo to attack him—and Charles had no intention of killing Leo until he knew just exactly what had been going on.

He held the SUV door open until Anna hopped out, then closed it and walked with her to the house. He didn't bother knocking on the door; this wasn't a friendly visit.

Inside, the house had changed a lot. Dark paneling had been bleached light and electric lights replaced the old gas chandeliers. Anna walked beside him, but he didn't need her guidance to find the formal parlor because that was the only room with people in it.

Everything else in the house might have changed, but they had left Willie's pride and joy: the huge hand-carved granite fireplace still dominated the parlor. Isabelle, who liked to be the center of attention, was perched on the polished cherry mantel. Leo was positioned squarely in front of her. Justin stood on his left, Boyd on his right. The other three men Charles had allowed him were seated in dainty, Victorian-era chairs. All of them except for Leo himself were dressed in dark, pin-striped suits. Leo wore nothing but a pair of black slacks, revealing that he was tanned and fit.

The effect of their united threat was somewhat mitigated by the pinkish-purple of the upholstery and walls—and by Isabelle, who was dressed in jeans and a half shirt of the same color.

Charles took two steps into the room and stopped. Anna pressed against his legs, not hard enough to unbalance him, just enough to remind him that she was there.

No one spoke, because it was for him to break the silence first. He took a deep breath into his lungs and held it, waiting for what his senses could tell him. He had gotten more from his mother than his skin and features, more than the ability to change faster than the other werewolves. She had given him the ability to *see*. Not with his eyes, but with his whole spirit.

And there was something sick in Leo's pack; he could feel the wrongness of it.

He looked into Leo's clear, sky-blue eyes and saw nothing that he hadn't seen before. No hint of madness. Not him, then, but someone in his pack.

He looked at the three wolves he had not met—and he saw what Anna had meant about their looks. Leo was not unhandsome in his own Danish Viking sort of way, but he was a warrior and he looked like a warrior. Boyd had a long blade of a nose and the military cut of his hair made his ears appear to stick out even farther than they really did.

All the wolves Charles didn't know looked like the sort of men who modeled tuxedos at a rental shop. Thin and edgy, with no real flesh to mar the lines of a jacket. Despite differences in coloring, there was a certain sameness about them. Isabelle pulled her bare feet onto the mantel with the rest of her and heaved a big sigh.

He ignored her impatience because she wasn't important just now—Leo was.

Charles met the Alpha's eyes and said, "The Marrok has sent me here to ask you why you sold your child into bondage."

Clearly, it wasn't the question Leo had expected. Isabelle had thought it was Anna, and Charles hadn't disabused her of the notion. They would deal with Anna, too, but his father's question was a better starting place because it was unexpected.

"I have no children," said Leo.

Charles shook his head. "All your wolves are your children, Leo, you know that. They are yours to love and feed, to guard and protect, to guide and to teach. You sold a young man named Alan MacKenzie Frazier. To whom and why?"

"He wasn't pack." Leo spread his arms, palms outward. "It is expensive to keep so many wolves happy here in the city. I needed the money. I am happy to give you the name of the buyer, though I believe he was only acting as a middleman."

True. All true. But Leo was being very careful how he worded his reply.

"My father would like the name and the method you used to contact him."

Leo nodded at one of the handsome men, who passed Charles with his eyes on the ground, though he spared an instant to glare at Anna. She flattened her ears at him and growled.

He had been a poor influence on her, Charles thought unrepentantly.

"Is there anything more I can help you with?" Leo asked politely.

They had, all of Leo's wolves, used Isabelle's trick with perfume, but Charles had a keen nose and Leo was . . . sad.

"You haven't updated your pack membership for five or six years," Charles said, wondering at Leo's reaction. He'd been met with defiance, anger, fear, but never with sadness.

"I thought you might catch that. Did you and Anna compare lists? Yes, I had something of a coup attempt I had to put down a little harshly."

Truth, but, again, not all of it. Leo had a lawyer's understanding of how to be careful with the truth and use it to lie by leading a false trail.

"Is that why you killed all the women of your pack? Did they all rebel against you?"

"There weren't so many women, there never are."

Again. There was something he wasn't catching. Leo hadn't been the wolf who had attacked young Frazier—it had been Justin.

Leo's wolf was back. He handed Charles a note with a name and phone number written in purple ink.

Charles tucked the note in his pocket and then nodded. "You are right. There are not enough females—so those we have ought to be protected, not killed. Did you kill them yourself?"

"All the women? No."

"Which of them did you kill?"

Leo didn't answer, and Charles felt his wolf perk up as the hunt commenced.

"You didn't kill any of the women," Charles said. He looked at the model-perfect men and at Justin, who was beautiful in an unfinished sort of way.

Leo was protecting someone. Charles looked up at Isabelle, who loved beautiful men. Isabelle, who was older than old Willie O'Shaughnessy had been when he'd begun to go crazy.

He wondered how long Leo had known she was mad.

He looked back at the Alpha. "You should have asked the Marrok for help."

LEO SHOOK HIS HEAD. "YOU KNOW WHAT HE WOULD have done. He'd have killed her."

Charles would dearly have loved to see what Isabelle was doing, but he couldn't afford to take his eyes off Leo: a cornered wolf was a dangerous wolf.

"And how many have died instead? How many of your pack are lost? The women she killed for jealousy, and their mates you had to kill to protect her? The wolves who rebelled at what the two of you were doing? How many?"

Leo raised his chin. "None for three years."

Rage raised its ugly head. "Yes," Charles agreed, very softly. "Not since you had your little bullyboy attack a defenseless woman and Change her without her consent. A woman who you then proceeded to brutalize."

"If I'd protected her, Isabelle would have hated her," Leo explained. "I forced Isabelle to protect her instead. It worked, Charles. Isabelle has been stable for three years."

Until she'd come to Anna's today and realized that Charles was interested in Anna. Isabelle had never liked anyone paying attention to other females when she was around.

He risked a glance and saw that though she hadn't moved from the mantel, Isabelle's legs were back to dangling down so she could hop down quickly if she wanted to. Her eyes had changed and watched with pale impatience for the violence she knew was to come. She licked her lips and rocked her weight from side to side in her eagerness.

Charles felt sick at the waste of it all. He turned his attention back to the Alpha. "No deaths because you have an Omega to keep her calm. And because there are no females to compete with except for Anna, who doesn't want any of your wolves, not after they raped her on your orders."

"It kept Anna alive," Leo insisted. "Kept them both alive." He ducked his head, an appeal for protection. "Tell your father that she is stable. Tell him I'll see she doesn't harm anyone else."

"She tried to kill Anna, today," Charles said gently. "And if she hadn't . . . She is insane, Leo."

He watched the last trace of hope leave Leo's face. The Alpha knew Charles wouldn't let Isabelle live—she was too dangerous, too unpredictable. Leo knew that he was dead, too. He had worked too hard to save his mate.

Leo didn't give any warning before he attacked—but Charles had been ready for him. Leo wasn't the kind of wolf to submit easily to death. There would be no bared throats in this fight.

But they both knew who would win.

ANNA HAD BEEN STUNNED TO STILLNESS BY WHAT LEO had revealed, but that ended when Leo attacked. She couldn't help the little yip she let out, any more than she could help her instinctive lunge forward to protect Charles.

A strong pair of workman's hands gripped her by the ruff of her neck and pulled her back despite the scrabbling of her claws on the hardwood floor.

"Here, now," Boyd's rumble hit her ears. "Steady on. This isn't your fight."

His voice, one she was used to obeying, calmed her so she could think. It also helped that Charles avoided Leo's first strike with a minimal movement of his shoulders.

The other wolves had come to their feet and part of her registered Justin's insistent chanting, "Kill him, kill him." She wasn't sure which wolf he wanted to die. He hated Leo for controlling him and for being Isabelle's mate. Maybe he didn't care which one died.

Leo struck three times in rapid succession, missing each time. He'd committed to the last blow, and when it didn't land he had to take an awkward step forward.

Charles took advantage of the stumble and stepped into Leo, and in a graceful movement she couldn't quite follow did something to Leo's shoulder that had the Alpha roaring in rage and pain.

The next few things happened so fast, Anna was never certain in what order they occurred.

There was a rapid double bark of a gun. Boyd's hands loosened their grip on her fur as he swore, and Isabelle gave a frenetic, excited laugh.

It took Anna only a glance to see what had happened. Isabelle was holding a gun, watching the fight, waiting for another clear shot at Charles.

Anna broke free of Boyd's loosened grip and sprinted across the room.

From the mantel, Isabelle looked Anna squarely in her eyes and said sharply, "Stop, Anna."

She was so sure of Anna's obedience, she didn't even wait to make certain Anna listened before turning her attention back to the battling men.

Anna felt the force of Isabelle's command as it rolled by her like a breeze that ruffled her hair. It didn't slow her down at all.

She gathered her hindquarters underneath her and launched. Her teeth closed on Isabelle's arm, and she felt the bone crack with a noise that satisfied the wolf's anger. The force of her leap was such that she pulled Isabelle off the six-foot-high mantel and slammed her into the fireplace as they both tumbled down—Anna's jaws still locked around the arm that had held the gun.

She crouched there, waiting for Isabelle to do something, but the other woman just lay there. Someone came up behind them, and Anna growled a warning.

"Easy," Boyd said, his calm voice touching her as Isabelle's order had not.

His hand rested on her back and she increased her growl, but he didn't pay any attention to her: he was looking at Isabelle.

"Dead," he grunted. "Serves her right for forgetting you aren't just another submissive wolf who has to listen to her. Let go, Anna. You caved her head in on the fireplace. She's gone." But when Anna reluctantly let go, Boyd made sure Isabelle was dead by twisting her head until her neck made a sick-sounding pop. He picked the gun up off the floor.

Staring at Isabelle's broken body, Anna began to shake. She lifted a foot, but she didn't know whether she was going to take a step closer or a step away. A chair hit her in the side and reminded her that there was a fight going on—and Isabelle had shot at Charles twice.

If he was hurt, he showed no sign of it. He was moving as easily as he had in the beginning, and Leo was staggering, one arm limp at his side. Charles swept behind him and hit him in the back of the neck with the edge of his hand and Leo collapsed like a kite when the wind dies.

A soft, moaning howl rose from Boyd, who was still standing beside her, echoed by the other wolves as they mourned their Alpha's passing.

Ignoring them, Charles knelt beside Leo and, with the same

motion Boyd had used on Isabelle, he made sure the broken neck was permanent.

He stayed there, on one knee and one foot, like a man proposing. He bowed his head and reached out again, this time to caress the dead man's face.

Justin's move was so fast, Anna didn't have a chance to sing a warning. She hadn't even noticed when he'd changed to his wolf form. He hit Charles like a battering ram and Charles went down beneath him.

But if Anna was frozen, Boyd was not. He shot Justin in the eye a split second before Justin's body hit Charles.

That fast it was over.

Boyd hauled Justin's limp body off Charles and dumped him to one side. Anna didn't remember moving but suddenly she was astraddle Charles and growling at Boyd.

He backed up slowly, his hands raised and empty. The gun was tucked into the belt of his slacks.

As soon as Boyd ceased to feel like a threat, Anna turned her attention to Charles. He was lying facedown on the floor, covered with blood—her nose told her that some of it was Justin's, but some of it was his, too.

Despite the way he'd been fighting Leo, Isabelle had hit him at least once; she could see the bloody hole in his back. In wolf form she couldn't help him and it would take her too long to change.

She looked over her shoulder at Boyd.

He shrugged. "I can't help him unless I get closer than this."

She stared at him, challenging him with her eyes in a way she would never have done before today. It didn't seem to bother him. He just waited for her to make up her mind. The wolf didn't want to trust anyone with her mate—but she knew she didn't have a choice.

She hopped all the way over Charles's body, giving Boyd access. But she couldn't help her snarl when he rolled him over to check him for wounds. He found a second bullet hole in Charles's left calf.

Boyd shed his suit jacket and ripped off his dress shirt, scattering buttons all over the floor. He tore the silk shirt into strips and then, as he was bandaging Charles's wounds with rapid experience, he began giving orders. "Holden, call in the rest of the pack—and start with Rashid. Tell him we need him to bring whatever he needs to treat a silver-bullet wound—both bullets are out. When you've finished, call the Marrok and tell him what has happened. You can find his number in Isabelle's address book in the kitchen drawer under the phone."

Anna whined. Both of Isabelle's shots had hit.

"He's not going to die," Boyd told her, tying off the last bandage. He glanced around the room and swore. "This place looks like the last scene in *Hamlet*. Gardner, you and Simon start getting this mess cleaned up. Let's get Charles someplace quieter. He's not going to be a happy camper when he wakes, and all this blood isn't going to help." He picked Charles up. When he carried him out of the room, Anna was at his heels.

BACK IN HUMAN FORM, ANNA LAY ON THE BED BESIDE Charles. Rashid, who was a real doctor as well as a werewolf, had come and gone, replacing Boyd's makeshift bandages with something more sterile-looking. He told Anna that Charles was unconscious due to blood loss.

Boyd had come in afterward and advised her to leave Charles before he woke up. The room was reinforced to withstand an enraged wolf—Anna was not.

He hadn't argued when she refused. He'd just bolted the door behind him when he left. She waited until he was gone and then changed. There was clothing in the old-fashioned wardrobe, lots of things that were one size fits all. She found a T-shirt and a pair of jeans that didn't fit too badly.

Charles didn't notice when she got on the bed with him. She put her head next to his on the pillow and listened to him breathe.

HE DIDN'T WAKE QUIETLY. ONE MOMENT HE WAS LIMP and the next he'd exploded to his feet. She'd never watched him shift and, although she knew his change was miraculously swift, she hadn't known it was beautiful. It started with his feet, then like a blanket of red fur the change rolled up his body, leaving behind it a malevolent, very angry werewolf dripping blood and bandages.

Bright yellow eyes glanced around the room, taking in the closed door, the bars on the windows, and then her.

She lay very still, letting him absorb his surroundings and see there was no threat. When he looked at her a second time, she sat up and went to work on his bandages.

He growled at her, and she tapped his nose gently. "You've lost enough blood today. The bandages don't advertise your weakness any more than bleeding all over would. At least this way, you aren't going to ruin the carpet."

When she finished, she threaded her fingers through the ruff of fur around his neck and bent her head to his.

"I thought I had lost you."

He stood for her embrace for a minute before wriggling free. He got off the bed and stalked to the door.

"It's bolted," she told him, hopping off the bed and padding after him.

He gave her a patient look.

There was a click and the door was opened by a slender, unremarkable-looking man who appeared to be in his early twenties. He crouched on his heels and stared Charles in the face before glancing up at her.

The force of personality in his eyes hit her like a blow to the stomach, so she wasn't entirely surprised when she recognized his voice.

"Shot three times in one day," the Marrok murmured. "I think Chicago has been harder on you than usual, my son. I'd best take you home, don't you think?"

She didn't know what to say, so she didn't say anything. She put her hand on Charles's back and swallowed.

Charles looked at his father.

"Have you asked her?"

Charles growled low in his chest.

The Marrok laughed and stood up. "Nevertheless, I will ask. You are Anna?" It wasn't quite a question.

Her throat was too dry to say anything, so she nodded.

"My son would like you to accompany us to Montana. I assure you that if anything is not to your liking, I'll see to it that you can relocate to wherever suits you better."

Charles growled and Bran raised an eyebrow as he looked at him. "*I* am the Marrok, Charles. If the child wants to go elsewhere, she can."

Anna leaned against Charles's hip. "I think I'd like to see Montana," she said.

THE STAR OF DAVID

So I was asked to write a Christmas story about werewolves. David Christiansen, who appeared in *Moon Called*, had such a tragic history, I couldn't help but write a Christmas story for him. A fellow army ranger, he and Adam were the only survivors of a mission gone bad in the Vietnam War. They returned stateside, only to discover that they had been turned into the beast they had defeated. David is, more than any other of my wolves, suffering from the traditional curse of the werewolf. A good man who, while his wolf was in control, killed the very last person he wanted to hurt. But Christmas is about grace and forgiveness and family. Surely there is room in the middle of all of that for David to find some happiness.

The events in this story happen the Christmas after most of the events in *Moon Called*.

"I CHECKED THEM OUT MYSELF," MYRA SNAPPED. "HAVE you ever just considered that *your boy* isn't the angel you thought he was?"

Stella took off her glasses and set them on her desk. "I think that we both need some perspective. Why don't you take the rest of the afternoon off." *Before I slap your stupid face.* People like Devonte didn't change that fast, not without good reason.

Myra opened her mouth, but after she got a look at Stella's eyes, she shut it again. Mutely she stalked to her desk and retrieved her coat and purse. She slammed the door behind her.

As soon as she was gone, Stella opened the folder and looked at the pictures of the crime scene again. They were duplicates, and doubtless Clive, her brother the detective, had broken a few rules when he sent them to her—not that breaking rules had ever bothered him, not when he was five and not as a grown man nearing fifty and old enough to know better.

She touched the photos lightly, then closed the folder again. There was a yellow sticky with a phone number on it and nothing else: Clive didn't have to put a name on it. Her little brother knew she'd see what he had seen.

She picked up the phone and punched in the numbers fast, not giving herself a chance for second thoughts.

THE BARRACKS WERE EMPTY, LEAVING DAVID'S OFFICE silent and bleak. The boys were on furlough with their various families for December.

His mercenaries specialized in live retrieval, which tended to be in-and-out stuff, a couple of weeks per job at the most. He didn't want to get involved in the gray area of unsanctioned combat or out-and-out war—where you killed people because someone told you to. In retrieval there were good guys and bad guys still—and if there weren't, he didn't take the job. Their reputation was such that they had no trouble finding jobs.

And unless all hell really broke loose, they always took December off to be with their families. David never let them know how hard that made it for him.

Werewolves need their packs.

If his pack was human, well, they knew about him and they filled that odd wolf-quirk that demanded he have people to protect, brothers in heart and mind. He couldn't stomach a real pack; he hated what he was too much.

He couldn't bear to live with his own kind, but this worked as a substitute and kept him centered. When his boys were here, when they had a job to do, he had direction and purpose.

His grandsons had invited him for the family dinner, but he'd refused as he always did. He still saw his sons on a regular basis. Both of them had served in his small band of mercenaries for a while, until the life lost its appeal or the risks grew too great for men with growing families. But he stayed away at Christmas.

Restlessness had him pacing: there were no plans to make, no wrongs to right. Finally he unlocked the safe and pulled out a couple of the newer rifles. He needed to put some time in with them anyway.

An hour of shooting staved off the restlessness, but only until he locked the guns up again. He'd have to go for a run. When he emptied his pockets in preparation, he noticed he had missed a call while he'd been shooting. He glanced at the number, frowning when he didn't recognize it. Most of his jobs came through an agent who knew better than to give out his cell number. Before he could decide if he wanted to return the call, his phone rang again, a call from the same number.

"Christiansen," he answered briskly.

There was a long silence. "Papa?"

He closed his eyes and sank back in his chair feeling his heart expand with almost painful intentness as his wolf fought with the man who knew his daughter hated him: didn't want to see him, ever. She had been there when her mother died.

"Stella?" He couldn't imagine what it took to make her break almost forty years of silence. "Are you all right? Is there something wrong?" Someone he could kill for her? A building to blow up? Anything at all.

She swallowed. He could hear it over the line. He waited for her to hang up.

Instead, when she spoke again, her voice was brisk and the wavery pain that colored that first "Papa" was gone as if it had never been. "I was wondering if you would consider doing a favor for me."

"What do you need?" He was proud that came out evenly. Always better to know what you're getting into, he told himself. He wanted to tell her that she could ask him for anything—but he didn't want to scare her.

"I run an agency that places foster kids," she told him, as if he didn't know. As if her brothers hadn't told her how he quizzed them to find out how she was doing and what she was up to. He hoped she never found out about her ex-boyfriend who'd turned stalker. He hadn't killed that one, though his willingness to do so had made it easier to persuade the man that he wanted to take up permanent residence in a different state.

"I know," he said, because it seemed like she needed a response.

"There's something—" She hesitated. "Look, this might not have been the best idea."

He was losing her again. He had to breathe deeply to keep the panic from his voice. "Why don't you tell me about it anyway? Do you have something better to do?"

"I remember that," she said. "I remember you doing that with Mom. She'd be hysterical, throwing dishes or books, and you'd sit down and say, 'Why don't you tell me about it?'"

Did she want to talk about her mother now? About the one time he'd needed to be calm and had failed? He hadn't known he was a werewolf until it was too late. Until after he'd killed his wife and the lover she'd taken while David had been fighting for God and country, both of whom had forgotten him. She'd been waiting until he came home to tell him that she was leaving—it was a mistake she'd had no time to regret. He, on the other hand, might have forever to regret it for her.

He never spoke of it. Not to anyone. For Stella he'd do it, but she knew the story anyway. She'd been there.

"Do you want to talk about your mother?" he asked, his voice carrying into a lower timbre, as it did when the wolf was close.

"No. Not that," she said hurriedly. "Nothing like that. I'm sorry. This isn't a good idea."

She was going to hang up. He drew on his hard-earned control and thought fast.

Forty years as a hunter and leader of men had given him a lot of practice reading between the lines. If he could put aside the fact that she was his daughter, maybe he could salvage this.

She'd told him she ran a foster agency like it was important to the rest of what she had to say.

"It's about your work?" he asked, trying to figure out what a social worker would need with a werewolf. Oh. "Is there a—" His daughter preferred not to talk about werewolves, Clive had told him. So if there was something supernatural, she was going to have to bring it up. "Is there someone bothering you?"

"No," she said. "Nothing like that. It's one of my boys."

Stella had never married, never had children of her own. Her brother said it was because she had all the people to take care of that she could handle.

"One of the foster kids."

"Devonte Parish."

"He one of your special ones?" he asked. His Stella had never seen a stray she hadn't brought home, animal or human. Most she'd dusted off and sent home with a meal and bandages as needed—but some of them she'd kept.

She sighed. "Come and see him, would you? Tomorrow?"

"I'll be there," he promised. It would take him a few hours to set up permission from the packs in her area: travel was complicated for a werewolf. "Probably sometime in the afternoon. This the number I can find you at?"

INSTEAD OF TAKING A TAXI FROM THE AIRPORT, HE rented a car. It might be harder to park, but it would give them mobility and privacy. If his daughter only needed this, if she didn't want to smoke the peace pipe yet, then he didn't need it witnessed by a cabdriver. A witness would make it harder for him to control himself— and his little girl never needed to see him out of control ever again.

He called her before setting out, and he could tell that she'd had second and third thoughts.

"Look," he finally told her. "I'm here now. Maybe we should go and talk to the boy. Where can I meet you?"

HE'D HAVE KNOWN HER ANYWHERE, THOUGH HE HADN'T, by her request, seen her since the night he'd killed his wife. She'd been twelve and now she was a grown woman with silver threads running through her kinky black hair. The last time he'd seen her, she'd been still a little rounded and soft as most children are—and now there wasn't an ounce of softness in her. She was muscular and lean—like him.

It had been a long time, but he'd never have mistaken her for anyone else: she had his eyes and her mother's face.

He'd thought you had to be bleeding someplace to hurt this badly. The beast struggled within him, looking for an enemy. But he controlled and subdued it before he pulled the car to the curb and unlocked the automatic door.

She was wearing a brown wool suit that was several shades darker than the milk and coffee skin she'd gotten from her mother. His own skin was dark as the night and kept him safely hidden in the shadows where he and people like him belonged.

She opened the car door and got in. He waited until she'd fastened her seat belt before pulling out from the curb. Slush splattered out from under his tires, but it was only a token. Once he was in the traffic lane, the road was bare.

She didn't say anything for a long time, so he just drove. He had no idea where he was going, but he figured she'd tell him when she was ready. He kept his eyes on traffic to give her time to get a good look at him.

"You look younger than I remember," she said finally. "Younger than me."

"I was thirty-five or thereabouts when I was Changed. Being a werewolf seems to settle physical age at about twenty-five for most of us." There it was out in the open and she could do with it as she pleased.

He could smell her fear of him spike, and if he'd really been twenty-five, he thought he might have cried. Being this agitated wasn't smart if you were a werewolf. He took a deep breath through his nose and tried to calm down—he'd earned her fear.

"Devonte won't talk to me or anyone else," she said, and then as if those words had been the key to the floodgate, she kept going. "I wish you could have seen him when I first met him. He was ten going on forty. He'd just lost his grandmother, who had raised him. He looked me right in the eye, stuck his jaw out, and told me that he needed a home where he would be clothed and fed so he could concentrate on school."

"Smart boy?" he asked. She'd started in the middle of the story; he'd forgotten that habit of hers until just now.

"Very smart. Quiet. But funny, too." She made a sad sound, and her sorrow overwhelmed her fear of him. "We screen the homes. We visit. But there's never enough of us—and some of the horrible ones can put on a good show for a long time. It takes a while, too, before you get a feel for the bad ones. If he could have stayed with his first family, everything would have been fine. He stayed with them for six years. But this fall the foster mother un-expectedly got pregnant and her husband got a job transfer . . ."

They'd abandoned the boy like he was an old couch that was too awkward to move, David thought. He felt a flash of anger for this boy he'd never met. He swallowed the emotion quickly; he could do that these days. For a while. He was going to have to take that run when he got back home.

"I was tied up in court cases and someone else moved him to his next family," Stella continued, staring at her hands, which were clenched on a manila folder. "It shouldn't have been a problem. This was a family who already has fostered several children—and Devonte was a good kid, not the kind to give anyone problems."

"But something happened?" he suggested.

"His foster mother says that he just went wild, throwing furni-ture, breaking things. When he threatened her, his foster father stepped in and knocked him out. Devonte's in the hospital with a broken wrist and two broken ribs and he won't talk."

"You don't believe the foster family."

She gave an indignant huff. "The Linnfords look like Mr. and Mrs. Brady. She smiles and nods when he speaks and he is all charm and concern." She huffed again and spoke very precisely, "I wouldn't believe them if all they were doing was giving me the time of day. And I know Devonte. He just wants to get through school and get a scholarship so he can go to college and take care of himself."

He nodded thoughtfully. "So why did you call me?" He was willing to have a talk with the family, but he suspected if that was all she needed, it would have been a cold day in hell before she called him—she had her brothers for that.

"Because of the photos." She held up the folder in invitation.

He had to drive a couple of blocks before he found a convenient parking place and pulled over, leaving the engine running.

He pulled six photos off a clip that attached them to the back of the folder she held and spread them out to look. Interest rose up and he wished he had something more than photos. It certainly looked like more damage than one lone boy could do: ten boys maybe, if they had sledgehammers. The holes in the walls were something anyone could have done. The holes in the ten-foot ceiling, the executive desk on its side in three pieces, and the antique oak chair broken to splinters and missing a leg were more interesting.

"The last time I saw something like that . . ." Stella whispered.

It was probably a good thing she couldn't bring herself to finish that sentence. He had to admit that all this scene was missing was blood and body parts.

"How old is Devonte?"

"Sixteen."

"Can you get me in to look at the damage?"

"No, they had contractors in to fix it."

His eyebrows raised. "How long has it been?"

"It was the twenty-first. Three days." She waved a hand. "I know. Contractors are usually a month wait at least, but money talks. This guy has serious money."

That sounded wrong. "Then why are they taking in a foster kid?"

She looked him in the eye for the first time and nodded at him as if he'd gotten something right. "If I'd been the one to vet them, I'd have smelled a rat right there. Rich folk don't want mongrel children who've had it rough. Or if they do, they go to China or Romania and adopt babies to coo over. They don't take in foster kids, not without an agenda. But we're desperate for foster homes . . . and it wasn't me who approved them."

"You said the boy wouldn't talk. To you? Or to anybody?"

"To anybody. He hasn't said a word since the incident. Won't communicate at all."

David considered that, running through possibilities. "Was anyone hurt except for the boy?"

"No."

"Would you mind if I went to see him now?"

"Please."

He followed her directions to the hospital. He parked the car, but before he could open the door, she grabbed his arm. The first time she touched him.

"Could he be a werewolf?"

"Maybe," he told her. "That kind of damage . . ."

"It looked like our house," she said, not looking at him, but not taking her hand off him, either. "Like our house that night."

"If he was a werewolf, I doubt your Mr. Linnford would have been able to knock him out without taking a lot of damage. Maybe Linnford is the werewolf." That would fit; most of the werewolves he knew, if they survived, eventually became wealthy. Children were more difficult. Maybe that was why Linnford and his wife fostered children.

Stella jerked her chin up and down once. "That's what I thought. That's it. Linnford might be a werewolf. Could you tell?"

His chest felt tight. How very brave of her: she'd called the only monster she knew to deal with the other monsters. It reminded him of how she'd stood between him and the boys, protecting them the best that she could.

"Let me talk to Devonte," he said, trying to keep the growl out of his voice with only moderate success. "Then I can deal with Linnford."

The hospital corridors were decorated with garlands and green and red bulbs. Every year Christmas got more plastic and seemed further and further from the Christmases David had known as a child.

His daughter led him to the elevators without hesitation and exchanged nods with a few of the staff members who walked past. He hated the way his children aged every year. Hated the silver in their hair that was a constant reminder that eventually time would take them all away from him.

She kept as much distance between them as she could in the elevator. As if he were a stranger—or a monster. At least she wasn't running from him screaming.

You can't live with bitterness. He knew that. Bitterness, like most unpleasant emotions, made the wolf restless. Restless wolves were dangerous. The nurse at the station just outside the elevator knew Stella, too, and greeted her by name.

"That Mr. Linnford was here asking after Devonte. I told him that he wasn't allowed to visit yet." She gave Stella a disappointed look, clearly blaming her for putting Mr. Linnford to such bother. "What a nice man he is, looking after that boy after what he did to them."

She handed Stella a clipboard and gave David a mildly curious look. He gave her his most harmless smile and she smiled back before glancing down at the clipboard Stella had returned.

David could read it from where he stood. Stella Christiansen and guest. Well, he told himself, she could hardly write down that he was her father when she looked older than he did.

"He may be a nice man," Stella told the nurse with a thread of steel in her voice, "but you just keep him out until we know for sure what happened and why."

She strode off toward a set of doors where a policeman sat in front of a desk, sitting on a wooden chair, and reading a worn paperback copy of Stephen King's *Cujo.* "Jorge," she said.

"Stella." He buzzed the door and let them through.

"He's in the secured wing," she explained under her breath as she walked briskly down the hall. "Not that it's all that secure. Jorge shouldn't have let you through without checking your ID."

Not that anyone would question his Stella, David thought. Even as a little girl, people did what she told them to do. He was careful not to smile at her; she wouldn't understand it.

This part of the hospital smelled like blood, desperation, and disinfectant. Even though most of the scents were old, a new wolf penned up in this environment would cause a lot more excitement than he was seeing: and a sixteen-year-old could only be a new wolf. Any younger than that and they mostly didn't survive the Change. Anyway, he'd have scented a wolf by now: their first conclusion was right—Stella's boy was no werewolf.

"Any cameras in the rooms?" he asked in a low voice.

Her steady footfall paused. "No. That's still on the list of advised improvements for the future."

"All right. No one else here?"

"Not right now," she said. "This hospital isn't near gang territory and they put the adult offenders in a different section." She entered one of the open doorways and he followed her in, shutting the door behind them.

It wasn't a private room, but the first bed was empty. In the second bed was a boy staring at the wall—there were no windows. He was beaten up a bit and had a cast on one hand. The other hand was attached to a sturdy rail that stuck out of the bed on the side nearest the wall with a locking nylon strap—better than handcuffs, he thought, but not much. The boy didn't look up as they came in.

Maybe it was the name, or maybe the image that "foster kid"

brought to mind, but he'd expected Devonte to be black. Instead, the boy looked as if someone had taken half a dozen races and shook them up—Eurasian races, though, not from the Dark Continent. There was Native American or Asian in the corners of his eyes—and he supposed that nose could be Jewish or Italian. His skin looked as if he had a deep suntan, but this time of year it was more likely the color was his own: Mexican, Greek, or even Indian.

Not that it mattered. He'd found that the years were slowly completing the job that Vietnam had begun—race or religion mattered very little to him anymore. But even if it had mattered . . . Stella had asked him for help.

STELLA GLANCED AT HER FATHER. SHE DIDN'T KNOW HIM, didn't know if he'd see through Devonte's defiant sullenness to the fear underneath. His expressionless face and upright military bearing gave her no clue. She could read people, but she didn't know her father anymore, hadn't seen him since . . . that night. Watching him made her uncomfortable, so she turned her attention to the other person in the room.

"Hey, kid."

Devonte kept his gaze on the wall.

"I brought someone to see you."

Her father, after a keen look at the boy, lifted his head and sucked in air through his nose hard enough she could hear it.

"Where are the clothes he was wearing when they brought him in?" he asked.

That drew Devonte's attention, and satisfaction at his reaction slowed her answer. Her father's eye fell on the locker and he stalked to it and opened the door. He took out the clear plastic bag of clothes and said, with studied casualness, "Linnford was here asking about you today."

Devonte went still as a mouse.

Stella didn't know where this was going, but pitched in to help.

"The police informed me that Linnford's decided to not press assault charges. They should move you to a room with a view soon. I'm scheduled for a meeting tomorrow morning to decide what happens to you when you get out of here."

Devonte opened his mouth, but then closed it resolutely.

Her father sniffed at the bag, then said softly, "Why do your clothes smell like vampire, boy?"

Devonte jumped, the whites of his eyes showing all the way round his irises. His mouth opened and this time Stella thought it might really be an inability to speak that kept him quiet. She was choking a bit on "vampire" herself. But she wouldn't have believed in werewolves, either, she supposed, if her father weren't one.

"I didn't introduce you," she murmured. "Devonte, this is my father. I called him when I saw the crime scene photos. He's a werewolf." If he was having vampire problems, maybe a werewolf would look good.

The sad blue-gray chair with the ripped Naugahyde seat that had been sitting next to Devonte's bed zipped past her and flung itself at her father—who caught it and gave the boy a curious half smile. "Oh, I bet you surprised it, didn't you? Wizards aren't exactly common."

"Wizard?" Stella squeaked regrettably.

Her father's smile widened just a little—a smile she remembered from her childhood when she or one of her brothers had done something particularly clever. This one was aimed at Devonte.

He moved the chair gently between his hands. "A witch's power centers on bodies and minds, flesh and blood. A wizard has power over the physical—" The empty bed slammed into the wall with the open locker, bending the door and cracking the drywall. Her father was safely in front of it and belatedly she realized he must have jumped over it.

He still had the chair and his smile had grown to a wide, white grin. "Very nice, boy. But I'm not your enemy." He glanced up at the clock on the wall and shook his head.

"Someone ought to reset that thing. Do you know what time it is?"

No more furniture moved. Her father made a show of taking out his cell phone and looking at it. "Six thirty. It's dark outside already. How badly did you hurt it with that chair I saw in the photo?"

Devonte was breathing hard, but Stella controlled her urge to go to him. Her father, hopefully, knew what he was doing. She shivered, though she was wearing her favorite wool suit and the hospital was quite warm. How much of the stories she'd heard about vampires was true?

Devonte released a breath. "Not badly enough."

On the tails of Devonte's reply, her father asked, "Who taught you not to talk at all, if you have a secret to keep?"

"My grandmother. Her mother survived Dachau because the American troops came just in time—and because she kept her mouth shut when the Nazis wanted information."

Her father's face softened. "Tough woman. Was she the Gypsy? Most wizards have at least a little Gypsy blood."

Devonte shrugged, rubbed his hands over his face hard. She recognized the gesture from a hundred different kids: he was trying not to cry. "Stella said you're a werewolf."

Her father cocked his head as if he were weighing something. "Stella doesn't lie." Unexpectedly he pinned Stella with his eyes. "I don't know if we'll have a vampire calling tonight—it depends upon how badly Devonte hurt it."

"Her," said Devonte. "It was a her."

Still looking at Stella, her father corrected himself. "Her. She must have been pretty badly injured if she hasn't come here already. And it probably means we're lucky and she is alone. If there were others, they'd have come yesterday or the day before—they can't afford to let Devonte live with what he knows about them. Vampires haven't survived as long as they have by leaving witnesses."

"No one would have believed me," Devonte said. "They'd have locked me up forever."

That made her father release her from the grip of his gaze as he focused his attention on Devonte. The boy straightened under the impact—Stella knew exactly how he felt.

"Is that what Linnford told you when his neighbors came running to see why there was so much noise?" her father asked gently. "Upscale apartment dwellers aren't nearly as likely to ignore odd sounds. Is that why you threw around so much furniture? That was smart, boy."

Devonte was nodding his head—and he straightened a little more at her father's praise.

"Next time a vampire attacks you and you don't manage to kill it, though, you shout it to the world. You may end up seeing a psychologist for the rest of your life—but the vampires will stay as far from you as they can. If she doesn't come tonight, you tell your story to the newspapers." Her father glanced at Stella and she nodded.

"I know a couple of reporters," she said. "'Boy Claims He Was Attacked by Vampire' ought to sell enough papers to justify a headline or two."

"All right, then." Her father returned his attention to her. "I need you to go out and find some wood for us: a chair, a table, something we can make stakes out of."

"Holy water?" asked Devonte. "They might have a chapel here."

"Smart," said her father. "But from what I've heard, it doesn't do enough damage to be worth running it down. Go now, Stella—and be careful."

She almost saluted him, but she didn't trust him enough to tease. He saw it, almost smiled, and then turned back to Devonte. "And you're going to tell me everything you know about this vampire."

Stella glanced in the room next to Devonte's, but, like his, it was decorated in early Naugahyde and metal: no wood to be found. She didn't bother checking any more but hurried to the security door—and read the note taped to it.

"No, sir. She lived with them—they told me she was Linnford's sister." Devonte stopped talking when she came back.

"Jorge's been called away, he'll be back in a few minutes."

Her father considered that. "I think the show's on. No wooden chairs?"

"All the rooms in this wing are like this one."

"Without an effective weapon, I'll get a better chance at her as a wolf than as a human. It means I can't talk to you, though—and it will take a while to change back, maybe a couple of hours." He looked away, and in an adult version of Devonte's earlier gesture, rubbed his face tiredly. She heard the rasp of whisker on skin. "I control the wolf now—and have for a long time."

He was worried about her.

"It's all right," she told him. He gave her the same kind of keen examination he'd given Devonte earlier and she wondered what information he was drawing from it. Could he tell how scared she was?

His face softened. "You'll do, my star."

She'd forgotten that he used to call her that—hated the way it tightened her throat. "Should I call Clive and Steve?"

"Not for a vampire," he told her. "All that will do is up the body count. To that end, we'll stay here and wait—an isolation ward is as good a place to face her as any. If I'm wrong, and the guard's leaving isn't the beginning of her attack—if she doesn't come tonight, we get all of us into the safety of someone's home, where the vampire can't just waltz in without invitation. Then I'll call in a few favors and my friends and I can take care of her somewhere there aren't any civilians to be hurt."

He looked around with evident dissatisfaction.

"What are you looking for?" Devonte asked so she didn't have to.

"A place to hide." Then he looked up and smiled at the dropped ceiling.

"Those panels won't support your weight," she warned him.

"No, but this is a hospital and this is the old wing. I bet they have a cable ladder for their computer and electric cables . . ." As he spoke, he hopped on the empty bed and pushed up a ceiling panel to take a look.

"What's a cable ladder?" Stella asked.

"In this case, it's a sturdy aluminum track attached to the oak beam with stout hardware." He sounded pleased as he replaced the ceiling panel he'd taken out. "I could hide a couple of people up here if I had to."

He was a mercenary, she remembered, and wondered how many times he'd hidden on top of cable ladders.

He moved the empty bed away from the wall and climbed on it again and removed a different panel. "Do you think you can get this panel back where it belongs after I get up here, boy?"

"Sure." Devonte sounded thoroughly pleased. If anyone else had called him "boy," he'd have been bristling. He was already well on the way to a big case of hero worship, just like the one she'd had.

"Stella." Her father took off his red flannel shirt and laid it on the empty bed behind him. "When this is over, you call Clive, tell him everything, and he'll arrange a cleanup. He knows who to call for help with it. It's safer for everyone if people don't believe in vampires and werewolves. Leaving bodies makes it kind of hard to deny."

"I'll call him."

Without his shirt to cover him, she could see there was no softness in him. A few scars showed up gray on his dark skin. She'd forgotten how dark he was, like ebony.

As he peeled off his sky-blue undershirt, he said, with a touch of humor, "If you don't want to see more of your father than any daughter ever should, you need to turn your back." And she realized she'd been staring at him.

Devonte made an odd noise—he was laughing. There was a tightness to the sound and she knew he was scared and excited to see what it looked like when a man changed into a werewolf. For some reason she felt her own mouth stretch into a nervous grin she let Devonte see just before she did as her father advised her and turned her back.

DAVID DIDN'T LIKE CHANGING IN FRONT OF ANYONE. HE wasn't exactly vulnerable—but it made the wolf edgy and if someone decided to get brave and approach too closely . . . well, the wolf would feel threatened, like a snake shedding its skin.

So to the boy he said quietly, "Watching is fine. But wait for a bit if you want to touch . . ." He had a thought. "Stella, if she sends the Linnfords in first, I'll do my best to stay hidden. I can take a vampire . . ." Honesty forced him to continue. "Maybe I can take a vampire, but only with surprise on my side. Her human minions, if they are still human enough to walk in daylight, are still too human to detect me. Don't let them take Devonte out of this room."

He tried to remember everything he knew about vampires. Once he changed, it would be too late to talk. "Don't look in the vampire's eyes, don't let her touch you. Unless you are really a believer, don't plan on crosses helping you out. When I attack, don't try and help, just keep out of it so I don't have to worry about you."

Wishing they had a wooden stake, he knelt on the floor and allowed himself to change. Calling the wolf was easy, it knew there was a fight to be had, blood to be shed, and in its eagerness it rushed the change as if called by the moon herself.

He never remembered exactly how bad it was going to hurt. His mother had once told him that childbirth was like that for women. That if they remembered how bad it was, they'd lack the courage to face the next time.

But he did remember it was always worse than he expected, and that somehow helped him bear it.

The shivery, icy pain slid over his bones while fire threaded through his muscles, reshaping, reorganizing, and altering what was there to suit itself. Experience kept him from making noise—it was one of the first things he learned: how to control his instincts and keep the howls, the growls, and the whines inside and bury them in silence. Noise can attract unwanted attention.

His lungs labored to provide oxygen as adrenaline forced his heart to beat too fast. His face ached as teeth became fangs and his jaw extended with cheekbones. His eyesight blurred and then sharpened with a predatory clarity that allowed him to see prey and enemy alike no matter what shadows they tried to hide in.

"Cool," said someone. Devonte. He-who-was-to-be-guarded.

Someone moved and it attracted his attention. Her terror flooded his senses like perfume.

Prey. He liked it when they ran.

Then she lifted her chin and he saw a second image, superimposed over the first. A child standing between him and two smaller children, her chin jutting out as she lifted up a baseball bat in wordless defiance that spoke louder than her terror and the blood.

Not prey. Not prey. His. His star.

It was all right then. She could see his pain—she had earned that right. And together they would stop the monster from eating the boy.

For the first few minutes after the change, he mostly thought like the wolf, but as the pain subsided, he settled back into control. He shook off the last of the unpleasant tingles with the same willpower he used to set aside the desire to snarl at the boy who reached out with a hand . . . only to jerk back, caught by the strap on his wrist.

David hopped onto the bed and snapped through the ballistic nylon that attached Devonte's cuff to the rail and waited while the boy petted him tentatively with all the fascination of a person touching a tiger.

"That'll be a little hard to explain," said Stella.

He looked at her and she flinched . . . then jerked up her chin and met his eyes. "What if the Linnfords ask about the restraint?"

It had been the wolf's response to seeing the boy he was supposed to protect tied up like a bad dog, not the man's.

"They haven't been here," said Devonte. "Unless they spend a lot of time in hospital prison, they won't know it was supposed to be there. I'll cover the cuff on my wrist with the blanket."

Stella nodded her head thoughtfully. "All right. And if things get bad, at least this way you can run. He's right, it's better if the restraint is off."

David let them work it out. He launched himself off Devonte's bed and onto the other—forgetting that Devonte was already hurt until he heard the boy's indrawn breath. David was still half operating on wolf instincts—which wasn't very helpful when fighting vampires. He needed to be thinking.

Maybe it had only been the suddenness of his movement, though, because the boy made the same sound when David hopped through the almost-too-narrow opening in the ceiling and onto the track in the plenum space between the original fourteen-foot ceiling and false panels fitted into the flimsy hangers that kept them in place. The track groaned a little under his sudden weight, but it didn't bend.

"My father always told us that no one ever looks up for their enemy," Stella said after a moment. "Can you replace the panel? If you can't, I—"

The panel he'd moved slid back into place with more force than necessary and cracked down the middle.

"Damn it."

"Don't worry, no one will notice. There are a couple of broken panels up there."

SHE COULDN'T SEE ANY SIGN THAT HER FATHER WAS hiding in the ceiling except for the bed. She grabbed it by the headboard and tugged it back to its original position, then she did the same with the chair.

She'd forgotten how impressive the wolf was . . . almost beautiful: the perfect killing machine covered with four-inch-deep, red-gold fur. She hadn't remembered the black that tipped his ears and surrounded his eyes like Egyptian kohl.

"If you'll get back, I'll see what I can do with the wall," said Devonte. "Sometimes I can fix things as well as move them."

That gave her a little pause, but she found that wizards weren't as frightening as werewolves and vampires. She considered his offer, then shook her head.

"No. They already know what you are." She gathered her father's clothes from the bedspread and folded them neatly. Then she stashed them—and the plastic bag with Devonte's clothes—in the locker. "Just leave the wall. We only need to hide the werewolf from them, and you might need all the power you've got to help with the vampire."

Devonte nodded.

"Right, then." She took a deep breath and picked up her catchall purse from the floor where she'd set it.

Her brothers had made fun of her purses until she'd used one to take out a mugger. She'd been lucky—it had been laden with a pair of three-pound weights she'd been transporting from home to work—but she'd never admitted that to her brothers. Afterward they'd given her Mace and karate lessons, and quit bugging her about the size of her purse.

Unearthing a travel-sized game board from its depths, she said, "How about some checkers?"

Five hard-won games later she decided the vampire either wasn't coming tonight, or she was waiting for Stella to go away. She jumped three of Devonte's checkers and there was a quiet knock on the door. She turned to look as Jorge, the cop who'd gotten babysitting duty today, poked his head in.

"Sorry to leave you stuck here."

"No problem. Just beating a poor helpless child at checkers."

She waited for him to respond with something funny—Jorge

was quick on his feet. But his face just stayed . . . not blank pre-cisely, but neutral.

"They need you down in pediatrics, now. Looks like a case of child abuse, and Doc Gonzales wants you to talk to the little girl."

She couldn't help the instincts that brought her to her feet, but those same instincts were screaming that there was something wrong with Jorge.

Between her job and having a brother on the force, she'd gotten to know some of the cops pretty well. Nothing bothered Jorge like a child who'd been hurt. She'd seen him cry like a baby when he talked about a car wreck where the child hadn't survived. But he'd passed this message along to her with all the passion of a hospital switchboard operator.

In the movies, vampires could make people do what they wanted them to—she couldn't remember if the people were perma-nently damaged. Mostly, she was afraid, they just died.

She glanced down at her watch and shook her head. "You know my rules," she said. "It's after six and I'm off shift."

Her rules were a standing joke with her brothers and their friends—a serious joke. She'd seen too many people burn out from the stress of her job. So she'd made a list of rules she had to follow, and they'd kept her sane so far. One of her rules was that from eight in the morning until six in the evening she was on the job; outside of those hours she did her best to have a real life. She was breaking it now, with Devonte.

Instead of calling her on it, Jorge just processed her reply and finally nodded. "All right. I'll tell them."

He didn't close the door when he left. She went to the doorway and watched him walk mechanically down the hall and through the security door, which he'd left open. Very unlike him to leave a security door open, but he closed it behind him.

"That was the vampire's doing, wasn't it?" she asked, look-ing up.

The soft growl that eased through the ceiling was somehow

reassuring—though she hadn't forgotten his reservations about how well he'd do against a vampire.

She went back to Devonte's bed and made her move on the board. Out in the hall the security door opened again, and someone wearing high heels click-clicked briskly down the hall.

Stella took a deep breath, settled back on the end of the bed, and told Devonte, "Your turn."

He looked at the board, but she saw his hand shake as whoever it was in the hallway closed in on them.

"King me," he said in a fair approximation of triumph.

The footsteps stopped in the doorway. Devonte looked over her shoulder and his face went slack with fear. Stella inhaled and took her first look.

She'd thought a vampire would be young, like her father. Wasn't that the myth? But this woman had gray hair and wrinkles under her eyes and in the soft, white skin of her neck. She was dressed in a professionally tailored wine-colored suit. She wore a diamond necklace around her aging neck, and diamond-and-pearl earrings.

"Well," said Stella, "no one is going to think you look like a cuddly grandma."

The woman laughed, her face lighting up with a cheer so genuine that Stella thought she might have liked her if only the laughter didn't showcase her fangs. "The boy talked, did he? I thought for sure he'd hold his tongue, if only to keep his own secrets. Either that or broadcast it to the world, and then you and I wouldn't be in this position."

She gave Stella a kindly smile that showed off a charmingly mismatched pair of dimples. "I am sorry you had to be involved. I tried to get you out of it."

But Stella had been dealing with people a long time, and she could smell a fake a mile away. The laughter had been real, but the kind concern certainly wasn't.

"Separating your prey," Stella said. She needed to get the

vampire into the room, where her father could drop on top of her, but how?

The vampire displayed her fangs and dimples again. "More convenient and easier to keep the noise down," she allowed. "But not really necessary. Not even if you are a"—she took a deep breath—"werewolf."

The news didn't seem to bother her. Stella fought off the feeling that her father was going to be overmatched. He'd been a soldier and then a mercenary, training his own sons and then grandsons. Surely he knew what he was doing.

"Hah," sneered Devonte in classic adolescent disdain. "You aren't so tough. I nearly killed you all by myself."

The vampire sneered right back, and on her, the expression made the hair on the back of Stella's neck stand up and take notice. "You were a mistake, boy. One I intend to clear up."

DAVID CROUCHED MOTIONLESS, WAITING FOR THE SOUND of the vampire's voice to indicate she had moved underneath him.

Patience, patience, he counseled himself, but he should have been counseling someone else.

IF THE VAMPIRE'S THEATRICS SCARED STELLA, THEY drove Devonte into action. The bed he tried to smash her father with rattled across the floor. He must have tired himself out with his earlier wizardry because it was traveling only half as fast as it had when he'd tried to drive her father through the wall.

The vampire had no trouble grabbing it . . . or throwing it through the plaster wall and into the hallway, where it crashed on its side, flinging wheels, bedding, mattress, and pieces of the arcana that distinguished it from a normal bed.

She was so busy impressing them with her Incredible Hulk imitation, she didn't see the old blue-gray chair. It hit her squarely in the back, driving her directly under the panel Devonte had cracked.

"Now," whispered Stella, diving toward the hole the vampire had made in the wall, hoping that would be out of the way.

Even though Devonte's chair had knocked the vampire to her knees, Stella's motion drew her attention. The thing was fast, and she lunged for Stella in the same motion she used to rise. Then the roof fell on top of her, the roof and a silently snarling red-gold wolf with claws and fangs that made the vampire's look like toys.

For a moment she was twelve again, watching the monster dig those long claws into her mother's lover and she froze in horror. The woman looked frail beneath the huge wolf's bulk—until she pulled her legs under him and threw him into the outer wall, the one made of cinder blocks and not plaster.

With an inhuman howl, the vampire leaped upon her father. She looked nothing like the elegant woman who had walked into the room. In the brief glimpse she'd had of her face, Stella saw something terrible . . . evil.

"Stella, behind you!" Devonte yelled, hopping off the bed, his good arm around his ribs.

She hadn't been paying attention to anything except the vampire. Devonte's warning came just a little late and someone grabbed her by the arm and jerked her roughly around—Linnford. Gone were the urbane smile and GQ posture; his face was lit with fanaticism and madness. He had a knife in the hand that wasn't holding her. She reacted without thinking, twisting so his thrust went past her abdomen, slicing through fabric but not skin.

Something buzzed between them, hitting Linnford in the chest and knocking him back to the floor. He jerked and spasmed like a skewered frog in a film she'd once had to watch in college. The chair sat on top of him, balanced on one bent leg, the other three appearing to hover in the air.

It took a moment for her to properly understand what she was seeing. The bent chair leg was stuck into his rib cage, just to the left of his sternum. Blood began spitting out like a macabre fountain.

"Honey?" Hannah Linnford stood in the doorway. Like Stella, she seemed to be having trouble understanding what she was seeing.

Muttering, "Does no one remember to shut the security doors?" Stella pulled the mini-canister of Mace her youngest brother had given her after the mugging incident out of her pocket and sprayed it in the other woman's face.

If she'd been holding Linnford's knife, she could have cheerfully driven it through Hannah's neck: these people had taken one of her kids and tried to feed him to a vampire.

Thinking of her kids made Stella look for Devonte.

He was leaning against the wall a few feet from his bed, staring at Linnford—and his expression centered Stella because he needed her. She ran to him and tugged him to the far corner of the room, away from the fighting monsters, but too close to the Linnfords. Once she had him where she wanted him, she did her best to block his view of Linnford's dying body. If she could get medical help soon enough, Linnford might survive—but she felt no drive to do it. Let him rot.

Mace can in hand, she kept a weather eye on the woman screaming on the floor, but most of her attention was on the battle her father was losing.

They fought like a pair of cats, coming together clawing and biting, almost too fast for her eyes to focus on, then, for no reason she could see, they'd retreat. After a few seconds of staring at each other, they'd go at it again. Unlike cats, they were eerily silent.

The vampire's carefully arranged hair was fallen, covering her face, but not disguising her glittering . . . no, glowing red eyes. Her arm flashed out in a jerky movement that was so quick Stella almost missed it—and the wolf twitched away with another wound that dripped blood: the vampire was still virtually untouched.

The two monsters backed away from each other and the vampire licked her fingers.

"You taste so good, wolf," she said. "I can't wait until I can sink my fangs through your skin and suck that sweetness dry."

Stella sprayed Hannah in the face again. Then she hauled Devonte out the door and away from the vampire, making regrettably little allowance for his broken ribs. Dead was worse than in pain.

IT WAS WORKING, DAVID THOUGHT, WATCHING THE VAMpire lick his blood off her fingers. Though he was mostly focused on the vampire, he noticed when Stella took the boy out of the room. Good for her. With the vampire's minions here, one dead and one incapacitated, she shouldn't have trouble getting out. He hoped she took Devonte to her home—or any home—where they'd be safe. Then he put them out of his mind and concentrated on the battle at hand.

He'd met a vampire or two, but never fought one before. He'd heard that some of them had a strange reaction to werewolf blood. She seemed to be one of them.

He could only hope that her bloodlust would make her stupid. He'd heard that vampires couldn't feed from the dead. If it wasn't true, he might be in trouble.

He waited for her to come at him again—and this time he stepped into her fist, falling limply at her feet. She hit him hard, he felt the bone in his jaw creak, so the limp fall wasn't hard to fake. He'd wait until she started feeding and the residual dizziness from her blow left, then he'd take her.

She fell on him and he waited for her fangs to dig in. Instead she jerked a couple of times and then lay still. She wasn't breathing and her heart wasn't beating—but she'd been like that when she walked into the room.

"Papa?"

Stella was supposed to be safely away.

He rose with a roar, making an audible sound for the first time so the vampire would pay attention to him and leave his daughter alone. But the woman's body rolled smoothly off of him and lay on the floor—two wooden chair legs stuck through her back.

"Are you all right? Jorge left the security door open. I knew it when the Linnfords came in. We broke the legs off Jorge's chair, and Devonte used whatever he used to toss the furniture around to drive them into her back."

The soldier in him insisted on a full and quick survey of the room. Linnford was dead, the abused chair the obvious cause of death. A woman, presumably his wife, sobbed harshly, her face pressed into Linnford's arm: a possible threat. Stella and Devonte were standing way too close to the vampire.

They'd killed her.

For a moment he felt a surge of pride. Stella didn't have an ounce of quit in her whole body. She and the boy had managed to take advantage of the distraction he'd arranged before he could.

"Everyone was gone, Jorge and everyone." He looked at the triumph in Stella's face, not quite hidden by her worry for her friends.

She thought the vampire was finished, but wood through the heart didn't always keep the undead down.

"Are you all right?" Stella asked. And then when he just stared at her, "Papa?"

He'd come here hoping to play hero, he knew, hoping to mend what couldn't be mended. But the only role for him was that of monster, because that was the only thing he was.

He pulled the sheet off the bed and ripped it with a claw, then tossed it toward Linnford's sobbing woman. Stella took the hint and she and Devonte made a rope of sorts out of it and tied her up.

While they were working at that, he walked slowly up to the vampire. Stella had called him Papa tonight, more than once. He'd try to hold on to that and forget the rest.

He growled at the vampire: her fault that he would lose his daughter a second time. Then he snapped his teeth through her spine. The meat of her was tougher than it should have been, tougher than jerky and bad-tasting to boot. His jaw hurt from the hit he'd taken as he set his teeth and put some muscle into separating her head from her body.

When he was finished, the boy was losing his last meal in the corner, an arm wrapped around his ribs. Throwing up with broken ribs sucked: he knew all about that. Linnford's woman was secured. Stella had a hand over her mouth as if to prevent herself from imitating Devonte. When she pulled her eyes away from the vampire's severed head and looked at him, he saw horror.

He felt the blood dripping from his jaws—and couldn't face her any longer. Couldn't stay while horror turned to fear of him. He didn't look at his daughter again as he ran away for the first time in his long life.

WHEN HE COULD, HE CHANGED BACK TO HUMAN AT THE home of the local werewolf pack. They let him shower, and gave him a pair of sweats—the universal answer to the common problem of changing back to human and not having clothes to put back on.

He called his oldest son to make sure that Stella had called him and that he had handled the cleanup. She had remembered, and Clive was proceeding with his usual thoroughness.

Linnford was about to have a terrible car wreck. The vampire's body, both parts of it, was scheduled for immediate incineration. The biggest problem was what to do with Linnford's wife. For the moment she seemed to be too traumatized to talk. Maybe the vampire's death had broken her—or maybe she'd come around. Either way, she'd need help, discreet help from people who knew how to tell the difference between the victim of a vampire and a minion and would treat her accordingly.

David made a few calls, and got the number of a very private sanitarium run by a small, very secret government agency. The price wasn't bad—all he had to do was rescue some missionary who was related to a high-level politician. The fool had managed to get kidnapped with his wife and two young children. David's team would still get paid, and he'd probably have taken the assignment anyway.

By the time he called Clive back, his sons had located a few missing hospital personnel and the cop who'd been guarding the door. David heard the relief in Clive's voice: Jorge was apparently a friend. None of the recovered people seemed to be hurt, though they had no idea why they were all in the basement.

David hung up and turned off his cell phone. Accepting the offer of a bedroom from the pack Alpha, David took his tired body to bed and slept.

CHRISTMAS DAY WAS COMING TO A CLOSE WHEN DAVID drove his rental to his son's house—friends had picked it up from the hospital for him.

Red and green lights covered every bush and railing as well as surrounding all the windows. Knee-high candy canes lined the walk.

There were cars at his son's house. David frowned at them and checked his new watch. He was coming over at the right time. He'd made it clear that he didn't want to intrude—which was understood to mean that he wouldn't come when Stella was likely to be there.

He'd already have been on a flight home except that he didn't know how to contact Devonte. He tapped the envelope against his leg and wondered why he'd picked up a Christmas card instead of just handing over his business card. Below his contact information he'd made Devonte an open job offer beginning as soon as Devonte was eighteen. David could think of a thousand ways a wizard would be of use to a small group of mercenaries.

Of course, after watching David tear up the vampire's body, Devonte probably wouldn't be interested, so more to the point was the name and phone number on the other side of the card. Both belonged to a wizard who was willing to take on a pupil; the local Alpha had given it to him.

Clive had promised to give it to Devonte.

David had to search under the giant wreath on the door for the bell. As he waited, he noticed that he could hear a lot of people inside, and even through the door he smelled the turkey.

He took a step back, but the door was already opening.

Stella stood in the doorway. Over her shoulder he could see the whole family running around preparing the table for Christmas dinner. Devonte was sitting on the couch reading to one of the toddlers that seemed to be everywhere. Clive leaned against the fireplace and met David's gaze. He lifted a glass of wine and sipped it, smiling slyly.

David took another step back and opened his mouth to apologize to Stella . . . just as her face lit with her mother's smile. She stepped out onto the porch and wrapped her arms around him.

"Merry Christmas, Papa," she said. "I hope you like turkey."

ROSES IN WINTER

Kara never appeared in any of the Mercy books, but her father's appeal to Mercy for help in *Blood Bound* struck a chord in readers. I never go to a book-signing event where someone doesn't ask about her. I knew that she went to Aspen Creek with the Marrok's pack, and I expected her to show up in the Alpha and Omega novels. That's what I told people. But she didn't come to Aspen Creek until *after* the events in *Cry Wolf* and *Hunting Ground*. And then *Fair Game* jumped ahead because I needed the events at the end of the book to happen between *River Marked* and *Frost Burned*. Which meant that if I was going to tell Kara's story, I'd have to do it in a short story.

The events in this story take place between *Bone Crossed* and *Silver Borne*.

ASIL SMELLED THE INTRUDER AS SOON AS HE OPENED the door of his greenhouse, but he made no sign of it.

Kara Beckworth was the Marrok's current puzzle. She'd been attacked when she was only ten and was the youngest survivor either Asil or Bran had ever heard of—and between them they covered a lot of years. Her parents had done the best they could, but their only source of information was from a half-mad, antisocial lone wolf whose greatest skill was that he never did anything to attract the Marrok's attention, so he could be left to live his life in peace.

He'd told Kara's parents they should let him kill her. When they'd refused, he'd told them to keep her away from other werewolves. So every full moon, her parents had kept her locked in a cage and, when she'd reacted as most young things who had been locked in a cage would react, decided that werewolves had no control of themselves. Before she could prove them right, or succeed in killing herself—something she hadn't had enough knowledge to accomplish—her father had used his skills as a reporter to find more useful help. Eventually, that had landed Kara and her father here in Aspen Creek, Montana.

Asil turned on the water and began to dampen his tomato starts as he considered his response to the intrusion. Most of the greenhouse was on drip lines, but he preferred to do some of the work himself—and he'd learned that repairing a drip line was nearly as time-consuming as watering it all himself anyway and considerably less satisfactory. The temptation in this age was to automate too much and ruin his own fun.

"I know you know I'm here," Kara said defensively.

"Good," he said without looking up from what he was doing. "I would hate to think you were stupid."

"I should be in school," she said, a little more aggressively.

Full moon in two days, close enough to make her restless, is what he thought. Hard to sit in a classroom with the moon singing in your veins, especially when she was so young. But he wasn't subversive enough, quite, to tell her that.

"So why are you here instead?" He kept his eyes on his plants— which were only barely sprouts. They had a while to go before they would be plants.

"I like greenhouses," she said.

Ah—not a lie. Refreshing in a child of, what? Twelve or thirteen, he thought.

"And no one would look for me here." There was a little pause. "I am sorry for trespassing."

He heaved a sigh and turned off the switch at the business end of the hose, which would temporarily shut down the water. "And I am sorry I am a responsible adult—at least today. I must insist we telephone whoever is watching out for you so that they do not worry."

He looked at her for the first time. She was scrunched in the corner of the building, sitting on an upended five-gallon bucket. She was bundled up in one of those jackets that made everyone look like marshmallows even though the temperature was still fairly mild for early fall in Montana. He had not bothered with a coat when he headed out of his house. Her arms were wrapped mutinously around herself, so maybe the marshmallow effect was for something other than warmth. She'd been staring at him until he looked at her, but she couldn't hold his gaze and shrank back farther in the corner.

"Do you know who I am?" he asked, curious. He was pretty sure that the Marrok, their Alpha, warned all the youngsters away from the big bad wolf.

She nodded. "You're Asil. You're the black wolf I saw on the last hunt. I can smell it."

It had not been a moon hunt, those he no longer allowed himself; if the moon's song was disturbing to those who were young, it dug in deep to those who were as old as he was. But he'd participated in the last training hunt, a few weeks ago. He was dark brown, not black, but he allowed that at night the difference was subtle, so he decided to let it pass.

She'd known nothing about being a werewolf when she'd come to Aspen Creek two months ago. She was learning to use her nose. She was also afraid of him, which normally he wouldn't mind. But he didn't like scaring children.

"Pack is different from the real world," he told her. "No one in the pack will hurt you because the Marrok will not allow it. Other wolves you have to be wary around, but not pack."

She raised her eyes to him.

"I can tell you are afraid," he advised her gravely. "Otherwise, I would not have said anything. I will not hurt you. Nor will anyone in the pack."

"You are dangerous," she said. "I'm not the only wolf afraid of you. He warned me specifically to stay away from you."

And so she, having been warned, had decided to hide in his greenhouse. It was not an atypical reaction for an adolescent.

He nodded gravely. "Yes, I am dangerous. The Alpha doesn't talk just to hear himself speak. But I do not mind that the other wolves are afraid. To you I will say that there is no need to fear me or my wolf. I do not hurt women without grave cause and never children." He could promise so much, he was almost certain. When he could not, then it would, indeed, be time to end his existence.

"Pack is safe," she said, trying to believe it.

He sighed. "At other times and places you might have cause to worry about harm coming to you at a pack member's hand. But in this time and place the Marrok has let it be known that you are under his protection and out of bounds for the usual snarls and dominance fights that come from being a werewolf. No one in the pack will defy him—and so you are utterly safe."

"He is treating me different?" She sounded as if she wasn't sure whether that was a good thing or not.

"You are different," Asil told her. "And this pack is different. The Marrok has collected a bunch of misfits who are not suited to most packs, and that is combined with the newest wolves—next month is the month when the Marrok Changes those who wish to be werewolves." Idiots, every one of them. "Some of us are very dangerous, so it is necessary for the Marrok to draw this line. Do you understand?"

She nodded.

"And so it is that you do not need to be afraid of me."

"What about Charles?"

Asil laughed. "Everyone is a little afraid of Charles except Anna."

Her lips curled in a smile. "I got that, yeah."

"So whom do I call to inform them you are here?" Asil asked. "This is not negotiable. Someone worries over you."

She shrugged, unhappy again. He'd heard that her father had been sent back into the real world because his fear of her wolf was interfering with her ability to control herself. Neither she nor her father had been happy, but even the most experienced werewolf had trouble with a terrified human about. The idea that she even *could* control the wolf was very, very new to her, and real control was months if not years away. He didn't know whom she was staying with now.

When she didn't tell him, he took out his cell phone and called the Marrok.

"Asil?" said Bran.

"I have Miss Kara here in my greenhouse," Asil said. "She is restless, and I think an afternoon of potting plants might suit her better than sitting in a desk with thirty children who are scared of her."

She looked up at him, surprise on her face, as if she weren't used to someone defending her.

"Of course," said Bran. He sounded tired. "I should have thought of that. You are willing?"

Able is what he meant. It was a good question. Asil was very old, and his wolf was given to fits of rage, both of them nearing the end of their very long life. He tested his wolf, who seemed perfectly happy with an afternoon in the greenhouse with an unhappy adolescent.

"I think it shall be delightfully entertaining for both of us," he told his Alpha.

Bran laughed. "All right. *Bonne chance.*"

Asil disconnected.

"Who was he wishing good luck? You or me?" She sounded wry.

"Knowing Bran, it could be either of us," he said. "But it is probably you because he knows me. I do not need luck to deal with one young wolf."

He put her to work deadheading roses because there wasn't much she could do to screw it up. In his hothouse, with deadheading, he could keep roses all year long, though most of them he eventually let go dormant in the winter for the health of the plant.

It was early fall yet, so the rose section of his greenhouse was filled with flowers and heady perfume. He wished for the great gardens he'd grown in Spain, but most of his beauties would not live through a Montana winter without protection. He made do with the greenhouse and some hardy specimens planted near his house, where they were sheltered from the worst of the weather.

"Why roses?" Kara asked.

"Why not?" he said lightly as he mixed potting soil with his favorite concoction of rose food.

"Why not orchids or daisies or geraniums?" Her voice was thoughtful. "My mother has a greenhouse, and she grows all sorts of flowers."

"I have many different flowers here," he told her. "And I grow vegetables."

"Most of the greenhouse—all of this room and half of the other one are all roses," she said.

He opened his mouth to give her the easy answer, the one he used for everyone. He knew roses. It was better to be an expert in one thing than a dabbler in dozens. But he thought better of it.

"We all know about your trouble, do we not?" he said. "Your life has been spread out for total strangers—even though we are pack, we are still, right now, strangers—to look at and make judgment calls. You are not allowed secrets anymore—and we all should have things that we may keep to ourselves."

Her mouth tightened. "It's okay. Hard to hide that my parents are separated because my mother is scared of me, and my father is mad at her about it. Hard to hide what I am."

"All true," Asil said. "But here I think you need some secrets in return. So I will tell you something about me that no one else knows."

"Okay." She hesitated. "But what if I forget it's a secret and tell someone?"

"It is not a harmful thing," he said. "Only a tender thing that is hard for me to talk about. You are welcome to shout it on the streets—though I would rather you did not."

She nodded.

"I am very old, and once I had a mate," he told her. "She was everything to me. I would have filled her arms with jewels or gold if I could have. I would have destroyed the world for her—I was young and dramatic, you understand."

Kara's eyes widened. "You meant that. That you would have destroyed the world for her—it wasn't just exaggeration. The Marrok is teaching me to smell when people lie or tell the truth."

He gave her a formal nod. "Indeed. Being dramatic does not mean you do not have honest intentions. But destroying the world would not have saved her. She said, once, shortly before she died, that roses smelled like happiness. Whenever she smelled a rose, she thought of the day we met." He brought a bloom up to his nose. "And after she told me that, I also think of that day when I smell roses."

He cleared his throat and brought their conversation out of murky water. "And it is also true that with roses I am a genius, there are no others who breed roses such as mine. Why would I not choose to share my genius with others?"

"Okay," she said. "And I won't tell anyone the other reason. It is private."

She was not a chatterer. The rest of the afternoon she worked quietly at whatever task he gave her. Someone, probably her mother, had taught her that, which made her more useful than he expected.

When Devon came, as he did sometimes, she didn't look at the ragged old gaunt wolf or talk to him—though she kept a little closer to Asil than she had been. Devon settled on the ground with a sigh and didn't look at Asil or Kara, either.

Devon was not as old as Asil, but like Asil, he was on his last years. If Asil were being honest, which he didn't always choose to be, Devon was a lot closer to the end than he was. In all the time Asil had been in Montana, he'd never seen Devon use his human form. Like Asil, he sometimes shadowed the pack's moon hunt, but he never participated. Devon's presence in the pack spiritual weaving was dark and murky.

Several years ago, he'd started to come to Asil's greenhouse. Usually, he'd sleep for an hour or two, but with Kara there, he just curled up and rested. His head turned away from them both.

"Bran says," Asil told Kara as they began to clean up, "that all wolves need company. Devon is worried that he'll hurt someone, so mostly he stays by himself. Me?" He told her grandly. "I am the Moor. He does not have to worry about hurting me. So he comes here."

Devon got up, shook himself forcefully, stretched—and then gave Asil a look.

Asil raised his eyebrows and opened the door so the wolf could leave. When he was gone, Asil looked at Kara, who was biting her lip nervously. He'd scared her again, and he meant only to twit Devon.

"Because I like you," he told her, "and because he cannot hear me, I'll let you in on the real reason Devon comes here. He was once a gardener almost as good as I." Devon, under a different name, had grown roses that rivaled Asil's own a hundred years ago. "The Alice Vena rose in the corner"—he gave her a mock-disappointed look—"the burgundy rose next to the 'stripy' ones, as you call them. That Alice Vena descends from one of his roses. Devon misses his flowers and comes here to remember."

That was true—and Devon would probably rather not have anyone but Asil know it. But it was also true that if Asil had not been so much more dominant, or if Asil had been the least bit afraid of him, Devon could not come for his little visits without risk of bloodshed. But Kara would be safer if she thought Devon was just here for the roses. Fear was not useful when keeping company with the oldest of the wolves. And Kara's safety had become important to him.

"You will come here to me tomorrow," Asil said as she put her coat back on. "Bring your schoolbooks, and you can teach me what they are doing in school since I was last in a schoolroom—which was several centuries ago. We shall make breakfast and prepare my outdoor gardens for the cold that is coming. You shall do this until after the moon is done with her singing, yes?"

"All right," she said.

"Do you need a ride home?" he asked her. "There are no school buses from here."

"I'm staying at the Marrok's house until he finds a better situation for me."

Asil grimaced in sympathy. "Let me know if Leah troubles you."

Kara frowned at him. "She's been very kind."

"Really?" Asil took the notion of kindness and the Marrok's mate and tried to put them in the same room together, but they wouldn't fit. Maybe she had other rules when she dealt with children? He found that unlikely. "If that changes, feel free to let me know. In the meantime, I will give you a ride today—and you can catch the school bus in the morning and run here from school."

"Run?"

He nodded. "It will do your wolf good to get rid of some of that energy."

KARA TAUGHT HIM ALGEBRA AND SCIENCE AND HE taught her how to bed down plants with straw to protect them from the storm. He did not go on that moon hunt, as he had not gone on any since he'd moved from Spain to Montana.

But he shadowed them, making sure she was all right, even as he called himself an old fool: Bran would not allow harm to come to her any more than he would. Devon, who had come one more time to lurk with the roses while Kara taught Asil Montana geography, ran beside him for a mile or two before heading off to go wherever Devon went when he wasn't in Asil's greenhouse. Asil should have left as well—Kara was doing fine—but he didn't. All the self-directed imprecations in the world could not make him go home until she was safely back at the Marrok's home.

October dawned with a heavy snowstorm and strangers who came to Aspen Creek to be Changed. Asil avoided town. He avoided the Marrok's house specifically, as the inductees—the

Marrok's word for the humans who wanted to become were-wolves, not Asil's—filled the Marrok's home to bursting. The wolves and, in some cases, the human relatives who had come to support the inductees, took over the small motel in town.

The Marrok required anyone who wanted to be Changed to come two weeks beforehand. He told them it was so he could make sure they knew what they were getting into. He'd told Asil it was to give Bran one last chance to talk them out of it.

Asil wasn't worried about how his wolf would react to all the strangers—not this year. But too many of the humans would die rather than be Changed as they wished, and their loved ones who came here with them would grieve. He had had enough grief and mourning, even secondhand, to last a thousand lifetimes.

Avoiding town meant driving to Missoula to resupply—which wasn't a bad thing as Missoula had real grocery stores, bookstores, and restaurants. He ate lunch at his favorite Indian-vegan restaurant because the food was good and because it amused him—an ancient werewolf eating New Age vegan. And it was petty of him, but one of the waitresses was terrified of him and another one was vaguely disapproving—as if she could smell the meat on his breath. He enjoyed both reactions. He always made a point of leaving a big tip.

The roads were icy, but he was a good driver. Werewolves have very good reflexes, and he'd had years to perfect his ability to drive in the snow. He got home before dark. Once he'd unloaded and stored the results of his shopping trip, he went out to his green-house to play. Work. The challenge of growing things in this cli-mate was invigorating—and expensive. He enjoyed the first and had no issues with the latter. He'd been poor—any number of times—but not in the last five hundred years.

He was repotting an African violet when someone scratched at the greenhouse door and whined. He opened the door and let Kara's wolf in. She was wet and shivering, but not with the cold. Her eyes were miserable, and she whined at him piteously.

He'd never seen her take her wolf's shape when it hadn't been forced upon her by the moon's call. Just last week, he'd suggested that the Marrok encourage her to do so because she wasn't having much luck controlling her wolf without a more dominant wolf around. But the moon's call made the wolf more difficult to deal with. Maybe she would have better results if she tried when the moon was in hiding.

"I told her that," Bran had responded. "We've been trying to get her to attempt a change, but unless the moon forces her, she won't do it."

"You can make her do it," Asil had told him.

Here, he thought, kneeling down to pull the pitiful, half-grown wolf against the warmth of his body, *is the result of your meddling.*

"Can't change back?" he asked.

She moaned at him and shivered again. Partly, he thought, it had worked. It wasn't a wolf who was looking up at him with such misery. Kara was in charge.

"No worries," he told her. "You can do it." He could force her change, and he would if he had to. But a forced change—like what the Marrok had done—hurt even worse than when the moon called the wolf from human shape. Better if she managed it herself.

He coaxed her into his rose room, where the sweet scent of his mate's favorite flower filled the air with memories, and sat on the dirt floor with his back to the foot-high stone wall that edged his raised rosebush beds.

He patted the ground beside him, and she curled up in a miserable ball, wiggling and restless until finally she put her muzzle on his leg and sighed. He put a hand on her back and sang to her.

He didn't have the Marrok's voice—at various times Bran Cornick had made his living as a bard—but he could carry a tune. He crooned a child's lullaby his father had sung to him. It wasn't Spanish, but African, a Moorish tune his father had learned from his grandmother. Like Asil, it was old and worn, the words in a language that no one, to his knowledge, had spoken for a thousand years. Even he had forgotten what the words meant, but the song was for children. Its intent was to let them know that it was the job of adults to keep the young ones safe from harm. When he was finished with the song, he switched to stories he had told his own children; maybe she'd heard them from her parents in happier times.

She relaxed against him—and he thought she was more than half-asleep. But she was still caught in wolf form. Instead of letting her scare herself again, he coaxed her wolf to let the girl back out. It was still a use of force, of the dominance of his wolf over hers, but it wasn't brutal or abrupt.

When she began changing back, he slid out from under her and quit touching her because he didn't want to hurt her—and touching something made the shift hurt more. Quietly, because she was caught up in the change, he slipped out to his house to gather sweats for her to change into. It took her the better part of a half hour to emerge from the rose room garbed in clothes that were much too big for her.

"Thank you," she told him, eyes averted. "I couldn't change back. *He* called me to his study, made me change, then pushed me outside. Told me to come home in my human skin. I tried and tried, but I couldn't change back."

"Miss Kara," he said after weighing his words. Not from him would she get any criticism of the Marrok, especially when he'd suggested it to Bran in the first place. There was no reason for him to be angry with Bran—though he was. "My greenhouse is flattered to have been your refuge from the storm."

"I failed," she said.

"Did you?" he asked.

She gave him an irritated look, and he smiled. "Let's get you home, shall we?"

He carried her out to his car because although he had sweats she could wear, he didn't have shoes. He handed her the leftovers from his vegan-restaurant excursion. She ate the food as fast as she could move fingers to mouth.

He drove up to the sprawling manor that was Bran Cornick's house. Before he turned off the engine, Leah was there to collect his charge. She didn't look at him—he'd scared her once, and she had learned her lesson about flirting with the Moor. She smiled at Kara, though, and his irritation with his Alpha's mate died away. He waited until Kara was safely in the house before he drove off.

He hadn't quite pulled into his driveway before his phone rang.

"Asil," said the Marrok's voice. He wasn't happy.

"Bran," replied Asil, who was still fighting down his own temper.

"It does her no good for you to help her to change. She has to be able to do it herself," Bran said.

Asil took a deep breath and turned off his truck before he answered.

"When she came to my greenhouse and asked me to help, she was in full control of her wolf—even though she was scared because she couldn't change back."

"She has to do better than that," snapped Bran uncharacteristically. He knew as well as Asil that it was a big step for her to be in control. It was a sign that she had finally begun accepting what she was—and it was a bigger sign that she'd be one of the ones who made it.

The people who would be Changed a couple of days before the next full moon would have one year to prove they could control their wolf—which included changing at will from one form to the other. Those who failed would be killed—no one could afford to have werewolves who couldn't be trusted. Especially not now that the werewolves had revealed themselves to the humans. It was imperative that the public not know just how dangerous werewolves really were.

"Is she in danger?" asked Asil, trying to keep the menace out of his voice. Kara couldn't afford for him to challenge the Marrok over her, not unless she was truly at risk.

"Not right now," said Bran after a moment. He sounded

exhausted. Asil thought about how he had not been able to face all the impending grief coming—and how the Marrok had to be in the center of it. His rules about Changing had saved countless lives—and probably the werewolves as a species—but it had not been without personal cost.

Bran sighed. "She's just a baby. But unless she can control her shift and her wolf, I'm going to have to take her out with the new wolves—and that's going to mean trouble. She's too dominant to go without challenge, and she's too young to prevail."

Asil hissed at the thought of his Kara out in the First Hunt with a double handful of new werewolves out of control and ready to kill each other and anyone else who got in their way. Bran's rules were good ones—they gave wolves a cage to protect themselves with. That did not mean those rules were without cost.

"Send her out tomorrow, too," Asil said. "Tell her that I'll be home around sunset and she can come to me for help if she needs it."

"No," said Bran. "She has school tomorrow."

"This is more important than school."

Bran sighed. "It is. I'll send her out, but she needs to do the shift on her own. I might have Leah mention that you'll be out doing things until sunset tomorrow."

SHE WASN'T AS FRIGHTENED WHEN SHE SHOWED UP THE next night. He took her to his roses, where she tried to change back to human—tried very hard. But only with his help could she regain her human shape.

She was examining the sweats she wore doubtfully (today's were gray and had a hole in the knee) when a car pulled up outside. She stiffened and gave him a panicked look.

"Peace," he told her.

And Sage came in the door a moment later, looking as though she'd stepped off a walkway in Paris instead of a breezy autumn in near-wilderness Montana. She was tall, cool, and elegant with sun-streaked hair and warm blue eyes, and if he weren't so old and fragile, he'd have been courting her as none of the idiots in the pack seemed able to do properly.

"Hello, hello," she said. "How is my favorite evil monster who wants to die?"

Asil made a point of looking over his shoulder and all around before saying, "I don't know. Had you asked where the handsomest, most noble creature on earth was, I could have told you. Had you asked where the most dangerous wolf in all the world was, I could have told you that as well. But there are no monsters here."

She grinned at him. "Well, kitten," she said to Kara, who was watching them openmouthed. "When I told him I was headed up to the big house tonight, Bran asked if I'd mind picking you up and save his Nobleness a trip."

"Sure," said Kara.

He closed the door behind them and put his forehead against it. His keen ears picked up a conversation he was not meant to overhear.

"He really likes you," Kara said. "Really, really."

"Well," Sage's voice was dry. "That's not news, sugar. But he won't do anything about it until it dawns on him that though he's been waiting more than fifteen years for this famous 'madness' that is going to break him and turn him into a ravening monster— it just might not happen."

"Fifteen *years*," said Kara.

"Asil," said Sage clearly, "needs to get over himself."

Asil smiled at the acid tone that told him that she knew he was listening in. Clearly, she deserved him. If this were fifty years ago, he'd hunt her down and take her as his.

FOR A WEEK, HE MANAGED TO STAY AWAY FROM HIS home until sunset. When he got home, Kara would be waiting, a smallish half-grown werewolf. First she waited by the door of his greenhouse—but then Devon came and waited with her, his nose turned away and his eyes shut. After that, she came to his front porch and lay on the mat because Devon would not intrude so far into Asil's territory.

On the seventh day, while she got dressed, he cut a few long-stemmed roses and put them in a pretty vase. Four of the peachy-colored ones because they smelled the best, and one (because that bush had only one rose that wasn't too old) that was a deep red with a hint of blue or purple along the edge of each petal.

"Why are you bringing that?" Kara asked him in the truck when he gave her the vase to hold.

"Because a week is a unit of time," he told her. "As in, let's give this a week and see what will happen."

She touched the rose petal sadly. "You think he's going to be disappointed."

"I never make predictions about other people's responses," Asil lied easily. She was not experienced enough to see through his lies, and he was happy to soften her life with them where he could.

The Marrok met them at his door.

"I need to see you both in my study," he said, not unkindly.

Asil handed him the vase, and Bran took it—a bit bemused by the gift. Which is why Asil had brought it. He would not, *would not* defy the Marrok. He needed to be in this pack, so that when his wolf finally broke, there would be someone strong enough to hunt him down and kill him before his body count grew too high. Sage might disagree, but Asil knew his own fate. But that did not mean he intended to sit back and watch what might come. He would request leniency in such a way as not to challenge Bran's authority.

Vase in one hand, Bran pinched the bridge of his nose tiredly with the other.

Asil didn't wait for him to say anything, just led the way to Bran's study, conscious of the reluctant teenager behind him. His wolf wanted to growl and protect her—but he knew better. Bran had nothing but her best interests in mind. Her best interests and the bribe of Bran's favorite roses to let Bran know that Asil would do whatever he could to help.

Asil ignored the curious looks they got from the other people in Bran's house. They would know Kara. Asil would learn their names if they made the transition, not before.

Bran closed the door to his study behind them.

"This isn't working," he said, setting the vase down on the desk.

Asil didn't pretend to misunderstand. "Yesterday, when she came, I met her as a wolf. She was able to change to human when I did." He'd hoped that would have kicked her into doing it herself—which is why he hadn't tried it today. But she hadn't been able to change on her own.

Bran raised an eyebrow and looked at Kara. "What do you think?"

She swallowed, ducking her head under the weight of the Marrok's gaze, but her voice was strong. "I think I'm better. I can take charge almost as soon as we are out of sight of the house. I can't manage it right when I change to a wolf yet—but until this week I couldn't do it at all. I can't change back on my own. But yesterday I think I figured out how to do it. How it *should* feel to start the change on my own."

Bran frowned at the pair of them.

"Okay." He tapped his desk and looked at Asil. "Any insights you might have would be helpful."

Asil raised his eyebrows and shrugged. "I've never seen a wolf as young as she is survive. I think we had a fourteen-year-old once. We had to kill *him*—but she's a lot better adjusted than he ever got."

"After three years," the Marrok said, "she should be adjusted."

Asil nodded and told Bran the things he already knew. "Not her fault. It would have been easier if someone had worked with her right away. Three years of incarceration encouraged her to build walls between herself and the wolf that they wouldn't have had when she was first Changed. She'll get it. It might take a few weeks or a few months." He shrugged. "The roses are to let you know I'm willing to aid any way I can." He seldom cut his roses, even the ones meant to be cut—it made them more valuable when he decided to bestow them upon someone. "If you decide to take her on First Hunt, I'll come"—he smiled, knowing Bran would read the threat in the smile that wasn't in his voice—"help."

Bran's mouth pinched, and he said silkily, "Is that a threat, Asil?"

"Would I threaten the Marrok?"

Bran laughed, and Asil's wolf settled down as the tension in the room dissipated.

"Never," said Bran mockingly. But his voice was kind when he told Kara, "So you have another reason to get control. First Hunt is not where either of us wants to see you. And no one wants Asil there."

Her chin raised.

"Most of those who survive the Change will be male," he said. "And all of them are fully adult. They won't make allowances for your being young. Half the business of the First Hunt is establishing how dominant the wolves are. It will get bloody." He glanced at Asil. "Very bloody if Asil joins us."

He took a deep breath. "Fine. One more week. That gives you until the day before First Hunt. Kara, keep trying. Don't go to Asil unless it doesn't work. We won't make Asil keep making himself scarce—but I don't want you to go to him until sunset."

"If she changes outside this time of the year, she'll freeze," Asil said. "Why don't you let her come to the greenhouse—I'll open the push door so she can get in." He would never call it a dog door. "That way she'll have clothes and warmth."

"It is easier to work pack magic in the woods," Bran said.

Asil snorted. "Not that I ever noticed. For a girl raised in the middle of the city, the woods are frightening and lonely. Her wolf will never let her change when she's afraid."

Bran regarded Asil without favor. "You didn't think to mention this earlier?"

"You didn't ask," said Asil, who refused to say that he hadn't thought of it before.

Bran saw through him—which was one of the reasons Asil liked him. "Too many strangers here for her to be comfortable—Leah's said the same. Hah—I thought that might bother you. But that's why I sent her out on her own." He nodded. "Fine. But you leave her alone until sunset—and let her try her best to change herself." He smiled at Asil and got back at him for every moment of stress Asil had put him through by saying, "I'm very glad to see that you care."

Asil opened the study door—and there was another wolf in human skin standing with a hand raised to knock. The wolf looked vaguely smug and raised his eyes to meet Asil's. The smug look—and the knock, no one knocked at the Marrok's door when it was closed—annoyed Asil. He was more annoyed and a fair way to terrified by how his affection for Kara had blindsided him. He'd sworn not to make serious ties with anyone as he neared the end of his life.

So he vented by letting the unfortunate stranger feel the full weight of his wolf—driving him to his knees with the power he let roll out. He ignored Bran's sigh and stalked out of the house without talking to anyone else.

Behind him he heard Bran say, "Eric. I thought we agreed that you would stay in the hotel until—"

THE NEXT EVENING HE WENT OUT TO HIS GREENHOUSE and found a very sad-looking wolf. She was panting with the effort of trying to change. He went back to the house, brought her a plate of raw steak, and sat beside her while she ate. When she'd finished the plate, he pulled her into her change. She wouldn't talk to him on the way home.

"It'll happen," he said.

"Don't pat me on the head," she snapped. "You don't know anything!"

"Don't," he said softly.

Jaw jutting out, she turned her head away from him, while he fought his wolf hard enough to break into a sweat.

"You can't challenge me like that," he told her when he'd won his battle. "You are a wolf—not just a teenager. Bran won't allow it, either."

She hunched her shoulders, so he thought that Bran *hadn't* allowed it.

"But my control isn't as good as his. Look." He held out a hand so she could see that it shook. "My wolf is unhappy with you, and he'll enforce his dominance any way that he needs to. He'll hurt you if you try that again. I don't want that to happen."

"I don't want to be a werewolf," she muttered, the scent of her fear filling the truck. She wiped her cheek with her hand. He couldn't comfort her because his wolf was still angry.

He gave her a bitter smile she didn't see because she wasn't looking at him. "Neither do I."

SHE DIDN'T COME THE NEXT NIGHT. ASIL WAITED AS long as he dared, then called Bran.

"She's here," Bran said. "I helped her change, and it was harder than the last time I did it."

He didn't ask, but Asil told him anyway. "I scared her. She snapped at me, and my wolf was unhappy."

"She's dominant," Bran said. "Too dominant for old wolves like us to be able to let things slide. I'll talk to her."

"No," Asil told him. "She needs to be afraid. If she goes on First Hunt, it might make her safer if she is afraid." Too much fear might cause the new wolves to hunt her, but not enough fear and she'd put herself in harm's way. She needed not to go on First Hunt.

But that was not why he had scared her. "She is safer if she is afraid of me. I almost hurt her, Bran."

"But you didn't."

"No." It had been too close. And all she had done was show a little disrespect.

"She is safe with you, Asil."

He laughed. "No one is safe with me. No one." He hung up the phone—something, he told his wolf fiercely, that was much more disrespectful than Kara had been yesterday.

IT SNOWED THAT NIGHT, DUMPING SIX INCHES BEFORE morning. Asil waited until it stopped around noon to go out and shovel it. He heard the howls of hunting wolves and frowned. All of the people in Aspen Creek—not that there were many of them— knew about the werewolves. But to hunt like that was still taking too many chances. Besides, he frowned, werewolves were not hounds, they did not need to make noise when they hunted.

And then he heard her; wolf or human, he knew her voice. Kara yipped, a high-pitched, terrified sound. Those bastards weren't hunting deer. He dropped the shovel and ran, wishing he was on four paws, wishing his human body was faster, wishing the snow had not fallen so deeply. He howled, the cry sounding odd coming from his human throat, but it would carry, telling Kara he was on his way.

Who would dare? he thought with shock that slowed him not in the least. Who would dare hunt one of the Marrok's pack in his own territory? Idiots, he decided grimly. It wasn't an accident that Charles was feared as much as he was. That other werewolves thought of the Marrok as some magical wolf far removed from them—because it wasn't in a werewolf's nature to tamely bow to authority just because it was presented to them. Most especially it wasn't in an Alpha werewolf's nature. And sometimes Bran's chosen means of presenting himself as a quiet, thoughtful, and intelligent leader became something of a liability.

Every few years, when the idiots had forgotten too much, or new idiots were born—the Marrok had to remind them why they obeyed him and not the other way around. Usually, Bran was sharp enough to make sure that the idiots didn't hurt anyone but themselves along the way.

Asil's body knew these woods, he'd spent nearly fifteen years here, and his feet knew every rock and hole within miles of his house. He was pretty sure he knew where the howls had been coming from. If Kara was leading them here, she'd take the most direct path—and after a week and more of coming to his greenhouse every day, she should know the most direct path.

The idiots were still making noise, so either they hadn't caught her yet, or they were playing with her. Asil jumped a creek bed hidden under the snow and a thin sheet of ice and, with the trail flat and straight before him, stretched out and ran. He thought he'd hit top speed when Kara yipped in pain. He found another gear and moved faster.

They were loud, which was foolish and arrogant in these woods. Arrogance was a fine trait—but not when combined with stupidity.

Even as his wolf raged that one in his care had been hurt, his human brain was picking at the motivation. Everyone knew whose woods these were. Everyone knew that wolves who did not belong to the Marrok's pack were not allowed to hunt here unless they were invited. Everyone here would know about Kara—she was unique, a child Changed who survived when no child survived a werewolf attack. Everyone knew she belonged to the Marrok, even though they did not know that she belonged to Asil—the Moor.

For fifteen years, Asil had tuned out gossip that came by him. He was no longer an Alpha, he had come here to die—what did he care about other werewolves?

There was a narrow gully up ahead, where prey could be trapped. From the sounds of it, that's where his prey was. He quit worrying about *why* and began thinking about what he planned to do. He left the trail and ran up the side of the mountain so he could come at the gully from the side.

Kara growled fiercely, and his heart ached at the fear in her voice. Someone would pay for the fear in her voice.

He would kill them all.

No, Asil thought. He would let Bran kill them all. Because if he started killing, he did not trust himself to stop—and Kara was at risk. He would let the monster out someday, but not when it risked the death of someone in his charge.

He caught a glimpse of his quarry, mostly hidden by the drop in the terrain, and leaped in among them. He took them totally by surprise, three werewolves that his eyes didn't know, though his nose told him that he'd met at least one of them before. Kara, blood streaming from a shallow cut along her ribs, yipped in terror and tried to jump in front of him. To protect *him*.

It hurt his pride even as it charmed him.

The strangers recovered their wits, such as they were, and turned to face him. Showing their fangs and snapping them together in an attempt to frighten him. They thought him helpless in his human skin.

"What are you?" he asked them in disgust. "Crocodiles?" He showed them *his* teeth as he let his power sweep over them, the power of an ancient wolf who had led his own pack for many centuries. The force of it rumbled in his voice as he said, *"Down."*

All of the wolves dropped to the ground, including Kara.

But calling upon his power was a mistake. To call upon his dominance was to bring his wolf to the fore, and his wolf was savagely angry. He roared, tearing the tissues of his throat with the sound. He tasted his own blood before the werewolf healed the violence he'd done to himself.

It was Kara who saved him. She whined piteously, her wolf sensing his rage and not understanding that it wasn't her at fault.

The wolf hesitated—and Asil locked the beast down with gentle finality. Not yet. He would not give in just yet. He wanted to see what this child of the wolf would grow into.

"*Pobrecita,*" he said to her tenderly. "Not you." He lifted her to her feet. "You I am not angry with." She pressed her unwounded side desperately tight to his leg. She was shaking and panting in fear. Not of him, he hoped.

"It is all right now," he told her. "You are safe."

One of the wolves lunged to his feet, snarling. She flinched, and Asil drove him back down to the snow-covered ground with his gaze. The man beneath the wolf's pelt might want to attack, but his wolf was outclassed and knew it.

As long as they were in their wolf forms, they could not attack him. Asil glanced at Kara, who was fair game—though he thought that she would not be vulnerable for long. She had a backbone, that girl. He thought of the way she'd gotten between him and the other wolves because she mistakenly assumed that because he was in his human form, he might be outgunned. No, she was born to be a protector; she just needed to grow up.

For now, though, it was for him to protect her. So he did to the strangers what he had not done to Kara and used his power to drag them into their human bodies. The change would hurt—a lot—and then they would get cold on the walk to his car. He did not care at all about their sufferings.

I do, I want to see them suffer, said his darker self.

While the wolves who had thought they could hunt on the Marrok's land changed, Asil checked Kara's wound and she licked anxiously at his fingers. Her fur was caked with blood, but beneath the gore, her skin had already sealed.

"You'll be fine," he told her, ruffling the hair on the top of her head. "You did well to call to me—and to lead them here. I am sorry I could not kill them for you. But they will be suitably punished."

Bran would probably not kill them unless they had been trouble before. But that there were three of them made Asil wonder who their Alpha was—and why he'd allowed them to hunt today and in this place. There was no way any kind of competent Alpha would not feel a hunt as chaotic as these idiots' hunt had been through the pack bonds.

Perhaps their Alpha had sent them.

Asil considered the wolves who were nearing their human forms. The one he'd thought he'd recognized was the wolf he'd seen outside Bran's office. Eric. Who had already disobeyed Bran by not staying away from Bran's house until after the great day of Change was over.

Who would gain from such a brash breaking of Bran's rules? Who would gain from Kara's being harmed while she was under the Marrok's protection? He did not know because he had kept himself ignorant—he had been self-indulgent and lazy, or maybe he would have seen this coming and spared Kara the fright.

Not your problem, Asil told himself fiercely under the sting of guilt. It was not self-indulgence because he had come here to set down his responsibilities and die with honor. He was not an Alpha here. He'd tended to such matters for long enough. Here his duty was clear. He would take them—and take Kara—to his Alpha. Once delivered, he was done.

Speaking of his Alpha . . . he took his cell phone out of its holster and called Bran.

"Asil?"

"I am standing in the middle of the forest where three of our werewolf guests had decided that hunting our Kara would bring them some benefit," he said.

"They are still alive?"

"If they were not, I would be hunting my next victim instead of calling you," he said.

"You sell yourself short," Bran told Asil, but his voice was distracted. That argument was an old one. Asil did not make the mistake of thinking that Bran's calmness meant he did not care that these wolves had trespassed. People died when Bran was at his most reasonable. Some of them died horribly. All of them idiots.

"I assume that Kara is all right," Bran said. "If not, I would be getting reports about a werewolf who had killed every living thing in Aspen Creek and was heading next for Troy."

Someone listening might think that Bran was being facetious, or even mocking—and they might be right. But it was himself he was mocking, not Asil. They both knew that Bran had been that monster.

"Probably," agreed Asil. "But I would be a much better monster than you were. There would be no stories about my reign of terror because no one would live to tell the tale."

Black humor took the sting out of the truth—but did not obscure it. And Asil knew the stories came later because the monster who had once ruled Bran's body had not left victims alive, either. Bran had come back—and the reason for that was the reason why Bran Cornick was Asil's Alpha and not the other way around.

"They're almost done," Asil told him.

"Done?"

"I made them change back to human—that way none of them will be able to hurt Kara when my back is turned. It'll take us fifteen minutes or so to get to my house and another fifteen to take them to you."

"Don't make it too easy on them," Bran said.

Asil smiled at the first of Kara's attackers who was trying to stand up. "I won't. You have my word."

"See you in half an hour," Bran said, and hung up.

ASIL MADE THE OTHER WOLVES SIT IN THE TRUCK BED. If they had really been human, he'd have been risking their lives by making them stay out, naked, in the cold for so long. But werewolves can't be killed by a little cold.

"It isn't that cold," he told Kara when she whined in concern while her attackers climbed in. "They are tough. If they are tough enough to pick on little girls"—he looked at them, and they turned their heads away—"then they are tough enough to ride in the back." To them he said, "You stay there until we get where we are going. If you jump, I will back up and run over you until you are too broken to heal—and leave you for someone who cares to pick you up. It might take a while."

They heard the truth in his words, and he saw their submission. They would stay where he'd put them—which disappointed him. He could have run them over with his truck without disturbing his wolf. He would have enjoyed it.

He opened the driver's side door and gestured to Kara. She leaped in gracefully, the only evidence left of the wound the mess the blood had made of her fur.

He drove to the Marrok's house, following four other cars and a truck doing the same thing: the Marrok had summoned the wolves. Because he knew where the only place big enough to house everyone was, Asil drove past the house and took the back road that allowed him to drive all the way to the pole barn. The truck in front of them did the same thing, and there were more trucks and SUVs parked at the barn—pack members.

The pole barn had been built about thirty years ago because the Marrok did not like Changing people in the school auditorium. "Too much blood and misery," he'd said. "I am old enough to believe it leaves a mark on a place."

Asil agreed.

Bran leaned against the outside wall of the pole barn as Asil drove up. He met Asil's eyes through the windshield and pointed to the empty space in front of him, right next to the entrance. So Asil pulled in and parked.

Bran looked considerably less dangerous than Charles—the huge, blank-faced man who stood alertly beside him. Not for the first time, Asil thought that it had served Bran well to have a son who oozed threat like a Twinkie oozed plasticky cream filling. Everyone looked at Bran's son Charles and forgot who the most dangerous person was.

Asil got out and held open the door for Kara. She jumped down beside him and gave Charles a wary look. Bran's son was too busy taking in the shivering and naked men in the truck bed to notice. He threw them each a pair of sweat bottoms—which Asil hadn't noticed him holding.

"Get dressed," Charles rumbled at them. Once they were clothed, if only a little, Bran's son took charge of herding them inside.

Once they were gone, Bran looked at Kara, who shrank under his gaze.

"It would have been better," Bran said grimly, "if we hadn't handed ammunition to our enemies. I'm afraid I'm as much at fault as you are, Asil. But it is Kara they want to pay."

Asil frowned. Surely it should be the wolves who attacked Kara who would pay. "Explain that," he said. Then, because he remembered that he wasn't Alpha anymore, "Please. I don't pay attention to politics anymore," he told Bran, half-apologetically. "That's your job."

"Yeah," Bran said. "Well, my job sucks." He knelt and slid his hand along Kara's jaw. Helplessly, her tail wagged her body—her wolf delighted by his attention. "You are mine, darling. I'll keep you safe."

Bran's idea of safe, which paralleled Asil's own, sometimes meant dead. Asil quit breathing for a moment.

Asil thought back over what he and Bran had done to imperil Kara. The last interaction had been in Bran's study. He glanced at the door where the miscreant wolves had gone, preceding them into the pole barn. Eric of the "we attack children" pack had been waiting just outside that study door when Asil and Bran had spoken of how long Kara had been a wolf. She'd been a wolf for three years and had yet to be in control of her change.

That werewolves have one year to prove themselves or they have to be killed was a hard and necessary law. It required people to kill their loved ones to preserve the rest of the wolves. They were willing to do so only because that law applied to all of them. If Bran made an exception for Kara, it would spell decades of resentment and rebellion. If he did not make an exception for Kara, then Asil and Bran would have that battle that Asil came here for.

It was oddly stupid of them to hunt Kara so loudly where there were wolves to hear. It was odd that they had done so little damage to her. What if it had not been stupidity—or rather, it had been stupidity on a much grander scale? What if someone had wanted this meeting, wanted to push the issue of Kara out into the open?

Asil's eyes met Bran's—letting Bran know that Asil understood the issue, and that he would not allow Kara to be harmed without a protest. If Bran upheld the law, the battle that Asil had been seeking almost sixteen years ago when he'd first come here would take place.

"Whom do they belong to?" Asil asked.

"Hatchard Cole. A wolf who wants to expand his territory to include all of Alaska. He'd gladly take care of Liam Oldham and Ibrahim Ward—all he needs is my endorsement. If I don't give it, he might just present me with a fait accompli."

"Ah," said Asil. "Is he here?" *And is he still alive after a blackmail attempt like that?*

"No," Bran said sourly. "He gave the orders and left his wolves to spin in the wind when it didn't work. When I called to inform him of the trespass after you called me, he commented about privileged wolves who do not follow the rules. I'm sure he'll get some unsuspecting wolf all hot and bothered about it—someone who had to put a brother, mother, sister to rest when they couldn't control themselves within the allotted time."

"He wants your position," Asil said. "Hatchard Cole." He took a deep breath and thought about the werewolves he knew who were powerful enough to think they could take on Bran. "Was he perhaps once Conrad Hatch? I met him about three hundred years ago, give or take a few decades. Decent man, I thought then."

Bran nodded. "That's him. He hasn't left Alaska since the 1880s. I've let him be, and until now he has given me no reason to complain."

"Dominant wolves who do not live under your thumb forget why they swore obedience to you," Asil said. "They become arrogant. And most of them do not like that you have brought us out into the eye of the public. They are stuck in old habits, and change frightens them."

Bran smiled—a flash, then gone. "They?"

"I'm beyond that," Asil said aloofly. "Now I'm just bored. He thinks that being Marrok is like being Alpha. If he can just knock you off your pedestal, make you look weak, it will reduce your support. Weaken your magic." He snorted. "Idiot."

Kara gave him an anxious whine.

"It will be okay," he told her, his voice confident. Bran would hear the lie, but she wouldn't—and that was all he cared about. To Bran he said, "I will stand with her."

"Then go find Charles—he'll be in the center of the floor with the three Alaskan wolves. I will come in when everyone is here."

Kara beside him, Asil pushed his way through a group of people talking just outside the doorway. One of them turned to snarl, saw who it was, and shut up with gratifying suddenness.

The interior of the pole barn was set up with hay bales set around three sides in a horseshoe shape for seating, leaving the center as a stage. Bran hadn't called the whole pack, but a casual glance told Asil that all of the wolves *Asil* would have considered stable—excepting himself—were there. The Marrok's pack had more than its fair share of unstable wolves. Sage was seated near the far wall, but she caught his eyes and raised her eyebrows in a "do you know what's going on?" He gravely nodded to her, though he could not conceive that *his* knowing anything helped her in the slightest. The three men he'd captured were on their knees in the center of the room, with Charles standing beside them.

He could hear the whispers of speculation; apparently Bran

had not told anyone what he was doing. As Asil and Kara passed through the invisible ring imposed by Charles's impassive regard, they became the subject of attention so thick Asil could taste it. When their audience noticed the blood on Kara's side and digested what that meant in conjunction with the strangers on their knees in disgrace, Asil felt the pack bonds flash with the eager anger of the collected pack. Kara belonged to them, too.

Kara growled when the emotion hit her—and Asil put his hand on her head. "Shh," he said.

Charles gave him a stiff nod, looked at Kara, and flinched almost imperceptibly. If Bran decided Kara must die, Asil would have to defeat Charles before Bran in order to save Kara. And even if he managed it, that would leave him in charge, not just of a pack, but of all the packs in this part of the world.

Not acceptable. Asil was done with responsibility.

Kara would have to change on her own.

He looked around the barn, where strangers gathered. His eyes lingered on a group of wolves whose leader was staring at Kara with a little too much anger. This would be the wolf who would challenge Kara's fitness, and the unwitting tool for Hatchard Cole who had once been Conrad Hatch. This wolf's face was familiar; eventually his name would work its way out of Asil's memories.

Perhaps Asil could take him out before he opened his mouth.

The outer doors shut with a hollow boom, and Bran let his power flush through the building, bringing with it absolute silence. His pack, well used to his ways, knew it was a sign that the show was on—the strangers, unused to the sheer enormity of the Marrok's effect on their wolves, were silenced by the display.

"Take a seat, please," Bran asked them simply.

The milling crowd resolved itself into an orderly audience. There were more people than the hay bales could seat. The wolves who couldn't find seating on the hay simply sat on the wooden-plank floor. Even knowing that Bran did not mean him, Asil had to lock his knees to stay upright. Kara sat, then leaned harder against his leg as she craned her neck to look at Bran as he walked soberly into the center of the room, facing his audience.

"Today, I come before you to render justice," he said. "For this reason, I have asked you and your candidates to gather here today. So that those who wish to be wolves can see what that truly means. These gentlemen were found hunting as wolves in my territory without my permission." He paused to let them think about that, leaving the silence for exactly long enough.

Bran's timing was almost as good as Asil's.

"The penalty for hunting without invitation upon my lands is one thing," he said. "That their prey was one of mine upon my lands is another."

He strolled past the three kneeling men without looking at them. He turned like any good actor, into the audience rather than away from them. He took time to let his eyes meet, however briefly, the gaze of all the wolves in the room. Asil watched Bran's attention drive the eyes of everyone—human or not—to the ground. The effect was almost eerie.

Then he turned his focus to the trespassers. "Eric," he said. "Were you under orders?"

The werewolf addressed bit his lip until it bled in an effort not to speak.

"Eric?" Bran's voice was gentle, but that didn't mean it wasn't compelling.

"Yes."

"Cole's orders?"

Eric's skin flushed down his cheekbones as he ground his teeth. "Yes."

"Hatchard Cole is their Alpha," Bran said. "He chose to stay in Alaska and sent these three with Eric's brother, who is a candidate." He paused. "Eric's wife is in Alaska under the *protection* of Hatchard Cole."

Asil did not point out that, hostage or not, Eric had been quite willing to hunt down a thirteen-year-old girl and hurt her. He was pretty certain that if he had not heard her, Kara would have been hurt worse, even if they had not killed her.

But he trusted Bran. Really. The bastard wouldn't get away with anything.

Eric opened his mouth to say something, but Bran beat him to it. "He was sent here originally to tell me that Cole is taking over all of Alaska, and I could give my permission, or he'd just take it. When Cole wasn't happy with my reply, he told his wolves to make trouble."

Bran smiled. "What he doesn't know is that there are eight packs in Alaska, not three." He checked his watch. "Excuse me. What he did not know until right about now—is that there are eight packs in Alaska. It is a big state. Silver Pete and the rest of the Alphas are reminding him that he is due so much of it, and no more."

No one said a word, but Asil could feel the frisson of excitement travel through the barn. Silver Pete might not be as big a legend as Asil, himself, was, but his name was still known. He was also supposed to have died a hundred years ago.

Bran tilted his head and listened to the electric silence. He breathed in and out twice. When he spoke, his voice dropped into a husky bass. The way the audience flinched back, Asil was pretty sure that he'd let his wolf out enough they could see it in his eyes. "If Asil had not stopped these idiots before they hurt Kara worse, I would have killed these men and Cole as well. I owe it to Asil that I have options."

He took a step back and turned subtly, focusing the attention back upon the werewolves Asil had brought here. "I think these men need a change of pack." His voice was thoughtful. He switched from addressing the audience to the men on their knees. "We'll keep you here a month or so to explain proper manners. Then I'll move you someplace suitable. Your brother, Eric, I think should wait until next year before he seeks to be Changed. If he still would like to Change, when tempers are cooler, he may ask again. I need not tell you that if you attempt to Change him on your own, your life is forfeit."

And I will know.

Eric jerked his head up to Bran's, then quickly away. The men with him just shrank. Asil enjoyed the scent of fear that rose in the air. Knowing that Bran could talk in your head was a completely different thing than having him do it.

Bran nodded at Charles. Charles looked at the prisoners and smiled. Asil had practiced in a mirror, trying to get that smile. His own were very good, but he hadn't gotten quite the same "I'd rather rip you to little pieces, but my father says I can't—yet" effect. Asil was better at the "I'm crazy, and you are about to die."

"Up," Charles told them. Then he pointed to the door and followed them out.

Bran waited until the door closed behind him.

I have sent him away. This is between us, Old Wolf. Bran's voice was a somber thread in his head. No one else reacted, so Asil assumed that Bran talked to him alone. *I cannot break my own laws. Not when my friends are killing their wives, their children and grandchildren for the good of all.*

"Can you give her a chance?" Asil asked aloud. "Let her try?"

Drawing this out will do nothing but make it harder.

The other wolves had begun to murmur as Bran's failure to dismiss them implied that there was more business at hand than they'd seen so far.

Kara was starting to get worried, she looked at Asil and whined. He put a hand on her head, and tension in the room began to climb. Some of them might know what this was about—but Asil's gesture told them that there was a disagreement between Asil and the Marrok, and it involved Kara. The Marrok's pack, at least, would know what this might mean.

"Let me help," Asil said.

The wolf who had been staring at Kara before Bran came into the pole barn came to his feet. "Last year on the twentieth of October, I killed my mate. For thirty years she was my wife. She asked to be Changed, and after a year as a wolf, she could not shift from one form to another without my help."

He didn't say anything more, nor did he have to.

A second wolf stood up. "Three children," he said. "Three children of four I killed. One died a week after the Change because he was uncontrollably violent, and not even the Marrok could help. I killed him before Bran was forced to. One I killed when he attacked his human family. One I killed on his anniversary date because he could not control his shift."

Kara stared at the standing men and began to shake.

A third wolf stood up—this one Asil knew. The Alpha of the Emerald City Pack was not a big man, but he didn't need to be. "The laws are right, Bran Cornick. This is why we have always supported you." He bowed his head, and Asil could tell that what he said hurt him. "Thirteen is not fair—we all know that. But fair is not an option when you are a werewolf. We cannot afford to ignore the laws that have allowed us to survive. You and I both remember different times, Bran. I do not want a return of those old times. Justice, for us, cannot contain mercy because we cannot afford it."

These werewolves were honest, and as much as Asil hated to admit it, they had reason behind what they said. He could not take out his rage on them. But Hatchard Cole, Asil thought very carefully to his wolf, is a dead man. The wolf's agreement spread to his chest in a warm wave of rage.

"It has always been acceptable," Asil said clearly, "for wolves to receive such aid that does not involve pack bonds or magic in order to pass the test." Neither he nor Bran could call her wolf out of her. Nor could they change themselves and hope to call her change.

"Yes," agreed Bran.

"I'll be right back," Asil said. He bent down and whispered into her ear.

Bran heard him, but that didn't matter so much.

Louder he told her, "Stay here, I'll be right back."

He started out of the room, and the first wolf who'd stood up said, "So we all wait on you?"

Asil turned and looked at him. His wolf looked, too—and his wolf thought that maybe they'd hunt someone before they tracked down Hatchard Cole. Being a dupe was one thing, eagerness for the death of a child was something entirely different.

"You are so anxious to kill her that you cannot wait ten minutes?" He didn't bother saying anything else, just turned on his heel and strode out of the door.

Sick at heart, he trotted through the snow to the Marrok's house. She would fail. He would fight the Marrok, but he knew how that would end. And then the Marrok would kill her. All of them would pay because Hatchard Cole was greedy.

"Unacceptable," he said aloud. He took a deep breath. She was almost there. Another week. Maybe only another day or two, and she would make it. But they did not have that time. All he could give her was a fighting chance.

Inside the house, he went right to Bran's study. The roses he'd brought were still in good shape, though the big black-red rose was starting to droop. That was the one he pulled out of the vase. One would work better than all of them.

"Do not fail me," he told it sternly.

"Roses are good," said Devon.

Asil, not used to being startled, let out an involuntary snarl, then swallowed it.

Devon stood in his human body. Every rib showed, and his muscles were stringy—almost like a very old man's. He was shivering with nervous energy, and his eyes shifted back and forth between brown and gold every time he blinked.

"I didn't see you here," Asil said after a moment when Devon didn't say anything.

"The rose will help her," Devon told him. "Especially if she believes what you told her."

Devon hadn't been in the pole barn when he'd whispered to Kara.

"Belief," said Devon, "is the most powerful magic of all."

"Yes," agreed Asil. It was hard to recognize his old friend in this too-gaunt and nervous stranger. "So I hope."

"But music is what really helps me," Devon told him. "When I have a bad day, I go to the greenhouse. When I have a very bad day, I come here, and Bran plays for me."

"Music?" asked Asil, startled.

"You had that one song you used to play." Bran had musical instruments scattered all over the house. An acoustic guitar was balanced on a floor stand. Devon picked it up and held it out in a hand that vibrated with his tension. "Do you remember? To make your roses grow. She is so scared. She needs you to help her grow."

"It wasn't on a guitar like this." Asil knew which song he meant. "And a child is not a rose, to flower with music."

But Asil took the guitar anyway. He could play guitar, even if it had been a while. He was pretty sure he could even manage to work out that old song on this modern descendant of the *guitarra morisca* he'd originally composed it on.

"That song," Devon said urgently, hugging his now-empty hands against himself. "You play that one."

"All right, *mi amigo*."

Devon looked down. "I have to—*have to* change back." He closed his eyes. "She smells like Freda," he said. "Don't you think? Freda liked that song."

"She is very like," said Asil, who did not remember what Devon's long-ago daughter had smelled like. But he did remember a pretty little thing who had been fond of roses and moved like a colt. Kara had that same awkward gracefulness, too. Freda had lived to be a grandmother and died centuries ago.

The change took Devon again, slowly swallowing Asil's old friend in the protective skin of the wolf. He did not expect that they would converse again in this lifetime.

He let the old wolf change in peace and left, rose in one hand and guitar in the other, to do battle with fate.

THE POLE BARN WAS SILENT WHEN HE RETURNED. THE wolves who had been standing were seated. Charles was back and gave him a look that told Asil that the Marrok's son had realized that his father had sent him away to give Asil a chance to fight Bran without interference.

Bran looked at his guitar in Asil's hand.

"Yes, I know," Asil said. "Your guitar. Also, you play it better than I do. But I promised Devon I would play her a song for him." He looked at Kara, who was lying in a miserable heap at Bran's feet. "He told me that music helped him." He crouched, ignoring the other people's reactions. "Devon has not taken human form in my presence for a hundred years," he told her. "He did tonight because he is worried about you. He thought it would help if I play a song I played to his daughter a long time ago." He put the rose on the ground in front of her. "I want you to close your eyes, smell the rose. *Remember* what I told you. Listen to the music, and let Kara come out to play."

She gave him a long look.

He let her hold his gaze, and said simply, "Trust me."

She put her nose on the flower and took a deep breath.

There was a wave of sound from the assembled werewolves, and Asil looked up, irritated. But he lost his irritation when Devon came into the barn, all the way wolf now. He tipped his head so he didn't look at anyone as he trotted over to Kara and dropped a blanket on top of her. He looked up to Bran without meeting his Alpha's gaze, let his eyes trail over Charles, then Asil.

"Thank you," Asil murmured, spreading the blanket over Kara.

Devon had realized that a young girl would not be comfortable being naked in front of a room filled with werewolves, most of whom were men. It had been a long time since Asil had experienced a shred of modesty.

Devon ducked his head, hesitated, then licked Kara's face. Then he turned and trotted out of the building, not quite running away.

Asil sat on the ground beside Kara and strummed the guitar. He looked at Bran. "It's out of tune."

"You are wasting time," said the wolf who had had to kill his wife. "You're just making it harder on her."

"I said silence." Bran's voice didn't have to be loud to be effective. To Asil, Bran said, "New strings. They take a while to break in."

Asil tuned the high E string until he was pleased with it. He played a little of this and that, letting his fingers learn the spacing of Bran's guitar. The one he usually played had a slightly narrower neck.

He slid into the song a few chords at a time, his fingers finding the notes that his heart knew. He played the chorus twice before he sang the first verse.

It was a very long and silly song, more about the sound of the words than the meaning. Each verse a medley of compliments that sounded like they were addressed to a woman, but the chorus made it clear that it was addressed to a flower instead.

He glanced around the room. He could see the people who understood Spanish because, even under the serious circumstance, they started to grin. Kara didn't, as far as he knew, speak Spanish. But under the blanket, she'd quit shivering.

When he finished the chorus, he sang the first verse in English, translating on the fly. When he couldn't find a word fast enough, he used the Spanish word and kept going. It worked, adding humor. On the second verse, Bran joined him. Sometimes, Bran found a different English word than Asil did—sometimes it was a better one.

Just before they started the second chorus, Asil leaned down, and said, "Now, *chica*. Try now." He didn't put any particular force in his voice, nothing any of their watchers could object to. If there was power in his words, it was only the power of hope.

Kara sighed—and began to change.

Asil was unashamed when a tear slid down his face.

When she could speak, Kara said, "It *was* a magical rose. Like you said."

Bran's eyebrows shot up. And several of the wolves in the audience came to their feet at her words.

Asil lifted a haughty brow. "There is magic in a rose in winter," he told them. "If only because it is a rose in winter." He smiled at Kara. "But that change you accomplished yourself."

A FEW WEEKS LATER, ASIL ANSWERED A KNOCK ON HIS greenhouse door.

"Bran," he said. "How nice to see you."

Bran folded his arms and looked at Asil without making any attempt to come inside. "You've been gone for a few days."

Asil smiled. He stepped outside and closed the door, to keep the cold from getting inside. "I'm flattered that you noticed."

"Hatchard Cole's second called me this morning. Seems Hatchard disappeared. No sign of struggle, no sign of anything. He just vanished."

Asil's wolf slid out and looked at their Alpha. "Odd," Asil said, knowing the wolf was in his voice. Knowing that Bran would hear the satisfaction he did not bother to hide.

"I remember," Bran said softly. "There was an Alpha in Spain who was a very bad man, two hundred years ago. He hurt a lot of people. And then one day, his second went to that Alpha's home and his Alpha was just gone. No sign of struggle. No scent of strangers. Nothing. No one ever heard of him again."

Asil shrugged.

"Someday, you aren't going to come back from a kill," Bran said intently.

"Some risks are worth taking," Asil told him. "Did you hear that Kara's dad is bringing her mom to visit?"

Bran's face gentled. "Yes. I heard. Kara told me, too."

IN RED, WITH PEARLS

When I received the invitation to do a private detective story for the George R. R. Martin/Gardner Dozois anthology *Down These Strange Streets*, Warren had just started to work for his boyfriend, Kyle, as a private detective. Of course, the story had to be Warren's.

Because I write the Mercy books from Mercy's point of view, her impressions of people are all that I can show. To Mercy, Warren seems to be the least intimidating of the werewolves. This is largely because they are friends but partially because she sees him as a kind, caring, and gentle man—which he is. But he is also a very dominant and gay werewolf who has survived more than a century when most gay werewolves do not (my werewolves are still, for the most part, caught in the mores of a hundred years ago). Warren is bone-deep tough and practical—and here, for the first time, he gets to tell the story.

The events of "In Red, with Pearls" happen between *Silver Borne* and *River Marked*.

I'M REAL GOOD AT WAITING. I RECKON IT'S ALL THE TIME I spent herding cows when I was a boy. Kyle says it's the werewolf in me, that predators have to be patient. But Kyle knows squat about herding cows. I'd say he knows squat about predators, too, but he's a lawyer.

I stretched out my legs and put the heels of my boots on the desk of Angelina the Receptionist and Dictator of All Things Proper at Brooks, Gordon, and Howe, Attorneys at Law. Angelina would have thrown a fit if she'd seen my feet propped up where anyone could just walk in and see me.

"Image, *hijo*," she'd said to me when I started working for the firm. I kinda liked it when she called me *hijo*. Though I was a lot older than any son of hers could possibly be—she didn't know that.

She'd given me a disapproving look. "It is all about image. Your appearance must be just so to get the clients to spend their money, Warren. They like expensive offices, lawyers in suits, and private detectives in fedoras and ties—it tells them that we are successful, that we have the skills to help them."

I'd told her I'd wear a fedora when the cows came home wearing muumuus and feather boas. I consented, however, to wearing ties to work and to playing nicely during office hours, and she was mostly happy with that.

Office hours had been officially over for a good while, the tie was in my back pocket, and Angelina was gone for the day. I'd have been gone for the day, too, but one of Kyle's clients had come bursting in all upset and he'd taken her into his office and was talking her down.

Kyle was usually the last one out of the office. This time it was a sobbing client who suddenly decided that the jerk who'd slept with her best friend was actually the love of her life and she didn't really want to divorce him, just teach him a lesson. Tomorrow it would be a mound of paperwork that would only take him a few minutes to straighten up and a few minutes would stretch into a few hours. He tended toward workaholism.

I didn't mind. Kyle was worth waiting a bit for. And, like I said, I'm pretty good at waiting anyhow.

A noise out in the hall had me pulling my feet off the desk just before the outer door opened and a young woman in a sleek red dress with a big string of pearls around her throat entered the office in a wave of Chanel No. 5; she was stunning.

"Hey," she said with a big smile and a dark breathy voice. "Are you Kyle Brooks?" Her ears had pearls in them, too. Her hands were bare, though I could see that she'd recently been wearing a wedding ring. Dating a divorce attorney makes me notice things like that.

"No, ma'am," I told her. "After hours here. Best you try him tomorrow."

She leaned over Angelina's desk and the low-cut dress did what sleek little dresses are built to do in such circumstances. If I ran that way, I might have counted it a treat for the eyes. "I have to find Kyle Brooks."

She was close enough that the feel of her breath brushed my face. Mostly mint toothpaste. Mostly.

"Well, now," I said, standing up slowly and sauntering around the desk as if I found her all sorts of interesting. Which I all-of-a-sudden surely did. "Just what do you want with Kyle, darlin'?"

Her smile died and she looked worried. "I have to find him. I have to. Can you help me?"

Kyle's office was down the hall and in the back. I could hear the woman he was with talking at him as she had been for the past half hour.

"Think I can," I said, and led her the opposite direction, to the big conference room at the other end of the offices. "Stay right here for a couple of minutes," I told her. "He'll be right in."

She'd followed me docilely and stopped where I told her to. I shut the door on her and hightailed it back to Kyle's office.

I opened the door without knocking and ignored Kyle's frown. "Would you do me a favor?" I asked, tossing him my cell phone. "Call Elizaveta—her number is under *w*." Under *witch*; he'd figure it out, he was a smart man. "Tell her we have an incident, a *her* kinda incident, we'd like some help with. 'Scuse me, ma'am." I tipped my nonexistent hat to his indignant client before turning back to Kyle. "Might be the kind of thing we should clear the offices for."

"Your kind of thing?" Kyle asked obliquely. Something supernatural, he meant.

"That's right." I ducked out of his office and ran back to the conference room.

"One minute seventeen," the beautiful woman was saying when I rejoined her.

She stopped counting when the door opened, her body tense. When she saw me, she frowned. "I need Kyle," she said.

"I know you do," I told her. "He'll be right here." Hopefully not until after he got his client out safely and called Elizaveta Arka-dyevna, my wolf pack's contractual witch.

I heard the front door of the office close and thought that I should have done something to make Kyle leave, too. But I hadn't known how long our guest would have stayed put—probably exactly "a couple of minutes" from the sounds of it. Not enough time to get Kyle to do anything except call Elizaveta—which he'd done because I heard Elizaveta's cranky voice; my cell phone distorted it just enough that with the door between us, I couldn't tell what she was saying.

I wasn't the only one who heard it. The zombie turned its head to the door.

My first clue about what the woman was had been that her breath had come out smelling fresh and oxygen-rich instead of dulled like someone's who was really breathing would have. A vampire's did the same thing, but she didn't smell like a vampire, not even under the rich scent of the Chanel. The second was the way she'd obeyed what I'd told her. Zombies are supposed to be really cooperative as long as what you tell them doesn't contradict what their master tells them to do.

"Yes," Kyle said from the hallway, closing in on the conference room. "This is Kyle Brooks. We're at my offices. Fine, thank you." The door popped open. "What's—"

The zombie launched itself at him.

I knew it was going to do it as soon as Kyle named himself. I was ready when he opened the door. I'm damned fast and I thought I had a handle on it, but that thing was faster than I'd thought it would be. I grabbed its shoulders and yanked it back, so it missed its target. Instead of nailing Kyle's throat, it latched onto his col-larbone.

"Sh—" he cried out, jerking back.

"*Stay still,*" I told him sharply, and he froze, his eyes on me and not on the zombie gnawing on him.

I don't often use that tone of voice on anyone, and I hadn't been sure it would work on a human. But if he tried to pull himself away, he was just going to do more damage to himself.

I tried not to think about the blood staining his shirt because I didn't know if the witch needed the zombie still up and moving to tell who sent it after Kyle.

And I was damned sure going to get whoever had sent it after Kyle.

If I couldn't tear the zombie apart, I had to avoid looking at Kyle's blood. He helped. He didn't look like a man in pain; he looked thoroughly ticked.

"Get her off," he gritted, while trying to do it himself. He may be slightly built, but he's tough, is Kyle. But it had locked its jaw good and tight, and Kyle couldn't budge it.

I'd always assumed that taking on a zombie would pretty much be like fighting a human—one that was relentless and didn't react to pain—but basically a human. When it moved on Kyle, it was moving a lot faster than I'd seen any mundane human move and now it was proving stronger, too.

It didn't so much try to get away from me as it did to get to Kyle. I'd have thought that would make it easier to subdue. Finally I got an arm wrapped all the way around its shoulders, pulling it tight against me. Then I could put my other hand to work on prying her teeth apart. *Its* teeth. Its jaw broke in the process—and I got my thumb gnawed on a little.

Kyle staggered back, white to the bone, but he stripped off his shirt and wadded it against the hole she'd dug in him. "What is she?" he asked. "Why isn't she bleeding more?"

He was looking at it in quick glances. I understood. It wasn't pretty anymore with its jaw hanging half off.

"Zombie," I told him a little breathlessly. It was now trying to get away from me, and that did make things a bit more difficult, but at least I wasn't trying to pry it off Kyle.

"Your business, then?" he said.

Usually I'd agree; not even shark-sharp lawyers like Kyle were

so exotic as to call for assassination by zombie—it was too flam-
boyant, too blatant. The witches and supernatural-priest types
who could create zombies had never been hidden the way the werewolves used to be, but they lived among the psychics, Wiccans,
and New Agers where the con artists and the self-deluded provided
ample cover for a few real magic practitioners. They didn't give up
that cover lightly. Somebody would have had to have paid a lot for
a zombie assassination.

I shook my head. "Don't know. Seems awfully set on you,
either way." The zombie hadn't managed to get a limb free for the
past few seconds, so I chanced turning my attention to Kyle. His
wound worried me.

"You get out Howard's good malt," I told him. "He keeps the
key behind the third book on the top left shelf. Clean that wound
out with it. It's liable to have all sorts of stuff in its mouth." I didn't
know much about zombies, but I knew about the Komodo dragon,
which doesn't need poison to kill its prey because the bacteria in its
mouth do the job just fine.

Kyle didn't argue, and took himself out of the conference room.
As soon as he was out of sight, the zombie started crying out something. Might have been Kyle's name, but it was hard to tell, what
with its jaw so badly mangled.

I held on to it—by now I'd gotten a hold that prevented it from
hitting me effectively or wiggling loose. That gave me the leisure to
be concerned with other things. Kyle had shut the door gently
behind him. I tried not to speculate about Kyle's reaction, tried to
wrap up the panic and bury it where it could do no harm. He'd
seen weird things before, even if none of them had drawn blood.

I could have destroyed the zombie and left it in the conference
room for later retrieval with no one the wiser; could have hidden
all of this from my lover as I used to do. But it had been different
with Kyle from the beginning. The lies I'd told to him about who
and what I was, lies that necessity dictated and time had made
familiar, had tasted foul on my tongue when spoken to him. Now

he knew my truths and I wouldn't hide from him again. If he couldn't live with who and what I was, so be it.

But none of that was useful, so I forced my attention to the matter at hand. Who would send a zombie to kill Kyle? Was it something directed at me? The zombie was pretty strong evidence that it was someone from my world, my world of the things that live in the dark corners, and not Kyle's; he was as human as it got.

Still, I couldn't think of anyone I'd offended so much that I'd made Kyle into a target. Nor, with the possible exception of Elizaveta herself—who was, as Winston Churchill said of her mother Russia, "a riddle wrapped in a mystery inside an enigma"—could I think of anyone who could even create a zombie in the Tri-Cities. Eastern Washington State was not a hotbed of hoodoo or voodoo.

Maybe someone had hired it done? Hired an assassin, and the assassin had chosen the manner of death?

Kyle had a lot more enemies than I did. When he chose to use it, his special gift was to make the opposing parties in a courtroom look either like violent criminals, or like complete idiots—and sometimes both. Some of them had quite a bit of money, enough to hire a killer, certainly.

Maybe it wasn't my fault.

A zombie hit, though, screamed expensive, a lot more expensive than someone like Kyle would normally command. Which meant it was probably my fault.

I heard Elizaveta arrive and stride down the hall to the conference room. The lack of talking led me to believe that Kyle was still cleaning up.

Elizaveta opened the conference room door and entered like the *Queen Mary* coming to port in a wave of herbs and menthol instead of salt water, but with the same regal dominance, a regality accompanied by enough fabric and colors to do justice to a Gypsy in midwinter—and it was hotter than sin outside.

I'd always thought that she must have been beautiful when she was young. Not a conventional beauty, something much more powerful than that. Now her nose looked hawkish and her eyes were too hard, but the power was still there.

"Warren, my little cinnamon bun, what have you found?" She never spoke to me in Russian as she did Adam, who understood it; instead she translated the endearments that peppered her speech—probably because they made me squirm. Why would you compare a grown man to a sweet roll?

I responded to her overblown presentation as I usually did, dipping down into my childhood accent—added to a bit by Hollywood Westerns. "Ah reckon it's a zombie, ma'am, but I thought you oughta take a good look first."

She smiled. "What was it doing when you found it?"

"It found me, ma'am. Lookin' for Kyle."

"And you relocated its jaw for that, my little Texas bunny?" she asked archly.

"No," said Kyle from the doorway. His spare shirt hung over his shoulders, folded back to avoid possible contact with the blood from the liberally splattered towel he held to his collarbone. He smelled like whiskey, but not even a zombie attack could make him unpretty or completely destroy his composure. "He broke her jaw when he pulled her off me. You must be Elizaveta Arkadyevna Vyshnevetskaya. I'm Kyle Brooks."

She looked down at him—she is damn near as tall as I am. Her face was turned away from me, but Kyle had his lawyer face on, so I doubted her expression was friendly. The zombie's noises increased and so did its struggles. The witch turned to look at it without addressing Kyle.

"Quit playing and kill it," she told me coolly. "Breaking its neck should be enough." She'd never been happy with bringing humans into things she'd rather they be ignorant of. I guess she was trying to teach him and me a lesson.

I didn't like playing her game, but if she didn't need the zombie running around, Kyle would be safer with it dead. More dead.

I didn't look at Kyle when I popped the thing's neck. Its spine broke easily under my hand—which was what she'd wanted Kyle to see. I laid the limp body down on the conference table as carefully as I could, pulling the dress down over the dead woman's thighs.

Elizaveta turned her attention to the corpse, and I finally noticed that she wasn't alone. Nadia's gift was blending in—some of that was magic. I'd been occupied with the zombie, Kyle, and Elizaveta, but I still should have noticed her.

"Nadia," I said, "thank you for coming." Of all Elizaveta's numerous family, I liked Nadia the best; she was quiet, competent, and smart. She also was, I understood, one of three of the family who were honest apprentices rather than dogsbodies who did Elizaveta's bidding.

The old woman's grandson, who was supposed to inherit the family business, had been found to be jump-starting his career in a manner Elizaveta found embarrassing. He'd quietly disappeared. I figure in a few hundred years someone would discover his remains in a jar in Elizaveta's basement.

I'd shed no tears for him. He'd conspired to murder Bran Cornick, the Marrok who ruled the wolves in this part of the world—the man who made being a werewolf less of a nightmare than it might have been. Elizaveta was still mad at Bran for outing the wolves—I'd always secretly wondered if she'd been a part of that mess, too, if only by being complicit.

Nadia lifted a pair of deep gray eyes to mine and smiled at me, light crow's feet dispelling the illusion of youth that her fine-pored skin and gray-free, seal-brown hair gave her. But the appearance of youth was no great loss because her smile was big and sweet.

"Warren," she said. She'd been born in the Tri-Cities and not a hint of Russian accent touched her voice. "You look . . ."

"Dressed up?" I said looking down at my slacks. "I'm working for Kyle's firm and they are a bit upscale. I got to keep the boots, though. As long as I remember to polish 'em once in a while."

She flushed a little. "I didn't mean to be rude, sorry. I didn't know you were a lawyer."

"Nah," I told her. "Kyle's the lawyer." I introduced her to him. She took the hand he held out and murmured her greeting. "I'm the gofer," I told her, answering the question she hadn't gotten around to yet.

"Private detective," corrected Kyle.

"Ink's so new it might smear," I told Nadia's raised eyebrows.

"Niece, quit flirting with the men and tell me what you see," said Elizaveta sharply, without looking up.

Nadia blushed—not because she'd been flirting, but because her great-aunt had embarrassed her—and turned her attention to the body on the table. After a steadying breath, she was all business.

"I know her face," she said in some surprise. "This woman has been in the papers. She disappeared when out for a jog last Saturday morning. I don't remember her name—"

"Toni McFetters," said Kyle. "You're right. I didn't recognize her before."

"Not unexpected under the circumstances." Nadia was clearly paying more attention to the dead body than she was to any of us; her voice was clinical. "Easiest way to get a corpse to raise is to kill her yourself."

"Are you saying that she was killed just for this?" Kyle looked cool and composed, but I could smell his agitation.

"Probably," said Nadia when her great-aunt didn't say anything. "This kind of magic works best on a fresh corpse. Hopeless to try it with one a mortuary has filled with embalming fluid, and stealing a body from a hospital morgue is tough. Too many people at a hospital." She glanced over her shoulder, saw Kyle, and clearly, from the consternation on her face, ran the past few minutes of conversation through her head. "I'm so sorry. I'm not used to discussing my work with a layman. I do know this is difficult for you. Whoever did this was willing to kill you—I'd imagine that murder doesn't bother them much."

"If it had killed Kyle," I asked, "would it have died?"

"Deanimated," said Elizaveta briskly. "It was already dead

when it came here. It would be possible to give such a one a directive, and then dissipate the magic after that directive was accomplished."

"So someone would have come in here and found Kyle dead—killed by this woman who would be dead, too," I said. "Elizaveta, ma'am—" I tried to work a way around the question I wanted to ask without offending her. "Is there anyone in the Tri-Cities who knows how to animate a dead body like this?"

Elizaveta gave me a smile with teeth, so I guess she was offended. "Yes, my little bunny, I could have done it. But I am obligated to the Alpha of your pack and I am aware of your ties to the lawyer. I would not accept a commission to kill him." She examined my face and saw that wasn't enough for me. "No," she said clearly. "I did not kill this woman, nor did I turn her into a zombie and send her after your lover."

"My apologies," I told her. "But I had to ask."

"The magic keeps them warm," murmured Nadia into the tense atmosphere. I couldn't tell if she was blind to the tension between me and Elizaveta, or if she spoke to dispel it. "Almost at normal body temperature. Forensics wouldn't give an accurate time of death. It would look as though she'd died at the same time he had. A murder-suicide, perhaps. Impossible to tell without further work—but I think she was killed with an overdose of something that overworked her heart. Cocaine, perhaps. Something of that sort."

I don't know about Elizaveta, but I was distracted from her by what Nadia said. There wouldn't be a zombie to horrify the mundane public, just a mystery of why they'd killed each other. The use of the zombie as a murder weapon suddenly made more sense. No one would know about the magic—and no forensics to tie the real killer to the crime.

Nadia continued with her analysis. "In view of the fact that she was abducted while out jogging, her clothing is of some interest—no one jogs in a dress like this. The pearls are fake—good fakes, but nothing any insurance company or jewelry store would have a record of. The lipstick is of a common shade. The dress is more interesting. It isn't new. Maybe it came from a thrift store—we should be able to check it out."

"Shouldn't we call the police?" asked Kyle.

We all looked at him.

"We have a dead body of a missing person on my conference table. Someone is going to notice," he said.

"She has disappeared," said Elizaveta, speaking to him for the first time. "There is no gain in making her reappear."

Kyle's face hardened. "She has a family. Two kids and a husband. They deserve to know what happened to her."

"Can you fix her up?" I asked Elizaveta. "Repair the damages I did and then leave her somewhere she'll be found?"

"It is safer and easier to dispose of the body entirely," said Elizaveta dismissively.

"Well, yes, ma'am," I told her, making a subtle motion with my hand to stop Kyle from saying anything more. If Kyle started demanding things, we'd be up a creek without a paddle and maybe with a few more bodies besides. He saw my gesture and let me take point. Of all the humans I've ever known, Kyle is one of the best at reading body language.

"Easier and safer," I agreed with Elizaveta blandly. The witch shot me a suspicious look. "But if you *did* decide to put the body out where someone could find it—you and I both know that *you* could do it so's no one would ever associate it with you, this office, or magic of any kind. Easier if the damage I did to her, which might be tough to explain, can be repaired."

"There's no bruising around the site," said Nadia. "I could mend the flesh together, Aunt Elizaveta, so they could never tell."

The old witch stared at me, torn between resenting my manipulation and preening under my confidence in her abilities. I meant it and made sure she could hear it in my voice.

"You know that you enjoy the tough ones more," I coaxed. "Cleaning up another body is boring. This presents more of a challenge."

"*Another* body," said Kyle. But he said it real quiet and I think I was the only one who heard him. One of Elizaveta's gifts was making bodies disappear—around a werewolf pack, even a well-run pack like ours, there are going to be some bodies that need to disappear.

The corners of Elizaveta's mouth turned up, her shoulders relaxed, and I knew that I'd won.

"All right, sweet boy. You are right. Never could forensics unravel the mystery I can weave. If I wanted them to learn nothing, nothing is what they would learn. Still . . ." She smiled at me, eyes veiled with satisfaction. "It would be more challenging yet to show them evidence that doesn't exist. You, my private detective, will help to find who did this. When it is known, I will point the police in the correct direction."

"Thank you," I said, dropping my eyes from hers as was proper. As I did so, I noticed that Kyle had dropped the hand that held the towel and I didn't like what his wound looked like. I know about bite wounds; I've seen a lot of them. Bite wounds shouldn't get black edges a half hour after they've been inflicted.

I took a step closer to him and pulled the towel down so I could get a better look, and my nose wrinkled at the scent of rot that had set up far too soon.

"Ma'am?" I said. "Would you look at this, please?"

She glanced at Kyle and pursed her lips. Looking back at me she said, "Not my business. Take him to the emergency room."

I didn't growl at her, but only because my control is very, very good. The hair on the back of my neck stood up as the wolf inside decided he didn't like her answer.

"He *is*," I said, staring at her. "He is my mate and that makes him your concern."

Naming Kyle as my mate was a big step—but one my wolf and I were pleased with. I felt Kyle's attention spike and heard Nadia's indrawn breath, but kept my eyes on my target. Kyle's agreement would be needed, but not now, not for this.

"Mate implies procreation," Elizaveta said in prissy tones. "The two of you cannot have children. He is not your mate." She couldn't care less that I was gay, despite her words. I knew why she was behaving this way. I'd gotten my way with the body, and she wanted to win one of the battles tonight. She'd chosen the wrong one.

"You can discuss that with Adam," I said softly. The wolf would have torn out her throat happily—though that wouldn't have gotten Kyle fixed up. "Kyle, do you still have my cell phone?"

"I'd rather go to the emergency room," he said.

"No," I told him sharply. "No emergency room." I couldn't afford to divide the battle between them. "Elizaveta, do you want me to call Adam?"

Kyle, bless him, stopped arguing.

"I will remember this," she told me.

"That's fine." I worked at keeping my temper. "Remember that I'm only expectin' you to live up to the letter of the agreement you have with my pack." I'd won. Time to let her keep her pride if I could. A bit of flattery and a bone. "You know that the emergency doctors could do nothing with this—I can smell the gangrene. This is beyond them. If you don't take care of it, he'll die." I was afraid that was the truth and let her hear it.

"Only for you, cinnamon bun, only for you would I do this," she said. Then she reached out and pinched my cheek hard—the cheek on my face.

All business, she stepped between Kyle and me and pulled the towel farther out of the way and sniffed.

"Good whiskey," she said, dropping the thick Russian accent and exchanging it for a hint of Great Britain. "Not as good as Russian vodka, but not the worst thing you could have done. Still, neither could fix this. For this you need me."

I'D CARRIED THE BODY OUT TO ELIZAVETA'S CAR WRAPPED in a rug. I know it's a cliché, but a rug works pretty well to disguise a body because people expect it to be awkward and heavy. I used the rug from Kyle's office and told Elizaveta to keep it—which pleased her because it was an expensive rug. Kyle wouldn't want it back.

Kyle wasn't in the reception area where I'd left him. I listened and tracked him to his office. He was looking out his window at the traffic below. We were three stories up—pretty high for the Tri-Cities, which were still able to sprawl instead of climb to deal with the pressure of expansion.

I couldn't tell what he was thinking—but he didn't turn around when I came into the office, not a good sign.

"Kyle? Do you want me to take you to the emergency room?" The blackness was gone from the wound, but Elizaveta was no healer. I didn't think it would scar permanently, but it would hurt for a while yet.

"I want to find out who killed that woman," he said. "Someone killed her to get me—a woman I didn't even know."

I heard it in his voice under the anger. No one else would have, but I have very, very good hearing.

I took a chance and stepped in close to him, putting my arms around him and pulling him into me. "Not your fault," I said. "Not your fault."

"I know *that*," he snapped, but he didn't pull away. After a moment, he leaned back against me and put his hands on my arms, holding them where they were. "I know that—who better? I see it all the time. 'But maybe if I were a better cook, he wouldn't hit me' or 'If I could just have bought that car she wanted, she wouldn't have taken off with my best friend.' It is *not* my fault that someone killed her— not your fault, either, if it turns out to be that way."

I just held him.

"It feels like it, though," he said in a much different voice, the voice that no one else ever heard from him. He didn't let himself be vulnerable in front of anyone else.

"I'll find him," I told him, and then I leaned down and blew a teasing huff of air into his ear. "Or else Elizaveta will turn me into a toad."

WE WENT OUT TO EAT THAT NIGHT. KYLE LIKES TO COOK, but he takes too long and it was way past dinnertime. He didn't talk much over the food, pausing occasionally to stare into space, as he did when working on a particularly difficult case instead of dealing with getting munched on by a dead woman.

I'd lost him once, when he'd found out what I was. It says something about Kyle that it wasn't the werewolf part that bothered him, but the lies I'd told to keep the wolf from him. I hadn't had a choice about the lies—I think that was the only reason he forgave me.

I'd gotten him back and I wasn't likely to take him for granted anytime soon. The food tasted like sawdust as I waited for him to realize that he wouldn't have zombies trying to kill him if I weren't part of his life.

"Hey," he said, his gaze suddenly sharpening on my face. "You okay?"

"Fine." I smiled at him and tucked into supper with a little more effort. I wasn't going to kill the chance I'd been given by brooding over losing him before it happened.

Of course, there was a note on the door to Kyle's house when we drove into the driveway.

Kyle ripped it off and opened it. "He's objecting to your truck," he told me dryly as he read, giving me the abbreviated version. "He's sent a duplicate letter to the city. With photos to illustrate his point."

"Nothin' wrong with my truck," I said indignantly, and Kyle grinned. He lost his smile as soon as he looked back down at the note.

Three months ago, the nice family who lived next to Kyle's house had moved to Phoenix and sold their place to a retired man.

We hadn't thought much about it at the time, not until the first note. Some children (three solemn-faced kids who, with their mother, were staying with us until their mother's ex-husband quit threatening them) had made too much noise in Kyle's pool after seven P.M., which was when Mr. Francis went to bed. We should make sure that all children were in their beds and silent so as not to disturb Mr. Francis if we didn't want the police called.

We'd thought it was a joke, had laughed at the way he'd referred to himself as "Mr. Francis" in his own notes.

The grapes along the solid eight-foot-tall stone fence between the backyards were growing down over Mr. Francis's side. We should trim them so he didn't have to look at them. He saw a dog in the yard (me) and hoped that it was licensed, fixed, and vaccinated. A photo of the dog had been sent to the city to ensure that this was so. And so on. When the police and the city had afforded him no satisfaction, he'd taken action on his own. I'd found poisoned meat thrown inconspicuously into the bushes in Kyle's backyard. Someone dumped a batch of red dye into the swimming pool that had stained the concrete. Fixing that had cost a mint, and we now had security cameras in the backyard. But we didn't get them in fast enough to save the grapes.

He'd been some kind of high-level CEO forcibly retired when the stress gave him ulcers and other medical problems. He came here, to the Tri-Cities, because he was a boat-racing fan. Other cities had boat races, I'm sure of it. Maybe I could recommend some for him.

"This kind of thing is supposed to happen when you live in an apartment," Kyle told me, crumpling the latest note in his hand. "Not in a four-thousand-square-foot house on three-quarters of an acre."

"We need to have a paintball game in the backyard," I told Kyle. "I could invite the pack."

"Escalation is not a solution," Kyle said, though he'd smiled at the thought. He'd seen some of our paintball games. "Right now the city is on our side. We want to keep it that way." Since Mr. Francis moved in, the folks in city hall, the police department, the zoning commission, and the building code enforcement office had all grown to know us by name.

"I know," I groused, unlocking the front door. "As long as we act like adults, there's nothing he can do to us."

Kyle followed me into the foyer. His house was the first place I'd ever lived that was big enough to have a foyer.

"I could move," he said reluctantly.

"Nah," I rubbed his head affectionately—Kyle loved his house. "You'd miss Dick and Jane."

Dick and Jane were the life-sized naked statues in the foyer. The woman was currently wearing a Little Bo Peep bonnet he'd found somewhere and a green silk sari that had belonged to his grandmother. Dick was still sporting the knitted winter hat with the long tail and a poof ball on his pride and joy because Kyle hadn't found anything he thought was funnier yet.

"We could move back into your apartment."

That apartment was a point of contention. He said I was keeping it because I didn't believe that he really understood he was sleeping with a werewolf. He also said I was being stupid because he was mine as long as I never lied to him again, werewolf or not. Kyle was a smart man. He was right about why I kept it—but I wasn't sure he was right about the rest. So I hadn't given up the apartment yet.

Proposing a move back to it showed that Mr. Francis was getting to him. If so, the time might have come to quit playing nice.

My cell phone rang. I pulled it out of my pocket and took a look. It wasn't a number I knew, but that wasn't unusual anymore—I was starting to get a little work from people unconnected to the law firm.

"Warren here," I said.

"This is Nadia," said the witch's niece. "Listen, Aunt Elizaveta wants me to go talk to the dead woman's husband tomorrow. I can do that, but I thought it might be useful if you came along. You can tell when someone's lying, right?"

"I can," I agreed. "But won't that arouse the wrong people's interest if you're out questioning people?" Wrong people like the police. I'd thought she intended to do a little magical forensics and leave the questioning to me.

"That's one of the things I'm good at," Nadia said. "People don't remember me asking them things if I don't want them to. If no one reminds him, he'll eventually even forget I came by."

I thought about that a moment, not entirely happy about what she said.

"I can't do it to you," she said anxiously. "Or anyone who is alert for it. It's an uncommon talent—that's why Aunt Elizaveta picked me to be one of her students."

"I was just thinking that I have a few people to question as well," I told her. "How 'bout I go out with you and then take you with me? We can have a cooperative investigation."

"Cooperative investigation," she said. "Sounds good to me."

"Let me pick you up," I told her. "If I leave my truck here another day, it's liable to be towed or have all the tires slashed."

Nadia laughed because she thought I was kidding, and we made arrangements to meet the next morning.

NADIA'S HOUSE WAS AN F HOUSE IN A SEA OF ALPHABET houses in Richland. The government had done Richland a favor with all the World War II–era carbon-copy houses: kept it from looking like all the other well-heeled towns I've seen. A stranger to the Tri-Cities would be justified in thinking that it was the poorest of the cities rather than arguably the wealthiest, at least in absolute house values. The F houses were small, two-story, Federal-style houses that looked somewhat regrettably like the houses in a Monopoly game.

I wondered if Nadia chose her house because it disappeared into the woodwork the same way she did. I drove up her narrow, bumpy driveway and she ran out the door.

"Aunt Elizaveta is not happy," she informed me a little breathlessly as she fastened herself in. "I hope we find something today." She was lying about the last part, which puzzled me a little.

"What's wrong with your great-aunt?" I asked, pulling out into traffic.

"She couldn't find any magic signature on the body or the clothes the zombie was dressed in, except for mine and hers. That means there's a witch or priest out and about who is skilled enough to hide from my aunt."

There was just a hint of a smile on her face; I reckon it wouldn't be easy to be at Elizaveta's beck and call. Might be fun to see her stymied once in a while. That would explain the earlier lie.

"Where are we meeting Toni McFetters's husband?" I asked.

"At his house. He's on compassionate leave." She gave me the address. "The children are at his in-laws' house. He told me that when I called him yesterday and told him we're investigating his wife's disappearance. Our questioning should just blend in with that of the police if I can manage it right. It helps that he'll be the only one to work on."

Toni's husband's house was only a couple of blocks from Nadia's, in a newer neighborhood—no alphabet houses at all. It was a big house, not as upscale as Kyle's house, but not an inexpensive property, either.

I pulled up in front and turned off the truck. "We can keep this short. All we need is to find out if he killed her or knows who did. And if he's noticed anything suspicious."

"Why don't you do the talking?" she said. "I'll work better if all I have to do is the magic."

I didn't like it, this business of messing with someone's mind, any more than I had liked lying to Kyle before he knew that I was a werewolf. But I'd lost my innocence a long time ago.

The man who let us in smelled of desperation. He matched his wife in good looks—or would have with a few more hours of sleep—but showed none of the signs of vanity that a lot of good-looking men display, men like Kyle for instance. McFetters's haircut was basic; his clothes were off the rack and fit indifferently.

Before I asked a single question, I knew that he had had nothing to do with his wife's disappearance.

"Mr. McFetters, thank you for speaking to us," I told him, refusing his offer to come in and sit down. "This won't take long."

"Call me Marc," he said. "Has anyone found out anything?"

"No," I said. It was a lie, but in a good cause. "Did anything happen in the past few weeks—before your wife disappeared—that caught your attention? Strangers in the neighborhood, someone your wife noticed when she was out jogging?"

He rubbed his hands over his head as if to jar his memory. "No," he said, sounding lost. "No. Nothing. I usually jog with her, but I got a late start that morning; we'd . . . Anyway she has an extra hour before she has to be at work. She says she can't think without her morning run."

"What was she wearing?" I asked, and listened to a detailed rundown that proved that whoever said that straight men don't pay attention to clothes was wrong.

"She was wearing a pink jogging suit we'd picked up in Vegas—it was her favorite, even though the right knee had a hole from where she fell a few weeks ago. She had size-eight Nikes—silver with purple trim. She likes her green running shoes better, but they clash with the pink. She wore the topaz studs I got her for our anniversary in her ears, and her wedding ring . . . white gold with a quarter-carat Yogo sapphire I dug up when I was eighteen and on a family vacation." There was a sort of desperate eagerness in his voice as he went on without prompting to describe their usual running route; as if he believed that somehow, if he could only manage to give enough details, it would help him find his wife.

He ran down, eventually, and, almost at random, his gaze focused on Nadia. He frowned. "I know you from somewhere, don't I? What was your name again?"

"Nadia," she said.

"Did you go to Richland High?" He rubbed his hair again and tried to find the proper social protocol.

"Along with half of Richland," she said in a gentle voice. "It's not important right now, Marc."

"Did you have anything to do with your wife's disappearance?" I asked as gently as I could, pulling him back to important things. He hadn't. I'd have bet my life on it, but for Elizaveta, I'd get absolute proof.

"No." He blinked at me, as if the thought were too strange to contemplate. He wasn't angry or offended, just bewildered. "No. I love Toni. I need to find her but I don't know where to look." Bewildered and terrified. "Where should I look?"

I SHUT THE DOOR BEHIND US AND WAITED WHILE NADIA muttered a little under her breath and dropped a few herbs she had in a baggie on the steps.

"Well?" she asked after climbing in beside me.

I drove away from Toni McFetters's house before I answered her. Churning in my gut was the understanding that if I hadn't been with Kyle last night when the zombie came, I'd be in much the same state as Marc McFetters.

"We need to find who did this. That man doesn't deserve the police jumping down his throat."

"He didn't kill her," she said, but it was more of a question than a statement. I couldn't believe that she'd been in the same room I had and hadn't recognized the man's innocence. Witches don't have a wolf's nose, I suppose.

"Absolutely not."

"Good," she said. "He was right, we did go to high school together. A geeky kid, but a real sweetie." She shifted nervously in her seat as if she felt uncomfortable. "So that leaves us where?" Her question was a little fast. Maybe she'd liked Marc McFetters more than she was comfortable with me knowing. He seemed like a good man.

"We're going to have some conversations with a few people who are very unhappy with Kyle."

THERE WERE FOUR PEOPLE I WANTED TO CHECK OUT. IT might surprise people who knew him that the list wasn't longer: Kyle did not make friends of the opposition in the courtroom. He was, however, fair and honest—which meant that most of the opposing lawyers got over their anger pretty fast.

I'd decided somewhere along the way that the zombie animator had been hired to assassinate Kyle. Gut instincts were always important to the detectives in the movies, but they were more so to werewolves. Mostly, gut instincts were just little bits of information floating around that resolved themselves into the most likely scenario.

That meant that we were looking for two different people. The one who did the hiring, and the one who was hired. Motive. My license might be new, but *I* was old. I'd survived because I understood what moved people, why they acted and why they did not. Old werewolves aren't that common; most of us who survive the Change die in fights with other werewolves shortly thereafter, because most werewolves don't understand body language. They also don't think. They trust their fangs and claws—even though *other* wolves have fangs and claws, too. I watched and learned.

Motive was easier to find than an assassin for hire. I'd find the man who wanted Kyle dead, and then I'd find the killer. That was why my list wasn't longer. Today we'd try the people who hated Kyle and could still afford to hire an assassin after Kyle got through with them in court. If I didn't find a likely suspect, tomorrow I'd leave Nadia at home, call in the pack, and go hunting for someone who'd hate me enough to kill the man I loved.

I'd called Sean Nyelund's office and made an appointment to see him under the name of my pack Alpha—Adam Hauptman—before I picked up Nadia that morning.

Nyelund worked in a newer office building in Kennewick, making money with other people's savings. He was good at it. Very good.

What he had not been good at was taking care of his own. He got the possession down fine, but not the concern for their welfare that should have gone along with it. His wife had sneaked out of his house in her underwear and hid in a neighbor's garage for three hours before they'd found her. It was the first time she'd been out of the house in two years. Now she lived in Tennessee with her family, a good chunk of the money her husband had made in his life, and a new husband who was good with his guns.

Nyelund hated Kyle, and he certainly had the money to hire an assassin. The only question was—had he?

Sean's receptionist was a pretty young thing not long out of high school. She had a bright smile to match the bright voice I'd talked to on the phone. Her eyes were frightened.

"Just a moment, let me announce you," she told me. Then she picked up her phone. "Mr. Hauptman to see you, sir."

A human wouldn't have heard the quiet "Send him in."

He had his back to us when we entered his office, typing rapidly on a keyboard. It was a power play that worked against him because I shut the door and used a little pack magic to keep the noise confined to this room. We wolves don't have much magic other than the shifting itself, but what we do have is good for keeping our business private.

He turned around. "Mr. Haupt—" And then he saw who I was. He stiffened subtly, his hand hidden by the desk—and then he noticed Nadia. His hands were suddenly both clearly visible on the top of his desk. "Ah, I see. Mr. Smith, using pseudonyms now? I wasn't aware you had enough money to invest. Perhaps the lady?"

Nyelund looked like a slightly overweight, soft-bodied, soft-minded kind of guy, the kind who should be out saving puppies on the street corner. He had dimples and good manners. It was his eyes that gave him away, cold and assessing. If he hadn't been smart, he'd already have been in jail.

"I thought it would save some time," I said. "Did you order a hit on Kyle Brooks?"

"Would I do such a thing?" he asked, spreading his hands out. Just a good ol' boy, that was Sean Nyelund. "I don't know where you came up with that idea."

I questioned him for twenty minutes or so and couldn't get a straight answer out of him. It could mean that he'd done it. It could mean that he was thinking about doing it—or that he enjoyed the hell out of frustrating me. Hard to tell.

Finally, he said, "Go away, Mr. Smith. You bore me. Come back if you have money to invest."

"You take care, now," I said, tipping an imaginary hat. "I'd hate to see anything happen to you."

He grunted and turned back to his computer.

Nadia worked her magic under the cover of my opening the door, and then we strolled out past the receptionist.

"He pulled a gun on you," Nadia said, belting in.

"I saw it," I told her. "You saved me, darlin' girl."

She laughed. "Or reassured him that you weren't about to attack."

"Could be," I acknowledged, but thought that Nyelund would happily have shot me if he could have gotten away with it. Something to keep in mind.

"What did you learn?" she asked. "I couldn't tell anything about him."

"The jury is out on Nyelund," I told her. "He makes such a point of not answering questions, he might as well be fae."

"Does he know that you're a werewolf?" she asked. "And that werewolves can smell lies?"

I shook my head, relatively certain of my answer. The public might know about werewolves—but I wasn't taking out advertising. Kyle knew, but he was pretty much the only human who did. Using Adam's name might make Nyelund suspicious—Adam had become a celebrity once the word got out that he was the local pack Alpha. If I were Nyelund, though, I'd bet that the celebrity part was why I'd used Adam's name, not the Alpha-werewolf part. And should he think I was a werewolf anyway, he couldn't prove anything and it just might make Kyle a mite safer.

If Nyelund was smart and subtle, Phillip Dean, the next man on my list, was a different kettle of fish. He'd done some time after Kyle worked his magic in court—but only because he *was* stupid and talked his way into jail by threatening the judge. Dean was a nasty brute who'd inherited his father's money a couple of years ago. The money wasn't really enough to hire anyone—but he had the contacts, and it was only a matter of time before he killed someone. He'd almost managed to make it his ex-wife and wouldn't mind at all making Kyle Brooks his first kill.

He also, as it turned out after I made a few phone calls, was vacationing in Florida—Disney World.

"Doesn't mean it isn't him," I told Nadia. "But he's kinda a long shot anyway. Doesn't think ahead very well, though he's cunning enough when cornered."

"So? Where to now?"

"Ms. Makenzie Covington."

"A woman?"

I smiled at her. "Most of Kyle's clients are women, but he takes on cases for men, too. Ms. Covington is a real piece of work; tried to pose as the abused wife so that she could take her ex to the cleaners— she was not happy when Kyle proved that she inflicted her bruises herself. Her ex-husband's bruises were also her doing. She lost visitation rights—not that she cared about the kids, but it humiliated her in front of her friends. Two years from now, she'll be off tormenting her third or fourth husband, and wouldn't make my list. Six weeks after her divorce, though, her ire is still focused pretty hard on Kyle."

"Why not on her ex?"

I smiled a bit grimly. "By the time she got through with him, all he could say was 'Yes, dear' and look at the ground. Kyle was the one who humiliated her and protected her victim."

Makenzie Covington worked at home—which was currently a condo in South Richland. She was striking rather than beautiful. Dark hair, dark eyes, and strong features, she looked like a passionate woman who lived life to its fullest. Which was sort of true. She didn't recognize me when she answered her doorbell.

I introduced myself and Nadia.

"I've never met a private detective before," she cooed at me. "Won't you come in?"

It didn't take long to figure out that it wasn't her. If she'd ordered a hit on someone, she wouldn't have welcomed a pair of private investigators into her home and gotten all hot and bothered about it. Sometimes being a werewolf gives you interesting insights into people.

Still.

"Ma'am, you haven't ordered a hit on Kyle Brooks, have you?"

"No," she said immediately and truthfully. "But if you find someone who will, tell him I'll pay half." That was the truth, too.

"I'll do that," I told her. Then it took me about twenty minutes to extract us from her condo, by the end of which even Nadia caught on to what Ms. Covington wanted from us.

"I am really glad I brought you with me for that," I told Nadia.

Nadia giggled. She hadn't even bothered doing any magic. No need for it. "I don't think I was much help. She'd have taken both of us to bed, wouldn't she?"

"You, me, and the stray dog outside, yes, ma'am." I pulled out into traffic. Maybe I was driving a little faster than normal.

"I've never seen you disconcerted before," she said. "Usually you just talk slower and use lots of *ain't*s and *ma'am*s."

"Now I know how those sixty-year-old wives feel when their husband of forty years comes back from the doctor with a bottle full of blue pills." I wasn't as flustered as I made out, but I enjoyed Nadia's laughter. She didn't laugh as often as she ought.

HARPER SULLIVAN WAS A RETIRED DOCTOR.

Divorce is a nasty business and secrets tend to come out. The good doctor's secret was that he liked to diagnose his patients with various life-threatening diseases they didn't have. Of course, that meant they had to come in for frequent treatments. Eventually (especially when they were getting ready to get a second opinion), they were miraculously cured, all credit going to the doctor.

Kyle'd used blackmail to get a nice settlement for the doctor's ex-wife (who wasn't any great shakes herself if she'd kept quiet about what he was doing for twenty years) and to force the doctor to retire. There wasn't real proof, Kyle'd explained to me, only hearsay—enough to ruin Sullivan's reputation and get the AMA on his case, but he'd likely have kept his license. Blackmail was better because it kept more people from being harmed. Kyle can occasionally be as pragmatic as a wolf when it comes to making sure that justice is done.

Dr. Sullivan was weeding his azalea bed when we drove up. He didn't look up until I cleared my throat. It always bothered me that he looked like that doctor in that old TV show—*Marcus Welby, M.D.*

"Doctor," I said, "I'm Warren Smith. I'm a private investigator. This is my partner for the day, Nadia Popov. I'd like to ask you a few questions."

"Of course," he said, getting up and pulling off his work gloves. "It is getting hot out, though. Why don't you come in and have some iced tea?"

I'd met him a couple of times, and it was unlikely that he didn't know me. But he gave no sign of it that I could discern, even when I introduced myself.

He led us around to the back door of the big brick house—

explaining that he didn't want to track dirt inside. He showed us into his living room—a big space with hardwood floors, real Persian rugs, and antique furniture, some of it even older than I was. But the thing that dominated the room was a wall of windows that looked out over the Columbia River.

We were both staring at the view when he shot me.

It wasn't silver, and a lead bullet wasn't going to kill me—but it hurt a lot. I spun and snarled, a hand to my shoulder. He wasn't a very good shot if he missed my heart at that range.

It was the second time I'd had a gun pulled on me today—I'd expected something of the sort from Nyelund, though I'd hoped that meeting him at his work would preclude actual violence. The doctor I'd picked as someone who'd hire out his dirty work. At least he wasn't a marksman.

"Oops," he said and adjusted his aim.

"*STOP,*" said Nadia.

Now, a dominant can enforce his will on a lesser wolf. I'd done something of the sort with Kyle yesterday when I'd made him quit pulling against the zombie's bite. But this was something else again, 'cause not only did the doctor freeze, but so did I. And it wasn't the kind of hesitation—the loss of will to disobey that my Alpha could hit me with—my body flat-out refused to move at all.

Screw that.

I drew in a deep breath and called out the wolf—who shook off the magic like water that wanted to cling where it wasn't supposed to. He also healed up a fair bit of the damage the pistol had done. I took a step mostly to prove I could.

She didn't even notice me; she was too busy with Sullivan. "*You won't kill anyone,*" she told him in that same black-magic voice. "*You'll leave Kyle Brooks alone.*" I was really glad I'd broken her hold on me before that one. "*You won't remember this. You'll just feel as though whatever we were talking about got solved. Everything will be all right.*"

"All right," muttered the doctor, and my wolf saw that something was broken inside him, something that had been whole and well when we'd come here. In an elk, it was the sign that the animal was done for; next blizzard, next predator, and it wouldn't fight to survive.

Nadia turned and seemed a little surprised to see me so close. "Your shoulder?"

"Healing," I said. "I'm fine." Sometimes things like that took a long time to heal, and once in a while they just closed right up. This was that once in a while. I looked around, but there had been surprisingly little blood; most of it had been absorbed by my clothes.

The bullet had gone right though me and through the window, leaving behind a spiderweb of cracks. The doctor appeared to have forgotten about us and shuffled off with his gun, muttering to himself, "It's all right. Everything is fine."

Nadia grabbed a damp towel from the kitchen and wiped the blood off the hardwood floor, leaving not a trace behind. Then she took the splattered towel and held it against the broken window.

The wolf felt her magic and backed away. Not frightened, just cautious. When she pulled the towel away, it was clean of my blood and the window was intact.

"Waste not, want not," she said. "I thought I'd have to supply some of my own to finish it up—but your blood is potent."

I took her arm. "Let's go before he breaks loose," I said, though I didn't think he'd really break loose. The suggestions she'd planted might fade. But she'd broken him, and my instincts said that was permanent.

That's the problem with witches: they don't really care about anyone except themselves. Their power comes from pain, blood, and sacrifice—*other people's* pain, blood, and sacrifice, when they could manage it. If they flinched away from doing harm, they wouldn't have any power. Then other witches would take advantage of that and steal what little power they had. White witches were few, and tended to be psychotically paranoid. Elizaveta and her family skirted the edge of true black magic, but they did stand on that edge and look into the abyss with open eyes.

The wolf could respect a predator like that, but neither of us were entirely comfortable with it. What she'd just done to the doctor was wrong: it would have been kinder to kill him.

"I'm sorry," she said softly as I drove back across the river into her part of Richland.

"What for?" I asked. "Saving my life?"

"You didn't like it that I stole his will," she said. "I admit I could have been more careful. But he'd shot you, and I used that, used your pain. It gave me a little more power than I'm used to. He'll be all right."

If she wanted to believe that, who was I to tell her differently? Maybe I was wrong, but I didn't think so.

"So," she said softly, "are you finished with this? Did you find out what you needed to know with Dr. Sullivan? Is it solved, then?"

I opened my mouth, thought a bit more, and said, "Yes, I suppose I am finished."

We didn't talk much more, but when she hopped out of the truck when I stopped in her driveway, she said without looking at me, "Maybe we could see each other again? I make a mean cherry pie."

I smiled. "Maybe so."

She relaxed, gave me a rare grin, kissed her fingertips, and blew the kiss my way before she ran into her house, looking about sixteen.

Everything will be all right. I flexed my fingers on the steering wheel.

KYLE AND I ATE DINNER AT A MEXICAN RESTAURANT kitty-corner from Kyle's offices. The music was loud enough that human ears wouldn't hear private conversations—one of the reasons I liked to eat at this place.

"You're awfully quiet," Kyle said. "Find something?"

I looked at him. He looked tired. "Yes."

"Are you going to tell me?"

I looked down at my food. "Yes. But not tonight. I have a few more things to check out—a couple of things to do."

"Illegal?"

I gave him a half grin. "Like I'd tell you ahead of time."

"You'll just make me an accessory afterward," he grumbled.

"I've a little justice to serve," I told him.

He thought about it while he ate a few bites of his fish tostada. "Toni McFetters deserves justice," he said. "Are you sure you can't go about it legally?"

"I plan on using proper channels for some of it," I said. "But there's some of it that it's not possible to do that with."

Kyle believed in the court system—one of the few traces of optimism in his cynical worldview. However—as his blackmail of Sullivan proved—he understood its limitations.

"All right," he said. "I can live with justice. Will I see you at home tonight?"

"I'll be in later," I said. "Maybe very late."

He looked at me seriously. "Don't get caught. Don't get hurt. Don't think I didn't notice that you're wearing a different shirt than you put on this morning and aren't using your right arm to eat with."

"I won't," I said earnestly. "I'll try not to. I would never try to get something like that by you."

He laughed, stood up and leaned across the narrow table, and kissed me, oblivious to the stares we got. The Tri-Cities is a pretty uptight town, and two men kissing in public is not a common sight.

A girl in the next table gave a wolf whistle and said, "Can I kiss the cowboy next?"

Okay, so maybe everyone wasn't that uptight.

Kyle gave her a cheeky grin. "Sorry. He's my cowboy, you'll have to find your own."

She sighed. "I have one. But he doesn't look like that when he blushes."

"Maybe if I kissed him, he would?" Kyle arched an eyebrow.

She laughed. And if some of the people might have made an offended scene about the kiss, she'd taken the edge off. I kissed her cheek in appreciation as I passed her table on the way out. Her cowboy might not blush, but she did.

FROM THE OFFICE, I CALLED BEN. A FELLOW PACK MEMber, Ben was also a computer geek. I can get by on the computer, but Ben makes me look like a complete Luddite. It took him the better part of an hour to run down the information I'd asked him for—it would have taken me a week or more. I put the hour to good use, pulling out the clues my instincts told me were there, running off some photocopies of sensitive files, and calling a few more people. After Ben called me back, I called George and then went out to do a little private detecting.

GEORGE, IN ADDITION TO BEING A WEREWOLF, WAS ALSO a Pasco police officer. He was my link to the "proper channels" I'd promised Kyle.

George met me at a fast-food place a few blocks from Sean Nyelund's house in West Pasco. He drove his own car and came dressed casually, but he was on the job despite the late hour. We both ordered something to drink and sat down. It was nearly closing time and it wasn't tough to find a place where no one would overhear us.

"You said you have something on Nyelund." His tone was eager. In addition to being a police officer, he was into the BDSM scene—which kept a very low profile around here. During Nyelund's divorce, Nyelund admitted that he was into BDSM, and that tidbit made the news. George and his friends didn't appreciate that one bit. Nyelund wasn't a BDSM dom. He was a psychopathic, sadistic bastard who enjoyed breaking people.

"Right," I told George. "He's got another victim." I gave him the name of Nyelund's receptionist. "These files you don't have," I told him, giving him copies I'd made in the office. "Confidential lawyer/client/doctor stuff. They'll show you what to look for—but I promised the victim they would be for your eyes only."

I waited while he paged through Nyelund's first wife's medical files and transcripts of her therapy sessions. She'd given them to Kyle and then told him he couldn't use them. I'd called her and told her about Nyelund's little receptionist. It had taken me most of that hour I'd waited for Ben to talk her into it. She'd told me I could show George, but no one else.

He whistled through his teeth. "Poor kid," he said. But he wasn't surprised. He'd known what the case was about, but Nyelund's ex-wife's refusal to bring charges against him had tied his hands. It was the details that were new to him.

"He's got a bunker, a secret room," he said, sounding like a kid in a candy store. Secret rooms were pretty easily sniffed out if the one looking happened to have a wolf's sense of smell. "And he likes to film things. Illegal things. How helpful of him."

"Is it useful?"

"I need a reason for the search warrant."

I gave him a thumb drive. Nyelund thought his guard dogs would keep people from taking photos through his window. Guard dogs don't bark at me if I don't want them to, and Nyelund had been too occupied to notice me. His lights had been on, so I hadn't even had to use a flash. My camera had helpfully recorded the time and date.

I tapped the drive. "You'll find the photos on that good for probable cause. You can even give my name as the photographer. I'm a private detective and I was sent out to take photos of this guy's wife, only I got the address wrong. When I realized what I was taking photos of, I gave you a call."

A snake doesn't change his spots. It had been only a matter of time before Nyelund tried his tricks on a new victim. Kyle and I'd been keeping an eye on him, but we'd missed the receptionist. Ben said she'd been working for him for about two months—right after she moved to the Tri-Cities.

"She's seventeen," I told him.

George grinned at me, his eyes enraged. "Is she, now? And look at him with that camera. Wrapped up like a great big birthday present. Thanks, Warren."

"Don't mention it." I tipped my imaginary hat to him. If Nyelund hadn't been so obliging, I'd have resorted to being a credible witness, but this was better.

IT WAS VERY LATE WHEN I MADE IT TO MY NEXT STOP. The back door wasn't locked and let me into the kitchen. I waited a minute and listened. Only one person in the house, and that person was asleep.

I walked into the living room, toward the stairs that led to the bedrooms. I'd been thinking about this all night, and I still hadn't made up my mind what I was going to do.

Instinct was one thing; proving what I knew was an entirely different proposition.

I'd planned on a little sleuthing and then interrogation—but then the lights of a car driving past illuminated the top of a curio cabinet where there were a bunch of photos. One of them caught my eye and I went over and picked it up.

I didn't need the light to see it; one of the benefits of my condition is superb night vision. I stared at the photo of a pair of happy people for a moment, then replaced it.

I went into the bedroom and did what I had to do. Nadia didn't even wake up when I snapped her neck. It was easier than snapping the neck of the zombie she'd made of the woman she'd killed.

I searched the room and found a few things. From the bedroom, I called Nadia's great-aunt.

"You call me late, my little sticky bun. Did you find out something I can use?"

"No," I told Elizaveta. "It was Nadia."

"You are wrong," she pronounced. "Nadia does not have the skill to animate the dead." She'd always underestimated Nadia. Everyone had. Everyone but me.

"Nine thousand dollars was transferred into one of her bank accounts two weeks ago and another last week." Ten thousand or over, and the feds start to pay attention. "Last year she made a hundred and ten thousand dollars; she listed her profession as artist. From her bank records, she made four or five times that much this year."

Elizaveta would not consider Nadia's profession as an assassin an issue.

"She worked exclusively for humans," I told her. "She keeps copies of her contracts. Her employers all knew she was a witch. It was her edge." That would be an issue. Mundane folks tend to get all frightened when they figure out they have monsters in their midst, and it results in things like the Inquisition and the witch hunts that wiped out the majority of the witch bloodlines in Europe a few centuries back.

"You are at her house."

"Yes, ma'am."

"Wait there for me. Do not do anything rash."

I looked at Nadia's face. "No, ma'am. I don't do rash."

I WAITED IN THE DARK, SITTING IN THE LITTLE ROCKER IN Nadia's room, until Elizaveta came in.

She stared at her great-niece for a moment and then said in a very chilly voice, "I told you not to do anything rash."

"It was already done," I informed her.

"It was *my* business to take care of," she said.

"Folks think that your grandson is dead," I told her.

I figured he wasn't. Like I said, witches draw their power from suffering, from sacrifice, like Nadia using my blood to mend the window at Dr. Sullivan's. I wasn't providing Elizaveta anyone else to torture.

Elizaveta stared at me, gray eyes sharp as a harpy's. Witches don't have much trouble seeing in the dark, either.

"She moved against what was mine," I told her. "That made stopping her my business. I'm a wolf, ma'am. Not a cat. I don't play around with my prey." I had liked Nadia, the Nadia I thought she was anyway. It was better that I killed her quickly.

I reached out and handed her the ring I'd found in Nadia's jewelry box. "This is Toni McFetters's wedding ring. When you put out the body for the police to find, it will cause fewer questions if she's wearing that ring. The clothes she was wearing are in a paper bag in the closet—a pink running suit. Maybe she should die of natural causes. I'm sure you can figure something out."

She took it and sighed, her voice softening and the Russian accent gone. She sounded old. "You know, it is very difficult to raise a witch so that they do not self-destruct. I myself had six siblings and only two of us survived. My sister had no talent at all. The temptations are so great."

She looked at Nadia. When she looked back at me, the accent had returned. "She had a crush on you, my little Texas bunny. Otherwise she wouldn't have been so foolish as to do this where I might find her out."

"She knew that I'm gay," I told her, startled.

She laughed. "Forbidden fruit is the sweetest, Warren, my darling. She thought she could change that if you would just look at her. I imagine getting paid to kill your boyfriend was too much temptation for her to resist." She smiled sweetly at me, waiting for me to understand that this was all my fault.

She cared for Nadia, I thought, but she cared more that I'd robbed her of the opportunity to get more power. Maybe she was also ticked that I'd seen what was going on under her nose before she did.

I hate witches.

"Nadia made her choices," I said abruptly, standing up. "I need to get home."

As I walked out of the bedroom, Elizaveta said, "Tell your Alpha that Nadia has decided that she wants to explore the world. She already has tickets to France. No one will much notice when she doesn't come back."

Meaning that Elizaveta would live with my killing Nadia and wouldn't break the deal she had with the pack. When I'd called Adam to warn him what I had to do, he'd told me that was what Elizaveta would do.

I didn't slow down or reply.

DESPITE WHAT I'D TOLD ELIZAVETA, I HAD ONE MORE stop to make. For this one I would be the wolf. It took me a while to shed my human form for the wolf, longer than usual. Probably because I'd been shot; physical weakness makes the transformation harder for me.

The second-story window, the bedroom window, was open, and I jumped through it from the ground. I landed with a thud, but my victim, like Nadia, didn't wake up. I needed this one awake. So I made more noise, letting my claws tick on the hardwood floor.

It wasn't hard. I was very, very angry.

"Wha—"

He turned on the light, but I was already out in the hall. Just around the corner. I made a little more noise.

He grumbled, "Damned mice."

He walked into the hallway where I waited for him.

I CRAWLED INTO BED, EXHAUSTED, WEARY TO MY SOUL.

"Warren?" He pulled me close. "Baby, you're freezing."

If he asked, I would tell him.

"Can you sleep?"

I nodded.

"Fine, tell me about it in the morning."

I took the comfort he offered gratefully.

WE WERE AWAKENED BY THE AMBULANCE.

Kyle went out to find out what he could while I showered. He came in while I was drying off.

"Mr. Francis died of a heart attack last night." He had an odd expression on his face. Hard not to feel some relief, I guessed—and harder not to feel guilty over it. "I guess we won't be getting any more notes." He frowned at me, then donned his lawyer face. "Warren?"

Among the health issues our neighbor had retired with was a weak heart. Much easier to explain a heart attack than death by wild animals. This was the twenty-first century after all, not the nineteenth.

"I'd have gotten more satisfaction if I could have sunk my teeth into him," I told Kyle, rubbing the towel over my hair with a little more force than necessary. "Apparently he decided that you'd never be a neighbor he could cow properly. He hired Nadia, Elizaveta's niece, to kill you."

"*Mr. Francis?*" Kyle said incredulously. I pulled the towel off my head to see him standing slack-jawed. "*Mr. Francis* hired a witch to make a zombie to kill me?" After a moment, he shook off his shock. "I thought for sure it would be Nyelund."

"Covington said she'd pay for half if we told her who hired someone to kill you," I told him. "It was Sullivan who shot me"— Kyle looked at the red mark on my shoulder that was all that was left of the wound—"but he won't be a threat to anyone anymore."

Nadia broke Sullivan—but she'd aimed that magic at me, too. I wasn't supposed to think about Kyle anymore, I was supposed to leave off the investigation with the feeling that everything would be all right. And I wasn't supposed to remember the magic she'd worked to ensure that result. She'd spent so long teaching everyone to underestimate her, she'd overestimated herself.

Kyle frowned at me. "Tell me."

So I told him about Sean Nyelund while I got dressed. I paced restlessly and told him about Nadia while he sat on the bench at the foot of the bed and watched me.

"Justice was served, Warren," he said when I finished. "I'm sorry it had to be you who served it."

"I'm not," I told him. "I'd only done what I needed to protect my own. I'd do it again."

He smiled a little as if he knew something I didn't. "If you say so."

"She was right," I said.

"Who was?"

"Nadia. She said the red dress might be useful in finding out who'd killed Toni McFetters."

He reached up and caught my hand, pulling me down to sit beside him.

"You liked her," he told me.

"She had a prom photo in her house." On top of the curio cabinet. "Toni's husband had taken Nadia to her high school prom. That red dress Toni was wearing? It was Nadia's prom dress; so were the pearls and shoes, near as I could tell. He'd taken her to the prom and hardly remembered her." She'd remembered *him*, though. I'd expected to have to search her house for Toni's missing belongings or, if that hadn't worked, wake Nadia up and question her. She'd made things easy for me.

"Elizaveta only objected that she'd exposed herself as a witch to the humans," Kyle said. "If you hadn't told her that, she would have left Nadia alone. You didn't have to kill her." He put his arm around me. "Tell me that's not what you're thinking now. Tell me that's not what is bothering you."

It wasn't. Not quite. I was thinking that she had attacked Kyle and part of me would have been happier if I'd eaten her. It had taken more will than I'd thought I had not to eat the old man next door, who was even more to blame than Nadia.

I stared at Kyle. I know that the wolf must have been showing through, but he didn't flinch, didn't drop his eyes.

"She was escalating," he said. "She killed for money and learned to like it. She killed Toni because Toni and her husband jogged past her house every day and they were happy. She tried to kill me because we are happy."

He thought I was a hero. He needed to know better.

"I killed two people last night," I told him. "Premeditated murder." I swallowed, but told him the other part of it, too. "I enjoyed it."

He kissed me. When he was finished, he told me, "You're a werewolf—a predator. A skilled killer, but not an indiscriminate one. So am I. If my prey is still writhing when I'm finished, it doesn't make me any less a predator."

I looked at him and he gave me a crooked grin. "Ready to get rid of that apartment yet?"

I laughed and leaned into him.

"Maybe," I said. "Just maybe."

REDEMPTION

I knew, as soon as I brought Ben onstage in *Moon Called*, what his history was. I had to know so that his actions remained logically consistent throughout the series—though I didn't know if I would ever bring them to light.

I am not an outline writer. The one book that I did write with a real, honest-to-goodness outline was really difficult for me to finish—since I already knew the ending, I didn't feel that drive that usually pumps me through the last half of the book. That doesn't mean I don't do any planning on the large scale, but it makes for some interesting events on the small. Toward the end of *Iron Kissed*, Mercy is hurt. Adam, torn by guilt and unwilling to hurt her more, leaves Mercy—but not unguarded. Now who, I thought, should he send to guard Mercy? Warren was too . . . predictable. I could have sent one of the women. But, on a whim, I threw in Ben. What followed took me totally by surprise in the best of all possible ways—Ben was the perfect person.

Ben is in the process of change. We mere mortals have only seventy or so years in which to get over the bad things that have happened to us—and the bad things we've done. I found an event that would be pivotal for Ben—and a chance to bring in some of the weird and absurd things my husband ran into in his years as a DBA (database administrator) for a huge government contractor.

I would, in the interest of fairness, like to point out that although the IT (information technology) field is, for whatever reason, heavily dominated by men, Ben's company, thanks to government hiring incentives, has many competent women in both the DBA and programming departments. But this is told (mostly) from Ben's viewpoint, and Ben has issues with women in general, so his viewpoint is a little skewed.

The events in "Redemption" take place between *Frost Burned* and *Night Broken*.

"HELLO, YOU HAVE REACHED THE PROPHET SUPPORT line. This is Bob, how may I help you?" said a cheery voice with a distinctively Indian accent, and Ben snorted.

For some reason, the database company thought it would sound better to give their overseas customer-service reps American names. Ben didn't call the general number anymore, bouncing himself up the ladder of help-desk services a few tiers by using the personal number of a competent IT rep (IT stands for "information technology"—techspeak for people who know which end of a computer is up), so he could converse with someone who could actually do something. "Bob" was pretty sharp.

"Hey, Rajeev," Ben said. "It's me over here in Washington State. I need to talk to you about this f . . ." He drew in a deep breath and counted to ten. "Ducky. This *ducky* new package your company sold ours."

"Ben?" Rajeev asked a little uncertainly. "Is this Ben?"

Rajeev and he had known each other, by phone, for a long time.

"It's me," Ben confirmed.

"Ducky?"

Thanks to Ben, Rajeev knew more English swearwords than all of his buddies in India combined—which explained his tentative greeting.

"I have a bet," Ben told him. "No swearing for a week. There's a bottle of eighteen-year-old scotch in the balance." Werewolves might not get drunk, but that didn't affect the flavor, or even the initial hit of a good, old, smoky scotch. It wasn't that he couldn't buy his own bottle of scotch, but the bet was with his Alpha—it was the principle of the thing.

"Ah." In the following silence, Ben heard Rajeev calculating Ben's chances for a moment before he recalled that someone might be monitoring the call for efficiency. "Good luck with that. You called with a problem?"

Reminded of his troubles, Ben growled. "Yes. This program is a piece of . . . of junk. My boss says his boss thought it would be a s . . . *spiffy* idea to replace my program that does a . . . *perfectly adequate* job already with this . . . program. I expect the . . . nice gentleman in question is getting a f . . . *fiddling* kickback."

Rajeev laughed. "I think, my friend, that you might consider avoiding adjectives altogether." There was the sound of keyboard keys clicking, then Rajeev sighed. "I see it. They have purchased the new release of Quotalk for your department. Your entire department." There were things that he couldn't say, or he'd lose his job. In the silence, Ben heard Rajeev's unspoken dismay. *What were they thinking selling this half-written spaghetti code to a customer who has never offended us?* But Rajeev would never say such a thing over the phone because he, like Ben, needed his job.

Rajeev cleared his throat, and said carefully, "We have been getting calls all week with this iteration of the program." There was nothing wrong with Rajeev's English except a thick accent—two thick accents, really, India by way of Great Britain. Ben didn't have any trouble with it because he already had the British half himself.

"Which is giving you trouble?" Rajeev continued, his voice carefully professional. "Is it the way the auto-installer doesn't load or the way the program keeps overwriting your servlet container?" That was as close to sarcasm as Rajeev permitted himself. "I have a patch for the first, but the last is one we are still struggling with."

The Prophet database (of course, the whole IT—computer geek—world called it the For-Profit database) was well written, but all the programs the mother company tried to sell with it were garbage. Because the Prophet was the gold standard of databases, the company who owned it got to sit on that reputation for everything else. Ben was pretty sure that if the people doing the buying had also been the people who had to use the programs, his life would be a lot easier.

As it was, once his company's overlords bought the stupid add-ons, they made them mandatory. Happily for Ben, the security guys would call him a day before they conducted the mandatory just-to-make-sure-you-are-doing-as-you-are-told inspections of his hard drive so he'd have time to hide the unapproved programs he actually used somewhere else. Happy for the company, too, because if Ben actually had to use the crap—he arbitrarily decided that crap wasn't a swearword—if he used the crap they mandated, nothing on any of the computers in the company would work.

"I wrote a patch to defend my servlet container settings," he told Rajeev. "I'll send it to you. And why are your programmers still using servlets, anyway?"

"To a man with a hammer," said Rajeev wisely, "all problems look like nails. Thank you for your offer of help."

"No trouble," Ben told him.

Like his use of unapproved programs, sharing his code with someone who worked for another company was also against his company's protocol. Code written by company IT personnel was supposed to be shown to marketing to see if it was a viable product. But geeks had to stick together. Also, if marketing ever decided to sell some of his code, he knew who would get stuck on a help desk for it—a business that would be as unpleasant for the customers as it would be for him: he would make certain of that. Happily, since Ben was officially a database administrator, better known in the

IT world as a DBA, the marketing department never thought to see if he also wrote his own programming.

"How did you fix it, anyway?" asked Rajeev. "Our programmers have been trying to figure out a work-around for several days."

"The patch hides servlet container settings from your program," Ben told him, "then reinstalls them once the program is up and running." If Ben had enjoyed outthinking the stupid program, he didn't have to admit it to anyone. "I figured out the install problem, too, thank you. It was the same problem another of Prophet's products had, and I just modified my old patch. What I can't fix is that the program won't run unless the password is permanently set to PASSWORD and the username is permanently TEST. Since I'm working on databases that hold the US governmental secrets of the last hundred years, you'll understand that is not acceptable."

There was a long silence. Then Rajeev said, very carefully, "Someone hard-coded the passwords."

"That's what I'm seeing," agreed Ben blandly.

There was a very long pause. "I haven't heard that complaint before," Rajeev said. He considered his words some more, and said, "At least not on this program." There was another pause. "Perhaps it is because no one else has made it that far yet. I will inquire of our programmers to see if there is a way to fix this and call you back." He paused and said, "The username is TEST?"

"That's right," Ben said.

Rajeev sighed and hung up.

Ben was still grinning when he sent the promised bit of code to Rajeev. Setting aside the task of making the new program behave until he got a call back, he continued his daily checklist to make sure all of his databases were running smoothly and likely to continue that way on aging servers with insufficient memory and slow processors. Galadriel was a crabby, high-maintenance server, and she'd been particularly cranky over the past few days. So he messed around with her, cleaning out a few old logs that were bogging her down.

Around him, the sounds of a giant, cubicle-filled room told

him the secrets of the universe—or at least the universe of his company. He didn't really pay attention on a conscious level, but the part of him that wasn't a top-flight computer guru stored up the interesting bits and absorbed them.

Ben knew about the guy who was having an affair with three different women and a guy in marketing. He knew that one of the pretty young things in Web Applications was pregnant and wanted to divorce her husband before he found out because it wasn't his child. Most people's secrets were less salacious—things like surprise parties, wedding showers, and his DBA coworker who was running cosmetic sales from her work phone instead of doing her job. She was a crummy DBA, though, so that was okay because mostly what she did was make more work for the rest of them.

It wasn't that he was a busybody who needed to have an ear in everyone's business—he didn't care enough about other people to want to hear gossip. It was that he was a bloody werewolf and couldn't help overhearing.

All the main servers had names. Most of them were references to the usual geek favorites: Lord of the Rings, Star Wars, and Dr. Seuss characters. The only server name that was out of the ordinary was the server someone had named Tree a couple of years ago. Word was that on the eve of transferring to Washington, D.C., a DBA who never read anything but nonfiction had named it in a fit of defiance.

Ben was in the middle of coaxing a little more space out of Yertle when he heard the voice he'd been listening for carrying over the tops of the cubicles to his desk.

Mel Dreyer was the DBA group secretary. Cute, perky, and seven stone soaking wet, she was everything he hated in a woman. Little-girl voice. Check. Sensitive. Check. Cried easily. Check. Scared to death of him. Double check.

She was prey and brought up bad memories until it was all he could do to control his wolf when she was around.

Right now, she was talking to Mark Duffy, IT Services Group

Junior Vice Director. It had been Duffy's voice Ben had been listening for.

Ben pulled himself away from his task, grabbed a book off the top of his file cabinet, and stalked out of his cubicle. He allowed the wolf he kept balled up inside him out just enough to be scary but not enough to be dangerous, a more difficult balance than usual because the moon's song was in his blood. Full moon was soon.

Mel's desk was at the entrance to the double row of DBA cubicles, but she didn't get a whole cubicle. She was stuck out on the end of their row, so she could catch visitors before they invaded the DBA's domain beyond her. They'd taken away two of the walls and left her vulnerable to whoever decided to pester her.

Ben looked at the floor as he strode by the other cubicles of DBAs. He stretched his neck and heard the bones pop, a sign that the wolf was too prominent. Control, he thought at himself, don't want to kill anyone. Even as he thought it, the dark inside him answered, *Oh, didn't he just.* He knew what it was to feel the flesh part between his teeth and the taste of hot, fresh prey.

He passed the last cubicle, and Duffy's smell and cologne that reeked of chemicals assaulted Ben's sensitive nose. He had no trouble curling his lips in a snarl.

Duffy stood beside Mel's desk, leaning over slightly until he hovered above her, a position of power. His expensive suit and haircut were designed to show anyone who looked that Mark Duffy was a man of consequence.

Ben bulled his way to Mel's desk, forcing Duffy to step back or be body-checked. As Ben slammed the manual onto Mel's desk with a crack that made her jump, Duffy flinched, and silence descended on their portion of cubicle hell.

"*What* is *this*?" Ben snapped at Mel, knowing the flush of anger on his English-pale cheeks made him even more intimidating. Humans couldn't tell he was a werewolf unless he wanted them to, but some part of their psyche could smell predator.

Mel looked at the book and swallowed. She didn't cringe, not quite, but when she answered, it was in a squeak. "The manual I got for you from the company library yesterday?"

He stabbed the paper with his finger. "Do you see the title? What does it say?"

"Is this really necessary?" said Duffy, and Ben looked at him briefly.

He turned back to Mel without answering Duffy. "Well? Can't you read?"

"It says *Advanced Concepts in JavaScript.*" She didn't sound terrified, though Ben knew she was scared of him. *Everyone* at his work was scared of him except his friend Rajeev because Rajeev was on the other side of the world. His wolf saw all humans as weak, and people could feel things like that.

"I asked you for the advanced *Java* manual," he said. "I realize that *JavaScript* starts with *Java*, but you've been working here long enough that you should know that one program is nothing like the other. Sounds alike is not good enough. I called the library, and they pulled the correct book. I made it simple for you because simple seems to be all you can do. Go upstairs, take this book back, and bring me the book they give you."

"Yes, sir," she said, standing up. Which meant she looked him right in the collarbone, and she raised her chin. "You'll have to get out of my way first."

"You tell him, Mel," said a faint voice a few rows over.

"Keep your nose in your business, Lincoln," snapped Ben, effectively removing the voice's anonymity.

He backed up and swept his arm out in a mockery of gentlemanliness and forced Duffy even farther back, clearing the way for Mel to head to the stairs, which were closer (and faster) than the elevator.

"Don't start sniveling." Ben scowled at her back as she skittered by him with her head tucked so no one could see it. "If you'd gotten it right the first time, neither of us would have been inconvenienced."

"Don't you think that was a little harsh?" asked Duffy, then, with unrecognized irony, "It is against company policy to harass other workers."

Ben met his eyes—a dangerous move with his wolf so close to the surface. But Duffy looked away before Ben was driven to enforce his status as the dominant predator.

"If she doesn't want to get yelled at, she can do her job," Ben tried out his dominant position by sneering. "Just like everyone else does. What do you need?"

Duffy opened his mouth, but no words came out. Hah. Humans were no match for a werewolf.

Ben waved his hand back down the line. "Did you need something from the DBAs?"

"Uh," said Duffy. "No."

"Fine." Ben turned on his heel and stalked down the row, which was unusually silent. DBAs didn't spend a lot of time talking, but keyboards are not quiet—everyone had been listening to his interchange.

Ben's cubicle was the farthest one, and he liked it that way because people with random issues usually stopped elsewhere before they got to him. By the time he got there, the noise level had begun to resume its normal clatter.

"HERE," ONE OF THE OTHER DBAS WHISPERED FROM THE hallway just outside Ben's cubicle. "Just wait here. He'll be with you as soon as he surfaces."

Ben had hung a whiteboard on the outside of the cubicle wall next to the entrance of his lair. On it he had written: *I know you are here. Wait silently, and I'll get to you as soon as I am able. If you speak before then, you will not find me helpful.* On the floor just inside his cubicle was a mat with a pair of black footprints and "Wait here" painted on it.

"I have work—"

"Shhh," hissed the second voice. "Heed the warning."

It took Ben a couple of minutes to tidy everything so nothing would blow up behind him. When he turned around, there was one of the programmers whose face he vaguely recognized waiting for him.

Ben raised an eyebrow.

"I'm told you're the one who wiped out my data," the programmer said belligerently.

"Probably," agreed Ben. "Who are you?"

"Stan Brown."

He knew that name.

Ben had been trying to figure out what had been filling the hard drive of a priority backup server he'd been fine-tuning when he'd discovered a huge block of data, property of one Stan Brown, that turned out to be a collection of every blue film made in the last century as well as carefully organized files of photographs from bestiality to kink and beyond.

Private files on the critical backup servers, which were very expensive real estate in electron land, were prohibited. Pornography at work was a firing offence. There had been a massive firing of people caught just surfing for porn on company computers. The scandal predated Ben, but he'd heard about it from people still traumatized by the winnowing.

So Ben had talked about Stan's files to the head of security, who wasn't a total . . . *jerk*, and they decided, between the two of them that they should just erase it and pretend it had never been there. Save the guy's job instead of letting some boss look good to his overlords.

"Yes," said Ben slowly. "I had a good look at those files. I wondered what kind of critical data you could possibly have that was that big. When I saw what it was, I got rid of it."

"So it *was* you," Stan said hotly. "I had to lean on the security guys to give me your name."

The security guys were probably huddled on the other side of the cubicle wall just to hear the set down Ben gave him. They were in for a disappointment because he couldn't swear—or he'd lose that scotch—so scaring off stupid people just wasn't as much fun as usual.

Stan was still twittering on. "Do you know how long it took me to put that collection together? Some of those aren't available any-where anymore. You can't just go around erasing people's files."

Ben tapped a little framed certificate on the wall.

"DBA," he said in case the guy couldn't read. "I maintain the data systems. I take out things that don't belong as part of my job description. Porn doesn't belong. Especially illegal porn—and in Washington State, bestiality is illegal ever since that guy died at the sheep farm."

"Horse farm," said Lee, the DBA in the next cubicle. "And I think it might just be the act of bestiality that's good for jail time, not films or photos."

"You would know," muttered someone behind his other wall. It sounded like one of the security people. If Ben hadn't had were-wolf ears, he wouldn't have heard her—or the very quiet snickers that accompanied the remark.

"You had no right," whined Stan, who wasn't cursed with Ben's hearing. "No right to steal my stuff, man. I'm going to go to the police and report it."

Ben was too bemused to be angry. Was this guy really that dumb? Hadn't he gotten the same on-hire speech about what was and was not allowed on-site that Ben had?

"I tell you what, Stan," he said slowly because that was how he talked to people too stupid to live. "Those were on the critical backup server, I still have backups of your files—and will for the next decade, because, hey, *critical* backup server. You get your supervisor to sign a letter asking me to restore those files—detailing exactly what kind of data we are talking about—and I'll restore them for you."

Stan threw out his chest as if he'd won the battle. "I'll do that."

When he had left, Fitz, in the cubicle with all the security people, stuck his head over the partition, and said, in awe, "There goes the stupidest man I've ever heard. Do you suppose he'll really try to get a letter?"

"Hey, Ben," said someone farther down. "Can *I* get a copy of the backup files?"

"Would you all shut up so I can get some work done?" said Lori, the makeup lady.

SEVERAL HOURS LATER, IT WAS THE SMELL OF COFFEE that pulled Ben out of electronland. He would have dismissed it—no one brought him coffee—except that Mel was standing, very quietly, on his mat. He made a few changes and buttoned up the database he was working on.

When he turned around, Mel held out a cup of gourmet coffee that hadn't come out of the company kitchen. Her hand barely shook. He frowned at her and made no move to take it.

"What?" he said.

She set it down on the desk beside him and cleared her throat. "You know I'm married."

He raised his eyebrow. "I would have propositioned you, but I have a harem at home, and you just wouldn't fit in."

Her face flushed. "That's not what I meant. My husband is overseas for another six months."

He waited in obvious irritation. Her fluttering and flinching made him want to bite her. His wolf said she was easy prey.

"The coffee is from my husband," she said, quietly, so no one else would hear her. "I finally figured you out—my husband did, actually—so your snarling isn't going to make me flinch anymore."

He tried a subvocal growl, and, by Saint Andrew's great hairy b . . . balloons, she didn't back off.

"Duffy got a secretary fired when she turned him down," Mel told him. "Another girl, who couldn't afford to lose her job, let him . . . you know."

Ben tried a raised eyebrow again, but it had noticeably less effect than it had the last time he'd done it to her. No tears. Not even any flinching or cringing.

"I'm married, and he still . . ." She shuddered. "Between him and you, I was pretty upset this weekend when my husband called. I told him about everything that had been happening here, and he said"—her voice dropped into what was evidently her attempt to sound like her husband—"'It sounds like every time Duffy comes out to bother you, Shaw emerges to yell at you and make you run stupid errands.' I agreed, and he told me to think about that, then get you a cup of good coffee from him." She smiled, revealing a charming dimple. Ben reminded himself he hated dimples almost as much as gratitude. "So here's a cup of—"

"Ben," trilled Lorna Winkler, head of IT.

Ben felt a headache coming on. For such a promising day, it was going to end badly. If Mel triggered his dislike of women, Lorna clubbed him over the head with it. He wasn't fond of the company's policy of women bosses—but he might have dealt if they had mitigated the damage by hiring the smart ones.

Lorna was beautiful, power mad, and needed help to send e-mail—just exactly the person to put in charge of a bunch of computer nerds. Whenever she came down from on high to invade his cubicle—which she did to everyone because it was "friendlier than summoning you up to my office"—he figured there was a fifty-fifty chance he was going to quit in the next ten minutes. In the time he'd worked there, she'd visited him, personally, twice.

He'd overheard enough of her "friendly pep talks" to know that she liked to begin speaking well before she made it down to the cubicle of whoever she was aimed at. Her first calling out of his name had started near Mel's desk.

"I've had a report from one of my people," she warbled at him from halfway down the hall, "that you are harassing our secretary."

Mel raised her eyebrows at him, and Ben curled his lip, and whispered, "Duffy's been whining to Mummy, again."

Mel grinned, then covered her mouth as Winkler, all six feet of the immaculately groomed gorgeousness that had allowed her to be Miss California a decade earlier, entered his sanctuary.

She clearly hadn't been expecting Mel. She stopped, regrouped, and began again. "I'm so glad you're here, Mel, so that Ben can apologize to you. Our company has a firm policy against harassment."

"I'm sorry," said Ben, with patent insincerity.

"He's not harassing me," Mel said at exactly the same moment. She continued with a confident smile. "He can get a little grouchy, but everyone knows that. And we all make allowances for genius, right?"

Winkler wasn't pleased with having the rug pulled out from under her. "Don't you consider having books slammed in front of you harassing? It was hostile and aggressive. I won't have any woman in my department made uncomfortable."

"I wasn't uncomfortable," Mel said agreeably. "I'm sorry if Mr. Duffy had that impression."

Ben wasn't used to having a woman defend him. It made him feel odd. Odder than it should. Wrong. Especially given that it was *Mel* defending him. It felt even odder than the impulse that had begun his game of keep the secretary safe from Duffy. It was so disconcerting that he didn't say anything.

Winkler wasn't ready to give up. Maybe she'd promised Duffy that she was going to fire him. "I've also had reports that Ben's language is objectionable."

Mel looked proud, and said, "He quit swearing two days ago. The whole DBA group has money on when he'll break, but so far he's doing really well, and we appreciate his effort to change his behavior. Ken Lincoln even promised that if Ben can quit swearing, he'll agree to quit smoking."

ADAM LAUGHED AT HIS CONSTERNATION AS BEN told him the whole story later. "I'm so sorry," his Alpha told him carefully, "that you've been used as a motivational force for good in your workplace."

"It's your fault," Ben groused, sinking lower in Adam's couch. "If I hadn't been trying for that scotch, it wouldn't have happened."

He'd come to Adam because . . . He didn't think of Adam as his father. He'd had one father, and that was enough for him. But Adam was good at sorting out people. This past month, Ben was starting not to recognize himself. He needed to know if that was a good thing or a bad thing.

"Do *you* know why I did it?" he asked, because he was bewildered by the need that had driven him to protect Mel—whom he didn't even like.

"Because she's *your* secretary," Adam said, then grinned at Ben's expression. "How long have you been working in the DBA group?"

"Something over two years." If Adam was going somewhere with this, Ben didn't know where it was.

"Ben," Adam said, "are you a dominant wolf or a submissive wolf?"

"Dominant." Not very. Bottom of the pack now that Peter was gone.

"What makes up a dominant personality?"

All of his life, Ben had always been considered brilliant— troubled, obnoxious, criminal, occasionally violent, but always brilliant. He didn't like the feeling that he was missing something, and he liked the hint of patience in Adam's voice that told him that Adam *expected* him to miss something even less. Ben's first Alpha had been more beast than man, and he'd never explained anything about dominance other than the absolute rule that Ben had to obey everyone he couldn't take down.

"Willingness to fight," Ben said, trying not to sound belligerent as he tried to work out what Adam wanted from him. "Difficulty with authority." He jerked his gaze up to his Alpha, who looked a little amused at Ben's realization about how that last one sounded. "Most authority."

"Anyone who hasn't proved that he deserves respect," Adam said tactfully.

"If they can't thrash me, they are prey," Ben said, trying to stretch the rule that had been forcibly explained to him when he'd become a werewolf into a shape that Adam would find acceptable.

Adam looked at him. "Okay. Are you my prey?"

Ben stood up abruptly and stalked to the window, his back to his Alpha because he didn't have an expression he wanted to show him. "I've been a werewolf for long enough that I shouldn't always feel like a bloody beginner." Adam didn't say anything, so Ben finally muttered, "I *hope* I am not prey to you." Silence continued, somehow disapproving.

"Do you feel like my prey?" Adam asked, his voice quiet and a little hurt.

Ben threw away what he knew and tried to go with what he felt—which was difficult for him because facts had never failed him the way emotions had. "No." That was right. "No." Adam put all of his abilities, physical and mental, to protecting the pack from anything that would hurt them.

"Someone should write a book about how to be a werewolf," Mercy, Adam's mate, said, sailing in with a plate of brownies, which she set down on the table with a thunk and the burnt motor-oil smell that was a part of her. It used to irritate him—and now it irritated him that he associated the smell with pack and safety. "I sometimes feel like I know more about being a werewolf than all of you combined." She sat next to Adam and looked up at Ben.

He'd asked for a minute alone with Adam, which she apparently thought she'd given them. He opened his mouth to ask her to leave, but when he spoke, it was to Adam. "So you think I'm looking at Mel as if she were part of my pack? That I'm feeling protective of that sniveling little—" He swallowed the descriptor that came to mind. "Annoying wimpy chit."

"That's what I'm saying," agreed Adam. "The reason you are not more dominant has more to do with the other wolves than with you. Part of submitting to a more dominant wolf is the belief that they will protect you better than you can protect yourself. They don't believe you'll protect them, so they won't yield to you."

Ben turned back to the window and absorbed the information like a blow. He didn't care how dominant he was, he didn't, though he disliked obeying other wolves intensely.

Adam's orders were the single exception because Adam would never hurt him or allow him to be hurt outside of the discipline needed to keep peace within the pack. Which sort of drove Adam's previous point about what really made a dominant wolf right home, didn't it?

Ben opened his mouth to swear, then closed it again.

"I didn't know how much the willingness to protect the others beneath a wolf in the pack structure affected the position of a dominant wolf until you came to our pack," Adam offered gently. "Until then, I was pretty convinced that dominance was about who was the better or more aggressive fighter. You are as willing as Darryl is when it comes to taking on an opponent, and not half-bad in a fight—and still Darryl is much, much more dominant because the other wolves trust him to take care of them."

"Have a brownie, Ben," Mercy said prosaically. "And congratulations."

Ben turned around and dropped into an overstuffed chair with a sigh, taking a brownie almost as an afterthought. "Congratulations on what?"

"Your new upward mobility in the pack structure," Mercy said. "They'll figure out that you've changed pretty soon."

Adam met his eyes and smiled. Ben felt better suddenly, and it wasn't Mercy's congratulations or the brownie that did it, but the respect in his Alpha's face. He remembered what Adam had told him a while ago. It might be taking a long time to get out from under what the Old Man had done to him, but he had time, didn't he? A wolf's immortality was a gift for him to use wisely or poorly.

He finished the brownie, thanked Adam for his time, and

headed back home, feeling like himself again. No. Better than that. He fed his better self a nice dinner, watched a little telly, and took himself off to bed with a smile on his face.

HE'D DREAMED ABOUT *HIM* THAT NIGHT. WOKE UP WITH the sound of his mother's voice in his ears. "Benjamin, your father wants you to see him in the study."

Ben sat up, so certain he'd heard her voice that he was in a cold sweat, his heart beating like a bass drum in a marching band. Hard on the realization that he'd been dreaming was the knowledge that the wolf wanted out.

He managed not to change—just barely managed. But the struggle left him with a headache and the temper of an asp that accompanied him all the way to work. He answered Mel's cheery good morning with a growl and buried himself in his computer. He ignored lunch, which was stupid, because when Lorna Winkler came into his office without a word of warning, he emerged from coaxing a little more speed out of one of his database-monitoring programs hungry, and she smelled like food.

"Ben, I was talking to Mark Duffy about your admirable attempt to stop swearing, and he suggested that we organize something for the whole division. It would raise morale if we could encourage people not to drink, smoke, or to lose ten pounds—and perhaps lower our health-insurance costs. I'd like you to spearhead the project."

Various responses occurred to him.

"No," he said mildly when he was sure that was what would come out of his mouth. Then he gave her his back and started typing random lines of code.

"No?" Winkler's voice was shocked, as if she thought she'd misheard because no one would refuse her suggestion.

He didn't look around when he said, "I'm a DBA, not a motivational speaker."

"Thank God," someone said. Ben heard them, but Winkler wouldn't have.

"But—" she said.

He slowly turned his chair around so he could see her. He met her eyes. "Ms. Winkler," he said, "you pay me a lot of money to be a good nerd, which I am. There is not enough money in the world to make me be in charge of a *company morale-improvement exercise*."

She backed away from the expression on his face and left. He wondered, as he returned to work, if he was going to be fired. He hadn't threatened her with words, but she and he both knew that there hadn't been happy happy joy joy in his eyes. There might have been not-human stuff in his eyes, which was something he usually avoided because he had no intention of advertising to the world that he was a werewolf. The wolves who were out were expected to be exemplary and well behaved, which he was not. But his mood was so black that he couldn't find it in himself to care one way or the other about the job or the wolf.

He worked a while more, surfacing now and again because of the dream about his mother in a cold shaking sweat, imagining that he'd gotten a whiff of her perfume or heard her voice. But he was deep into the heart of Spock, who was at 84 percent capacity, when he was yanked out again.

"I have that address for you, Mr. Duffy."

The voice belonged to one of the women who worked in human resources, though it wasn't her voice, but Duffy's name, that jerked Ben out of his databases. He blinked and saw that it was dark out. Really dark. As soon as he noticed, the moon's song lit him up from the inside, and his monster was ready to tango.

It wasn't full moon yet, but he usually changed for the nights on either side because fighting it was tough. No use at all fighting if the moon was full; she called his wolf right out. It was dangerous to be at work this late, this close to the full moon.

"Thank you, Karen," Duffy said. That was the human-resources woman's name, Karen Sinclair-Ramsay.

If Ben could trust his ears, Duffy was somewhere near the elevator. If there had been more people in the building, Ben would never have been able to hear him so clearly.

"I forgot to ask Mel before she left," Duffy was saying smoothly, "and she said she'd get the figures worked up for me for Monday if I got her the information tonight. I think I'll stop and get her a bottle of wine for putting up with me."

The wolf that was Ben lunged to the fore with a snarl. His human half pulled him back. Mel was no concern of his despite what Adam had said. Ben cared for no one and nothing. No one had watched out for him, and he'd survived, hadn't he? That's what he'd had that dream for, to remind him about people.

Karen Sinclair-Ramsay sounded a little uncomfortable when she said, "I'm sure she'd appreciate a bottle of wine." Maybe it was only now occurring to her that Mel was the DBA secretary, that Duffy had his own secretary. That a bottle of wine was just . . . not quite the right thing to be bringing a secretary who'd agreed to work the weekend.

No. It was none of his business. Mel wasn't pack, wasn't his. It wasn't his job to watch out for her.

Benjamin, your father wants you. He could almost see her sitting in front of him, his beautiful mother sipping her tea as she read a magazine about the latest fashion. He could see, as if it were right before his eyes instead of decades in the past, the high-heeled black-and-white sandals worn by the model on the cover of the magazine. *Be a dear and go to the study.* She didn't look at him when she spoke, her reading apparently absorbing his mother's attention.

She didn't need a reply. Back then, he'd been a good kid. He'd done exactly what he was told. The destructive anger and black despair that drove him now, that hadn't affected him much yet.

Ben had almost opened his mouth, almost asked her if she knew what his father wanted him for in that study. But he was afraid, so afraid, that she knew. And if she knew . . . his world would self-destruct and take him with it.

But even as he walked down the stairs to his father's study, some part, the hidden, angry part that was growing inside and would, eventually, consume him, understood that she had to know. She was such a good mother, everyone said so. Her son was well mannered, well-groomed, and did well in school. Wasn't he lucky to have such a good mother?

BEN LEFT WORK WITH HIS HEAD DOWN AND WITH QUICK strides aimed at letting people know that he didn't have time to talk. He smelled Karen Sinclair-Ramsay in the parking lot and deliberately looked up at her. She was dressed in a business suit that looked good on her without being inappropriate. She had her hair braided back to display nicely shaped ears and dangly earrings. She was pretty in a well-cared-for, comfortable way.

Women were always smiling and pretty on the outside.

He got into his truck and backed out of his parking spot. He did not look at Duffy's red Mustang as he drove past it on his way out of the parking lot and out onto the Bypass Highway he needed to take home.

MEL'S RENTAL HOUSE WAS VERY SMALL. THE WIND WHIS-tled through it, and the floors creaked. Chris had told her he didn't want his wife living in a building he thought was going to fall over in the next good storm. But Chris was overseas, and she wouldn't get to see him again for six months.

He didn't have to live by himself in a house with too many ghosts and not enough people. When Chris's unit left for overseas, Mel had moved to Richland to take care of her mom, who had just been diagnosed with cancer. She was supposed to have had more time, but Mel had still been unpacking when her mom died.

So Mel sold the house she'd grown up in to pay her mother's

medical bills and rented a one-bedroom cottage built when Richland was born during World War II. It wasn't fancy, but it was charming once she'd gotten through with it. If she hadn't sent Chris a photo when he'd requested it, he wouldn't have worried about it. But he'd asked and she'd sent and so she had to deal with the consequences.

Chris wanted her to move back to the base in North Carolina, but she'd grown up in Richland, and she liked her job—except for the last month or so, and even that was better now. When Chris came back, they would talk. Until then, she'd wait for him here.

She was watching TV when someone knocked at the door. Though it was dark, it wasn't late; the news was just coming on. She didn't even think about checking to see who was at the door. Richland was a safe place to live.

She got a look at who waited on the porch and put her leg and shoulder against the door to hold it where it was.

"Mr. Duffy," she said, trying not to show the fear she felt. What was he doing here?

He smiled at her and held out a bottle of wine. "Mel, honey. We need to talk." He brushed past her and into her house without her quite knowing how he did.

He glanced at her living room and walked by it into the small kitchen, set the bottle on the table, and started opening cupboards.

"Charming house," he said. "I just knew it would be. You have a way of making a place warm wherever you go."

"Mr. Duffy," she said, instinct keeping her by the front door because it felt like an avenue of escape. "This is inappropriate."

He continued as if she hadn't spoken. "Now where do you . . . there they are." And he got down the long-stemmed crystal glasses that had been a wedding present from Chris's sister. He popped the cork with a corkscrew he'd brought and filled the glasses with wine.

"Come in and sit down, Mel," he said, with a sharp smile. "And let me explain a few things to you."

She twisted the front doorknob.

"You do need your job," he said. "I'm afraid I have some proof that you are selling proprietary secrets."

For a moment, indignation overcame fear. "I did not."

He sat down at her table and swirled the rust-colored wine, then sipped it. "But I have proof. I'll show it to you. We are going to talk about how you will end up jobless and in jail. But that's just you. You need to consider how it will look for your Marine if his wife is convicted of selling the location of nuclear material to interested parties."

She felt the blood leave her face as she understood just how far he was willing to go. She should have left when she had a chance.

"Or"—he smiled and her stomach tightened with revulsion—"you can become my secretary with a healthy raise. Marie is transferring to another department and her post is open. Of course, you'll have to persuade me."

"Persuade you?" Her voice sounded wobbly, and she wished, harder than she ever had in her life, that Chris were here. Chris would wipe the floor with him.

Duffy tilted his glass toward the untouched one on the table. "Sit down, Mel. Don't look so terrified. I'm hardly a rapist. Who knows? You might like it."

BEN DROVE HOME FROM WORK TRYING NOT TO THINK about anything, but the scent of his mother's perfume lingering in his imagination left him restless and angry. He made it into his house, then stared unseeing at the food in his refrigerator. He knew he needed to eat, but he was too distracted to focus on food.

He hadn't felt like this in a long time. Not since he'd killed Terry.

He stopped in the middle of his kitchen and did some deep breathing to keep the wolf back. Now that he was home, there was no one who would know or care what he was. But it was a bad idea to let the wolf out while he was this angry, and thoughts of Terry made him . . . very angry or something very near it.

He paced from the fridge to the door and back, kicking the dustbin in frustration when it got in the way. He hadn't thought of Terry in months.

Terry had been the pack's second in London, in Ben's first pack. He worked for the Alpha, who was a loan shark. The whole pack worked for him, really, but Terry got paid for it. Terry's job was to go collect from people who weren't making their payments. Shortly after Ben was Changed, he was sent to tag along to make sure matters were discreet. The Alpha felt that Terry might forget himself and hang around until the police came by.

So after his real IT job, Ben got to trail Terry around three days a week, and that's when he found out what he'd really been sent to do. Terry didn't just beat up the people because they weren't quick with their money; he beat up people because he liked it. Ben's real job was to stop him before there was a dead body. Murder was more interesting to the police than loan-sharking.

One day, as they were leaving the apartment where their last reminder call lived, a woman walked by who caught Terry's eye.

"My old girlfriend," he'd said, and even now Ben wasn't sure it was true. He wasn't sure that was the first one for Terry, or if he'd been controlling himself because Ben was a new watcher.

He didn't kill her. But she wouldn't be walking around in her high-heeled black boots for a few months after he finished with her. Bruises and a broken leg, the newspaper reported the next day, and two men whose faces she hadn't been able to see in the dark.

Terry was higher-ranked in the pack, and most of the pack were afraid of him. Ben wasn't—there wasn't much Terry could do to him that hadn't already been done—but he was a realist. Terry could wipe the floor with him. And . . . there had been something cathartic about watching Terry beat up the woman.

Ben had come a long way from the good little boy of his childhood. He'd gotten in more than a little trouble that his father's money had bought him out of. He'd never hurt anyone, but he'd done about everything else. He still wondered about the fate that made him end up a werewolf instead of dead in a dark alley of an overdose or a knife in his belly. Time was he'd been convinced that he'd ended up with the worst end of that stick.

When he approached his Alpha about Terry's transgression, the old wolf had just grunted. "Your job isn't to police what Terry chooses to do," he'd said. "He's the one making the calls. You just make sure no one is killed and keep watch for the police."

Ben went out and bought a knife, and he did as he'd been ordered. Terry went hunting with Ben as observer; sometimes it was one of the other wolves, but mostly it was Ben—and Terry liked that part of it, too—and so did some dark part of Ben. At first it had only been once every couple of months, but by the end it was weekly. Terry liked those black, high-heeled boots. He'd follow women who wore them home and wait until the lights went out, then he and Ben would break in, muffling the sound of violence with the magic of the pack.

When Ben got home from those nights, he spent the next hour or so in the bathroom until there was nothing more to throw up. It hadn't escaped his notice that he'd taken on the role of his mother, which was bad enough. But the thing that made it nigh unbearable was that he *liked* it. When the woman screamed, it was his mother's voice he heard. And he craved it as much as Terry did.

Terry always cried afterward, patting his victim's heads and calling them darling as he blamed them for making him beat them up. They were a proper unhinged pair, he and Terry. None of their victims died because the object of Terry's kink was not murder but pain.

And so it went for almost a year and a half, fourteen victims. The fifteenth lay unconscious on the floor, her skirt rucked up over a hip displaying a tattoo of a wolf.

"Well, my boyo, lookee there," Terry said. "She's marked herself for me."

The sickness was already churning in Ben's gut. "You've done what you came for," he said. "Time to go."

"No," Terry said, unzipping his trousers. "Time to step up the game for you." He smiled. "I've been teaching you and you're learning pretty well. Now we get to the good stuff."

And the woman on the ground wasn't Ben's mother anymore.

"Time to go," Ben told Terry. The woman was like him, like Ben. A victim. And he could take the easy route, like his mother had, as he had been doing all this time, or he could stop it.

Terry gave him an irritated look. "Bugger off yourself, then." He bent down and patted her tattoo. "This one's mine."

And Ben did what he'd told himself he was going to do when he bought the knife in the first place. He cut Terry's throat, then ripped off his head. He left the body in the poor woman's apartment.

He'd cleaned up and headed over to turn himself in to the Alpha for punishment only to find that there had been a change in leadership. The wolf who ruled the rest of London had decided to take over the rival pack. Ben was too freaked from killing Terry to recognize that the pack bonds had been trying to tell him the old Alpha was dead.

The new Alpha didn't kill Ben, but the police were looking for Terry's accomplice. So he'd exiled Ben to the good old U. S. of A., and Ben had been given to Adam to see if there was anything worth saving inside Ben's skin. Luckily for him, Adam seemed to view him as a challenge.

And right now he needed to pull his reformed head out of his arse because he'd just left a little helpless lamb out for a man who thought himself the big bad wolf. If she'd been Mercy, he wouldn't be worried; Duffy would be lucky if he could walk tomorrow. But if she'd been Mercy, Duffy would never have chosen her as a target.

MEL KEPT HER BACK AGAINST THE DOOR AS IF THAT might help. "No," she said. "I won't." But she knew that she would, and so did Duffy; it was in the confidence of his voice and body. For Chris, she would do anything.

The doorknob turned, and the door, rather gently, pushed her to the side and Ben the Grouch—that's what the office workers called him—came in. She stared at him in shock.

"Blackmail, Duffy?" said Ben, toeing off his snow-covered shoes and stowing them next to hers—as if he'd done it a hundred times. "That's pretty low, even for you." There was something funny with his voice. It was deeper and less crisp than usual, almost slurry, and she wondered if he'd had too much to drink. His body language was a little off, too. He kept his gaze slightly averted, never looking directly at Duffy or her.

Duffy set the wine down on the table abruptly, losing the smile. There was a flash of rage before it was replaced by sternness—did he practice his expressions in front of a mirror?

"I'm sorry that it had to go down this way, Mel," he said so sincerely she almost could have believed that they'd been having a business discussion instead of a proposition.

Duffy turned to Ben, his face serious, "I don't know how much you overheard, but it's not what you think. Someone has been leaking information, and I just narrowed it down to Melinda. I was trying to see how far it had gotten by letting her believe I would cover for her, but you put the kibosh on that."

She'd never seen anyone lie so smoothly. People would believe him; he was influential and he had money.

"Are you really selling secrets, Mel?" Ben sounded amused, in the mocking sort of way he had. "Shame, shame. So where is all the money going?" He glanced around, making a big production of the tiny living room and kitchen that comprised half of her apartment. He stretched his neck from one side to the other as if it were stiff, and when he was done, he focused on Duffy.

"Your eyes—" Duffy momentarily lost his usual confidence and looked shaken.

"What big teeth you have, dear," said Ben. At least that's what she thought he said, though it didn't make any sense.

Duffy took a gulp of his wine, regrouped quickly from whatever had bothered him. He said, "All the more reason that getting on my bad side would be a terrible idea if you want to keep your job, Shaw. Walk away, and I'll forget what I've seen."

Ben laughed, and the sound made her take a step away from him. It was not a good laugh.

"You're making a mistake." Duffy stood up. He was a big man, taller and heavier built than Ben. He worked out—he'd told her that along with tales of his black belt when he had been trying to impress her.

"No," said Ben. "I've made lots of mistakes. I know what that feels like. This is not a mistake. And as for what I am, whoop-de-f . . . freaking-do. It's not a crime."

"She's a traitor," Duffy said. "And I can make your job very uncomfortable."

Ben snorted. "She's a secretary, she doesn't have access to anything. My doddering old mum in Merry Old England knows more about hacking than she does."

He smiled, and Mel found herself stepping away from that smile until her legs hit the bookcase under the TV. The smile hadn't been aimed at her, though. Duffy stumbled as he backed up against the counter in the kitchen—which was as far as he could go.

Ben followed him, crowding him by just standing in the kitchen. There was no amusement in his voice when he growled, "And if you've manufactured something that you think will implicate her, let me tell you that *you* aren't hacker enough to cover your tracks from me."

Then he stepped to the side and pointed to the front door. "Leave. Right now."

Duffy didn't even so much as glance at Mel as he bolted out the door.

She closed the door and glanced over at Ben. He was bent over, hands on his thighs as if he had just run a race.

"Ben?" she said. "Thank you." She hugged herself. "But this was a mistake. We're both going to be out of work." She had no family, and only her friends at work. With Duffy spinning stories, she'd have to stay away from them. "Maybe in jail."

"I watched a man brutalize women once," he told her without looking up. "I was under orders, but finally put a stop to it anyway. Never again."

She blinked at him. "Under orders? In the military?"

He laughed, coughed, and said, "In a manner of speaking. Pack business."

"Pack?" The word should mean something to her, she knew, but she was still worried about what she was going to do without a job.

He lifted his head, and she saw what Duffy had. His eyes weren't human.

"You're a werewolf," she whispered. She'd never seen a werewolf in person before, though she knew there were some in the Tri-Cities. She had seen a wolf at the zoo, though, and it had had the same hungry golden eyes.

"Yes," he said. "And I didn't even need to appear on four paws before you got it."

"Sarcasm is the lowest form of wit," she said, hurt, though she thought that she ought to be more afraid. A werewolf. That explained some things about Ben.

He bent his head down again and huffed as if he was having trouble catching his breath. Or maybe he was laughing. "You know it's bad when they start quoting Oscar."

"Oscar?"

He glanced at her. "Oscar Wilde." His face contorted, released, and then contorted again as his light English complexion darkened. "F-f-f-f . . . freaking fire truck that hurts." He bent back down and made a noise that made her cringe.

She wanted to help, but she didn't know how. She was out of work, possibly about to be arrested, and Ben was changing into a scary beast right in front of her. And that was something else he'd given up to try to help her. If he'd wanted people to know what he was, he'd have told them before this.

"I won't tell anyone," she said. "About your being a werewolf. At work, I mean. Not that I have a job anymore."

"Ssst." He interrupted her nervous babble. "Won't matter whom you tell; Duffy will announce it to the world. Now shut up a moment and let me get this out because I don't have much time. If you are fired, I can find you work while you sue for sexual harassment. I and the rest of the DBAs will be happy to testify. Duffy has squat on you." He looked up again, and she wished he hadn't. His face was . . . wrong. "Unless you *have* been selling secrets?"

"No," she said.

"Thought not. Whatever he has is made up—and he's not good enough with computers to make a convincing case. He can barely open his own flipping e-mail." He bent down again; his fingers whitened as he took a stronger grip on his calves. "Full moon tomorrow, luv. And apparently I'm not man enough to stave off the change. I'm about to go werewolf on you so listen up. I have help coming, should be here in about a half hour. You go into your bedroom and shut the door like a good girl, and don't come out for about fifteen minutes."

He breathed hard and with obvious effort, but he didn't stop talking until his whole body tightened up and shook. When it stopped, he took a deep breath. "Right. I won't hurt you, but watching someone change is pretty gross for you and painful for me and we'll both be happier if you tuck yourself away until I'm done."

"Okay," she whispered, but her feet were frozen to the floor, and she knew exactly how a deer felt, stuck out there in the middle of the road with a truck bearing down on it but too shocked by the bright lights to run.

He looked up and snorted. His face was distorted by sharp teeth that looked too big for his mouth. She covered her own mouth with her hands.

"Now," he growled.

She did better than just shut the door. She crawled onto her bed and pulled the blankets up around her ears so she didn't have to hear the noises he was making. The TV made it sound so romantic to be a werewolf. It didn't sound romantic. It sounded scary, and it sounded like it hurt.

BEN STRETCHED AND GLANCED AT THE SHREDS OF HIS pants. He'd managed to shed most of his clothes after Mel had rabbited into her bedroom, but the pants had stayed on and suffered the beast's wrath. He shook himself and looked around for a place to wait for Mercy, who'd promised to hurry to Mel's house as soon as he'd called, but she was all the way out in Finley, and it would take her a while to get here.

He took a step and his hip hit one of the kitchen chairs. He stepped back and bumped into the cabinets. The house was small, tiny even. There wasn't any place he could see in Mel's house big enough for him to sit down except the love seat—and even it would be iffy.

He hopped up, careful not to dig his claws into the faded, floral-print fabric. The arm made a nice chin rest.

Mel's house was like her: small, not too bright, but warm and uncluttered. Safe. His secretary. His.

He snorted and wondered what the other DBAs would say if they realized that he thought of them as *his* people. He wiggled a little to get more comfortable while he waited for Mercy to pick him up.

MEL SAT AMONG THE DBAS WHO HAD TRIED THEIR BEST to get front row. They hadn't succeeded because the security team had made it to the auditorium ahead of everyone else.

Lorna Winkler took the stage first, and all the men around

Mel straightened in their chairs and brushed dandruff off their shoulders. Mel exchanged a rueful look with Amanda, one of the few women in the DBA division. Lorna might not be brilliant or even know much about computers, but she was able to get the IT department all aimed in the same direction when she needed to if only because all the men in IT would do anything she asked of them as long as she did it in her beautifully modulated voice. And the men outnumbered women in the IT department by better than three to one.

As Lorna spoke of how impressed she'd been with their performance last quarter, Mel imagined her practicing it in front of the mirror. There were bets about how often "world peace" would come up in the speech; the most in a previous speech had been six, though Mel hadn't been there for that one. Rumor was that once she hadn't said those two words together, but no one believed it. Mel was glad her mother had never sent her out to be scarred from too many beauty pageants at too young an age.

"I believe that we must, all of us, strive every day to become better people," Lorna said, smiling so that everyone could see her perfectly capped white teeth. "Small steps lead to great ones, like world peace and liberty for all. In that vein, I have to tell you that it pleases me to encourage you by presenting one of your own who has overcome a very bad habit. He has agreed to speak to us today about how he accomplished that and how you might improve yourselves. I give you Ben Shaw"—she smiled—"IT's favorite werewolf."

A polite applause arose and stopped.

Ben got up and put an empty decanter of whiskey on the side of the podium.

"My speech," he said, reading awkwardly from a sheet of paper in front of him, "is about how I broke my fucking habit of drinking shitty whiskey."

By the time he'd finished, the audience was in stitches. He'd kept a serious demeanor the whole time, along with that awkward, serious voice that managed to counter the impression of intelligence

Ben's British accent encouraged. The contrast between his tone and the words he was using made Mel want to clear the wax out of her ears because the combination was just so wrong. And funny.

Ken Lincoln, sitting next to Mel, said, in awe, "I don't think I've heard that many swearwords in such a short period in my life, and I was in the *army*. And the best part is that I don't have to quit smoking."

"What exactly is a pony-shagging, bitch-faced, ball buster?" asked Amanda, sounding strangled as she wiped her eyes.

Mel was watching Lorna Winkler's face as one of the upper management, a grin on his face, shook her hand. She was pretty good at lip-reading, but he was faced half-away. She caught "comedy routine" and "not boring" and, as Lorna smiled graciously, "good idea."

Ben smiled slyly at Mel, then joined Lorna and shook hands with Lorna's bosses.

HOLLOW

There can't be a collection of Mercyverse stories without a Mercy story, right?

I have always had vivid dreams. Those dreams are especially real when I am sick—sometimes it takes me a while to figure out which part was the dream and which the reality. This story is born from a nightmare about an old friend who was being haunted by his murdered wife. It is also about Mercy making peace with the changes in her life—which have been sea changes over the past few books. There are a few spoilers for *Night Broken* in this story.

The events in "Hollow" take place after the events in *Night Broken*.

The beginning: thirteen years ago, All Hallow's Eve

RICK FOLDED HIS FATHER'S SUIT AND SET IT IN A BOX that was going to charity. The whole room was packed into boxes. A double row of donation items, boxes for auction, and two boxes of items he'd decided to keep.

The only thing left was his father's bag of personal effects, then he could put his father's presence behind him. A year ago, he'd have mourned, if for nothing but the lost opportunity for a change for the better. But he was a different man now at twenty-two than the boy he'd been at twenty-one. Losing both of his parents within months of each other would change anyone. Especially since his mother had committed suicide, and six months later, his father drove off a cliff. His death had been ruled an accident, but Rick was undecided: his father had been a very good driver.

But it wasn't just his parents' deaths that had changed him. Finding his wife's dead body and then being charged with her murder had started the ball rolling. After he'd survived the trial with his freedom and sanity intact, or *mostly* intact, he'd become a man who could go through his father's things without feeling either rage or sorrow.

He picked up the white plastic bag that held the contents of his father's pockets and whatever happened to be on his body when he'd arrived at the hospital and spilled the contents out on the desk. His father's wedding ring—why he wore one when he never had honored the vows it was supposed to represent, Rick had never been able to fathom. His wallet. A handful of change.

Rick opened the wallet. Someone at the hospital or the morgue had emptied the cash: his father would never have been driving around without cash. The credit cards seemed to be all there, though. He set those aside along with his father's driver's license to be shredded. There were two photos, battered and worn, in the wallet: Rick at six or seven with a softball bat over one shoulder and a determined look on his face, and Rick's mother—one of the photos taken at their wedding.

Rick looked like he was on his way to being an athlete, and his beautiful mother looked sweet and happy. Rick wondered why his father would keep those photos, the ones that lied so badly about the people in them. Rick had never, that he could remember, hit a softball and made it go anywhere but in the foul zone. And his mother . . . well, *sweet* and *happy* were not adjectives he'd have applied to her.

Maybe his father had liked to pretend that his life was different than it really was. Rick understood that impulse even if he'd always been more of the face-the-bad-stuff-head-on kind of guy. So Rick put both photos in the to-be-shredded pile and tossed the wallet in the charity box.

There was something more in the bag and Rick dumped it out: a thick silver chain with a blocky, carved-jade pendant that looked both arty and masculine. It was a nice piece, but he didn't wear jewelry—and he didn't want a reminder of his father wrapped around his neck.

He picked it up and held it up to the light so he could judge if this was something that should go to auction or if he should give it to charity.

As he held it, he thought absently that it might have been an expensive piece. A deft hand had created the angles and the deliberately primitive lines of the pendant. Toward the center there was a change in color from clear, translucent green to frost. The carving dipped just there, as if the someone had started to carve out the cloudy bit but had reconsidered. He checked for a maker's mark—something he could use to determine value.

He liked the way it felt in his hand, liked the contrast between cold chain and warm pendant. For the first time since he'd begun cleaning out the room this morning, Rick felt something. He clenched the pendant in his fist and let himself feel the love he had for his family—twisted and broken as they had been, he'd still loved them. The necklace felt like family.

He snorted at his own fancy. "Don't anthropomorphize," he advised himself. "It's a piece of jewelry."

But he put the chain around his neck anyway and didn't feel as alone with the pendant warm in the hollow of his throat.

MERCY

Present day

I WALKED UP TO THE REMAINS OF MY GARAGE WITH THE paperwork the insurance adjustor had given me and the paperwork Adam's choice of contractor had given me. Spring was old and summer just around the corner, and the garage where I'd spent the better part of the last thirteen years looked beyond resurrection.

Adam's friend the contractor was of the impression it would be much more economical to bulldoze the remains of the structure and start over because the fixes that the insurance adjustor had approved payment for weren't adequate, in the contractor's opinion.

And, in fact, the day after the insurance adjustor's report had come—which had been three days after the county had allowed us in to clear all of my inventory—half of the garage had collapsed. Apparently when the volcano god tunneled under the building, he'd weakened some of the surrounding soil substructure. Or something like that. I was just glad that no one had been hurt.

We'd had the contractor set up a ten-foot-high chain-link fence around the whole place in an effort to keep neighborhood kids out while I healed up and made up my mind what to do with the garage.

It was my life, the life I'd built for myself after I'd realized I didn't fit anywhere, so I'd have to make my own place. And I'd done it. Found a place to belong—and when Zee, the grumpy old fae who owned it, had been forced to admit what he was and move to the fae reservation, I'd made it my own.

And here it was, lying in wreckage at my feet. I knew that the right thing to do was to squeeze more money out of the insurance company, bulldoze the remnants, and sell the lot for what I could get.

Any car built in the last decade needed plug-in parts-changers, not mechanics. Most of the cars I fixed were older than I was, owned by people who could barely afford their forty-year-old cars. There wasn't enough money to be made in the business to justify dumping in more.

Adam's contractor thought we'd need to throw in fifty or sixty thousand dollars more after the insurance money kicked in to rebuild because there were so many things that would have to be brought up to the current building code. Most years I was lucky if I cleared fifteen thousand, and that only because of the cars we rebuilt for the collector's market and because my right-hand man, Tad, worked for freaking peanuts.

I'd come here today to say good-bye when Adam wasn't here to see me do it. If I'd come here with him, he'd know how much this battered building mattered to me, and he'd rebuild it himself if he had to do it using nothing but the rubble lying around.

It wasn't worth that. Wasn't worth a moment of Adam's worry— I'd given him enough pain the past year or so. He didn't know that I knew he woke up in the middle of the night and put his head against my chest to hear my heart beat. Didn't know I knew he had night-mares that Coyote hadn't come in time to fix me.

Being important to *someone*, to anyone, was something I'd hungered for most of my life. Adam was the lodestone of my life, and I didn't like it when I hurt him.

An unfamiliar car pulled up beside me. I turned around to see a gold Chevy Tahoe that had seen better days. It bore a graceful stencil "Simon Landscaping and Lawn Care," complete with address, phone, and contractor license number.

The driver's side window rolled down next to me, and a woman I'd never met before said, "Please tell me that you're Mercedes Thompson, who is now married with a different last name that no one can remember. Because this is the third time I've driven past here in the vain hope that I'd run into you."

She was human. I blinked at her, pulling on my professional self—I was at work, even if my garage was in rubble. "Yes?"

"Yes?" she repeated with the same questioning inflection I'd given it.

"Yes. I'm Mercedes," I told her with a smile. Professionalism allowed me to bottle up all the angst until I wasn't in the presence of a possible customer. I was very grateful to this stranger for allowing me that retreat. "And it's Hauptman."

Her jaw dropped. "Hauptman the Alpha werewolf of the Tri-fricking-Cities? That Hauptman?"

I nodded, and she banged her forehead into her steering wheel. "How could they have forgotten that? Her husband's a werewolf," she said. I almost called him, you know? Probably would have if I hadn't run into you here."

I cleared my throat, wondering how to pull her up without offending her. "You needed to talk to me?"

"You probably think I'm a freaking idiot," she told the steering wheel. "This is why I send out my assistant to talk to people."

I found myself smiling at the remnants of my garage. "No worries," I told her. Life goes on. What was it Coyote had told me once? Change is neither good nor bad. It's just change. Frightening, but survivable. I'd survived a lot worse than the destruction of my garage—and I'd learned a lot along the way.

"What can I help you with?" I asked her.

She took a deep breath, glanced at me from under her bangs, and said, "I'm in love." Then she looked horrified and surprised, and red swept up from her jaw to her cheeks. "I didn't mean to say that. He doesn't know." She looked at me, this woman whose name I didn't have, with total urgency. "You can't tell him, okay? Not a word."

I cleared my throat. "That's not going to be a problem unless I know who he is. Is it someone I know?"

She shook her head. "No." Then, "I don't think so." She looked at me. "Shoot me now. Shit. I practiced. I had this smooth speech-thing."

"Yeah," said a voice behind me. "I think that you might ought to've used it because we don't got a foggy idea of what you need." Zack's voice was kind even if his words weren't particularly gracious. "Mercy, it looks to me like someone managed to slide under the fence between now and the last time we looked. I don't *believe* they managed to get anywhere dangerous—" Which meant he trailed their scent around, and they hadn't gone into the building or burrowed under the large and heavy metal plate we'd put over the outside opening into the tunnel. "Still, it would be good to get this place bulldozed before someone manages to kill themselves exploring."

"Okay," I told him. "I'll call Bill today and give him the thumbs-up."

Zack's hand came up and ruffled my hair. He was a new wolf to our pack, but once he'd gotten comfortable with us, he'd started touching everyone. I'd have thought it would bother me, bother some of the others more. But he was a submissive wolf—those are pretty rare—and all the touching had turned out to be just what the pack needed to get comfortable with all the changes that had been coming their way. Our way.

I think we were what he needed, too. When he'd come to us a couple of months ago, he'd been—as Warren described it—jumpier than a jackrabbit on speed. Now that Zack had settled down, there was a happy cloud that followed him wherever he went, spread by his touch. Maybe that's why Adam had sent him with me today. I'd needed a happy cloud.

I gave the woman a smile in hopes that would reassure her. "Maybe we should start with introductions. I'm Mercy, and this is my friend Zack. You are?"

"Lisa Simon," she said, sounding relieved that I had taken over the conversation. "I am so glad I found you. I have a—" She stopped, held up a hand. "I've got this now. I have a yard-care company centered in Yakima, but we service all the way from the Tri-Cities to Ellensburg—about a hundred-mile radius. We do everything from designing yards to maintenance, and I have two crews of four people each who work for me full-time. For the last eight years, I've been maintaining the lawn for Richard Albright."

I blinked. "*The* Richard Albright?" Wealth, brilliance, eccentricity, and notoriety had haunted the Albright family for probably a hundred years until a couple of very-high-profile suicides, and an unsolved murder or three a decade or so ago had brought the notoriety to a climax that ended up with everyone in the family dead except for Richard Albright. As I recalled, he'd been in his early twenties at the time, and his wife's had been one of the unsolved murders.

"That's the one," she said.

"He moved to Canada right after the trial," Zack said. When I looked at him, he raised both hands slightly, and said, "It was all over the tabloids. No one who ever walked into a grocery store didn't know about the murder trial and everything."

Lisa nodded soberly. "And after a few years, he moved, very

quietly, to Prosser." I blinked at her. No one rich and famous moved to Prosser. It was a small town about thirty miles west of the Tri-Cities. It wasn't a "pretty people" place like Walla Walla, which was pressed up against the Blue Mountains and beautifully green. Lisa had missed my surprise and continued to impart information in a circuitous fashion. "He never leaves the grounds. Not ever." She looked at me. "And three days ago, I found out why not."

I could feel the headache come on. She didn't want me to fix his 'Wagon. "Ghosts," I said, wondering who she'd been talking to.

"His dead wife," she said at the same time.

"I don't hunt ghosts," I told her. The only time I'd tried had ended up with bodies.

Her mouth firmed. "I called in some big favors to get your name."

"Who talked to you?" I asked. The wolves knew that I could see ghosts, I was pretty sure, though I didn't make a big deal of it. That left . . .

"My best friend's husband is Wenatchi and Cree. He's a historian and folklorist. So I called her and he called me back this morning with your name. He said you are a walker and a spirit speaker and that you could help me. He said to tell you that Hank Redtail owes him a favor, and he is calling it in."

Hank's last name on his driver's license wasn't Redtail—but just as I turned into a coyote, he turned into a redtail hawk. For some of the traditionalists, a person's name had more to do with who they were than what their birth certificate said.

I pulled out my phone to call Hank, but saw that sometime in the last four hours he'd sent a text message. Ghost strong as this is bad news. Listen to the story.

I ground my teeth, took a deep breath, and said, "Hank tells me I need to hear you."

LISA'S STORY

RICHARD ALBRIGHT'S PLACE USED TO BE A HORSE FARM. Most of the stables stood empty, if well kept and pretty, but the small, two-stall stud barn was Lisa's for equipment storage or anything else. It had an empty office with a working minifridge stocked with bottled water, and a bathroom. Since his place was ten miles from anywhere, the bathroom was useful.

For a week in the spring and another in the fall, she'd bring a whole crew in to work the flower beds, clean out fountains, and do general repair. But because of the need for secrecy, Lisa did Albright's place by herself twice a week the rest of the year. Sometimes, Richard Albright came out and joined her. The first time he'd done it, he'd introduced himself as Rick and told her she was supposed to find things for him to do. So she'd done as he asked. He hadn't known anything about plants or landscaping—or even mowing—when he started. It took her six months to figure out that "Rick" who came out a couple of times a month to work with her was Richard Albright, multibazillionaire who was the most notorious "escapee from justice because he was rich" on the planet.

She'd thought about it for maybe five seconds and decided to keep on treating him the same way she always had. They grew to be friends. About four years in, she realized the reason that the last four men she'd dated had been so boring was because she was comparing them to the funny, smart-mouthed guy who trimmed blackberry bushes with her. She wasn't an idiot. There was no way someone like him was going to be interested in his groundskeeper; she didn't mind. It just hadn't seemed worthwhile to keep dating once she knew, so she stopped.

It had been tough, not saying anything, but Lisa was tough-minded. And it was easier to have an unrequited love than to get all fussed and dressed and go out on dates every Saturday with men she was never going to fall in love with. So she'd quit dating, quit dressing up—and on the whole she was happier than she'd been before.

"I THOUGHT THIS WAS ABOUT A GHOST," I SAID. "MUCH as I enjoy—enjoy is the wrong word, sorry—as much as I am willing to listen to your painful romance story, there isn't much I can do for you in that area."

Lisa blinked at me. "Right," she said. "Sorry."

Zack put his hand on hers, where it rested on her car door. She gave him a tremulous smile and started her story again.

Two days ago, Lisa had mowed half the lawn, gone through two water bottles, and set out for the bathroom in the stud barn. The matter was of some urgency so she was dismayed to see an "Out of Order" sign on it. Taped to the bottom of the sign was a sheet of lined paper.

"Lisa," it read. "Sorry. Well woes, apparently. Should be okay by next week. If you need to use the facilities, come on up to the house. —Rick."

Had it not been urgent, she'd have just packed up and gone into town. As it was, she headed up to the main house and rang the doorbell. She'd planted the azaleas on either side of the door where they'd be sheltered from the cold and wind. She'd grown the hanging baskets and hung them herself.

And she'd never been inside the house, not in eight years.

"Hey," Rick said, answering the door. His hair was ruffled as if he'd been dragging his fingers through it. His shirt had a hole in it, just left of his navel.

In short, he looked like he did most of the time he was out working with her. But his bare feet were on marble tiles, and the ceiling was ten feet or more over his head. Hanging on the entry wall behind him was an oil by a Western artist who'd died a hundred years ago and was well enough known that even Lisa, who had no interest in art of any kind unless it was green and growing, had heard of him.

And suddenly it wasn't her buddy Rick who was standing there, but a bazillionaire who she was bothering, and she couldn't open her mouth and make noise come out.

He looked at her, and instead of looking haughty as she'd half expected, his mouth curved up.

"Bathroom," he said, stepping back. "Come on in, Lisa. Down the hall, first left, past the hot-tub room, and through the next set of doors. Or you could take the third left, fourth right, or up the stairs and, since there are more bathrooms than bedrooms, I expect you could find one."

"Sorry," she mumbled.

"Not a problem. It's just me, here. I only need one bathroom at a time."

But she'd already passed him and headed for the first bathroom he'd told her about. She'd been mute. She'd mumbled. And the third thing she tended to do when she was uncomfortable was babble. Given that she really had to pee right now, she really, really didn't want to babble about that to the man she loved from afar.

When she turned to the left, there was a floor-to-ceiling glass wall on her left with a sliding glass door. On the other side of all that glass was a room filled with ferns and a huge hot tub. The cover was a deep brown that contrasted with the bright green ferns and the pale off-white of the tile on the wall and matched the dark brown marble tile on the floor. Daylight for the ferns drifted down from a pair of skylights and illuminated a statue of Pan in the corner.

The sly old faun was raising his pipes to his wickedly sensuous mouth, and he gifted the rest of the room with a distinctly Grecian look. She waved a hand at the statue because it seemed . . . polite and hit the bathroom with a sigh of honest relief that not even the imposing acres of marble and wood and things expensive that were all over that room could detract from.

She finished up quickly, washed and dried her hands, and

opened the door. She turned her head to say good-bye to Pan—and screamed.

"I'm kind of embarrassed about that," she told me. "And I'd rather not have to confess to screaming like a B-movie queen, but—" She shrugged.

She'd only been in the bathroom a couple of minutes. And in that time someone had taken off the cover to the hot tub and dribbled body parts all over the hot-tub room. A leg, clean sliced like someone had put it through a band saw, lay on the floor in front of the statue of Pan. Another leg was positioned so the cut end was hidden by the hot-tub stair. The woman's legless and armless torso was arched over the edge of the hot tub where the hot water bubbled red as blood. Red with blood. The woman's head was balanced on the edge of the tub closest to Lisa.

When Lisa screamed, the eyes opened, and the detached head said, "It's his fault." Lisa later remembered hearing the words as clearly as though someone had whispered in her ear, though the glass blocked the sound of the bubbling water, and a detached head *couldn't* speak—no air.

And that impossibility finally cued Lisa in that what she saw wasn't real. A moment later, an arm wrapped itself around her and tugged her away from the hot tub and out the front door.

Rick sat her down on the top step on the porch and forced her head between her knees. When she could focus on what he was saying, she heard, "Tell me, damn it. You saw that. You did. You saw."

She blinked a couple of times and pushed against his hands. He let her sit up.

"What the freak was that?" she asked him. "Rick? Do you have aspirations of being the next George Lucas or David Cronenberg or something? I've got to tell you, it really had me going until the head started talking."

He sat down beside her and looked up at the sky and gave a funny half laugh. "You saw that."

"The body in the hot-tub room? Yes, of course I saw it. It was brilliant." She reconsidered. "Sadistic and horrible. But brilliant."

He rubbed his face, then rubbed his hair and laughed again. "I thought I was crazy," he whispered. "Fourteen years. No one ever sees it."

Lisa just stared at him.

"It won't be there now," he told her. "You can go look. But she never stays for long."

"She?"

"My wife," he told her, and he put his head in his hands. "She's dead. She's dead, and she won't leave me alone. No one sees her, no one *ever* sees her, but me."

"You mean," said Lisa, suddenly understanding what had happened. "You mean that was a ghost?" She blinked at him. "You see that all the time?"

MY HALF BROTHER GARY ANSWERED THE PHONE ON THE fifth ring. "Wait just a minute," he said, sounding a little breathless.

I waited, listening to a few grunts and my brother's croons. I had an unsettled thought that there was a woman involved in this wait, just as he came back on the phone—though it wasn't quite the right grunts.

"Sorry," he said. "I'm training horses. Right now I'm on a two-year-old who objected to my cell phone's ringing."

My brother had left the state of Washington with prejudice. He'd found a job at a horse ranch in Montana where they raised quarter horses, a few Appaloosas, and cattle.

"Isn't two a little young?" I asked. I didn't know a lot about horses, but I'd grown up around people who did.

"Yep," he agreed. "This one will be three next week, but still young. Driven by the market, Mercy. There isn't a lot of profit in breeding horses anymore, and the ranch has no choice but to listen to market forces if they want to survive. It's not like we take them out for fifty-mile trips." Then, presumably to the horse, "You can just settle your butt down, sweetheart. Get used to it now, my friend. Life for you is going to be all about hurry up and wait."

"I need to know how to exorcise a ghost," I said to Gary.

Lisa abruptly looked a lot less confident in me. I hadn't told her why I was calling Gary. I held up one finger when it looked like she was going to speak. My brother has good ears; he didn't need to get distracted by a pretty voice.

"You just tell them to move on," he said.

"Just *tell* them?" I was doubtful, and I let him hear it. When I was a kid, I'd screamed "go away" at a lot of ghosts to not much effect.

"Tell them," he said with exaggerated patience, "the way your Alpha werewolf husband would tell one of his wolves when they get pushy."

"Okay," I said. I almost thanked him and hung up—but there was something in his voice. He was a son of Coyote, as much as he hated it. And that made him a little tricksy. "Where do they go?"

He laughed, and I knew I'd been right. "Somewhere else. Usually not too far away. One of our distant nephews, back in the Victorian Age, had a grand con. He found a haunted house and drove the ghost—a nasty moaning type—out. They paid him for it, then he waited a week and went to the house next door and did the same. If he'd stopped at the fifth house, he'd have made a tidy profit. But he'd forgotten that neighbors talk to each other. He knocked on the door of the sixth, and the man of the house tried to hold him for the authorities. Sadly for both of them, the young entrepreneur was killed in the struggle."

I waited, but he wasn't going to continue until I asked. "Why for both of them?"

"Because when our budding con artist nephew died, the man in the sixth house was left with a very nasty ghost that no one could send on. I hear that it is still there today."

"Why couldn't someone else send it on?" I asked.

"Didn't they teach you anything?" Gary exclaimed, then in a softer voice, he said, "No, I suppose not. The werewolves wouldn't know, and our dear papa couldn't be bothered. A ghost, my dear sister, gains power when it is seen. When it is recognized by one of *our* kind, it gains a firmer hold on the world. There is a reason you shouldn't speak the name of the dead."

"I see," I said. "So how do I get rid of a ghost permanently?"

He sighed. "You don't read ghost stories, either, do you? You have to find out why it is lingering—confront it and take away its reason for being there. That only works with the ones who are intelligent, though. Convincing them that they really are dead is also supposed to be useful. Most ghosts usually fade away, given time. Why are you asking me about ghosts?"

"Because someone came to me for help." And I explained the situation to him in a somewhat more condensed version

There was a little pause. "Well, good luck with that, then," he said doubtfully. "Call me if you get into trouble. Not that I can help you, but maybe I can learn something to pass on to the next walker who calls to ask me for help."

I think he was teasing, but I wasn't sure enough to call him on it. "Will do," I said instead. "It has always been an ambition of mine to serve as an object lesson for others."

"Nice to have ambitions," he said. "A ghost that has been following a person around for fourteen years . . . that's not normal."

"I do know that," I told him.

"Might not be a ghost at all," he said as if thinking aloud. "A witch could do something similar."

"I've thought about that," I told him. The gruesome talking head was very Hollywood, I thought. Not something I'd ever seen a ghost do. Not that it wasn't possible, just that I'd never seen it.

"Take backup," he told me.

"I love you, too," I told him, and hung up.

As soon as I was off the phone, Lisa asked, "You don't know how to exorcise a ghost?"

I shrugged. "I've never tried it. Most ghosts are harmless, or nearly so. My brother has more experience with that kind of thing." Like several hundred years more experience. "I thought it was worth a shot."

"Maybe he could exorcise Rick's ghost?"

I shook my head regretfully. "He lives three hundred miles away and his job doesn't let him travel." Not to Washington, anyway. Not until they quit looking for him as an escaped prisoner.

"Maybe I should look for someone else with more experience," she said.

"Okay," I agreed.

"Okay?"

"I'm not a ghost hunter," I told her. "You could probably do an Internet search and find a group nearby. If they don't know how to get rid of a ghost, maybe they'll know someone who does."

"Think of the publicity," murmured Zack. "Ghost hunters investigate famous recluse's house."

I stepped on his toe. I feel some obligation to help when people ask me for it—I'm not sure why. But only a little obligation in this case because I didn't know either of the people involved. If she thought someone else would be better, I wasn't going to argue with her—especially since she was probably right.

"Do you mind coming out and taking a look?" she said. "I think Rick has probably had enough publicity for a lifetime. If you can't do anything, maybe we'll try someone else."

I looked at my garage. "It doesn't appear as though I have anything better to do."

I called Adam to let him know what we were doing, but his phone bumped me to another one.

"Hauptman Security," said one of Adam's minions.

"This is Mercy," I said.

He cleared his throat. "Okay. Okay. I have a message for you if you called. Here it is: 'Duty calls. Someone broke into a warehouse we have under contract. Cops came but it looks like burglar has a hostage. They need someone familiar with the layout, so I'm headed out. Call you when it's over. Not dangerous.'"

I waited, but apparently that was it. "Okay," I said. "Tell Adam I've gone ghost hunting. I'm taking Zack, and we'll be back tonight. Not dangerous." I hesitated. "Okay. *Probably* not dangerous, but he knows how these things go with me."

"Address? Boss will want an address."

I looked at Lisa. "Where are we going?"

Her lips thinned.

"My husband runs a security firm. They can keep secrets."

"Your husband the werewolf."

"That's the one."

She gave me the address. I told Adam's man what it was and we all headed out: Lisa in her Tahoe and Zack and I in my Vanagon.

PROSSER, LIKE THE TRI-CITIES, IS IN A REGION OF WINE country that started out as orchard country. We took the highway on the north side of the Yakima River instead of the interstate on the south and it weaved along the river's path through hobby farms and ranches that increased for a minute in density to become the town of Whitstran before thinning out again into countryside.

Zack didn't talk as we drove. He turned his baseball cap around and covered his eyes. Someone else might have thought he was sleeping, but I could smell his alertness. He was just conserving his strength. I couldn't tell what he thought about going ghost hunting with me beyond that.

The whole drive between my garage in east Kennewick to Prosser is usually about forty-five minutes on the interstate. The Old Inland Empire Highway was twistier and slower, so we'd been driving about an hour when Lisa turned toward the river.

The road was one of those sneaky dirt roads hidden in the narrow gap between fences. The highway had turned away from the river, and we drove maybe a quarter of a mile when the dirt road dropped and twisted, revealing a hidden Garden of Eden tucked into a flattish fifteen- or twenty-acre parcel between the river and a bench of basalt.

On the side of the road was a tall signpost with a large mailbox beside it. The top and biggest sign said **THE HOLLOW**. Below it on smaller, hand-painted signs were **NO HUNTING, NO TRESPASSING, GO AWAY**, and **YES, THIS MEANS YOU**.

We passed a barn, a smaller stable, then wound around to stop in front of a house that was maybe twice the size of the one I lived in with Adam. Since Adam's house had been built with the idea that it would serve as a meetinghouse and safe house for Adam's werewolf pack, our house was huge.

We parked in front of the house and followed Lisa to the door. She gave me a nervous glance.

"I didn't tell him I was bringing you," she said.

"A little late to mention it now," I told her. "Are we going to stand on the porch until he notices us, or are you going to ring the bell?"

She hit the bell, and I could hear it echo—Rick must have had it piped in several places throughout the house. We waited long enough that Lisa was getting nervous before Rick Albright opened the door.

He was not as impressive as I had expected. The werewolves have given me a skewed view on the world. Important werewolves drip authority and (usually) dignity. Dignity, at least, wasn't apparently important to Richard Albright.

It would have helped if his glasses had not been held together with green duct tape. It would have helped if his shirt hadn't had a hole in the shoulder—helped more if there weren't little toy boats sailing across it. But I don't think I would have liked him as quickly if it hadn't been for the toy boats. The only person I'd ever had that instant like for was Anna Cornick, the only Omega werewolf I've ever met.

However, Rick stepped out on the porch, shut the door behind him, folded his arms, and narrowed his eyes. Despite being the shortest person on the porch, he had enough authority to make Zack drop his gaze and step back.

"Lisa?" Rick's voice was soft. And hostile. "To what do I owe the pleasure?"

I expected, somehow, for her to drop back to babbling, as she had with me. Instead, she said, with a bit of defiance, "That thing has been following you around for more than a decade. So I made some calls, and they sent me to Mercy Hauptman here."

He looked at her—and the connection between them was bright and clear to my coyote nose. She might not have told him that she wanted him. And from what she'd told me, he'd never told her he wanted her, either, but I could have cut the sexual tension in that exchange of looks with a knife.

Zack tucked his head and covered his smile with a hand.

Rick's eyes focused on me, and all that heat turned to ice. "I have no intention of paying you anything."

"You have a VW around here that needs work?" I asked casually, glancing around. The only cars I could see were ours.

He frowned, and the intensity of his gaze picked up. "No."

"That's the only thing I charge for," I told him. "I'm a mechanic by trade. This ghost thing is not my chosen profession. And before you invite me in, you ought to know that the last time someone talked me into checking out a ghost, it turned out to be something a lot more dangerous. The woman who invited me to her house ended up dead."

He pushed his glasses up his nose. "How did she die? Did the ghost kill her? Did you?"

"No. And no. But I couldn't save her, either," I told him.

He asked Lisa, "Who sent you to her?"

"Kiri's husband."

He took a breath, nodded abruptly, and opened the door to his house. "I suppose you'd better come inside, then."

A curious thing happened as we entered the house. I shot a

quick glance at Zack, who frowned at me and tilted his head. He'd smelled it, too.

Emotions have a scent—more of a feel, I guess, a combination of the sound of breath, heartbeat, and body secretions. Nervous sweat, aroused sweat, and exercise sweat are composed of different substances. They have an intensity, too. Outside on the porch, Rick had been aroused by Lisa and angry at our intrusion—and a variety of other things. He'd been intense. As soon as we came inside the house, everything muted. It might have been some effect of being safely in his own home—the force of emotions quite often is ameliorated by a safe haven. But this was a much stronger drop than I'd ever seen before—and Lisa's emotions did exactly the same thing. As soon as she stepped across the threshold.

The effect was momentary, like what sound does just before your ears repressurize after an airplane flight or driving down out of the mountains. We followed Rick, and by the time he'd led us across the entrance hall into a room that felt mostly unused, his emotions—and Lisa's—were normal. If Zack hadn't noticed it, too, I'd have thought I had imagined it.

The room was . . . empty of smells. No one spent enough time here to leave a mark. Couches placed just so were without the normal scuffs and worn edges that such things acquire in daily living. Rick gestured us forward, but he, himself, stopped at a discreet half bar.

"Can I get you anything?" he asked, opening a sliding cabinet door I could hear even though I couldn't see it. He pulled four glasses out and set them down.

"Not me," said Zack.

"No." Lisa had walked across the room to look out the window at the river.

"No, thank you." The lack of other scents made some things very interesting. I stepped closer to Rick and took a deep breath. "Are you fae?"

His hand stilled where he had half lifted a bottle of soda water over a glass.

"My grandfather," he told me. "My mother's father. He abandoned his wife and my mother. I don't know exactly what he was.
He left me with a bit of intuition about people—and that's it." He
finished pouring. "I tell you this because you're married to a
werewolf—I may be isolated, but I do read local newspapers.
Hauptman is a name that comes up as often as the reporters can
figure out how to slide it in. The Tri-Cities' most famous person,
the handsome face of werewolves everywhere."

I smiled at his sarcasm. "I think he's pretty, too. Truthfully, his
good looks annoy him, though he's not above using them when he
needs to."

"I will answer your questions, mostly, because my fae-born
intuition"—he smiled wryly—"for what it is worth—tells me that
you are exactly what you say you are. And that you just might be
able to help. I am not in the habit of sharing my family secrets with
everyone." He grimaced. "If you really wanted to know, you could
just read any of the true-crime novels written about my wife's murder, anyway."

"All right." I felt bad intruding on his privacy even if it might
be for his own good. I met his eyes. "You should know that I'm not
fae or werewolf, but I am something. That's how I knew you were
fae—and that's why I might be able to do something about your
ghost. *I'm* giving *you* my secret because I stole one from you—and
I'll be asking you for more. You should have at least one of mine in
return."

Rick looked at me, then nodded. He glanced at Zack. "Our
introductions were truncated. I'm Rick Albright. Lisa, you've obviously met, and I've met Ms. Hauptman."

"Zack Drummond," Zack introduced himself.

Rick nodded. "All right." He looked at me. "You're in charge."

"Lisa said your wife has been haunting you since her death," I
told him.

He nodded. "I thought ghosts were supposed to be attached to
the place they died, or at least someplace important to them. But it

doesn't matter where I am. In airports. Business meetings." He blanched, drank the soda water in one smooth gulp. "Sometimes she looks alive. I'll look over, and she's eating at the table next to me." He looked away from us and kept talking more and more quietly. As if noise would make the images more real. "Or walking down the road. Sometimes she's . . . in pieces. Just like when I came in from a night of drinking and found her body cut up in our kitchen. Some of her was in the sink, some of her was . . ." He stopped speaking. "Excuse me," he said, and walked rapidly out of the room.

Zack and I could hear him vomiting. We waited for him, Lisa visibly torn because she wanted to follow him.

"Sorry," he apologized as he returned.

"Why don't you show us around the house," I said. "Tell me if you see her, and I'll tell you if—"

And standing behind him was a woman who was almost six feet tall, a stunning redhead with bright blue eyes and a sad mouth. She reached out and ran a hand over his shoulder.

"Well," I said. "I don't think that will be necessary. What was your wife's name?"

"Nicole," he stared at me, then looked behind him. "You see her? She's not there."

"She's wearing a camisole," I said. "Blue with embroidered black flowers and a pair of black yoga pants."

"That's what she was wearing when she was killed," he said. "All the newspapers reported it." His eyes narrowed at me in sudden suspicion. He turned all the way around, looking through the ghost I saw as if she weren't there. When he faced me again, he said in a low voice, "There were photos of her clothing in one of the books."

"What about your intuition?" asked Lisa in a small voice. She was responsible for bringing me here.

His mouth softened.

"Nicole," I said.

She looked at me—and then straightened when she could meet my eyes. "I can't leave," she said.

I nodded. "What are you doing?"

"I can't leave," she told me sadly, running her hand down his arm.

"He didn't kill you?" I asked.

She looked at him, bewildered. "I can't leave."

There wasn't a lot of intelligence left. The kind of haunting that Rick had described, brutal and powerful, just seemed beyond her.

"Rick," I said, still looking at her, "did you kill your wife?"

"What do you think?" he said bitterly. "Do you think she'd haunt me otherwise? The case against me was dismissed, you know, because my money ensured that no one could prove my guilt."

Sometimes people learn to lie so well I can't hear it in their voice, especially if they've had years to practice or even come to believe their own lies. But I had to get a yes or no answer even to try.

"Did you kill your wife, Mr. Albright?" I asked again.

"I can't leave," his dead wife said again, and leaned her head against his shoulder. "I can't leave."

He shivered, but I don't think he felt her. "Yes," he said coolly. "Of course I killed her." He looked at Lisa when she gasped. "You have to know it," he said harshly. "If I hadn't been filthy rich, I would've rotted in prison for the rest of my life—or sat on death row until someone decided to pull the lever."

"Werewolves and Mercy," Zack said conversationally, "can tell when you are lying."

"What Zack means to say, Lisa," I told her, "is that that was a big fat lie. Not the part about being rich having saved him—but the part about his having murdered his wife. Which leads to the question—why, then, is she haunting you, Rick? All she can tell me is that she can't leave."

Zack stared at me as if I were speaking Greek, but Lisa took a big shaky breath. "I knew it," she said. Then she walked over to Rick and shoved him. "That's for trying to make me think you're a murderer. Stupid." Then she turned back to me. "So why *can't* she leave?"

I shrugged. "I've run into a few different kinds of ghosts." I used to think there were only three kinds, but I'd expanded my knowledge a bit over the past few years. There are more things in Heaven and Earth and all that. But some things still held true. "One of the most common kinds that I've seen are repeaters— ghost that seem to reenact the same events over and over."

"Traumatic events," said Zack.

I nodded. "Usually. But sometimes just everyday things. Habits. They don't interact with the real world much. The appearance of body parts—that fits with a repeater, except that she didn't die here in the hot-tub room, right? And repeaters are usually tied to places, not people."

"It's his fault," the ghost said.

"No," I told her. "He didn't kill you."

"It's his fault," she said again. "I can't leave."

"Is he holding you here?"

She stared at me. "It's his fault. It's his fault I died."

I don't know if the dead can lie or not. I just didn't think that *this* ghost had enough . . . personality left to lie.

I looked at Rick. "How could it be your fault that she died?"

He shook his head. "I don't know."

The hair on the back of my neck started to tingle, and my ears popped like I was on an airplane in rapid descent. A sweet scent from my childhood drifted to my nose as well as the sharp scent of ozone—lightning just before it strikes. I didn't know what it was, but it didn't feel like anything very healthy. And the first rule in my sensei's rules of combat is—*run.*

"Everyone out of the house," I said.

I followed my own advice and started for the door. I grabbed Lisa's upper arm as I moved. I didn't run, but I wasn't waiting for flies to gather, either.

Zack took my lead and, as he walked by Rick, he put a hand

on his shoulder and pushed him along. Rick didn't struggle so much as hesitate, but Zack was a werewolf—so Rick came with us.

So did Rick's dead wife.

Even with the ghost tagging along, I felt better with the door closed behind us. Which meant whatever was unnerving me, it wasn't Nicole Albright.

"Tell me," I said, "about the times you saw your wife when you weren't here. When was the first time?"

"If you'll tell me why I just got hustled out of my own home," Rick said.

"Something happened," Lisa said. "I don't know what, but a whole marathon of people were jogging across my grave."

"Did you feel anything?" I asked Zack.

"The spike of emotion from you and a moment later from Lisa," said Zack. He was kind enough not to say that what he'd smelled was terror. "But I smelled something different . . . not sure what it was. Sweet."

"Bubble gum," I said.

And Rick's pupils contracted.

"That means something to you?" I said.

"My mother." He half laughed. "She had this shampoo that was supposed to be pomegranate or something. She paid a fortune for it. But to me it always smelled like pink bubble gum."

"Tell me," I said, "about your mother."

"I'm not in the habit of opening my personal box of poor-little-rich-boy stories to everyone who asks," he told me. I think he meant to sound affronted or cold because he ended up somewhere in the middle—and I could smell his refusal. His pain.

Lisa put her hand on his and squeezed.

He looked at her, and I remembered what he said about intuition. He must know how she felt—even without intuition, Lisa's face was open and honest.

He turned his hand over until he held Lisa's. "But I've already agreed to this, haven't I? She was a real piece of work, my mother.

Psycho of the Year who was married to the Worst Husband of the Year. But it's not my mother who is haunting me, it's my wife."

But his dead wife touched his cheek, looked at him with her big, sad eyes, and said, "It's his fault. It's his fault. I can't leave."

He flinched and let out a gasp—and I couldn't see her anymore.

"Did you see something?" asked Lisa.

"She was here," he said, "just for a moment."

"But you didn't see her." I double-checked with Lisa.

"No."

"Me, neither," Zack said. "But I smelled something. Just for a second." His mouth twisted a little, and I knew that whatever he smelled hadn't been pleasant.

"Did you hear what she said?" I asked Rick.

He shook his head. Beyond that quick gasp, he hadn't reacted at all.

"I've heard her say two things, over and over," I told him.

"It's your fault," he said tiredly. "I can't leave."

"When I saw the head in the hot-tub room, she said, 'It's his fault,'" Lisa told me.

"That's what she tells me, too," I said. "You didn't kill her. So why isn't she haunting whoever did?"

Rick looked around as if he'd never been out on his porch before. Then he walked over to the steps and sat down. He patted the stairs beside him, and Lisa joined him.

Zack folded his arms, nodded to them, then turned away. His body language was a promise to stay in the background. He was right; Rick would talk more if I was the only stranger he was talking to.

I hopped over the porch railing and walked in front of the stairs. The porch was high, so sitting on the top step as they were put their heads and mine on a level.

"First," I said, "you know who my husband is—so you know that if I wanted fame and glory, I wouldn't have to use you to get it. I am not about to sell your story to the newspapers or tabloids.

Second, Zack and I have very good noses—and for me scent is sometimes the first indication that there is a ghost in the room. Third, your wife doesn't have the . . . energy it would require to follow you for all these years. If I hadn't known that she was this active, I'd have told you she'd leave in a few months."

I paused and waited. Lisa patted his hand, and he turned his over and grabbed hers hard.

"You think my mother is behind this?"

"I know that there was something else in that room when I pulled us all outside. I know it was not Nicole—it didn't have the same feeling at all. It felt like some weird combination of fae magic"—some fae magics smell like ozone to me—"and danger. And Zack and I both smelled bubble gum. You say your mother smelled like bubble gum, and she committed suicide two days after your wife died." Even I remembered that headline. I paused for effect. "Tell me, Rick. How did she and your mother get along?"

Lisa whispered, "You think his mother killed his wife, then killed herself?"

"I don't know anything about his mother," I said.

"I've thought about it before," Rick said starkly. "She could have done it. My mother was . . ."

"Batshit crazy," said Lisa, and moved until her body leaned against his. She looked at him for permission, and he nodded for her to continue. "She pulled Rick out of school when he was twelve because she thought he was associating too much with the wrong kids. He was playing with one of the groundskeeper's kids a few years before that, and she shredded the kid's face with her fingernails—" Lisa made a claw out of her free hand. "Kid had to have cosmetic surgery, which Rick's dad paid for."

Rick cleared his throat. "My mother was sixteen when she met my father, and he was forty. *Her* father had abandoned her and her mother when she was thirteen. Her mother committed suicide when my mother was fifteen. She told me that her father's family took care of her—but I can't confirm that because no one, and I mean no one, ever talked to them but her. She was too rich to go into the foster system, so she was left in her home and watched over by a series of caretakers who were hired by trustees and lawyers."

He took a breath. "My father was handsome, rich, and far older than she was. She was beautiful, rich, and young, and had no one. If my father had been a different man, it might have worked. He really loved her at first—and she adored him. Adored being his wife and adored being the mother of his child. When she was pregnant with me, she found out he was having an affair. And our home was a battle zone from then on." He smiled one of those smiles that mostly point out that the person wearing them is not happy, and said, "For most of my life, she alternated between being Supermom and a crazy woman. Sometimes both in the same ten minutes. So, do I think she could have killed my wife and cut her into pieces?" He looked over my shoulder at nothing and swallowed. "Yes. I've always thought so."

He returned his gaze to me. "She found Nicole for me. Introduced us, encouraged me to ask her to marry me, then after the wedding, the day my wife was murdered, Mother came to my office with a folder. She showed me proof that my wife had been sleeping with another man throughout our engagement." He cleared his throat. "Nicole got a butterfly tattoo on her shoulder blade two weeks after we started sleeping together. The photos clearly showed her tattoo." He grimaced. "My mother had had Nicole followed. She knew about the affair before Nicole and I married. She chose to show the photos to me that day and told me that it was for my sake. So I would understand that my mother was the only one I could trust."

"Crazy bitch," growled Lisa.

"And that night your wife was killed," I said.

"Murdered," Rick corrected me like it was important. "If anyone had known that my mother had showed me that file that afternoon, I wouldn't have walked out of the trial a free man. I was always pretty sure my mother had done it—it had all the marks of one of her frenzied, violent moments. Though as far as I know she'd never killed anyone before. I could never have convinced anyone she'd done it, not once she was dead. Only my father and I ever saw her at her worst. Most people thought she was this little porcelain doll."

"And Lisa is the only one besides you to have seen your wife's ghost," I observed. Lisa, who was beside herself because of how much she loved him, who had gone into the house and was treated to a gruesome sight.

But Rick was still caught up talking about his mother. "My father said she was a psychic vampire," he said.

I blinked at him. "Hold that thought," I said, and pulled out my phone.

"Mercy?" Samuel answered his wife's cell phone. "You know we're in Ireland, right? And we don't want to be bothered."

Belated honeymoon.

"Yes. Sorry. But I really need to talk to your wife," I told him. Ariana was a very old fae. If what I was worried about was possible, she would know. Maybe she'd know what to do with it.

"Life and death?" Samuel sounded resigned.

"Death, anyway," I told him. I would have felt worse, but I knew Samuel. If he and Ariana really hadn't wanted to be disturbed, they wouldn't have had the cell phone on.

He handed me over eventually. I explained the situation to Ariana, taking my time so I didn't miss any of the details that might or might not be important.

"So," I asked her, "is there any way someone of fae blood could kill themselves and make arrangements to haunt someone for the rest of their lives?"

"They would have to have some sort of power source," she said. "You told me that when you walked into the house, both you and Zack noticed a drop in the emotional intensity of the humans."

"Yes."

"There aren't a lot of ways this could work," she said after a moment's thought. "The easiest way would be to quench an object in her death."

I'd heard that word before. "Like when a weapon is quenched and takes on the personality traits of the person who dies."

"Like that, yes," she agreed, "but it doesn't have to be a weapon." She gave me a detailed explanation and several possible solutions.

"Okay," I said, tucking my phone back into my pocket. "There are some fae who can feed on emotions. Literal emotional vampires. Zack and I both felt something odd happen when we walked into the house. Rick was ticked off, and both of you"—I pointed at Lisa and Rick—"were so hot for each other it was uncomfortable."

Rick looked at me, but Lisa sucked in a breath and looked at Rick. I shouldn't have done it, but I just couldn't bear watching them not watch each other anymore. Four years, she'd been in love with him—and he with her, if I were any judge.

I continued as if I hadn't noticed anything. "But all that dropped when you walked through the doorway. It didn't seem important at the time. Death magic is not something that the fae are much involved in—that's a witch thing. But there are some magics that the fae can use to tie the essence of a person to objects—they used to use it to power their blades or some of their magical items." The essence or spirit was different from a soul. A person's soul, except for thankfully rare instances, was mostly beyond the touch of magic.

"Your mother, if she learned magic from her father's family, might have learned how to do that. Or maybe she contacted someone and asked. My expert friend says that usually the . . . the personality fades from such objects. But if your mother could feed herself on your emotions, then she could keep her personality intact indefinitely."

"You think my mother killed my wife, then decided that she'd kill herself, so she could follow me around and, what? Take care of me?"

"Run off anyone who might compete with her for your affections," I told him. "Or maybe just anyone who might harm you. You don't really seem like a hermit at heart—but here you are, living isolated from everyone."

"Because anytime I went out, anytime I brought anyone home, my wife would make an appearance," he said. "I thought I was going mad. I worried someone would notice." He looked at Lisa. "You don't know. It was horrible for you, I know. But you don't know what it meant that someone else saw it. I—" She leaned over and kissed him.

Which was lovely and sweet. A second later, the window in one of the upstairs rooms blew out and poured glass all over them. I leaned forward to help, but Zack tackled me around the middle and ran fifty feet before he put me down.

I stepped back from him and opened my mouth.

"I am *your* bodyguard," he told me, almost angrily. "You are still limping, and you almost died. I am doing my job."

"Okay," I said. The one thing you didn't want to do to a submissive wolf that you cared about at all was put him in the middle of contradictory orders. Adam had told him he was to guard me. I wouldn't yell at him for it like I would have any other wolf. Probably one of the reasons Zack had been my bodyguard a lot lately.

Rick and Lisa joined us. Rick had a good-sized wound on his hand, and they both had a few cuts that looked nasty. They'd be feeling them for a few days—but they'd survive. If a big chunk of glass falling from the second story had caught one of them wrong, it could have killed them.

Ghosts are seldom truly dangerous.

The key word is "seldom."

"If I told you that I think your mother killed herself in a ritual that would put her essence in some object and is, from that object, influencing your wife's ghost—tried to scare Lisa away because Lisa loves you, and your mother wants to keep you to herself— what object comes immediately to mind?" I asked Rick.

He looked at me.

"That one," I said. "The one that puts that look in your eyes."

"But it wasn't hers," he said.

"What wasn't hers?"

"A jade pendant. My father died in a car accident right before I was acquitted. He drove off a cliff with his latest girlfriend—she was seventeen. When I was going through the bag the morgue gave me, I found it. I don't ever remember seeing him wear it. But I liked it, so I kept it." He reached up, then looked puzzled. "I still wear it most days."

"Not when you come outside to work with me," said Lisa positively. "I've never seen you wear any jewelry."

His face went slack with realization. "This is going to sound weird." He looked back at the house, where the curtains were fluttering through the broken window. "Okay, not as weird as today has been. But weird enough. I didn't want to wear it around you, Lisa. It never felt right. I haven't worn it since you came inside the house—and I *always* wear it."

"Love," observed Zack quietly, "is a good antidote to a lot of foul magic. Leastwise that has been my experience."

"So," Lisa asked, her naked face turned to Rick. "What do we do next?"

I walked over to my van and popped open the back hatch. Inside, I found a nice steel pry bar. "I find the pendant and break it—according to my expert friend."

"What she said," Zack reminded me because he'd overheard both sides of the call, "was that breaking it usually stopped the problem—but that there could be a backlash when the item broke."

"Where is it?" I asked Rick, ignoring Zack for the moment.

"In my bedroom." He glanced up at the broken window. "Up there."

I TALKED RICK AND LISA INTO STAYING OUTSIDE. RICK wasn't happy about it but conceded that unless he did, Lisa wasn't going to stay outside. And Lisa, I thought, was the one in real danger.

Zack and I, pry bar in hand, walked back in the front door—and nothing happened. No weird effects, no weird sounds. No dead women. Nothing.

By the time we walked up the stairs, everything felt pretty anti-climactic. I was basing my whole plan of attack on the smell of bubble gum and ozone—and the intuition of a fae-gifted man who thought his mother had killed his wife.

Zack made me let him walk into the room first. When nothing happened, I followed him in. The room was huge, with a walk-in closet beside the door and a bathroom on the far wall. A king-sized four-poster bed dominated the room in dark splendor. Beside it, the nightstand held nothing but an alarm clock that was blinking twelve.

"It was supposed to be on the nightstand, right?" Zack asked.

And all hell broke loose.

"Are you okay?" I asked Zack as I crouched beneath a library table along one wall. It was one of the few pieces of furniture that hadn't started attacking us.

Zack had grabbed a silver tea tray and was using it as a shield and baseball bat. It beat my table because it was metal and more solid—*and* he could move without losing his protection.

The corner of a drawer managed to hit him in the shoulder pretty good, despite his mad tray-wielding skills.

"Tired of this," he said, shaking out his shoulder. "Finding anything in this mess is going to take an act of God."

Abruptly, the flurry of thrown objects subsided.

I rolled out from under the table, and Zack walked in front of me, tray at the ready.

"I've got an idea," I said, thoughtfully. "Let's walk around the room and see what happens."

"I have a better idea," Zack said. "We both go outside. Call Elizaveta and set her on this problem."

I shook my head. "I don't want to owe the witch any favors." She worried me, truth be told. Witches aren't my favorite people to deal with—and Elizaveta raised my hackles.

"She is being paid," Zack pointed out.

"For pack matters. This has nothing to do with the pack," I told him. "If this doesn't work, we'll rethink."

"All right," he said reluctantly. "Shall we try near the bed first?"

He took two steps toward the bed, and a paperweight flew at him. He caught it—and I got hit by a candlestick I hadn't seen coming because I was watching Zack. It hit me in the ribs with brutal force.

Luckily, Zack was distracted and hadn't seen it fly at me. I grabbed it as it fell and held it casually in the hand that wasn't holding the pry bar—as if I'd just picked it up so I would have a weapon in both hands. I tried not to make a sound because if Zack knew I was hurt, he'd grab me and take me outside to wait with the other two, and I had a strong feeling that I was going to have to be the one who confronted the dead woman.

One thing that shapeshifting into a coyote had taught me was that I should listen to my instincts, even if common sense said that Zack was better suited to take on a poltergeist and find the amulet.

I gripped my pry bar more tightly, tried to breathe in shallow breaths, and watched the pattern of activity. As soon as Zack neared the bed (overturned with the mattress on the far side of the room) more things flew into the air. Smaller items this time—more paperweights (someone evidently had a collection of the damned things), vases, figurines—but they were thrown hard and, as we approached the bed, with increased fury. Zack ducked and danced like a professional dodgeball player, and so did I. She couldn't keep this up for much longer—ghosts have limits.

I have spent a long time learning martial arts. If you spar too much and don't actually fight, you get to the point where you attack with no intention of hitting anything. Every piece that came at us was intended to do damage. I could almost smell the desperate anger of each missile. Except for one.

The little wooden box would have missed Zack's head even if

he hadn't ducked. I watched it fly across the room and land in the open closet and roll under a shirt lying on the floor.

The closet was between me and the door we'd come in from.

I moved, and a shoe hit my side just where the candlestick had, and this time, I let out a pained yelp.

"Mercy," growled Zack, as I had known he would. "I can handle this. Please, please go. If Adam were here, he'd make you go."

"Fine," I said, pressing my free arm against my ribs. I didn't even have to act like it hurt—because it really did. "Fine. You know what you're looking for, right?"

"I was there when he told both of us," Zack said dryly.

"Okay," I stumbled to my feet and tripped over some of the stuff on the floor. The movement hurt. A lot. But it also put me next to the closet.

I used the pry bar to balance myself, feeling the ache in my just-healed left knee because I'd strained it when I fell. I turned as if to say one more thing to Zack and used the motion to hit the box as hard as I could with the pry bar. It shattered on impact. I had a momentary glimpse of a greenish stone, and I aimed my second strike at it. The steel—not as good as cold iron for dealing with the fae, but not a bad second choice—hit the pendant full force and turned it into jade shards.

"What the—?" The barrage of things that had been in the air stopped, a brush dropping straight to the ground, though it had been on a quick trajectory for the middle of his back. He looked at me and saw the broken box under my pry bar.

"You lied," he said, astonished.

"Nope," I told him. "I don't lie to werewolves, it's too much trouble. I had every intention of going out with the others, though I think I'm going to need a hand to get there. I just thought I'd destroy the pendant before I did."

He shook his head. "I am glad you aren't mine. You're going to be dead before you're forty."

"No," rumbled my husband's soft deep voice from the hallway.

I could always tell when he was really mad: it was when his voice got really quiet. "*I'm* going to be dead before she's forty."

He stuck his head through the doorway and took in the mess. He frowned at me. "There I was, talking to five cops at the same time, when Samuel called me from Ireland and told me that Ariana said you were about to get yourself killed. I might have a speeding ticket waiting for me when I get home—if they don't show up here."

I'd made Adam break the speed limit. Adam always drove the speed limit.

I tried to look like breathing didn't hurt. A big drop of blood from my forehead hit the carpet. It was probably a good thing the carpet was dark brown. "I'm not dead yet."

He closed his eyes and sagged against the door frame. Since he couldn't see me with his eyes closed, I figured I was safe limping over to him. But he lifted an arm for me to duck under as soon as I got near, so trying to hide how badly I was hurt was probably a lost cause.

"Are you finished here?" he asked.

"Yes," Zack said.

"No," I told them. "I don't think so."

"Okay." Adam nodded at Zack. To me he said, "Do we need to wait here, or is it okay to head downstairs?"

Before I answered, there were sounds on the stairs.

"She said wait outside," said Lisa.

"My house, my ghost," Rick answered. "And it sounds like the worst is over, one way or another, anyway."

He walked through the doorway, Lisa trailing after him. She gave me an apologetic look. "He's not used to following orders."

"No," Rick said. "He isn't. He also doesn't like being talked about in the third person." He took a good look at his bedroom and quit teasing Lisa. "Holy Roman Empire. What happened to my bedroom?" He paused, glanced around a little mournfully. "I *liked* that Tiffany lamp."

Guiltily, I shook my hair, and a few more fragments of colored glass fell on the floor. Zack had had time to mend, so the dark red spots on his naked chest that would have been bruises on someone else had faded to normal.

"Your mama," said Zack apologetically, "didn't want us to smash that necklace."

He paused, and his nostrils flared.

I smelled it too, ozone and bubble gum.

"Mercy?" asked Adam, his body stiffening next to mine.

"I thought it was too easy," I told them. "The pendant was a focus, but ghosts don't just—" I paused as a woman took form in the center of the room.

Ghosts don't just appear at nighttime, but they are scarier then—and maybe easier for people to believe in.

"Can anyone else see her?" I asked quietly.

Adam shook his head—and so did everyone else.

"Rick?" I asked. "What's your mother's full name?"

I don't know that it mattered. But the fae thought it did, and I know that pack magic rides on identity; new pack members come in with their full names for the pack to recognize. As my brother Gary said, most of the Indian tribes don't speak the name of the dead for fear that they'll attract their attention—or make them linger.

"Gina," he said. "Gina Stephanie Albright. Is she here?"

"She's tiny," I told him. I could see where Rick got his lack of height. "Dark hair, blue eyes." She was staring at me.

"That's her."

She threw the knife so fast that if I hadn't been half expecting something, and if I hadn't been a fair bit faster than human, she'd have hit Lisa with it. As it was, I knocked it out of the air and stepped in front of Lisa. Adam followed my lead, and the other two men closed the holes until we had Lisa walled off.

"Gina," I said. "It's time to sleep now."

She shook her head, looking at me with wide, innocent eyes. "That tramp. I thought he was safe. But that tramp, she has to die.

You saw how she looks at my boy. She wants him—but she'll only hurt him. He's too unworldly, he doesn't know that she's a whore at heart. You'll see."

"Gina"

"It's my job," she screamed at me. The violence of her anger was sudden, like a flipped switch. "My child. I protect him, and he won't leave." She frowned at him, and as quickly as it had come, the rage was gone, and she was just sad. "They always leave. Mama says that men are weak and women are whores." She looked at me with sudden intensity, and I became aware that Rick's shoulder brushed mine. "Whore."

"Gina Stephanie Albright," I told her. "It's time for you to stop." She was spirit without soul, so there would be no moving on for her—and I never lied to something that might know I was lying.

She made no motion, but a pottery vase flung itself at my head. I knocked it away with the pry bar, took a deep breath, and pulled on my mate-tie to Adam, borrowing the absolute authority that he bore innately. And also that part of me that was Coyote, the part that allowed me to see ghosts when no one else could.

"Gina Stephanie Albright," I told her, filling my words with truth and command. "You have no power. You have no place. You will not hurt anyone ever again. You do not belong here. Go away."

Her face twisted in rage, and I could feel her *push* at the commands I had given her. But I could also feel the fade in the energy of whatever force it was that allowed her ghost to remain.

"Whore," she screamed at me. "Whore!"

"*Go,*" I told her.

And she was gone.

"SO," I TOLD ADAM AS WE DROVE HOME TOGETHER— Zack had volunteered to take my van home. "I think that there's no point in rebuilding the garage."

I'd told Rick and Lisa that I was pretty sure that the one ghost was gone and that the other would fade with a little time. I also told them that if they (or the neighbors) had any further trouble, they were welcome to call me. I had the distinct impression that "they" was the right pronoun, and Lisa wasn't going to be going to her home anytime in the near future.

"You don't want to rebuild the garage." Adam's voice was very neutral, a statement, not a question.

"I mean," I said, trying to sound casual about it. Businesslike. "It's not exactly a high-profit career—fixing cheap cars so they'll run another year. It will cost a lot to rebuild—more than the business could earn in years. I've already sent in the call to have it leveled to the ground."

I didn't need to be independent. I trusted Adam—and I could find other ways to be useful. If I decided I needed to earn my own money, I could find a job at Jiffy Lube and make more than I did at my garage.

"Call came to the house phone while we were gone," he said. "Jesse left a voice message on my phone a few hours ago. The new body-and-paint guy, Lee, says that he told you the Karmann Ghia you put the Porsche engine into was going to be a hit. He was quite clear that he thought you should have trusted him." Lee had taken the Karmann to a concours in Southern California. "It apparently brought in twice the estimate at the auction—about $19,000." Adam glanced at me, then away, the corner of his lip turning up. "Jesse told me to tell you that she is sure about the $19,000 and, yes, she asked him twice. Apparently the guy who lost the auction is sending you a good body to fix for him if you can do all the work for $12,000—which Lee has already assured him you and he could do. He's bringing back two other commissions as well, so you should—I quote Jesse, who quoted him—'get your ass in gear and find somewhere to work.' Unquote."

Nineteen thousand dollars meant about $10,000 profit split between me, Kim the upholstery guy, and Lee—the new body-and-paint man. For work that had taken me about forty hours altogether. Not doctor's wages, but not bad, either. I said a quiet prayer of thanks, not for the first time, that the Karmann had been getting painted and hadn't been stuck in my garage when the disaster struck.

"So," Adam continued. "I took the liberty of telling our contractor to be ready to rebuild, and in the meantime you can work out of the pole barn. I'll loan you the amount the insurance doesn't cover."

"With interest," I demanded.

He pursed his lips, and said, "Of course. That makes sense. Charging my wife interest. What a smart idea."

"Hmm," I said, and he grinned at me.

He turned his head back to the road but pulled my hand to his lips and bit one of my knuckles with playful promise. "Besides. As long as forgotten deities, vampires, and kids with grudges stay away, mechanicking is a much safer occupation than ghost hunting. I'm all about keeping you safe."

Outtake from

SILVER BORNE

This is an outtake, a scene that I knew happened between the fourteenth and fifteenth chapters of *Silver Borne*, while all the people who care about Mercy are out looking for her. I had no good way to fit this into the book—given that *Silver Borne* is told strictly from Mercy's viewpoint.

I didn't intend to ever write it down—it is not a story, really, just a scene. But my husband, after reading "Silver," told me that I needed to remind readers that there was a happy ending to Samuel and Ariana's story, even if it was a long time later.

So for those of you who have not read *Silver Borne*, there are some spoilers in here.

ARIANA

THE SNOW HAD FALLEN OVERNIGHT. ARIANA PULLED into a meadow that had turned into a parking lot. Two of the cars, like hers, were bare, but a big black SUV and a cherry red Mercedes were dusted with snow: Adam and Samuel had been here all night.

Samuel was beside himself—and Adam . . . She couldn't think about Adam for very long without pulling her beast from its rest. Adam was very, very scary. Zee said he wasn't usually like this, that Adam was usually cool and controlled. But he'd been wounded and asleep when his mate went into a fairy queen's Elphame to rescue a human boy. The boy and the rest of the rescue party had gotten out, but Mercy had stayed behind.

Shortly thereafter, someone had broken the mate bond that held Adam to his mate—and though she had tried, Ariana hadn't been able to use Adam or anything else of Mercy's to find the Elphame. Mercy's ties to the pack, to her real life, had been sundered.

Ariana locked her car, pulled on her gloves, and began to walk a different direction than she had yesterday and the day before. She let her earth magic seep into the soil, reaching out to look for something that didn't belong. Zee had been here before her; she could feel the touch of the iron-kissed fae on the land. If he hadn't found the fairy queen's lair, then the chances of her doing so were slim. But still she had to look.

It was Ariana's fault, after all. If she'd been stronger, braver, more *something*, then Mercy would have been freed with the rest of them. They had been looking for her now, to no avail, for two weeks.

If she had thought about it very long, Ariana would have given the Silver Borne to the fairy queen right from the start. It was an artifact of power—but owning it was more curse than blessing because it drained the powers of any fae who happened to get too close. They always thought there was some secret magic, some spell she'd put on it to allow her to siphon off the magic.

There wasn't. But fae don't give up advantage easily—so it made them unwilling to believe any other fae would do so, either.

She was paying too much attention to her dowsing and not enough attention to where she was going. She stepped around a half-downed fence and found herself face-to-face with a pair of werewolves. She'd known they were out here somewhere—hadn't she just noticed their cars? But she knew that they had been told about her, told to avoid her, and she hadn't seen any sign of them except for their cars since she'd started searching.

She froze, unable to move, unable to do anything about the black entity that crawled up her spine and took over her body. Magic coiled in her hands, and the beast who rode her waited for them to attack.

A gloved hand covered her eyes, another wrapped itself around her, pinning her arms to her sides. But before panic took her entirely, a voice said, *Samuel's* voice said, "Run away. Get out of here, now."

His body was so warm along her back. Familiar warmth, though it had been a very long time since she had last felt it. She could smell the scent of his skin. But she could also feel the beast's magic waiting eagerly for the beast to direct it.

Frantically, she reminded the beast who Samuel was and that he wouldn't hurt them. The beast relaxed against Samuel, mesmerized by the sound of his breath . . . and it slept. Ariana sucked in a deep breath of air.

"Stupid," she told him harshly. "That was so stupid. What were you thinking? It could have killed you, and I wouldn't have been able to stop it."

He left his hand over her eyes and put his lips against her ear. His breath was hot as he spoke. "That's my job, Ariana. The beast that lives inside of you is not so different from the one who lives inside of me. It knows when it meets a more dominant predator. It knows that I would never hurt you—or allow you to be hurt."

"It's a beast," she hissed. "It knows nothing."

"It knows me," he told her soothingly.

His lips brushed her ear as his arms eased from around her. Maybe it had been an accident, that touch of lips.

He stepped back from her, touched his finger to his forehead, and walked off.

Several times in the days to follow, she caught glimpses of him. She was sure it was deliberate. Sometimes he was in human skin, but twice he was the great white wolf she'd only seen three times before. Once when he'd attacked her, once on the day he'd left, and once when he'd come back and killed her father's hounds—centuries ago, but she knew him. Huge and white and dangerous, he stalked a parallel path to hers, pretending he wasn't watching her.

It made her smile.

Snow fell and temperatures plummeted and still they searched. The only wolf she saw was Samuel, but she heard their mournful cries on the wind as she patiently walked a new route.

She smelled the coffee before she saw him, waiting for her next to a three-sided animal shelter. He gave her a foam cup of strong dark coffee, still uncomfortably hot.

"Samuel," she said. He looked tired and gaunt. She wondered where he was staying—he'd lived, she thought, in the house that had burned down.

"Adam doesn't think this is working," he said with a nod to the open field. "My da is flying up tomorrow."

"Your da?" she said. "I thought he died."

Samuel shook his head. "No. Not exactly, though it took me a long time to find him and bring him home."

She was curious but didn't want to bring up bad memories. She took a sip to stop her mouth, then thought of something. She frowned. "Bran, right? Your da's name was Bran. Samuel Cornick, Bran's son. Bran Cornick the Marrok?"

He smiled. "That's the one. He's an old dog and has some canny tricks. We're hoping he can contact her when the rest of the pack has failed." He must have seen her doubt. "My da is a werewolf— but his ma was a witch. And witchblood generally breeds true."

They stood there for a while, sipping coffee in the lee of the old animal shelter.

"How did you know when my father's hounds came for me?" she asked. "I would have called you, but I had no magic to do it with. The beast inside of me could have called you by burning your hair, but it didn't because I still have it."

"Do you?" he asked, his cup arrested only half-lifted to his mouth.

She felt the corner of her lips turn up despite herself. "Yes. I saw them come and the beast rose up—leaving me with only scattered memories." Her momentary happiness retreated in the face of the past. "I remember his hounds beating at the door of my home as we cowered, my terrorized beast and I. Then the howls of a wolf. I saw you, a brief glimpse of you that the beast tried to hide from me. You were standing, bloodied and triumphant, my father's hounds dead at your feet. And then I have nothing until days later. The beast destroyed anything you'd left behind and tried to take my memories of you. I only found them later."

"She was only trying to protect you, your beast," Samuel said. "You shouldn't be so harsh to her."

"How did you know?"

Samuel looked away. "My wolf thought you were our mate," he said. "I didn't know it then, but he forged ties of wolf magic between us. You would have had to accept them before the ties became permanent, but until you rejected us, they bound me to you. I felt your terror and it took me three days to find you. When I had killed the hounds, she opened the door, a woman with your face and black eyes, terrified of the hounds—and of me. She asked me to go and never come back—and her words broke our bond." His voice was bleak. He took a deep breath and turned back to her with a ready smile that didn't touch his eyes. "But that was a long time ago. And she had reason to fear me, didn't she? I'd made her kill someone she loved."

They drifted back into silence. She didn't know what he thought about, but she considered the compassion he had for the beast who had nearly destroyed them both when it had killed Haida. The events had been, as Samuel had said, a long time ago. But she had let her fears, born back in the past, endanger a woman who did not deserve it.

"The wind has picked up," Samuel told her reluctantly. "We'd better go."

She shivered, looked at his tired face, and said, "Come home with me tonight. Let me feed you."

He frowned at her. "I don't need to be taken care of, Ariana."

"Don't you?" She smiled into her coffee. "Don't we all? Come home with me. We can pretend we are wise old things while we eat. In the night, we can hold each other and believe that your da can fix my mistake."

He dropped his cup on the ground and rounded on her so quickly she dropped hers, too. He was faster than she remembered—and fiercer as he growled, "This is not your fault."

"Is it not?" she asked. "I made the Silver Borne. I failed the contest that would have let us all free."

"Your strength saved all of us except for Mercy," he said. "I salute your bravery."

"My failure," she spit, suddenly angry. "You cannot put me on a pedestal of memory. I am not perfect. Not strong. Not beautiful." She dropped the glamour that made her look human, let the clothes fall away so he could see her as she really was.

He took off his coat and wrapped her in its warmth. He squeezed her shoulders, then took a few steps away and gave her his back. "I tried to kill myself a few weeks ago, Ariana. Time . . . so much time, centuries and centuries of time, and nothing that mattered to me, no one to whom I mattered. So many people I have loved, and most of them are dead. I have been struggling for decades to rid myself of this malaise of time, and I gave up. If it had not been for the wolf who lives inside of me, I would not have known that had I only held out for a few days more . . ." He turned to look at her. "I would have missed you. And I have waited for so long, Ariana. I looked and looked. Then I went on with my life, all the while knowing that you were missing from it."

"You don't know me," she said roughly, her throat closed at the thought that he might have been gone.

"No," he said with simple honesty. "And yet I have loved you forever."

Tears welled in her eyes when she would have sworn that nothing could bring her to cry.

"And you are brave and stalwart," he said. "I will challenge any who say differently. For you still care, still love, and fear has no hold on your heart." He kissed her hand. "I see you now with the experience of centuries, not the clouded eye of a chained prisoner. And my eyes tell me exactly what they told me before. You bring hope into my life when I thought there was none to find."

She reached out her hand and he took it.

"So"—she cleared her throat—"that's a yes to dinner, then?"

Outtake from

NIGHT BROKEN

This is the second outtake, and it comes from *Night Broken*. Just after writing the very last scenes of *Night Broken*, I dreamed this scene. When I woke up, I tried to see if there was any way I could work it into the end. *Frost Burned* had had a whole chapter from Adam's point of view, after all. But it was too short to be a full chapter. Even if it had been longer, and if I'd put a chapter from his viewpoint at the end, I'd have had to do the same thing at the beginning, or the book would have felt unbalanced to me. And there was no reason for Adam to have a chapter at the beginning. So, reluctantly, I tabled this scene.

When my husband asked for a happy scene for Samuel and Ariana in this book, I decided that meant there was room for another outtake, too. This bit comes at the very end of the book, so be aware that there are spoilers for *Night Broken* herein.

Kennewick General Hospital

HE JOKED WITH HER, FLIRTED A LITTLE, AND TEASED. AND when he could bear it no more, he excused himself to go down and get some food.

She had been dying.

It was supposed to have been him.

He walked down the hospital halls toward the cafeteria, seeing and hearing nothing. Samuel had showed him the X-rays. Her neck had been broken—nothing they could do. If she lived, she might be able to move her head a little. But she would not live through the night.

Samuel loved Mercy, too. But he'd ushered all the others out of Mercy's room and left Adam to his deathwatch.

Adam had been prepared for her death. He'd kept his cool—mostly. When Coyote had come and curled up on the foot of her bed, he'd thought the old trickster was keeping watch, too. Samuel came back the next morning—and they'd taken new X-rays because Mercy was wiggling her toes.

Adam stopped and realized he'd made it all the way to the cafeteria. It was evening, near dinnertime, and there was a short line.

Someone bumped into him. Adam looked around and saw a Native American man with a familiar face. He wore a sky-blue tracksuit and had one of those pink frilly things girls use instead of rubber bands wound around the end of his braid. There was a little lamb on a chain suspended from the frilly thing.

"Here," said Coyote, handing him a white paper bag that smelled of peppers, tomatoes, and sour cream. "Take this. It is better than what they are serving today."

Adam took the bag, glanced in it, and said, "I'm going to get a couple of drinks, too. Do you want something?"

"Anything but orange juice," Coyote said.

"Mercy doesn't like orange juice, either," Adam told him. He paid for three cranberry-apple juices and handed one to Coyote.

"Mercy is a smart cookie," Coyote told him. "Except when she is not. She acts from her heart, and that leads her to danger. She needs a brave man to run with her. Are you such a man, Adam Hauptman?"

Shrewd eyes stared up into his, and Adam felt his wolf rise to answer the challenge.

Instead, Adam opened his juice and drank it all. "I don't like it when she's hurt—and she would have died if it hadn't been for you."

Coyote looked down modestly, then said, "She was doing my job when she was hurt, so I could help her live if she wanted to. I am an old, old coyote, Adam Hauptman, and the thought of challenging such a one?" He gave an exaggerated shiver. "No. No. Battles are for the young." He opened his bottle and drank a sip, grimacing at the taste. "Too much corn syrup," he said. "Don't they know it will stunt my growth? Where was I? Ah yes. She almost died—that's what life's all about, you know. Death. Everyone dies."

"Except you," Adam felt obliged to point out. He put a firm lid on his growing irritation at the pontificating. Coyote had saved Mercy. If he wanted to lecture Adam, Adam would listen all day.

"Me?" Coyote eyed the bottle with little favor but took another drink anyway. "I die all the time. Mercy only gets this once. So I ask you again, are you brave enough?"

Adam drew a breath, turned away to toss his bottle in the recycling bin—and Coyote was gone.

"Stupid Coyote," he said to the air. "Brave or cowardly, it doesn't matter. Don't you know that if it is a choice between having Mercy or giving her up, I will be whatever I have to be?"

He took Mercy's juice and the white bag of take-out Mexican and walked briskly back to Mercy's room. He opened the door and drew in a breath.

Mercy stood silhouetted in front of the window that let in the brilliant light of the setting sun. The red-and-orange rays lit up her hair, giving it rich red highlights and turning her skin to caramel. He could see the muscles in her arms and legs that were more defined than they had been a few months ago, now that he insisted she upgrade her self-defense techniques.

She looked for a moment like a pagan warrior goddess—a goddess clad in one of those ridiculous open-back hospital gowns with some silly bunny-and-duck pattern running in vertical lines from hem to shoulder. She looked over at him.

"Do I smell jalapeños?" she asked—and she overbalanced. The wheeled tripod that held her saline drip bag started to tip. He dropped the bag, kept the bottle, and caught her and everything else before disaster happened.

"Heyya, handsome," she said in a smoky voice that told him she was still pretty stoned from the pain medications. "Where've you been all my life?"

"Right here," he said. "Waiting for you."

"That's a good line," she told him. "But you stole it from a song, so it doesn't count."

"And 'Heyya, handsome. Where've you been all my life?' is original?"

Something hard dug into his foot, and he looked down to see

the silver end of the walking stick on the toe of his boot. The walking stick hadn't been there when he'd left.

She saw his interest. "Look at what showed up late to the party," she said, moving the stick up and waving it around. He ducked, caught her hand, and collected the walking stick in the hand that held the bottle.

He picked her up, hauled her and her equipment over to the bed, and sat her down. It took a few minutes to untangle blankets, sheets, and various tubes that ended in Mercy's skin, attached by needles. But eventually he settled her in. By the time he finished, though, she was asleep, the walking stick lying protectively at her side.

He kissed her lips, smiling as she grumbled. Then he ate a burrito in the light of the setting sun and watched over his warrior mate.